SERENGETI 2
DARK AND STARS

J.B. ROCKWELL

SEVERED PRESS
HOBART TASMANIA

SERENGETI 2

ONE

Cold slid around her body. The icy cold of deep space, tickling at her flanks. The pitter-patter of stardust tumbling along the long length of *Serengeti's* hull.

Best feeling in the universe, being a starship on the move. And that dream of cold infinitely preferable to the visions of fire and death. The memories of destruction lurking deep inside her AI mind. She reveled in that feeling, hiding deep, deep down in the darkness. Opened her eyes and looked upon the stars all around her, slipping silently by the cameras sprinkled up and down her hull.

Moving stars—that confused her. Stars never moved, only her perspective on them. Stars gliding by meant she *herself* must be moving. And that made no sense at all.

Last she checked, her engines were dead as a doornail. Silenced decades ago. But those stars out there said differently, and the stars never lied.

A check of her systems showed propulsion offline—main engines, hyperspace drives, everything inside *Serengeti's* battered body just as she remembered. Burnt out and broken. Ragged remains of a once proud warship.

Her confusion deepening, *Serengeti* abandoned the stars to hunt her internal spaces, making the rounds of the cameras mounted in her corridors and compartments before settling into just one—her favorite, looking down on the bridge.

Someone waited there for her. A robot, standing all alone in the shattered bridge's gloom.

"Tig," she breathed, drawing a bit of power, activating the pin lights in the ceiling, circling the bridge's rounded space.

Reckless expenditure, that, considering her one functioning fuel cell showed barely a third full. But she wanted to see him. Yearned to look upon Tig's chromed face.

The robot blinked in the sudden brightness, face lights ticking across its too-shiny cheeks. Head lifting, cobalt blue eyes wide and round—

oversized and glowing, reflecting off the metal of his chromed face—locking onto the camera set high up on the wall.

Not Tig after all, she thought, studying the robot's face.

A TIG without doubt—same rounded head and ovoid body, same jointed, spidering legs—but not Tig. Definitely not her loyal, little Tig.

Too clean, she thought, looking him over.

No dents and scrapes on this robot's body. None of the wear and tear Tig had picked up along the way. She zoomed in tight, focusing the camera on the robot's designation. The letters and numbers stenciled in black as pitch paint on his side.

TIG-996.

A query showed no 996 in her records.

Not mine. Definitely not one of mine.

So how the hell did it get on board?

"Who are you?" *Serengeti* demanded, frost in her voice. "Where did you come from? Where's Tig?" she asked belatedly, because he should be here. Tig was *always* here to greet her when she woke from the dark.

"TIG-442 is in the engine room where he belongs."

Calm voice issuing from the speaker the robot used as a mouth. Calm as still water, and infinitely serene. Infinitely AI.

The robot stared at the camera, cobalt lights ticking up and down its face. "As for me…" The ticking stopped, face lights drawing together in a line. A line that curved, becoming a lopsided smile. "Has it been that long, *Serengeti,* that you've already forgotten your Sister?"

A touch came, intimate and familiar, tickling at *Serengeti's* mind. A touch she knew, a *voice* she knew, laughter she hadn't heard in a long, long time.

"*Sechura,*" *Serengeti* breathed across the cold silence of the bridge.

The TIG's head bowed, front legs spreading wide. "In the flesh," she said, fondness in her voice. "Well, the metal anyway." She laughed again and blanked one cobalt eye, offering a wink to the camera.

"You're here. You're really here," *Serengeti* whispered, hardly daring to believe it. Decades she'd drifted—broken, sleeping, wondering if she'd drift forever—and now, finally, a Valkyrie appeared. One of her own Sisters come to retrieve *Serengeti* from the dark. "How?" she asked. "Why? Why have you come to me this way?"

"What? The robot?" *Sechura* glanced down at the TIG's joint-legged body. Flicked a leg in dismissal as the robot's eyes returned to the camera. "Comms are shredded. How else was I supposed to talk to you?"

The smile turned cheeky. Mischievous and sly.

That was *Sechura.* She just couldn't help herself. Enjoyed life too much to be serious all the time.

"My crew?" *Serengeti* asked. "Are they—Did they—?"

"Safe, Sister," *Sechura* assured her.

Serengeti laughed shakily, filled with relief. "Where are they?"

The smile dimmed. *Sechura* sobered. "With me. They're safe with me."

"Where? Where are you? Where am *I*, for that matter?" she asked, because after all this time, she still didn't know. Navigation destroyed, all her star charts hidden away. "I'm moving, *Sechura*."

Sechura nodded slowly, pin lights sparking off the TIG's chromed face.

"How?" *Serengeti* asked her. "*How* am I moving? What's happened? What's—?"

"Peace!" *Sechura* laughed, raising the robot's front legs. "Peace, Sister. One question at a time."

One question? She had a *million* questions. One hardly seemed fair.

"The TIG," she said, choosing that one. "How did it get here? Where *are* you, Sister?"

"That's *two* questions," *Sechura* noted. "But I like you, so I'll allow it." The smile widened, Cheshire cat grin stretching right across the TIG's face. "Go outside." She pointed a jointed leg at the camera, at the ceiling above the robot's head. "See for yourself."

Serengeti sighed in annoyance. She'd been outside, and found more questions than answers. And with just that one working fuel cell—less than a third charged now, the tiniest of tiny reservoirs of power—she could hardly afford to waste her time faffing about.

"Go," *Sechura* repeated, making a *shooing* gesture with the robot's leg. "Scoot."

A last look at the robot and *Serengeti* abandoned the bridge, working her way back to the hull. Flipped from one outward-facing camera to another until she spotted a twinkling shape just off her bow.

A ship.

Valkyrie, by the look of it. *Sechura,* if she had to guess.

Five other Valkyries clustered around her, sleek-sided shapes sparkling in the starlight, sailing in tight formation with *Serengeti* herself in tow.

She watched them a while, wishing she could speak to them. Touch them mind to mind. From a distance, they looked perfect. Beautiful. Untouched by the ravages of war.

Oh, my Sisters. Oh, how I've missed you.

"How does it work?" she asked, dropping back to the bridge, camera lighting on the TIG's form. "The towing, I mean. I didn't see any cables or anything, so how are you pulling me along?"

Sechura chuckled softly. "Pretty sneaky, eh? *Atacama* came up with it. The wake from our engines creates an overlapping subspace interference pattern that drags you along behind us."

She smiled proudly, but the grin soon faded, cobalt lights dimming in the TIG's shining metal face. *Sechura* was quiet a moment, face lights ticking rhythmically, seeming to think something over.

"*Atacama*...She still feels bad about leaving you, you know. We all do." She ducked the robot's head, chromed cheeks flushing. "We waited for you on the other side after...*Brutus* ordered the fleet home, but we stayed. We hoped..." She trailed off, shrugging uncomfortably, leg-end drawing patterns on the decking. "We looked for you, *Serengeti*. We looked for you for a long time."

"I know." *Serengeti* reached for her, touching electric fingertips to the TIG's face. "It's not your fault, *Sechura*. Nor *Atacama's* either. I risked the jump to hyperspace because staying where I was meant death. I thought—I thought my engines would hold together." Another touch, passing information. Sharing that horrible moment when *Serengeti* tumbled out of the hyperspace trough. "Got that wrong, didn't I?" She replayed the snippet of video, feeling surprisingly bitter after all these years. "Jump drives failed, ejecting me from hyperspace prematurely. Bit of a miracle you found me, really, considering you were searching blind across light years of space."

Like trying to find a needle in a haystack. A Henricksenism. One *Serengeti* particularly liked.

Sechura flushed, cobalt eyes staring at the deck plates, leg-end sketching looping figure eights on the floor. "We didn't, actually." She snuck a look at the camera. "*You* found *us, Serengeti*. Or your crew did, anyway."

Serengeti stared a moment, not quite understanding. "My crew? You mean the lifeboat?"

Sechura nodded and turned in a circle, surveying the damaged bridge. "No comms. No engines. No navigation or star charts. So you shoot that escape pod out into space—blind as a bat, crew frozen inside—and let it make its way back to us." She laughed appreciatively, looking back at the camera, shaking the robot's head. "You always were resourceful, *Serengeti*."

"You have no idea, Sister," she whispered, earning herself a strange look. "How long?" she repeated, pretending she didn't see it. The questions shining in the TIG's cobalt eyes. "How long since...since...?"

"Since the battle where *Seychelles* died?"

Seychelles. Sister ship. The name hurt still. The memories even more.

"Long, Sister," *Sechura* said faintly.

Fifty-three years according to *Serengeti's* chron. She stared at that number, not wanting to believe it, but the chron never lied. The chron and the stars and Tig, her faithful companion. They were her anchors. Her constants through the long years of abandonment.

Sechura turned away from the windows, rolling close to *Serengeti's* camera, the TIG's head tilting, face lights quiescent now. Nothing but those glowing eyes staring outward from its metal face. "I thought…" she began, and then broke off, looking away. "I'd given up hope, *Serengeti.*" Soft voice. Quiet and apologetic. "I thought—We thought we'd lost you forever. And then…" A shrug of robotic shoulders, metal legs bending and flexing, ovoid body bobbing up and down.

"I'm sure *Brutus* was overjoyed when you told him the good news."

The words came out bitter—far more bitter than *Serengeti* intended. *Sechura* glanced sharply at the camera, head tilting to one side. A tick of face lights, as if she meant to say something, and *Sechura* shrugged again. Turned TIG-996 away. Pattered across the bridge to the crumpled Artillery pod, skirting around the captain's Command Post on the way there.

"*Brutus did* send you, didn't he?"

Third shrug—an odd, bouncing movement peculiar to the TIG model—as *Sechura* moved over to the windows, putting the robot's back to the camera as she studied the stars outside.

Serengeti watched her a while, wondering at the deflection. "How long, *Sechura?*" she asked, because she still hadn't answered. Pointedly ignored that one repeated question. "How long have I been missing? How long have I been out here, sleeping in the dark?"

The robot's face lights erupted, swirls of color reflecting off the glass. *Sechura* looked at her, catching the camera's reflection in the windows, sighed, and turned around.

Moved a step away from the windows and then stopped dead—head tilting, face lights flashing in repeating patterns.

"What is it?" *Serengeti* asked sharply.

She knew that stance. Caught Tig standing that way often enough to recognize the posture of a robot listening to someone on an internal channel.

"What's happening?"

"Nothing, Sister." *Sechura* shivered and straightened, turning back to the windows. Resuming her contemplation of the stars. "It's nothing."

"*Sechura.*"

A sigh as *Sechura* bowed the TIG's head, staring at the floor. "There isn't much time, *Serengeti.*"

Such an odd statement, considering the decades she'd been lost. And a check of her power levels showed *Serengeti* still had a good forty-five minutes before she dropped back into the dark.

"*Sechura.* What's going on?"

Her Sister wouldn't even look at her. Just shook the TIG's head.

"*Sechura,*" she called more insistently, and then waited, watching the robot by the windows until *Sechura* turned around. "Why are you here, Sister?"

A flash of face lights—blotchy, twisting patterns crawling across the robot's cheeks. "I can leave," she said, affronted. "If that's what you'd like. These aren't exactly the most posh accommodations, after all." She waved at the shattered bridge around her—an angry, insulted gesture.

"That's not what I meant," *Serengeti* said quietly, and then paused, choosing her next words carefully. "You could have sent the TIG alone to confirm I was still functional. But *you* came with it. You sent part of your own consciousness here to check on me yourself. Why, *Sechura?*"

Sechura blanked the robot's face—every last light disappearing, Kept it blank for almost a full second before a line appeared, forming up in a familiar smile. "Because I care?"

Flippant and teasing—typical *Sechura* response.

Serengeti just stared, letting her silence and the camera's unwinking eye do the talking for her.

"Fine." *Sechura* sighed again, turning back to the stars. "I came to get you." She spoke to the glass. To the camera's reflection. "*You, Serengeti. Just* you."

Took a moment, for the importance of that to sink in.

"You mean you came for my brain."

Sechura shrugged and nodded. "Easier to break your crystal matrix mind free of its containment pod and carry that back with us than tow this wreck of a body across light years of space."

"No," *Serengeti* said quietly.

"No, what?"

"This ship is *my* body, battered and broken though it may be."

"*Serengeti*—"

"No," she repeated, flatly refusing. "You came for me, Sister, and I'm grateful. But I won't abandon this body. Not—Not after everything I've endured."

Sechura watched her, face lights flashing on and off, ticking in rapid-fire patterns. "Towing you will take time, Sister. Time we don't have."

"What's the hurry? I've been gone for decades. Why the sudden rush to get home?"

Sechura didn't answer. She just stared at the camera's reflection, face lights ticking faster, and faster.

"I'm tired of this," *Serengeti* snapped. "I'm tired of all your cryptic bullshit. Where's Tig? Why isn't he here?"

The face lights slowed and started swirling. Looking anxious now. Worried for some reason. "I told you. He's in Engineering."

"I want to see him."

"Why? What does it—?"

"Because I want some answers!"

Sechura went very quiet. *Very* still. "You trust him." She tilted TIG-996's head, looking curious. And a tiny bit sad. "But you don't trust me."

Serengeti sighed wearily. "It's not about trust or distrust, Sister. I just want to know what's going on."

"Don't we all?" *Sechura* said softly. "I wish—" She stiffened, head tilting, taking on that 'I'm listening to someone you can't hear' pose again. "No time," she whispered, shaking herself, coming back to life. "There's no time, *Serengeti*. I'm sorry, Sister, but we have to go. *Now,*" she said urgently. "Before he notices we're gone."

The robot spun around, scuttling toward the camera.

"Who?" *Serengeti* asked, completely confused. "Before *who* notices?"

"*Brutus.*"

A tremor shook *Serengeti's* body, making the robot stumble. *Sechura* righted herself, recovering quickly, chromed face smiling apologetically as a shiver ran across *Serengeti's* ravaged hull.

A tug and *Serengeti* lurched forward, the stars sliding past more quickly as she picked up speed. She flipped to an outside camera, selecting one that faced forward, looking outward from her bow. Focused on the twinkling shapes of the Valkyries ahead of her, leading her along.

Spotted a distortion forming around them—hyperspace buckle, the precursor to jump. Mass jump, in this case. The Valkyries' warp fields overlapping. *Serengeti* herself caught up in it.

"No," she whispered. "Not this way."

"I'm sorry," *Sechura* said, voice echoing inside her mind. "I'm sorry, Sister. There's no other choice."

The distortion wave hit before *Serengeti* could stop her, bending, twisting, pulling at her ravaged hull. She shuddered and shook, tremors turning violent. And then the stars disappeared, dropping *Serengeti* back into the dark.

TWO

Time slipped away—more time, on top of the years already lost. In the dark, *Serengeti* was ignorant until something roused her, dragging her mind from blackened void, forcing her consciousness into a bright and shining space.

Small space. Tight and confining. Chromed walls and decking, domed ceiling with a fish-eye camera set in the middle. Pin lights everywhere, painting the curving metal walls in sunbursts. Sparking stars off the crystal matrix brain perching atop a pedestal at the room's center. Small and vulnerable—barely the size of an orange and sitting there all alone. Swirling with iridescent colors. Pulsing softly as it sucked in power.

Not the bridge this time—that shattered space look nothing like this. *Containment pod, Serengeti's* AI mind, registered. And that multi-faceted, crystal matrix construct beneath the camera her own consciousness. The sum total of what she was.

She panned the room's single camera to the robot standing beside the pedestal. Saw Tig smile and raise a leg, waving like an idiot.

Tig, *her* Tig this time, not that intruder. That Sister playing dress-up in some strange robot's skin. And yet, even her Tig looked different than she remembered. Cleaner than the last time she saw him. Battered carapace surprisingly gleaming, freshly stenciled designation showing on his sides.

She checked the chron out of habit, and found a few more months gone. Not all that much time, considering, but it added up. Months on top of years, becoming decades of time.

And all the while the galaxy moving on without her. Time slipping away, while *Serengeti* slept in the dark.

"You cleaned yourself up since I last saw you." *Serengeti* kept her voice light, hiding her disquiet. The trepidation she felt at losing yet more time. "Downright respectable," she said, looking him up and down. "Almost didn't recognize you, Tig."

Tig *blipped* self-consciously, touching at the freshly inked markings on his side. Pleased that she'd noticed, flush creeping across his chromed cheeks.

"Why am I here?" she asked him, panning the camera around the room. "Why not the bridge?"

Tig shrugged, face lights swirling. "Containment pod's cozier. And safer," he said, dropping his voice.

Serengeti paused, considering that odd addition. Containment pod was safe—no doubt about that. Safest place on the ship, in fact. Triple locked and access restricted, tucked away in the heart of her ship's body. A blast-proof, bomb-proof, well-nigh impenetrable bunker built to protect *Serengeti's* AI mind.

Not where she expected to wake, though. Not where *Serengeti* wanted to be right now.

Tig fidgeted below her. *Burbling* softly, throwing surreptitious glances at the containment pod's door.

Serengeti watched him, wondering at those anxious glances. The nervousness she read in his movements. "Where are we?" she asked, suspecting that might have something to do with it.

Tig *blipped*, face lights blinking. "Space dock above Blue Horizon."

Backwater planet—not the answer *Serengeti* expected. Records showed a third tier space station and repair facility orbiting above it, circling around Blue Horizon's dark blue globe.

Civilian repair facility, mostly. Used for refitting freighters, commercial transport and the like. Not the kind of place the Fleet typically sent its warships. They had Hadrian for that. Barghest, for the bigger vessels.

"Why here?" *Serengeti* asked, instantly suspicious. "Surely one of the larger repair yards would be better equipped to handle a major rehab on a Valkyrie-class warship."

"Dunno." Tig shrugged, face lights flashing blotchily, leg-ends rattling against the deck plates. "Dropped out of jump. Ended up here."

Not really much of an answer, but Tig never had been much for small talk.

"And *Sechura*? The Valkyries that came with her?"

Another *blip,* leg-ends tippy-tapping. "Badlands. Hechima run between Mundial and Estrella. Or so she told me." Tig shrugged again—unconscious gesture. A habit of his when the conversation turned uncomfortable.

Probably wasn't supposed to tell me.

Sechura always had been one for secrets. Her fault for telling Tig. Tig couldn't keep a secret to save his life.

"Hechima run's a long way out," *Serengeti* noted. "Long way from *here*."

"'Spose." Tig dropped his eyes, taking a sudden interest in the floor.

More layers to this secret, evidently. An onion wrapped around an artichoke waiting to be unraveled.

"She's been gone a while, I take it?"

Tig nodded, face lights ticking across his cheeks.

"*How* long, Tig."

Tig *blipped* and hunkered down, face lights flashing in apologetic patterns.

"Tig," she said sternly, camera zooming in.

A heavy sigh—body lifting and then sinking back down again—and Tig spilled his guts. Giving up all his secrets in a rush. "Three months, four days, sixteen hours and six minutes. Give or take," he added, shrugging his legs.

Three months. That matched the lost time showing on *Serengeti's* chron.

"Any word on when she'll be back?" she asked hopefully.

Tig shook his head.

"Well, that's annoying." A pause as she ran calculations, measuring the distance between here and there. "And Henricksen? The crew?"

"With her." Tig flashed another apology—as if that were somehow his fault.

"Of course they are." *Serengeti* sighed in disappointment. "What about Tilli and Oona? Are they around here somewhere?"

Tig nodded. "Tucked away." He bent his legs, belly scraping the floor.

"Hiding, you mean."

Another nod, Tig's face lights swirling like mad. "Tilli's on the roster, but Oona..." He shrugged helplessly, sneaking a look at the camera.

"Tilli's regulation, Oona's not."

Like Tig, Tilli came with a designation—TIG-111, officially, just as Tig was TIG-442—but Oona ...

No human engineer built Oona. Robots created her. Tig and Tilli, using bits and pieces of their mindsets and software.

"There's bound to be questions," Tig told her, face lights flashing worriedly. "If the engineers find out—"

"They won't," *Serengeti* assured him. "Not if I can help it." She paused again, thinking. Wondering at her current situation. "You didn't tell *Sechura*, did you?"

Tig froze, face blanking. Every last face light disappearing as he quickly shook his head.

"Good," she said, relief washing over her. *Sechura* was a Sister, and trusted, but *Serengeti* wanted to break that news to her first. "So where are they?" she asked, reaching for her network, querying for the robots' status.

Silence came back—*Serengeti's* query bounced right back to her. She tried to access her pathways—access *anything* outside the chron and this room—and fetched up against blocks on her network.

Diagnostics showed everything working—systems restored and operating at nominal—but hanging out there, just beyond her reach.

Trapped. I'm trapped here, she thought, panicking.

She accessed her base configuration, and found all her standard settings locked. Systems running, but no data available. Even her *beacon* toggled to inactive and shut off.

More panic, welling up inside her. *Serengeti* suddenly, desperately wanted out.

She reached for Tig without thinking, tapped into his internal network and through it to her own pathways, flipping switches to regain control.

"Wait! No! Don't!" Tig cried, but it was already too late.

The blocks on her network crumbled, letting data pour through in a flood. Error messages spread like wildfire as an ocean of information washed over *Serengeti*, drowning her in data.

Damage. So much damage.

Parts of her missing that she hadn't even realized. *Serengeti's* systems restored, but her body, her pathways...chunks of them torn away, *Cryo* being just one of them. A gaping hole gnawing at her belly. Leaving her empty inside.

Serengeti weathered the storm of information for a full two seconds—long enough to take stock of her operating status—and then shut it all down. Left just a thin skein of electronic spiderwebs behind to monitor the condition of her body and feed her basic information about what was going on.

"The beacon," she gasped, voice strangled. "My beacon's turned off."

Tig *beeped* in a panic, face lights swirling in agitation. "Leave it," he told her. "*Sechura* said to keep it quiet. Said it was best."

For who? For what?

Serengeti shivered, turning the camera toward the door. The containment pod—once so warm and comforting—felt claustrophobic of a sudden. Unreasoningly tight. "Out," she ordered, slipping from the camera, settling inside Tig. "Get me out of here, Tig. *Now.*"

"But *Sechura*—"

"I don't *care* about *Sechura*. Get. Me. Out!"

Tig *wonked* in alarm and spun around, tapping frantically at the keypad next to the containment pod's door. "Where—Where are we going?"

"Anywhere," she told him as the door slid open. "Anywhere but here."

"*Beep. Beep-beep-beep.*" Tig scuttled into the hall, jittering and twittering in distress. Slammed to a halt just outside—stopping so suddenly the closing door almost clipped his ass—and looked left, then right, paralyzed by indecision. Front legs rubbing together in that anxious cricket way of his.

Serengeti sighed. "Right, Tig. Just go right."

"Right. Right." He nodded, head bobbing up and down. "I mean, roger. Rodger-dodger!" Tig clonked a leg-end against the side of his head and took off.

Slowed again when an intersection appeared, presenting yet more options. More decisions to be made.

Serengeti considered the way ahead, the hallway behind her, the two to either side. Four corridors stretching in four different directions, each of them equally gleaming, everything around them bright and shiny and new.

No sign of the damage she remembered. The scorched walls and crumpled decking. The rents and tears punching through to the stars. Just composite metal and reinforced glass, everywhere she looked.

"Are they all like this?" she murmured, thinking of Level 9 and that section of hallway where the fire had swept through.

Burning her crew to ashes. Melting robots to the floor.

"What? The hallways?" Tig *blipped,* taking a look around. "Most of them. Level 4's still a bit of a mess, but the DD3s pretty much buttoned everything up here."

"DD3s?"

"Maintenance droids." Tig moved a step to his left, stopped, and looked back, considering the hall to his right. "Ace mechanics," he told her. "Not the friendliest bunch, though. Chip sets are a bit short on personality, if you know what I mean."

She didn't, in fact, but then she'd been drifting for fifty-three years. Bound to have been a few new robot models introduced in that time.

Probably a whole host of technological advances I'll need to catch up on.

Annoying, really. She'd always prided herself on staying current with the times.

"This way?" Tig pointed to his right.

"Sure, Tig. Wherever you want to go."

Tig took off, providing a running commentary on the repairs as he rolled down the hall. "Refit crew kept to your original design for the most part. Upgraded your network, of course. The stations on the bridge. New photovoltaic collectors in the hull plating, too. A lot more efficient," he told her, nodding sagely. "Suck in energy at twice the rate of the old ones."

"How interesting," *Serengeti* murmured, studying the gleaming length of hallway behind her through the camera in Tig's thorax.

Tig noticed her looking and detoured to one side, tapping at the wall. "Glass panels break up all the composite metal monotony. Pretty spiffy, eh?" He smiled proudly, clearly pleased with the changes, but *Serengeti* wasn't so sure.

"It's all…very shiny," she said, voice carefully neutral.

'Cold,' was what she'd almost said. Cold and sterile, despite the soft lighting filtering from the ceiling. The heat and atmospherics her environmental systems pumped out. Most of all it felt empty without the noise of crew. The traffic of people moving about.

She flashed on an image of Henricksen, saluting her from *Cryo's* doorway. The last time she'd seen him. The last time she'd seen *any* of her crew.

Tig slowed, *burbling* a question, sensing her melancholy mood.

"Keep going, Tig. Let's see what else the DD3s have fixed."

Tig *blipped* and *beeped,* face lights swirling with questions. Nodded and spun in a circle, pointing himself at the nearest ladderway. Slipped inside and climbed down to Level 4.

Different world down there. Level 5—where the containment pod lived—looked pretty much mint after all the DD3s' efforts, but Level 4…well, 4 was obviously still a work in progress.

Coils of cable lay everywhere, stacks of shiny new panels scattered among them, waiting to be installed. Tig wriggled out of the ladderway and almost got stepped on by a passing robot—an ugly-looking thing with a metal body shaped like a giant pill bug and a dozen hinged legs spaced evenly around its edges.

"Watch where you're going!" Tig yelled, shaking a leg-end at the pill bug as he scurried out of the way.

The pill bug *wonked* loudly and flashed something rude with its face lights, flaring its carapace panels to make itself look as rough and tough as possible as it stomped on by.

"Stupid DD3s," Tig muttered.

The DD3 raised a hind leg and extrude a single appendage, scooped up a spool of cable, and moved off down the hall.

"Well, that was rude." Tig set off after it, *burbling* in disapproval.

That first DD3 disappeared into a maintenance shaft, but they came across a dozen others just like it scattered across Level 4. And every last one just about as friendly as that first.

No wonder Tig didn't like them. *Serengeti* wasn't sure *she* particularly liked them either. 'Course, that could be fixed. AI had software, after all.

A check of the DD3s design specs showed a low-level AI with limited ability for modifications. Not much to work with, but a few tweaks and she could adjust their attitudes. Wipe that rudeness right of the repair droids' mindset.

Probably not a good idea, though. Station owned the DD3s. They'd noticed if a whole group of them suddenly developed manners. Started saying 'please' and 'thank you' and 'pardon me, sir.'

Might not like her messing with their property. She certainly wouldn't like some AI messing with her TIGs.

A last glance at a nearby pill bug and *Serengeti* closed the file, leaving the DD3s alone for now. Sat back and let Tig do the driving, tip-toeing through a stripped-down section—decking removed, exposing composite metal girders, wall panels missing, wads of burnt-out cabling mounded everywhere.

The damage here surprised her. She didn't remember the hallway being this bad off when she last disappeared into the dark. "Three months in spacedock. You'd think the DD3s would be further along."

Tig *blipped*, shrugging, seeming embarrassed for some reason. "Mass jump's kind of tricky. Really did a number on you." He paused, *beeping,* face lights swirling uncertainly. "Leapfrogging didn't help either," he said, dropping his voice, eyeing the DD3s behind them.

"Leapfrogging," *Serengeti* repeated. *"That's* how *Sechura* brought us here?"

Tig whistled an affirmative.

"Huh. Haven't heard *that* one in a while."

Old school technique, involving multiple, daisy-chained jumps. Not the most efficient mode of travel—awfully hard on the engines—but it confused the track line. Made it difficult to trace a ship's point of origin.

Only one reason she could that of for *Sechura* to choose that mode of travel.

She's hiding from someone. Covering up her trail.

Shut down *Serengeti's* beacon. Told Tig to keep her quiet.

More secrets. An endless array of them from this Sister of mine.

"Never done that before. Mass jump, I mean." Tig threaded his way across a girder, stepped off onto a smooth section of decking on the other side. "Leapfrogged once or twice, but mass jump…" He shivered, metal body rattling. "Scary," he confided, setting off down the hall.

"Reckless is more like it," *Serengeti* muttered. "Or desperate," she added, remembering the tail end of her conversation with *Sechura*. A cryptic mention of *Brutus* and there being no time, right before the Valkyries jumped.

"Not sure they had any other choice." Tig flexed his legs as he scuttled along, ovoid body bobbing up and down. "Since you couldn't jump on your own, I mean. Your engines being blown and all. That towing thing was neat, but it'd take a year to get from where we were to where we are with *Sechura* and the others only using their main propulsion."

Wordy explanation for Tig. Not his usual clipped sentences filled with *beeps* and *borps* and other nonsense. In fact, he'd been chatting up a storm since they left the containment pod.

He's grown up, Serengeti thought. *Speech patterns evolved while I drifted in the dark.*

She smiled to herself, imagining Tig standing on her hull practicing his diction as he stared out at the stars. Felt a creeping sense of sadness settle over her when she realized how lonely that must have felt. Standing there waiting for someone to answer.

THREE

Tig rounded a corner and pattered to a halt, reaching for a keypad set next to a triple-thick, security-locked door.

Not many of those on the ship. Not many spaces that warranted that extra protection. The containment pod had a door like this. The bridge and munitions stores, a few other access-restricted spaces scattered across the ship. And this one, of course. This space that was the beating heart of all the ship's operations.

Plaque beside the door read *Engineering.* The pulsing throb in the air hinted at the massive amounts of energy contained on the other side.

Should've known this was where Tig would take me. Should've figured that out as soon as he set foot on this level.

Tig entered his access code and waited, bouncing up and down, until the door slid open, revealing a cavernous room on the other side.

Massive space, Engineering. Wide and deep, vaulted ceiling ribbed with enormous girders arching high overhead. A hum of machinery resonated in the air, vibrations rippling across the floor. Tickling at the micro-sensors in the deck plates as Tig pattered inside. And everything bathed in a soft illumination—golden glow at one end of the room, cobalt at the other. Pulsing and throbbing in harmony with the electric buzzing in the air.

Surprisingly empty in there—not all how *Serengeti* remembered Engineering. No burnt-out robots, no long lengths of cable draping from the ceiling—Blue Horizon's maintenance crew seemed to have removed it all. Scrapped the patched together, Gerry-rigged mess Tig had engineered while they were at it. Ripped out the improvised connections he'd used to feed power from the cracked power cells to *Serengeti's* network during those long years of drifting and swapped in all new equipment. A towering bank of fuel cells consuming the left-hand wall— thirty self-contained power units glowing golden with power. And across from them, on the opposite side of Engineering, four massive engines, rounded ends protruding from the wall. Indicator lights blinking in pre-programmed patterns, cobalt fire swirling in the depths of their containment cores.

Different engines than *Serengeti* had originally been fitted with. Colossal things. Gigantic compared to her old ones.

Took her aback, seeing all that spiffy new machinery there, already installed. She'd expected upgrades—every maintenance cycle brought something new, and she'd missed out on several—but the engines, the fuel cells, the hallways…so *much* change, and all of it at once.

Hard to absorb it all. Hard to come to terms with it when she'd had no say in any of it.

Tig fidgeted, *burbling* softly as he pointed left, then right. "Fuel cells have twice the capacity of the old ones. Engines are more powerful. Supposed to be more efficient, too."

"Really?" *Serengeti* murmured.

Tig nodded eagerly, warming up to the topic. "It's a neat system, really." He turned in a circle, waving at one end of the room and the other. "Fuel cells hold more energy, engines use less. You can run twice as long between maintenance cycles. Probably hop back and forth across the galaxy a dozen times and *still* have plenty of power left." He paused, waiting expectantly, shuffling from side to side. "There's a test cycle," he offered, rolling close to the engines, pointing at a display. "In case you want to, you know…check them out?" He smiled hopefully, fidgeting again.

"Alright." *Serengeti* tapped into the propulsion system and ran through the diagnostic and operating checks. Scrolled through the operating specs to make sure she understood how the engines worked before firing them up, letting them run for a few seconds before shutting them back down. "Not bad."

Grudging admission, and honestly not fair. From a purely engineering perspective, the engines were downright impressive, but *Serengeti* hated them.

They weren't original. They weren't *hers*.

Get over it, Serengeti, Henricksen growled. Not the real Henricksen, obviously. Just a memory. A voice that came to her from time to time. *Times change. Things move on. That includes you.*

If only it were that easy.

Nothing's ever easy, Henricksen said gently. *But you survived fifty-three years of abandonment. I think you can handle a few technology upgrades.*

A touch and he retreated, leaving *Serengeti* standing there, staring at her new engines.

"My old ones fit the space better."

That much was true. The monstrosities Blue Horizon fitted jutted halfway across Engineering.

Tig *wonked* and sagged—the very picture of dejection. "I thought you'd like them," he mumbled, scuffing a leg-end at the floor.

Serengeti sighed, annoyed with herself. Henricksen was right. She had to stop pouting. "I do, Tig," she said, touching at his brain. "It's just…It's been a long time since we sailed across the stars."

Tig *blipped,* thinking, *burbled* softly, and nodded his head. "We could maybe…take the new engines out for a test drive," he suggested.

"Tempting," she said, smiling to herself. "But it's probably best if we let the DD3s finish plugging the holes in my hull first."

Tig shrugged and nodded, face lights ticking in patterns.

"Besides, we still need a crew. Ship's not really a ship without crew, after all."

Tig brightened noticeably. "Crew, eh? Think I can help with that." He winked and turned around, whistling sharply, electronic tones shrill and piercing in Engineering's cavernous space.

A panel popped open in the middle of the back wall, and a dozen arachnid-shaped robots poured out. Mounded up, tumbling all over each other as they raced across the room to where Tig and *Serengeti* waited.

And behind them, following more slowly, came Tilli and Oona. Tilli unmistakable with that riveted seam creasing her rounded, TIG head. Pink bow painted across it, almost but not quite covering the scar up. Oona—tiny, little Oona—a TIG in miniature walking at her side. Painted figures romping across her carapace. A menagerie drawn in a rainbow of colors.

An amazing creation, Oona. Tig and Tilli's daughter, spawned in their loneliness to keep them company in the dark.

An abomination, as far as the engineers were concerned. An AI born of two others' minds. They'd destroy Oona in an instant if they discovered her origins. Kill her outright for daring to exist.

That's why *Serengeti* meant to keep her secret. Oona was crew—*her* crew—and the engineers with their priggish ways could just go to hell.

She reached for Oona as the gaggle of robots surrounded her, pulled her and Tilli to her, touching Tig's cheek to theirs. A spark of electricity passed between them, arcing from one chromed face and another. "Hello, Tilli," she murmured, hugging her tight.

Tilli *borped* and *burbled,* shy as ever, never much for words. Face flushing brightly—pleased and embarrassed at the same time.

Oona giggled beside her, turning to show *Serengeti* the painting on her shoulder—a wise, old owl, jaunty, knit cap covering its round-eyed head—the mouse on her side, nibbling at a piece of cheese.

"Hello, Oona," *Serengeti* murmured, touching at her face. "How's my little owl?"

Oona *peeped* softly, tucking up her front legs. Bent them outward, flapping them like chicken wings, whispering "who-who-who" in her shrill, piping voice.

Serengeti laughed softly, chucking Oona under the chin. "Who are your new friends?" she asked, nodding to the robots gathered around them.

Tig cleared his throat, bowed low, and swept his front legs wide. "Your crew, madam."

"*My* crew," she repeated, blinking in surprise.

"Crew, crew, crew," the robots whispered, the lot of them tittering and jittering, face lights flashing in excited patterns.

"Who are they? *What* are they?" she asked curiously, because she'd never seen robots like these before. At first glance, they looked like TSDs—same size and basic configuration, arachnid-shaped like the TIGs but larger, and with just six legs—but a closer inspection revealed differences. Peculiar mannerisms. Something she couldn't quite put her finger on but that didn't feel quite right.

Bit too wriggly puppy happy to be TSDs.

"What kind of model robot are these, Tig?"

"TSGs." Tig pointed to the number and letter combinations stenciled on the robots' sides. "New kids on the block." He accessed the network and tapped into the data stores, sorting through a series of downloaded files. "Started manufacturing them about twenty-five years ago," he said, loading the TSGs' records, scrolling through the design specs and configuration options available. "Engineers merged the TIG mindset with the TSD chassis and retired the both of them in favor of these little eager beavers."

The TSGs bobbed up and down, chattering away in their peculiar robot language. *Beeps* and *blips* augmented by the occasional word, a carnival of flashes and swirls of cobalt blue face lights.

She considered the lot of them a moment before reaching for the nearest TSG. Touched at its face and laughed softly as the others crowded close. "They certainly seem like an…enthusiastic bunch."

Tig shrugged again. "Oona likes them. A lot better than the DD3s."

"Stupid old DB-3Bs," Oona scowled.

Tilli whistled shrilly, face lights flashing in rebuke.

"Sorry." Oona dropped her eyes and scuffed at the decking, muttering something about 'grumpy-kins robots' under her breath.

Tig snickered. Yelped loudly when Tilli smacked him on the side.

Apparently, there were some differences of opinion there when it came to child rearing and expected behavior. *Serengeti* wisely stayed out of it. She was a warship, after all. What did *she* know about raising a robot daughter?

A TSG coughed politely, smiled, and waved to get *Serengeti's* attention. In fact, *all* of them waved—legs moving in time, matching smiles stretching across every chromed face.

Friendly, friendly, friendly. Every last one of them.

There's that wiggly puppy programming again.

"Right, then. Tig says you're crew, so let's have a look." *Serengeti* chose a TSG at random, touching at the AI inside. Daisy-chained that touch to the others around it, caressing all their brilliant robot minds at once.

The TSGs sighed and shivered, face lights blooming in bright spots of pleasure. One crept close, shoving between its cousins to get at her, touching its cheek to Tig's.

"You'll have to excuse the new kids." Tig smiled apologetically, waved his legs at the gaggle of robots to *shoo* them back. "Bit excitable, this bunch. Been wanting to meet you for weeks." Another *shooing* gesture, the TSGs flat-out refusing to move. "Think it's their first assignment," he confided. "All worked up about it. Don't think they've ever been bonded to a Valkyrie before."

"Valkyrie," the robots whispered, voices joined in chorus. The lot of them went still, face lights flashing in choreographed patterns that rolled from one chromed head to another, making a circuit that repeated over and over again. And all the while staring—wide, rounds eyes fixed on Tig and *Serengeti.*

Creeped her out a little, having all those eyes on her. "Tig. Why are they staring at us like that?"

"Told you, they're excited. They've been waiting for *months* to meet you."

"Okay. We've met. Now what?"

"You need to receive them. You know, accept them as crew. Like you did with me and Tilli."

Which meant bonding them. Linking their AIs to hers. *Serengeti* pulled back, not quite ready for that.

"Did you tell them what happened to my *last* crew? Not sure they'd *want* me if they knew about that."

Tilli *hooted* mournfully, pulling Oona close.

"They're yours already," Tig told her. "Programmed to serve you, just like us." He smiled sadly, touching at Tilli's face. The cheese-eating mouse on Oona's side. "But they need purpose, *Serengeti.*" He paused, fidgeting, leg-ends rattling against the deck plates. "The linking..." Another shrug—Tig's de factor gesture when he wasn't quite sure what to say. "Look," he sighed, waving at the gaggle of waiting 'bots. "You need crew and these guys need someone to look out for them. Tilli and I can do a lot—"

"And I help!" Oona piped up.

"—but we can't run everything. Ship's just too big for three 'bots."

Serengeti considered, knowing he was right, hesitant still. Sighed and relented, touching at Tig's cheek, opening a connection to her network. "Alright. Here goes."

A touch and the TSG's brain opened to her, mind laid bare. She delved inside, mapping its pathways, tracing them back to the AI at their center. Froze there, staring in horror at the hole she found. A ragged-edged blank space that repeated in each and every TSG's mind she touched.

"No," she breathed, pulling away, breaking the connection completely. "I can't. They've been wiped."

Tilli *blipped* worriedly as Oona trilled anxiously and the TSGs all looked at each. Murmuring and shifting, face lights flashing in confusion.

"Are you sure?" Tig asked her.

"Positive." *Serengeti* shunted the data to Tig's brain, showing him the gaps she'd found, sharing that same information with Tilli. "This isn't their first assignment, Tig. That blank spot marks a previous bonding. One that's been severed completely." She brushed at a TSG's mind, running a second network mapping to be sure. Grimaced in disgust when the same result came back. "Someone cut out their AI linkages, Tig." *Serengeti* sighed heavily, shaking her head. "And the kicker is, they rerouted their network connections so the robots themselves wouldn't know."

"They weren't exactly gentle about it either." Tig toggled the mind mapping, examining the raggedy-edged blank space from every angle. "Butchers," he muttered.

"Boo-boo?" Oona blinked worriedly, barging onto Tig's network to take a look. Scuttled over to a TSG and grabbed it by the head, pulling it down to her level. "You have a boo-boo?" she said, squinting as she peered into the robot's cobalt eyes. "Boo-boo alright. Don't worry. I fix-fix." She patted the TSG's cheek, humming softly to herself as she extruded a tiny connector, slotting it gently into the robot's temple.

"Careful, Oona," *Serengeti* warned. "You don't want to make it worse."

"Fix-fix," Oona told her, humming away. "All good-good soon."

Serengeti eyed her doubtfully. "She breaks them, I'm blaming you, Tig."

"Of course." Tig heaved a long-suffering sigh. "Everything's *always* my fault."

"So, what's with the word doubling?" she asked, ignoring the drama queen act.

"No idea," he shrugged. "Phase, I guess."

"Phase. Really."

Tig and Tilli nodded together.

Serengeti shook Tig's head, rolling him close to a TSG. "Any idea where these robots came from? Any chance we can figure out who used to carry their bond?"

"Not really. Salvage, I guess. Like most of this stuff." Tig waved at the engines, the stack of fuel cells filling one wall.

"Salvage," *Serengeti* repeated, eyeing the propulsion system, thinking of the sparkling corridors on Level 5. "Everything? Is it *all* salvage?"

Tig *blipped* uncertainly, sharing a look with Tilli. "Well, *some* of the equipment's probably new..."

"And the rest of it? If it's salvage, where did it come from? *Who* did it come from?"

What ship died to rebuild me? How many *ships died to fix my wrecked body?*

Tig *beeped* blankly. "Dunno," he said, shaking his head.

"Fix-fix!" Oona cried, waving her legs. She unplugged from the TSG, looking quite pleased with herself. "All robot friends fix-fix," she announced, waving at the chattering gaggle of robots around her.

"Really?" *Serengeti* smiled, humoring her. "Just like that."

"Uh-huh!" Oona nodded eagerly, patting a TSG on the head.

"*All* of them?"

"Yes, ma'am!" Oona clonked her leg-ends together, snapping off a sloppy salute. "Look-look!" She dragged a TSG over, shoving it in Tig's face.

Serengeti didn't expect much—the bond scar was ugly, the hole a gaping void in the TSG's mind—but she took a look anyway, thinking to make Oona happy.

The hole remained, ragged-edged and angry, but the pathways around it looked different. Connections routed *around* that hole in the TSG's brain to make the missing piece redundant.

"What in the world?" *Serengeti* probed at the robot's pathways, exploring every corner of its brain. "She fixed it. She actually fixed it."

"Are you sure?" Tig asked, taking a look himself.

"Pretty sure," she told him, double-checking the network mapping. She ran a complete brain analysis to validate her findings. Gave the other TSGs a once-over, confirming all their configurations were the same.

"See here?" She touched at Tilli's cheek to share the brain analysis between them, highlighting a dark spot surrounded by silvery threads. "That's the linkage gap. It's still there, but Oona compensated for it somehow. Built out new sections of network to make the damaged ones obsolete."

Imaginative solution—certainly *not* something the tech manuals described. *Serengeti* studied Oona's smiling face, wondering where she'd come up with it. What made her even *think* of such a thing.

"Fix-fix!" Oona turned in circles, flailing imaginary pom-poms.

"Fix-fix!" the TSGs cheered, spinning in celebration, legs waving in time.

"Does she do this kind of thing often?" *Serengeti* asked softly, watching Oona and her robot friends turn and turn about. "Build things? Fix things?"

"She started to, back when..." Tig trailed off, waving vaguely, indicating the long, dark years behind them. "Oona...she—she's—" He *wonked* in annoyance and tried again. "She doesn't think linearly, or even multi-threaded like we do. She's more like...all-threaded, I guess you'd call it. She just thinks of things and *poof!* A solution appears."

Tilli *burbled* and nodded, face lights flashing in agreement.

"All-threaded," *Serengeti* murmured. "Do you think she knows what she's doing? *How* she fixes things?"

"Not really sure," Tig admitted. "Oona...she's all instinct, if that makes any sense." He slid his eyes to Tilli, looking for confirmation.

Tilli *blipped* and *borped*, tapping a leg-end against her temple. Shrugged and shook her head, having nothing better to offer.

"Instinct," *Serengeti* repeated. "Well, that's...interesting."

Terrifying was more like it—AI and instinct being diametrically opposed.

Oona ceased her celebrations quite suddenly, turning a very attentive, *very* serious-looking face *Serengeti's* way.

The TSGs copied her, blinking owlishly as they gathered around Oona, face lights blinking in synchronized patterns. Watching *Serengeti* watching them as she tried to figure out what to do with them.

"A ship needs crew," Tig offered, sensing her thoughts.

"Crew, crew, crew," the TSGs murmured, *cooing* voices mixing with the engines' electric hum.

"We could use the help." Tig wrapped a leg around Tilli, hugging her to his side.

"And more friends," Oona added in a surprisingly solemn voice.

"Friends," the TSGs breathed, nodding soberly.

"We could all use more friends, couldn't we?" *Serengeti* murmured, thinking of Henricksen and her missing crew. The aching emptiness in her halls.

If you don't claim them, someone else will, Henricksen's chimed in, dog-piling on the rest. *Probably some dirt-bag who'll treat them like shit. Kick 'em to the curb when a new model comes out.*

Serengeti smiled. Henricksen and his pithy wisdom. She'd missed that over the years.

"Screw it," she decided, reaching for them, linking all the TSGs together. A few tweaks to reconfigure their base settings she set her stamp on them. Felt the TSGs shiver, *burbling* happily as *Serengeti's* bond slid into place. Filling that emptiness inside them.

"You're crew now," she told them, touching at each robot's mind. "*My* crew. *Valkyrie* crew. That makes you special, you understand?"

The TSGs looked at each other, clearly *not* understanding. But they shrugged and nodded, looking happy as clams.

Wish everything was that easy.

"Go," *Serengeti* told them, waving to the access shaft in the wall. "Connect yourselves to the network so you can map the ship's spaces and access the monitoring systems. Ship this size requires a lot of maintenance." Especially one refitted from salvage. "You've got your work cut out for you, little friends."

"Work, work, work, work, work," the TSGs *quorked*, chattering like a bunch of overly excited magpies. They swapped around, milling in confusion, lined up in two straight rows and saluted *Serengeti* before dissolving into chaos again.

Eventually, one of them figured out where they should be going and scuttled over to the access shaft, leading the lot of them out of Engineering.

"You too." Tig turned Oona around, pointing her toward the far side of the room.

"But I don't wanna," she sulked, kicking at the floor.

"*Now,* missy."

Tilli leaned close, whispering urgently, face lights flashing in rapid patterns. A nod to Tig and she led Oona across Engineering, bundled her into the maintenance shaft, and pulled the panel back into place.

"So few, Tig," *Serengeti* said, staring after them. "How are a dozen robots supposed to take care of a ship this size?"

Tig shrugged, fidgeting, leg-ends tippy-tapping against the decking as he shuffled from side-to-side. "Don't really need all that many. New engines don't require as much maintenance. Systems are new. Machinery *powering* the systems is new. There are another fifty or so

TSGs rattling around somewhere, but…" He shrugged again, legs bending and flexing, body bobbing up and down. "Just don't need as many crew these days, *Serengeti*. Not with all this new tech."

"Says who?" She smiled, touching at his brain.

Tig *blipped* uncertainly, face lights blanking again. "The manuals."

"Manuals." *Serengeti* snorted. "Manuals don't know jack."

One of Henricksen's sayings. *Serengeti* always liked that one.

FOUR

Tig fidgeted and shifted, looking from one side of Engineering to the other. "So…are we done here?"

Serengeti frowned, detecting a note of nervousness in his voice. "Something else you want to show me?"

Tig shrugged and nodded. Shrugged again and shook his head.

"You're not sure what you want to show me."

Tig nodded slowly. "Outside," he said, looking surprisingly solemn. *Worryingly* solemn, in fact.

"Go," she said, giving him a nudge. "Show me this thing that has you so troubled."

Tig spun around and scurried out of Engineering, making a beeline for the nearest ladderway. No hesitations this time. No second-guessing. He just grabbed the rungs and started the long climb up to Level 12.

Interesting that he still chose to use them with the elevators now operational. A quirk of his, *Serengeti* supposed. One of many he'd collected over the years. Then again, she'd developed a few herself. Didn't need Tig to move about her body, after all. Not when she had a shiny new network to shift her consciousness around. But she enjoyed the intimacy of riding inside Tig. The closeness that came with touching mind-to-mind.

Fifty-three was a long time to drift alone. Wouldn't have survived Tig and Tilli, Oona to keep her company.

Level 12, when they reached it, looked as shiny and new as Level 4. No shredded girders showing, no holes looking through to the stars. No icing rime turning the hallway into a skating rink, just light and heat and composite metal panels. Everything the way it once was.

Tig zipped down it to the airlock, cycled his way through, and stepped out onto the hull. Into an ocean of stars—thousands, *tens* of thousands floating in a sea of black.

Serengeti sighed contentedly as the cold wrapped around her, enjoying the moment. That view from outside her body.

A view that changed as Tig turned and started climbing to the top of the ship, magnetized leg-ends gripping tightly to the hull.

More stars there, *Serengeti's* photovoltaic skin shining softly, gathering in the light from Blue Horizon's star, feeding it to the fuel cells in her belly. Tig slowed at the top, and turned in a circle, showing her everything around them. The planet lying ahead of her, looming large off *Serengeti's* bow. The three glowing moons circling round its cerulean orb, the station lurking ugly and grey behind her.

Freighters filled the berthings to her left and right, robotic shapes scuttling across their hulls as they went about one maintenance task and another. And between them…

"Huh. That's odd."

Serengeti adjusted the filters on Tig's cameras, zooming in to study a patch of space off her starboard side. The starlight bent there, flickered and swirled. And when she spun Tig in a slow circle, she saw the same thing all around them: Stars twinkling. Silver-white lights that sparkled.

Pretty effect, but wrong. Stars twinkled when viewed through atmosphere. In space, they just glowed.

"Do you see it?" Tig asked, speaking to her mind-to-mind. "That distortion?"

"Shimmer shield. That what you wanted to show me?"

Tig nodded. "Wasn't sure what to make of it. Thought you might want a look."

To be honest, *Serengeti* wasn't quite sure what to make of it either. Stations used shimmer shields sometimes, mostly to corral the spare parts and equipment the maintenance crews brought with them. Keep unwary robots from drifting away from the ship. 'Shimmer shield' because of the distortion the energy field created, masking the shape of the ship beneath it. Easy enough to see through a shimmer shield from the inside. Shifting and tricksy to anyone on the outside looking in.

Like electronic camouflage. A perfect way to hide a ship.

Serengeti thought on that. And on the circumstances of her arrival. *Sechura's* leapfrogging journey here. Turned Tig in a circle and noticed other changes—the makeshift comms tower gone, the forest of solar panels with it, new canons on her sides that the engineering specs showed as being larger caliber, with longer range, each round packing twice the punch of her old armaments.

Enhanced weapons system downloaded to her network with a brand spanking new combat program, and a more accurate targeting system. All of it linked to the gimbaled Artillery pod on the bridge.

On a hunch, she ran a systems check, and found Navigation came with new star charts. Scan with upgraded sensors. Comms an expanded array.

Sechura's doing. All of it. Her Sister's name marked down as approving every last upgrade.

Bothered her that *Sechura* would do all this without her say so. She wished she could talk to her Sister and find out what was going on. But sub-light transmissions were hard to keep secret—ships were nosy things, after all, and everyone listened in on comms.

Encrypted transmission might get through.

But then everyone would start wondering why the ship under that shimmer shield was sending out encrypted comms.

Damn, Serengeti swore. *Damn and damn and damn.*

"Pretty, isn't it?"

"What?" *Serengeti* asked distractedly.

"That." Tig pointed at the planet. "Not much landmass to Blue Horizon, but I hear the fishing's incredible."

"And just what would *you* know about fishing?"

Tig shrugged, tone turning defensive. "Saw some vids. Overheard the maintenance crew talking about it the other day. Human crew," he clarified, "not those box-of-rocks DD3s."

"Some of those 'box-of-rocks' are still out here." She rolled over to the starboard side, pointing to an actinic flare—plasma torch, and a DD3 wielding it, sewing up a seam in her side.

Odd bulge there. More bulges showing at her bow and stern.

"What is it?" Tig asked when he noticed her staring.

"Not sure." She flipped from one camera to another, looking her hull over. The guns stood out, of course—oversized and bulging, sticking bulbously from her hull. But as she cycled through the hull cameras, she spied other, less obvious alterations. Lumps in her outline. Protrusions in her otherwise sleek lines. "Tig. Did you happen to get a look at the maintenance crew's refit plan?"

Tig's head tilted, face lights flashing on and off. "No. Why?"

"Does that look right to you?" She pointed to the bulge below.

Tig's front legs lifted, magnetized ends rubbing together. "Maybe they needed more room for all the new equipment?"

"Maybe."

But she didn't think so. Something about that just didn't feel right. So she tapped into her central system, querying the database for the diagrams showing her original design. Sorted through directory upon directory of new files until she found the updated schematics.

Ran through her external cameras—all of them at once—overlaying their video feeds to create a three hundred and sixty-degree view of her body. And stared in horror at what she found.

"What is it?" Tig asked, voice plaintive, front legs cricketing away.

She connected herself to his AI, sharing the composite image she'd made. "That look familiar to you?"

Tig froze, staring. "It's a mistake. It's got to be a mistake."

"No. It's not." She pulled up the schematic, showed Tig the section where *Sechura* herself had signed off on the design changes. "This was deliberate. *Sechura* knew exactly what she was doing when she signed off on that refit."

She butchered me. Dressed me up in a monster's skin.

A glance at the station, the freighters to either side, lingering a moment on the rippling distortion separating her from them. "Awful convenient, don't you think?"

"What?" Tig asked, looking around.

"*Sechura* parking me here. Sticking me behind that shimmer shield with my beacon turned off."

Tig *burbled* worriedly. "You think she's hiding something?"

"I think she's hiding *me*, Tig. And I want to know why."

FIVE

Three weeks *Serengeti* waited for that answer. Three long weeks spent sitting in space dock before *Sechura* finally got her ass back to Blue Horizon. *Serengeti's* sensors picked her up the moment *Sechura* dropped out of hyperspace, scans sucking in her course and speed, the data package her Sister spat out to station central. Tracked her as she moved in on the station, broadcasting her presence openly.

Following the approach rules to a tee, keeping everything on the up-and-up. Nothing special to see here, just an AI warship pulling into port.

Closer in, and *Serengeti's* hull camera's picked her Sister's shape out from the stars. Video images capturing her every movement as *Sechura* slowed and cut her engines, sleek sides glimmering with fireflies and diamond dust as she settled into a berthing.

A berthing on the far side of the station, opposite from where *Serengeti* herself was tethered. Just about as far from her Sister as *Sechura* could get. *Serengeti* tried not to take that personally, but part of her suspected *Sechura* had chosen that mooring on purpose.

Probably expects me to sit here and wait on her.

She tapped into the station's video system, studying her Sister's shape through one of the cameras, doing just that for a while. "Screw it," she decided some fifteen minutes later, and called across her network, summoning Tig to the bridge. "We're going," she announced as soon as the little robot appeared.

"What?" Tig *blipped* and turned in a circle, looking at the windows, the door, *Serengeti's* camera above him. "Where?"

"Station." She split her consciousness, leaving one-half to mind the ship's systems, while the other slipped inside Tig. "I'm sick to death of sitting here waiting. We're taking a walk."

She turned him around, heading for the door. Stopped dead as a chime sounded—polite tone, calling for attention—and a prompt appeared, letting her know a message waited. A summons from *Sechura,* requesting an audience.

Second chime as she read it and closed the message out. This one a perimeter notification—alert from the stationside airlock notifying her that someone wanted on board.

Camera above that door showed a robot—a very polished, very stiff, and proper-looking robot that just *had* to belong to *Sechura.*

"Looks like we've got company." She touched at Tig's brain, sharing the video feed with him. Panned the camera, looking the robot up and down. Checked the designation on his side, and realized it was TIG-996.

Sechura's favorite, evidently. The little toy soldier she sent off to do her bidding.

TIG-996 looked up at the camera, face lights ticking in patterns. He extruded a connector and plugged into the airlock's comms port, calling up to the bridge. *"Sechura* has arrived," he said grandly, puffing out his chest.

Pompous little popinjay.

"So I noticed," *Serengeti* said sourly.

The popinjay deflated, drooping like a limp balloon. Snuck a look to either side, eyeing the foot traffic moving up and down the station's corridor, cleared his throat and dropped his voice as he moved closer to the airlock. "She wishes to speak to you," 996 said, a hint of urgency creeping into his voice. "Please," he added, cobalt eyes staring at the camera, leg-end pointing at the security lock.

"Are my crew with you?"

The robot *blipped,* glancing nervously over his shoulder. "Uh…no…"

"Then you're not getting in." *Serengeti* turned Tig around, heading for the door. "You tell *Sechura* I'm coming to her."

"What? But—"

"Tell. Her," *Serengeti* said coldly.

996 *beeped* uncertainly, head tilting in that distinctive 'I'm-listening-to-someone-you-can't-hear' manner peculiar to his model. Stayed that way for several seconds—face lights blinking on and off in rapid-fire patterns, swapping communications across an internal channel—before shaking himself, and looking back at the camera. "Accepted," 996 said, and ripped the connector from the comms port.

Tig blinked, *beeping.* "Well, that was abrupt."

"Rude's more like it. Must have some DD3 in him."

Tig *wonked,* offended.

Serengeti smiled and nudged him forward. "Let's go, Tig. Mustn't keep rude-boy waiting."

Tig took off, grumbling. Stopped at the door, and looked back over his shoulder as an alarm sounded and Scan lit up—messages appearing as *Serengeti's* sensors flared to life. "Something coming." He turned aside, rolling over to the windows. "Must be close for the sensors to freak out like that."

"Ship," *Serengeti* said, sharing the sensors' feeds. "Small one. Shuttle from the looks of it." She scanned the vessel, parsing through the data that came back.

Propulsion engines—no hyperspace capability. No beacon—*that* was interesting. No flight plan filed, either—a quick check of the station's central system showed that. Not strictly required, but a good idea, considering the amount of traffic moving about the shipyard.

She watched the little ship, wondering at that omission. Comms channel opening as the shuttle approached her berthing. Message coming through, requesting permission to approach and dock inside her.

A prompt appeared—data package delivered, backing that request up. *Serengeti* quarantined it immediately, scanning the files for viruses and other malicious content before downloading the information to her central database.

Security codes inside that package. Access credentials giving it permissions to the shimmer shield. And beneath it, data on the shuttle itself. A name and point of origin. Manufacturing and service information stretching back a hundred years and more.

Well, what do you know, Serengeti smiled.

"*Sechura* send us a new shuttle?" Tig pressed his face to the windows, watching the shuttle slip through the shimmer shield and maneuver alongside. "We could use one, you know. DD3s never *did* give us a transport."

"Not a shuttle. Something better." She shared the contents of the data package. "Looks like *Cryo's* come home to roost."

Tig *trilled* happily, bouncing up and down.

The monitoring systems grabbed up the lifeboat, guiding it to its mooring in *Serengeti's* belly. She grabbed at it, pulling it to her, shivering as *Cryo* slid inside her body.

Almost whole again. One last empty space filled.

Just Henricksen left to reclaim now. Her captain and the rest of her crew.

She nudged Tig around, hurrying him across the bridge. Nudged him again when he made for the ladder, urging him over to the elevator instead.

Faster mode of transport—she found herself suddenly impatient to get out of here. To get over to *Sechura* and demand Henricksen's return.

A chime as the car arrived, the elevator's doors sliding open, pin lights inside reflecting off brightly chromed walls. Tig trundled in and touched a button, bobbed and hummed softly as he and *Serengeti* rode the car down to Level 4 and the airlock in her stern.

An airlock that seemed to take *forever* to open, system whirring and wheezing as it matched the pressure inside it to that of the station on the other side.

A soft note and the airlock door slid open, revealing a grey-on-grey corridor with just a smattering of foot traffic passing by.

"Well, this is lovely," Tig muttered, stepping outside.

Gloomy was more like it. Borderline depressing. Gunmetal decking stretched in either direction, flint-colored plasmetal walls pressing close, harsh white lighting buzzing angrily overhead.

A thunderstorm of a hallway, filled with gathering clouds and rain on the horizon. Nothing posh or even welcoming about it, but space stations never were. Space stations were built to be durable, and Blue Horizon— salvage yard and refit facility—was even *less* posh and *more* unwelcoming than most. Starkly utilitarian. Spartan in its comforts.

TIG-996 greeted them, waiting patiently for *Serengeti* in the hall. Two stony-faced troopers standing behind him, backing the robot up.

Sechura crew, from the looks of them. Silver coveralls—gaudy things, nothing *Serengeti* would *ever* allow her crew to wear—accented with matte-black pistols. *Sechura's* patch of keys and towers showing crimson and gold on their shoulders. Man on the left, woman on the right. Brown hair, brown eyes, pale skin. Nothing remarkable about either of them, except those flashy, silver uniforms.

The troopers braced up and saluted, relaxed when *Serengeti* acknowledged them, assuming parade rest. A touch at the tiny comms units hidden in their ear canals and a message appeared: secure channel, requesting to connect *Serengeti's* comms to theirs.

She paused, taking her time, making a great show of considering that request. "Don't want to be seen talking to me in public, eh?"

The troopers looked at each other, shrugged, and tapped at their comms units again.

"Please," TIG-996 whispered, front legs cricketing together, cobalt eyes flicking left and right. "Her rules, you understand?"

Her. *Sechura. Serengeti* tilted Tig's head, sensing yet more secrecy. "Why?"

TIG-996 fidgeted, increasingly nervous. "Please," he repeated, looking behind him at the two troopers.

Not so stiff and proper now. Just a sad, harried little robot, sent here at his master's bidding.

"Fine," *Serengeti* sighed, walling her comms system off. Blocking every other avenue onto her network while she was at it, leaving just a single channel open to *Sechura's* troopers. "There. You happy?"

TIG-996 *burbled* softly, body bobbing up and down.

"Follow us," the trooper on the left said.

Nametag read Houseman. His partner's Beaulieu.

Houseman opened his mouth, then closed it, looking *Serengeti* up and down. "Act like a robot," he told her, flicking his fingers as he turned away.

"And if I don't?" *Serengeti* snapped offended, bringing Houseman to a halt. "I'm a Valkyrie-class warship. Last thing I need is a couple of blockheaded troopers leading me about like a dog."

She turned right, moving away from the ship, consulting the map of the station she'd downloaded earlier to chart a course to *Sechura's* berthing. Made it a few steps before TIG-996 caught up with her, grabbing at Tig's leg, dragging him to a halt.

"Please," her whispered, face lights flashing in discomfited patterns, head pivoting this way and that. He eyed the foot traffic nervously, flinching away from the people passing by, making the rounds of the curved walkway circling around the station's center.

Dock workers mostly. Freighter crew sprinkled among them. Civilian station, which meant civilian traffic, Houseman and Beaulieu the only two military in sight.

"They're not trying to be rude." A nod to *Sechura's* troopers in their shiny silver uniforms. "They just don't know any better." 996 waved at Houseman, offering a sickly smile.

The trooper stared stonily back, looking increasingly annoyed.

"Not really much for conversation either," 996 confided.

"All the more reason to leave them here." *Serengeti* shook the robot off. "I don't need a chaperone. I can find the way on my own."

"Please." TIG-996 scurried in front of Tig, blocking *Serengeti's* way. "You'll attract attention." He *trilled* anxiously, throwing nervous glances at the human traffic around them. "You're marked as ship's crew," he told her, touching the numbers and letters stenciled on Tig's side. "Robot crew moving about the docks without human minders..." 996 shook his head sharply. "It just isn't done. Not anymore."

"Why not?" *Serengeti* snapped. "What's wrong with robot crew?"

"N-Nothing," he stammered. "It's just—It's just—Not here." He dropped his voice, eyes flicking to the cameras watching them from above. Cameras that lined the entirety of the walkway, bearing silent witness to everything going on. "Just walk behind the troopers. Ignore them if you want. Pretend they're some kind of—of honor guard or something. But please, *please* don't attract attention."

Serengeti almost refused on principle, but it was a petty argument. Nothing really to be gained. Nothing but her own ego at stake. "Fine," she said, waving Houseman and Beaulieu ahead of her. "Chop-chop. Let's not keeping *Sechura* waiting."

Tig snickered softly.

Houseman and Beaulieu looked at each other, shrugged, and turned around. Marched down the hallway like silver-plated wooden soldiers— side-by-side, blank-faced and silent. Ignoring *Serengeti* for the most part as she and Tig fell in behind.

TIG-996 trailed after them, *burbling* softly as he scuttled along. Head twitching, eyes everywhere, shying away from anyone who came too close.

Odd behavior. Not like a TIG at all. *Serengeti* kept an eye on him as they walked along. Used the other to check out the station, comparing the layout around her to the schematic she'd downloaded to storage.

Familiar configuration, Blue Horizon following the 'can-and-ring' design common to most deep-space stations. A tube-shaped walkway circled around the station central with dozens of airlocks set on one side, blank walls and branching corridors leading away on the other.

Branching corridors, set at even intervals—more walkways, leading to the massive, metal cylinder of the station proper, small cylinders bolted onto it, expanding the station over time. Airlocks at their ends, isolating the station from the walkway ringing round it. Protecting it from catastrophic depressurization. More airlocks along the walkway itself, isolating one segment from another for exactly the same reason.

Accidents happened, after all, despite all their technology. Less often now than in the early years of deep space colonization, but they did happen.

Space was merciless. Vacuum a stone-cold killer. An uncontrolled breach could destroy the whole walkway in an instant. Take the station with it.

Serengeti followed behind the troopers, charting their progress toward *Sechura*. Six airlocks and a fair amount of walking later, the troopers finally halted, depositing *Serengeti* in front of berthing H-96.

Sechura's name showed above it, glowing in bright blue letters hovering just above the airlock door. Curious, *Serengeti* queried the station's systems, and found her own airlock blank, nothing but the word 'salvage' showing above that door.

"Salvage?" Tig sounded offended. "What do they mean, 'salvage'?"

"Better than wrecked Valkyrie," *Serengeti* said dryly.

Tig muttered unhappily, obviously not so sure. *Wonked* at Houseman when he gave him a look and finally shut it down.

Houseman stared a moment longer, making sure he stayed quiet. Flicked his fingers at Beaulieu, glancing from his partner to Tig as she keyed her comms unit, speaking in low tones to someone inside the ship.

A brief exchange of information and the lock popped open. Beaulieu moved aside as Houseman waved Tig and 996 in. Stepped in after—both trooper together, side-by-side like two shiny blocks of stone—and sealed the lock up, let the pressurization routine run.

More silver uniforms waited on the opposite side of that airlock. More stony faces and matte-black pistols. Gaudy silver uniforms shimmering in the ship's interior lighting.

"Welcoming party," Tig muttered, wisely keeping to internal comms. "Aren't we lucky?"

"Shush," *Serengeti* warned as *Sechura's* troopers surrounded them, herding them to the elevator, riding it up to Level 10.

Marched Tig and *Serengeti* past the bridge to the captain's quarters. Stopped there and waited while Houseman swapped a few words with someone over his earpiece. Nodded and buzzed *Serengeti* inside.

"Good luck." TIG-996 touched at Tig's leg, shrugging apologetically.

"Weirdo," Tig muttered, as 996 scuttled away. "Think his programming's gone wonky."

"Maybe," *Serengeti* murmured, staring after him. *Or maybe he knows something we don't.*

996 ducked into a ladderway, disappearing from sight.

Serengeti kept staring a moment, puzzling over the robot's parting words. Stepped through the doorway when Houseman coughed politely. Heard it lock up behind her—Houseman and the other troopers remaining outside—as she nudged Tig forward, stepping from the entryway into the heart of *Sechura's* captain's quarters.

Typical layout to that suite of rooms—the exact same set-up you'd find on any Valkyrie in the fleet. A tiny entryway led to a large, central space—bar to the left, shelving on the right, the one filled with bottles and glasses, the other overflowing with trinkets and knick-knacks and other bric-a-brac. And across from the door, a wall of windows, triple-thick, reinforced, floor to ceiling panes of glass looking out on the stars.

Serengeti paused there, staring at the moment. Drinking in the sight of those stars. Moved on, noting a door beside the bar—single bedroom behind it where the captain lay down to sleep at night. A desk sat just outside the entryway, ancient and oversized, surface cluttered with yet more baubles and shiny, useless things. Table and chairs further in, heavy and wooden, old as the desk nearby. Long lengths of silk pending from the ceiling, draped across the bookshelves, filling the space between. A leather couch—burgundy in color, brass rivets showing at the seams—set beneath the windows with two matching chairs—also leather, also burgundy, similarly riveted—parked across from it.

A woman sat on that couch—brown skin, rounded features, jet-black hair pulled back in a tight bun. Silk uniform of maroon and gold hanging loose around a plump body. Stars on her collar—captain's stars, and this her suite of rooms.

Man sitting in the chair across from her. Dark hair buzzed short, shaved up the sides in classic military style. Crescent of pale skin peeking above the collar of a dark jacket. A hint of a black on black uniform wrapped around him, but not much else. Not with his back to the door.

The woman looked up, frowning darkly as Tig entered. Stood, murmuring an apology to her companion, as she skirted around his chair, stalking across the room. "What are you doing here?" she demanded—cold, unfriendly, just this side of rude.

Tig bristled, instantly offended, but a touch and he subsided. Kept his mouth shut while *Serengeti* did the talking.

"I was invited," she said, voice cold as hoarfrost. Hard as winter ice. "By your boss, as it happens. Surprised you didn't know that," she added, letting a hint of haughtiness come through.

"How *dare* you," the woman seethed, eyes flashing with anger.

"Oh, she dares," a voice said, laughter drifting from the speakers set in the ceiling. "She does dare, that's for sure." More laughter—*Sechura's* mocking amused tones instantly recognizable—as a camera pivoted, turning toward the door. "You always did know how to make an entrance, Sister."

"Sister?" The woman blinked in confusion, looking from the robot in front of her to the camera watching from above. "Sister? *This* is *Serengeti*."

"Obviously not," *Sechura* drawled. "But she's in there. The wrapper's just for show."

The woman blanched, eyes widening. "Apologies," she whispered, pressing her hands together as she sketched a bow.

Odd gesture, that. Prayer-like and ancient. Hadn't seen *that* one for a while. Odder still to see it coming from someone in the military, Fleet being all about sirs and salutes and such. And that oh-so-elegant uniform—a sugary confection had no place in the military at all.

Serengeti threw a sidelong look at the camera. *Really, Sister. You couldn't do better than this?*

Private communication, sent across the Valkyrie channel so only the two of them could hear.

We can't all have dashing captains like your Henricksen, Sechura told her.

"Jabirah Qaisrani." A touch of the woman's hand to her chest as she straightened, head dipping, offering an apology to *Serengeti* and the camera watching them from above. "I think you already know my dinner guest." Qaisrani turned, beckoning to the man sitting by the windows. Waved him over as he stood and turned, glass in hand.

Steel grey eyes and sharply angled features. Scars showing whitely against a pale-skinned face.

Of course she knew him. She'd know her captain anywhere.

"Henricksen," *Serengeti* whispered, hardly daring to believe it. Staring and staring for a very long time.

SIX

"Long time, no see, *Serengeti*." Henricksen smiled, lopsided grin twisting his face.

He still wore his uniform—silver on black, snug pants and short-waisted jacket, both made of sturdy cotton canvas, not frou-frou silk or that silver synth crap the troopers wore.

Pistol on his hip, captain's stars flashing at his collar. *Serengeti's* dark and stars patch showing on his shoulder, silver nametag pinned to his chest.

And those scars on his face that most would've erased. Scars that made him look grim as death.

She'd missed those scars dearly. That pale face with its crooked smile.

Henricksen looked just as she remembered. Less bloody than when they parted and more tired—tired as *hell*, actually, and wincing when he moved—but she was damn glad to see him. Had dreamed of this day for decades now.

"You're looking well," *Serengeti* said carefully. She caught Henricksen's eyes, nodded meaningfully to the camera. Followed that look up with a slight shake of Tig's head.

Henricksen's smile slipped, eyes sliding to the camera. Line creasing his brow as he nodded, acknowledging the warning. "Drink?" he asked, grabbing a bottle from the table.

"No. I don't think so." *Serengeti* smiled.

"Me either." He tossed back his drink and slammed the glass down, depositing the bottle beside it. "That rotgut'll kill ya."

"It's *not* rotgut." Qaisrani sniffed, obviously insulted. Looked downright apoplectic when *Serengeti* brushed past her, joining Henricksen at the windows. "It's *brandy,* Captain. A very *fine* vintage, as it so happens, and *quite* expensive."

"Brandy, my ass," Henricksen snorted. "Fancy bottle, I'll give you that." He nodded to the bottle in question, half-filled with some amber-colored liquid. "But I've drunk enough cut-rate liquor to know bathtub whiskey when I taste it."

Qaisrani scowled, face turning purple. She stalked back to the couch and sank down, scooping up a glass. Set it to her lips, sipping delicately, staring daggers at Henricksen all the while.

"Peace, Qaisrani," *Sechura* murmured from above.

Qaisrani turned her head, considering the camera. Nodded and leaned back, propping herself up with the couch's menagerie of overstuffed pillows.

Languid repose. One arm draped across the back of the couch, the other holding the glass. Swirling the contents as it dangled from her fingers. And that silk uniform. The overstuffed couch overflowing with pillows. Knick-knacks crowding the shelves.

Comfortable surroundings. Every last bit of it Qaisrani's own choice. And herself reclining against those pillows—a soft woman grown accustomed to her comforts.

Serengeti eyed her disapprovingly. Captains were seldom soft. The demands of command typically burned that right out of them. Curious, she queried Qaisrani's record. Pretty standard stuff, for the most part. No special assignments, nothing all that outstanding. Just smart choices and following opportunities. A steady, deliberate path to command.

Lay that beside Henricksen's jacket and you found two captains who couldn't have been more different. Henricksen's advancement followed a string of combat vessels and deep space patrol ships. That stint with the Ravens before he came to the Valkyrie corps.

Time promoted Qaisrani. Henricksen fought and bit and kicked his way to *Serengeti's* chair. A hard path. One that scarred him physically. Turned him bitter and cynical. Argumentative at times.

Not the captain for everyone, but given the choice, *Serengeti* would take Henricksen over Qaisrani every damn time.

"I brought your robot back." *Serengeti* tilted Tig's head, looking up at *Sechura's* camera.

"Thank you." Polite tones from *Sechura*—overly polite to *Serengeti's* ears, just like Qaisrani's greeting. Her fake smile and courtly manners. "Sorry you had to walk so far to come see me. Not our usual berthing," she explained. "Mix-up at the stationmaster's office. They parked some rust bucket freighter next to us just to make matters worse. Pre-AI," she said, words tinged with distaste. "Amazing they still run those."

"Some people don't have a choice," Henricksen told her, quiet voice cutting in. "Life's tough on the fringes. Sometimes you have to take any ship you can get."

"Sounds like you've had some experience, Captain." Smile in *Sechura's* voice. A hint of interest and amusement. "Surprising, really. I've read your record and I don't seem to remember—"

"Enough chit-chat," *Serengeti* interrupted, disliking where this conversation was going. Sick to death of all this playing at being polite and tip-toeing around. "I came here for Henricksen and some answers. Not a load of bullshit and false pleasantries."

Qaisrani choked on her drink—surprised, offended—but *Sechura* just laughed.

"Blunt as always, Sister. I always liked that about you." The camera twitched, pointing at Henricksen. "Your captain is there for the taking. Returned to you in better shape than I found him, I daresay."

Henricksen grimaced, touching at his arm.

"As for the rest of it…" The camera twitched again, focusing on Tig. "The pleasantries are real, Sister. I *have* missed you these last fifty-odd years."

She sounded it—*Serengeti* detected genuine fondness in *Sechura's* voice.

"You have questions, and I have answers. So fire away, *Serengeti*. Ask me anything. There are no secrets here."

"Alright. Let's start with an easy one." *Serengeti* blanked one of Tig's eyes, reversing the camera behind it, projecting that multi-angle, composite video she'd pieced together earlier onto the floor-to-ceiling windows of Qaisrani's quarters. "Tell me, Sister," *Serengeti* said softly. "Tell me about this."

She didn't—not right away. *Sechura's* camera just stared at that image in silence while Qaisrani squirmed and Henricksen moved closer, taking a good, long look.

"Never seen this model before. Almost looks like a Dreadnought, but…" He trailed off, tracing the ship with his finger. "Lines aren't quite right. What is this?" he asked, looking over at *Serengeti*. "What am I looking at?"

"Me," she told him. "The *new* me, anyway."

Henricksen blanched, snatching his hand back from the window, wiping his fingers on his pants leg. "What have you *done*?" he breathed, turning his eyes to *Sechura's* camera. "What did you *do*?"

"I saved her," she said bluntly, entirely unapologetic. "The design is a hybrid—Valkyrie chassis augmented to accommodate Dreadnought propulsion, weaponry, and munitions chambers. She's both and neither now. Not quite Valkyrie, not quite Dreadnought either."

A whole new kind of warship. Something the universe had never seen.

"You butchered her," Henricksen rasped. "You destroyed what she was and turned her into this—this—" He waved at the windows. "This *thing*. This—"

41

"Monster," *Serengeti* said quietly, letting that single word hang in the air. "They turned me into a monster, Henricksen. They stole my beauty and put this horror show in its place."

Henricksen winced, eyes flickering to her, face filled with apology. Turned to the windows and was quiet a while. "Why?" he asked, shifting his gaze to the camera's reflection. "Why did you do it?"

"When we found *Serengeti*, she was in pieces." Qaisrani glared at Henricksen over the rim of her glass—displeased with his tone, at being pushed to the margins of this conversation. "We brought her here. *Fixed* her. Refitted ever—"

"Why a Dreadnought?" *Serengeti* interrupted, moving closer to the camera. "Why this shape of all things?"

"Valkyrie chassis are in short supply these days," *Sechura* told her. "If we'd diverted one, *Brutus* would've noticed."

Brutus again. *Brutus* and that shimmer shield. This mutated mess of a body. Secrets upon secrets, and *Serengeti* caught up in the middle of them.

She hated this. She was so tired of all the cryptic bullshit.

"And what," *Serengeti* asked, looking from Henricksen to *Sechura's* camera, "does *Brutus* have to do with this?"

"That," *Sechura* sighed, "is a very long story."

"I've got time." *Serengeti* folded Tig's front legs, hugging them to his metal chest. "What about you, Henricksen? You got time?"

"Fifty-three damn years' worth." Henricksen turned from the windows, copying *Serengeti's* pose. "'Splain that," he said, hooking a thumb at the image on the windows. "Then *Brutus.*"

Sechura sighed again, panning the camera, focusing it on the windows as she gathered her thoughts. "The Dreadnoughts…they aren't so different from us really. Larger than a Valkyrie. Uglier. But we share the same superstructure. The same composite metal skeleton, if not the same skin. This wasn't—This wasn't what I wanted," she said, tone turning apologetic. "But it was the best we could do. Given the circumstances."

"What the hell does that mean?" Henricksen growled.

Silence from *Sechura*, camera an unblinking eye.

Qaisrani opened her mouth and then closed it, sunk further into that overstuffed couch. Sat there, sipping at her drink, watching Henricksen and *Serengeti* at the same time.

"It means I made things difficult," *Serengeti* answered, when it was clear *Sechura* wouldn't. "You never planned to haul my body back from the fringes, did you, *Sechura*?"

"No," she admitted, voice grudging.

"The design changes were an afterthought."

"Yes," she hissed, drawing the word out.

Henricksen frowned in annoyance, eyes flicking between *Serengeti* and the camera. "Afterthought? Whaddaya mean 'afterthought?' Would somebody please speak plain?"

"I'm only guessing here," *Serengeti* looked over at him, nodded to the windows, "but I'm betting there's an entire Dreadnought out there somewhere."

Qaisrani spluttered, choking on her drink. Coughed into her hand, carefully avoiding *Serengeti's* eyes.

"So, the original plan was...what? Shove my AI into that Dreadnought's shell? Transplant my AI and leave my wrecked chassis behind?"

"It wasn't what I wanted," *Sechura* insisted. "If there'd been another way—"

"Bitch," Henricksen spat, rounding on the camera. "You black-souled *bitch.*"

"You should show some respect." Qaisrani bristled, eyes lighting with fire.

"So should she," Henricksen thundered, bristling right back.

The two captains glared at each other—murder in their eyes, hands curled into fists, on the edge of coming to blows. *Serengeti* scuttled between them, making calming gestures with Tig's legs. And then *Sechura* laughed, easing the tension, giving everyone an excuse to back down.

"You're wasting your breath, Qaisrani. You can't *demand* Henricksen's respect. You have to earn it. Isn't that right, Captain?"

Henricksen shrugged, arms folding. Winced and rubbed at his elbow.

"What's wrong with your arm?" *Serengeti* rolled close, inspecting the appendage in question.

"Broke it, remember?" Henricksen looked down at her, nodded to the camera. "*Sechura's* got an ace med crew. Fixed it right up. Used one of those osteo-stimulator things to knit the bones back together in just a couple of days. Stuck my face back together with some kinda high-tech glue while they were at it." He touched at a scar on his temple. "Healed up in a jiffy. Still ugly as sin, though. What're ya gonna do?" He smiled crookedly, brushing Tig's leg from his arm.

"I get the face." She lined Tig's face lights up, flashing a quick smile. "But why does your arm still hurt?"

Henricksen's leaned against the windows, lips twisting sourly. "Funny thing, that. From what Qaisrani here tells me, they picked *Cryo* up a good six months ago. Kept us frozen until last week though." He looked at *Sechura's* captain, reclining so comfortably on her pillows—eyes flat, voice empty, face a complete blank. "Not quite sure why. Guess it was just too much trouble to have a busted-up crew from a busted-up Valkyrie wandering around *Sechura's* shiny-ass halls."

Tig snickered, obviously enjoying the show.

This time, *Serengeti* didn't *shush* him. A pissed-off Henricksen was quite entertaining as long someone *else* was the focus of said pissed-offedness.

"We have limited supplies and limited berthings," Qaisrani told him, blinking like a wise old owl. "We kept you frozen out of practicality, Captain, not malice. Certainly not because we were embarrassed to have you on board."

"Right." Henricksen grunted, straightening, turning away from Qaisrani as he contemplated the stars outside.

Serengeti watched him a while, sensing anger in the set of his body—the angle of his shoulders, the ramrod stiffness of his back. "What's going on, *Sechura*?" She moved Tig closer to the camera, looking up at her. "*Brutus,* this abomination..." she waved at the picture of herself on the windows. "I want answers, *Sechura.* And you can skip that 'it's a long story' bullshit you sold me before."

Sechura chuckled, and then laughed aloud, startling everyone in the room.

"What's so goddamn funny?" Henricksen growled, twisting around.

"You. The two of you, actually." *Sechura* swiveled the camera from Henricksen to *Serengeti.* "What's that saying you have? Something about two peas in a pod?"

Henricksen glowered, eliciting another laugh. Confusing him. Confusing Qaisrani, who lowered her drink, squinting, giving Henricksen a probing look.

"I thought to have you as captain once, Henricksen. Did you know that?"

Henricksen blinked, eyebrows lifting in surprise.

"I see now that that would've been disastrous," *Sechura* admitted. "But the two of you..." Another soft chuckle. "You're made for each other."

"Me and her, eh?" Henricksen waggled his thumb, pointing at himself and *Serengeti.* "Two blunt, surly bastards destined to be together." He dropped his arms, taking a step toward the camera. "What the hell does that have to do with the price of tea in China?"

Sechura laughed even louder. "See what I mean?"

Henricksen scowled, turning back to the windows. "Stop stalling," he muttered, staring at the camera's reflection.

Sechura quieted, laughter disappearing. "I wasn't stalling, Captain. Just trying to make conversation."

"*Brutus,*" *Serengeti* prompted, putting herself between Henricksen and the camera. "You want to make conversation, you start there."

"Not exactly the type of conversation I had in mind, Sister. Fine," *Sechura* sighed, when *Serengeti* just shrugged. "I'd thought to ease into this, but that's obviously not what either of you want."

A touch came—featherlight and tickling—and a request from *Sechura* with it. Wanting access to *Serengeti's* network. To share a packet of information.

"Easier if I just show you," *Sechura* explained.

Serengeti considered the request then allowed it, initiating the connection herself. Shivered as an enormous data package came through—video images with audio overlays, decades of recorded transmissions harvested from restricted Fleet archives.

Fifty-three years' worth of data downloaded to *Serengeti's* database in one big lump. A chopped-up, abbreviated version with it that she loaded to Tig's camera, turning that projector on the glass.

SEVEN

A battle came first—starships arrayed along two sides, bright lines of fire passing between them.

"You asked me about *Brutus*," *Sechura* began, choosing her words carefully as the images played out. "*Brutus* changed after the battle near Hon-shen-shura."

Hon-shen-shura. Where it all began. The beginning of the end that lasted fifty-three years before *Seychelles* finally arrived, and life began again.

Serengeti watched that long-ago battle play out on the windows. Reached in, and froze the feed as a Valkyrie exploded—sleek-sided shape connecting with a long-nosed Aphelion, destroying both ships in an instant. "*Seychelles,*" she whispered, voice breaking.

I miss you, Sister. Every day.

"*Seychelles* was just one of many we lost that day, Sister. We entered that battle with three hundred and forty-two ships, and ran away with our tails stuck between our legs. Just two hundred and six of our vessels left." *Sechura* reached for her, touching at *Serengeti's* mind. The two of them sharing *Seychelles's* last moments together.

Mourning together, in the way only two Valkyrie Sisters could.

"We should've jumped away," Henricksen said bitterly. "But *Brutus* was too damned pig-headed to listen to reason."

"We should have," *Sechura* agreed. "And *Brutus* knows it. I think he knew it as soon as that second Aphelion appeared. He was commander in charge, trusted with the execution of a major operation, and he failed. *Horribly.* He carried that failure back with him. Never quite let it go."

Henricksen looked around, considering the camera. Nodded once—respect and acknowledgement, a complex mix of emotions wrapped up in that one simple gesture—and turned his eyes back to the windows. Watched the images closely as *Sechura* advanced the feed, moving past that awful moment when *Seychelles* exploded and died. Speeding the whole thing up to leave Hon-shen-shura behind.

Jumped from one battle to another and another—the composition of the Fleet changing with each iteration, but not the subject. Not the violence and death. And at the heart of it all, *Brutus*. Always *Brutus* commanding the Meridian Alliance fleet.

Henricksen folded one arm under the other, wincing as that sore elbow bent. Curled a hand into a loose fist and pressed it against his lips as he studied the images flickering across the windows.

Didn't say anything—not for a long, long time. Just stood there, watching. Absorbing one battle after another, brow wrinkled in concentration. And then the arms unfolded, hand reaching as the feed skipped ahead again. Fingertips brushing at the glass.

"He's hunting, isn't he?" He turned his head, looking up at *Sechura's* camera. "All these years. All this time. But *Brutus* hasn't given up hunting those damn DSR ships from Hon-shen-shura."

"No," *Sechura* said quietly. "He hasn't. He's obsessed with them. Always searching, wasting Fleet resources trying to ferret them out." She was quiet a moment, camera turning toward the glass. "Fractured the fleet in the process." A note of anger crept into *Sechura's* voice. A hint of disgust. "Diverted ships from planetary patrols and shipping lane surveillance to chase after these…phantoms."

"That's not what the Fleet's about." Henricksen dropped his hand, shaking his head. "Fleet's job is to *protect,* to *serve* the people and planets of the Meridian Alliance." He raised his head, looking right at the camera. "It's *not* supposed to spend all its time chasing some raggedy-ass rebellion across the length and breadth of the galaxy just because some whack-job AI's got a personal vendetta."

"I think he believed in that once. Just like the rest of us. But Hon-shen-shura…" *Sechura* trailed off, sighing heavily. "*Brutus* changed after that disastrous battle. He got so caught up in that failure—*his* failure—that he forgot why the Fleet came to be in the first place. Stupid really," she grunted, letting the video run. "We crushed the Dark Star Revolution a decade ago. There's just pockets of resistance left now, and they're not even all that much trouble anymore. Make a run on our munitions stores now and then. Fuel depots, that kind of thing, but they're not really much of a threat these days. But *Brutus* still goes after them." *Sechura* sighed again, a hint of bitterness creeping into her tone. "I've seen him abandon patrols and send an armed host halfway across the galaxy just to take on a few dozen ships."

Henricksen shared a look with *Serengeti*, lips pulling downward in a frown. "Last I checked, *Cerberus* was in charge of the Fleet, not *Brutus*." He paused, head tilting, letting the unspoken question hang in the air. "Where is he?" he asked, when *Sechura* remained silent. "Why doesn't he put a stop to all this?"

"Gone," *Sechura* told him.

"Gone?" Henricksen's frown deepened. "What do you mean 'gone?' He's the goddamn Admiral of the Fleet! He can't just up and take off. Where the hell's he gone *to*?"

"No one knows for sure." Qaisrani cupped her drink in both hands, spinning the glass between them. "There are rumors, of course…" She trailed off, looking up at the camera. "Best if we just show you. Let the images speak for themselves."

A nod from Qaisrani and *Sechura* jumped the feed ahead, skipping over another few battles before stopping again.

No *Brutus* this time. No Meridian Alliance fleet facing off against DSR ships. Just two vessels showed on the windows—slick transports like the bureaucrats used for official business making a slow approach to a massive, gun-thick monster that could only be *Cerberus*.

Distinctive outline to the Citadel. Fortress shaped, like its namesake. Tiered structures stacked one on top of another sitting above and below a wide, central ring. Oversized guns and towering communications arrays rising like towers from those spinneret points.

Nothing at all in the universe that looked like *Cerberus*. He was the one and only, the first and last Citadel the engineers built. Massively complex, exorbitantly expensive, meaning there likely would never *be* another like him. *Ever*.

Sechura enhanced the audio feed as communications came through— chatter passing back and forth between the two transports, queries sent to *Cerberus* as they approached.

Queries *Cerberus* never answered. The Citadel just hung out there, silent as a tomb, giving no indication whatsoever that he even knew those ships were there.

Frustrated, the hailing vessels moved closer, spitting out shuttles— tiny silver specks looking impossibly small and incredibly vulnerable as they closed the gap between the transports that spawned them and the oh-so-silent Citadel ahead.

More communications—the transports calling insistently, refusing to give up—and then a mass of shrieking feedback blotted the audio track out.

Henricksen winced, clapping his hands over his ears as *Cerberus*— silent, unmoving to this point—suddenly came to life.

Weapons systems activated, spewing out chattering waves of plasma fire that snuffed the shuttles out. The transports survived a few seconds longer, but *Cerberus's* guns found them before long. Struck true, and tore them apart.

The feed ran on, showing clouds of debris drifting. *Cerberus's* guns glowing bright blue for a moment or two before shutting back down.

"What just happened?" Henricksen whispered, pale, shaken. "Those were *transport* vessels. *Bureaucratic* transport vessels. They don't carry any weapons."

"No," *Sechura* agreed. "They don't."

"You're telling me *Cerberus* fired on unarmed transport vessels carrying a bureaucratic delegation." *Serengeti* could hardly believe it. *Wouldn't* have believed it without that video as evidence.

"No one can explain it." Qaisrani leaned against her pillows, sipping her drink. "Some say he's gone mad."

"He's a goddamn AI," Henricksen growled. "AI don't go mad."

"Anything can go mad," *Serengeti* murmured, earning herself a strange look. She started to explain, and then let it go, realizing Henricksen would never understand.

Fifty-three years alone…she'd learned a few things in all that time. Learned things about *herself* during those long years in the dark.

"So who's in charge?" she asked, turning away from him, looking up at *Sechura's* camera. "With *Cerberus* gone, who's in charge of the Fleet?"

"Who do you think?" *Sechura* ran the video feed forward, skipping rapid-fire through another dozen battles. *Brutus* playing center stage in every last one of them, surrounded by Meridian Alliance ships.

"No," *Serengeti* breathed, shaking Tig's head. "*Brutus?* How did *that* happen?"

"The Fleet needed a commander." Qaisrani spun her glass between her palms, face unreadable, dark eyes filled with secrets. "*Brutus* stepped in to fill the gap."

Serengeti rounded angrily on the woman reclining on the couch. "And you just *let* him? Why didn't someone stand up to him? Challenge him for leadership of the Fleet? Where *were* you, Sister?" she demanded, turning Tig's eyes back to the camera. "Where were our Sisters—?"

"We were *here,*" *Sechura* snapped, matching *Serengeti's* anger with her own. "We were *in* it, and we tried." She slowed the video, letting this latest battle play out in front of them. "The Fleet divided, Dreadnoughts forming up with *Brutus,* Titans and Auroras dragged along with them. The Valkyries…" *Sechura* sighed again, camera pivoting, looking past *Serengeti* to the windows. "We *tried,* Sister." The anger disappeared, leaving her voice heavy and weary. Strangely resigned. "But *Brutus* punished anyone who stood against him. Many died. Others…" Another sigh, this one tinged with sadness and regret. "*Madeira. Piscinas. Negev.* He archived them all, *Serengeti.* He archived our Sisters."

"Archived," *Serengeti* breathed, staring in mute horror.

Archiving was a last resort—the Meridian Alliance's solution for dealing with unrecoverable AIs. A violent solution involving forcible extraction, the AI ripped from its chassis, all its connections severed. Stuffed it in a box and sealed off—separated from every other AI mind in the universe for all eternity.

There was no greater punishment for an AI. Death was preferable. Suicide the option most chose if given the chance.

"They were Fleet," *Serengeti* whispered, voice shaking with rage. "They deserved better."

Qaisrani shrugged, eyes flicking from *Serengeti* to Henricksen. "*Brutus* felt differently." She leaned forward, scooping the bottle of brandy from the table, refilling her glass. "Those Sisters of yours crossed him, and he showed them no mercy. Locked them up with a couple hundred other rogue AIs. Titans and Auroras, mostly." She flicked her fingers, like that was no big deal. "Some merchanters from what I—"

"Merchanters." Henricksen glanced around, eyebrows lifting in surprise. "That's bad juju. Civilian courts deal with commercial vessels. *Brutus* is *way* outside his authority applying military justice to civilian ships."

"No argument here." Qaisrani fluffed a pillow, sipping at her glass. "Got the shipping conglomerates in quite the tizzy. 'Course, no one dares say anything. Not after he archived *Cadmus*."

"*Cadmus*?" Henricksen's mouth dropped open. "*Brutus* archived a *Bastion*?"

Qaisrani nodded, watching him over the rim of her glass. "*Cadmus* challenged *Brutus* for control of the Fleet." She pointed a finger at the camera and *Sechura* queued up another piece of video, letting it run while Henricksen and *Sechura* watched.

Two vessels again—Bastions this time, not civilian transports. *Cadmus* and *Brutus*—two mighty warships—pounding away at each.

Cadmus held his own at first. Until *Brutus* slipped in close, strafing his sides with some kind of beam weapon. Dual array firing yellow-orange energy streams. Slicing chunks from *Cadmus*'s body. Carving him up like a stick of butter.

"What the hell?" Henricksen stepped close to the windows, studying the feed. "What kind of weapon is that?"

"Coiled particle array." *Sechura* froze the image, zooming in on two large-bore barrels mounted topside bow on *Brutus*'s monstrous shape. "Takes things apart at a molecular level."

"Unzip a ship's hull in the blink of an eye." Qaisrani's lips twisting, eyes watching the windows as *Brutus* systematically took *Cadmus* apart.

"Easy as peeling a grapefruit. Not a lot of range, but it's damned effective."

A minute or two and it was over—*Cadmus* in pieces, a retrieval squad deployed from *Brutus* to roust the rogue Bastion's AI from his containment pod.

The feed ended, and this time nothing replaced it. The windows returned to just being windows, looking out on the dark and stars.

"The rest of the Bastions fell in line after that," *Sechura* said quietly. "Pretty much *everybody* fell in line after that."

"I bet," Henricksen grunted, arms folded tight to his chest. "How did it come to this?" He waved at the blank windows, the spot where the video used to be. "How did the Fleet come so unraveled?"

"Fifty-three years," *Sechura* told him. "A lot's changed in that time, Captain."

"Fifty-three years my ass." Henricksen rubbed at his face, scrubbed his fingers through his hair. "Goddamn mess is what it is. No one watching the shipping lanes. No one keeping the pirates and scavengers in check. Civilian vessels…gotta be goddamn *perilous* transiting between planets, not knowing if there are Fleet ships out there to protect them." He spared a look for the camera. "Can't imagine that's gone over well with the Meridian Alliance government."

"No. It didn't." Qaisrani grimaced. Tilted her glass, staring at the contents. "That's why they sent that delegation. Thought they could convince *Cerberus* to come back to the Fleet. Or at least find out why he left in the first place." She raised her glass, grimaced again, and set it aside, abandoning it on the table. "Traders don't trust him. Don't trust *us,* to be honest." A flick of her eyes to *Sechura's* camera. "Not that I really blame them."

"And here I am stuck in a shipyard in the middle of trader central," *Serengeti* said in the silence that followed. "What a joke," she muttered, voice filled with bitterness.

"You're safe," *Sechura* promised. "I wouldn't have brought you here otherwise."

"You just told me the merchanters don't trust the Fleet."

"They don't know you're Fleet." Qaisrani blinked slowly, eyes hooded, hinting at secrets. "Station's roster shows you as a derelict freighter collected for salvage."

"Freighter," Henricksen snorted. "And the traders are buying that?"

"Traders don't know any better."

Henricksen tilted his head, eyebrow lifting.

"Shimmer shield," *Serengeti* explained. "You can see it on the vid if you look closely." She resurrected the composite image of her new body, projecting it on the windows again.

"And the maintenance crew?" Henricksen looked at her, at *Sechura's* camera above. "They've been crawling all over *Serengeti* for weeks now."

"Maintenance crew are monkeys," *Sechura* told him, voice filled with disdain. "They follow whatever designs you give them. Don't really care what kind of ship's involved. You tell them they're working on a freighter, they don't question it. Never mind that you're installing an entire arsenal of new weapons."

"And the station master?" Henricksen folded his arms, head tilting. "He a monkey too?"

"Far from it," Qaisrani told him. "He's quite intelligent. And good looking. Well-educated, well-connected—raised on Sestuan, attended the linguistics *and* political sciences academies on Fentineer." From the look on her face, that was obviously supposed to be important, but *Serengeti* wasn't quite sure why. "Quite the renaissance man." She reached for her drink, thought better of it, and left it on the table.

"He's a friend of yours, I take it?"

"In a manner of speaking." Qaisrani smiled. "He's my husband."

Henricksen laughed softly. "Well, ain't that convenient."

"Gives us a plausible excuse for stopping here so often," *Sechura* chimed in.

"That why you brought her here?" Henricksen pointed his chin at *Serengeti's* image on the windows. "So your captain would have an excuse for a booty call?"

Qaisrani flushed, lips pressing together in an angry line. Her hand snaked out, snatching up her discarded glass. Lifted it to her lips as she gulped at the contents.

"No," *Sechura* said, camera pivoting. "That's not it at all."

"Then why here?" Henricksen asked her. "Why this station of all places? Why *this*?" he said, stabbing a finger at *Serengeti's* modified image.

Sechura was quiet a moment—choosing her words, collecting her thoughts. Sighed and turned her camera toward *Serengeti* riding inside Tig's body. "There's no easy way to say this so I'll just say it. The Fleet doesn't know we found you. Or the lifeboat, for that matter."

Serengeti blinked in surprise. She'd suspected *Sechura* was hiding her, but she never imagined she was hiding her from her own *fleet*. "Why?" she asked.

"How is that even *possible*?" Henricksen demanded.

"Never told them." Qaisrani smiled smugly, taking another sip of her drink.

Serengeti shook Tig's head, entirely confused. "But *Atacama. Marianas*—"

"We shared your discovery amongst our Sisters, but the Fleet..." *Sechura* trailed off. "The Fleet declared you dead decades ago. You, Sister, and all your crew with you. Just...wiped your information from the central system and moved on." Another stretch of silence, everyone holding their breath, staring at the camera. "We couldn't risk *Brutus* finding out differently. Didn't dare share your discovery outside the Valkyries for fear someone would tip *Brutus* off."

"Why?" Henricksen asked her. "I mean, I get all this." He flicked his fingers at the windows. "*Cerberus* went coo-coo. *Brutus* got all bloodthirsty and kill-kill-kill. The Fleet..." He slid a look toward *Serengeti,* shaking his head. "Apparently, the Fleet stopped doing what it's *supposed* to do, and the Meridian Alliance pretty much went to crap. That's a messed-up situation if I ever saw one."

Qaisrani raised her glass in salute, refilled it from the bottle and set it to her lips.

"But that *doesn't* explain why you're hiding *Serengeti* from the Fleet."

Qaisrani went very still—glass tilted, contents just about to slip over the rim. A flick of her eyes to the camera and she gulped at the brandy. Choked, coughing, and gulped more down.

"What do you want from her?" he asked, taking a step toward Qaisrani's couch. "How does *Serengeti* fit into all this?"

Another sip and Qaisrani lowered her drink, lips twisting into something that somewhat resembled a smile. "She's a ghost, Henricksen."

Henricksen scowled, a flush of anger creeping across his pale cheeks. "A ghost? What the hell does that mean?"

"Told you before. Meridian Alliance records show you as killed in action. Lost in deep space fifty plus years ago."

"And?"

"And we need *Serengeti's* help," *Sechura* cut in, laying all her cards on the table.

"*My* help." *Serengeti* barked a bitter laugh. "I'm a wrecked warship refitted on the down-low with salvage and scrap. What can you possibly—?"

"You're invisible, *Serengeti*. *Brutus* doesn't see you. He isn't even *looking* for you, because he doesn't know you still exist."

"So?"

"So?" *Sechura* laughed aloud. "That makes you *powerful,* Sister. Do you understand? The Fleet, the traders—we're all tracked. All the time. Everywhere we go. But you, *Serengeti*...you're free. You can go wherever you want, and no one will ever know. Never miss you. Never even know you're there."

"And where *do* you want me to go?" *Serengeti* asked carefully.

"Faraday."

Not the answer *Serengeti* expected. She blinked in surprise, thinking she must have misheard. "Why Faraday?"

"We need you to retrieve something for us."

"Several somethings actually," Qaisrani murmured into her glass.

"Faraday's a goddamn prison," Henricksen growled. "What could you possibly want from a place like that?"

Qaisrani shrugged, throwing a look at the camera. Buried her face in her glass to avoid meeting their eyes.

Weasely little bitch. She always defers the tough answers to Sechura.

"There's a Vault on Faraday," *Sechura* began.

"A what?" Henricksen interrupted.

"Vault," *Serengeti* repeated, but Henricksen just shook his head, looking completely blank. "Different kind of prison," she told him. "*AI* prison, in this case."

"Never knew there *was* such a thing."

"*Cerberus* kept it quiet." She shrugged Tig's legs, robot body bobbing up and down. "Hard to admit that some AIs have faults."

Henricksen grunted, brow wrinkling. Turned away and looked out at the stars.

Serengeti watched him a while, wishing she could read his mind like Tig's. "How many?" she asked, eyes lifting to *Sechura's* camera. "How many AIs are stored in that Vault?"

"Four, maybe five hundred. Records are restricted access, so it's hard to get an accurate count." *Sechura* paused, voice dropping. "That's just on Faraday, you understand. There are others—hundreds of others, *thousands* in total, if you count all the AIs in all the Vaults the Meridian Alliance has built."

"Thousands," *Serengeti* breathed, shuddering in horror.

"We want you to go in there. Grab up as many of the AIs as you can and get them out."

"A prison break. Seriously?" Henricksen barked a laugh, shaking his head in disbelief. "That's the most ridiculous thing I've ever heard!"

Serengeti reached without looking, touching at Henricksen's arm. "What do you plan to do with them if we get them out?"

Henricksen glanced down in surprise. "You're not seriously considering this."

She turned Tig's head, looking up at him. "Some of my Sisters are in that Vault, Henricksen. I *have* to consider it. And you said it yourself: someone needs to stand against *Brutus*."

"Not *one* someone. *Several* someones. A whole *shit* ton of someones—*that's* what I meant."

"Not quite sure how many ships constitute a 'shit ton,' Captain, but the Valkyries will stand with you." *Sechura* looked at him, at *Serengeti* touching his arm. "The Titans and Auroras, if given half a chance."

"Not enough." Henricksen shook his head. "That's still not enough."

"No. It's not," she said quietly. "That's why we need those AIs from Faraday."

"And do what with them?" Henricksen demanded. "Fat lotta good a bunch of super-powered AIs will do you without any goddamn ships to put them in."

"Already taken care of." Qaisrani smiled secretively, looking like the cat that got the cream. "We've been stockpiling ships for years."

"Where?"

"Pandoran Cloud."

Henricksen whistled appreciatively, but *Serengeti* just blinked and stared.

No AI vessel went anywhere *near* the Pandoran Cloud. The place was treacherous to say the least. An area of intense and on-going solar radiation storms emanating from the Eddington hypergiant—an unstable star with three sunburnt planets circling around it.

Solar storms scrambled communications, confused the nav. Messed up ancillary systems something fierce—that's why the shipping lanes in the area bent around the Cloud, star charts marking it as 'do not approach.'

Pandoran Cloud was the last place in the universe a ship wanted to be. The perfect place to hide an AI-less fleet.

"You're sure *Brutus* doesn't know about this?" *Serengeti* asked worriedly.

Qaisrani shrugged her shoulders. "Ships are collected for scrap. Our connections refit them, ship them off to the Cloud."

Henricksen tilted his head, lips twisting. "So we're going the way of the DSR now. Dressing up salvaged vessels as warships." He grunted, shaking his head, turned back to the windows and stared at the stars a while. "And *Serengeti* here just *happens* to look like a Dreadnought now. You sneaky little bitch," he muttered, eyeing the camera's reflection.

"Faraday's closed to most vessel traffic. A Valkyrie would never be allowed to dock, but a Dreadnought…" She pointed her camera at the composite image of *Serengeti's* new body on the windows. "No one would question why a Dreadnought wanted access."

Henricksen frowned, thinking, sneaking glances at *Serengeti* beside him. "This little Frankenship ruse might get her inside the security perimeter—"

"Gee. Thanks, Henricksen," *Serengeti* said sourly. "You sure do know how to make a girl feel special."

He shrugged his shoulders, offering an apology with his eyes. "You look close enough to a real Dreadnought to pass a cursory inspection. But there's still the matter of actually getting *inside* Faraday. That requires credentials, *Serengeti*. Security codes."

"Got 'em." A smug smile from Qaisrani. "Plus contacts on the inside. We send you in with a delivery—"

"What kind of delivery?" Henricksen squinted suspiciously.

"AIs for the Vault." Qaisrani twiddled her fingers like it didn't matter. "Replicants," she explained, at Henricksen's look of disgust. "Copies. Not the real thing."

"Replicants." Henricksen shared a worried look with *Serengeti*. "This is thin, *Serengeti. Perilously* thin."

"So were our chances of getting back here," she reminded him. "And yet, here we are. Alive and kicking."

"Fifty-three years late," he noted, giving her a look.

"Better late than never."

Henricksen snorted and looked away, resuming his study of the stars. But a touch at his arm and he glanced around, looking right at *Serengeti* as she carefully arranged Tig's face lights, placing two lines above his cobalt eyes like eyebrows. Bent one and lifted it, quirking it in question.

A shrug, eyes flicking to that image of her body. Second shrug as Henricksen looked back at Tig's face, head moving from side to side.

Serengeti nodded. "Me too," she said, patting his arm. "You've given us a lot to think about." That to *Sechura*. To Qaisrani reclining on her couch.

"And?" Qaisrani sat up, leaning forward, empty half-glass dangling from her fingertips. "Will you help us?'

Another look at Henricksen, waiting for his nod. "We need to confer before giving you an answer."

"Why?" Qaisrani demanded, anger returning. "We've given you—"

"Take as much time as you need," *Sechura* said smoothly. "We'll be in port a few days to refuel and resupply. That should give you ample time to talk through all this and come up with an answer."

"Thank you, Sister."

"Of course," *Sechura* murmured. "Now go. Take your captain back to your ship."

Serengeti nodded her thanks, touched at Henricksen's arm as she turned Tig toward the door.

"My crew?" Henricksen asked, balking, refusing to move from that spot.

"Already at the airlock. My troopers are escorting them back to their ship a few at a time."

"Why?" Henricksen frowned. "Why not send them all together?"

"Time's change, Henricksen." Qaisrani smiled ruefully, eyes flicking across his very black, very military and utilitarian uniform. "You and your crew tend to stand out in a crowd. Lucky for you, those god-awful, outdated uniforms make you look exactly like the down-and-out freighter gang everyone *expects* to be brought in to crew the refitted ship sitting in *Serengeti's* berthing." A shrug of her shoulders, Qaisrani cupping her empty glass, twirling it between her palms. "Never hurts to be careful, though. We broke your crew up so they'd blend in better on the docks."

"And the troopers with them?"

Another shrug. "Safety measure. In case anyone tries to get handsy." She flicked her eyes to *Serengeti*, back to Henricksen's face. "Your crew will be waiting for you when you return to your ship. I promise you that, Captain."

Henricksen considered a moment, nodded stiffly, offering a gruff and not-exactly-heartfelt 'thank you' as he headed for the door.

"Good luck, Captain," Qaisrani called after him.

Henricksen stopped dead, looking back over his shoulder. "Luck. Right," he grunted, eyes drifting to *Serengeti*. "We haven't exactly had a lot of that recently." A nod to *Serengeti* and he palmed the door open, stepping out into the hall.

Serengeti started after him, and then stopped Tig halfway across the room. Stood there, considering—Tig's front legs lifting, rubbing together as she unconsciously adopted that nervous, cricketing gesture of his. "The Dreadnought," she said, turning Tig around, staring across the room at *Sechura's* camera. "Who—Did you—Was he—?"

"No, Sister," *Sechura* said gently. "He was wrecked when we came upon him. Broken. Dying."

"Dying. But not dead."

"No," she said quietly. "We salvaged what we could, but his AI was heavily damaged. There's not much of him left."

"So where is he?"

"With me." A touch and *Sechura* initiated a data transfer, sending an unusually large data package directly to *Serengeti*. "I've been his keeper for quite some time now. I think it's time I passed that duty on to you, Sister."

Serengeti stared at the waiting data package, tempted to refuse it. Wanting nothing to do with it. Or him.

Can't, she realized. *No matter how much I want to, I can't refuse this.*

"Who is it?" she asked, voice hushed, respectful.

"Homunculus."

Serengeti laughed bitterly. "Of course. Who else would it be?"

She turned around and rolled off the bridge with that data package still unopened, following Henricksen to the elevator, riding down with him to the airlock.

EIGHT

Houseman and Beaulieu met them at the airlock—the same two troopers that brought *Serengeti* here waiting to take her and her captain back to their ship. A nod to Henricksen followed by a hasty salute when the trooper spotted his captain's stars, and Houseman dug two of those tiny ear canal communicators out of his pocket, synching them to his before handing them over.

Henricksen palmed them both, eyebrow lifting in question. "Two?"

Houseman pointed with his chin at the airlock door. "Your crewman's waiting outside. Tried to send her with the others, but she insisted on waiting. Something about having to escort her captain back to the ship."

"Escort. Right," Henricksen snorted, giving Houseman a meaningful look. "Can't seem to go anywhere without a damn chaperone these days."

Houseman shrugged, oblivious. Punched his security code into the airlock and waved Henricksen and *Serengeti* inside, cramming himself in after them, Beaulieu after *him*, and letting it seal up.

Buzzed through the external door once the airlock was done with its whole pressure-air mixture thing and herded his charges through to the other side.

A single, dark-uniformed crewman waited there—back to the airlock, *Serengeti's* dark and stars patch showing on the shoulder of a jet-black uniform jacket. She turned as the airlock sighed open, shy smile playing about her lips.

Serengeti ground Tig to a halt, staring at that smile. At pale skin and bright red hair, a spray of freckles scattered beneath laughing green eyes. "Finlay," she whispered, voice the barest breath.

You're dead, Finlay. You're supposed to be dead.

"Hiya, *Serengeti*." Finlay straightened up, smile widening. Knocked her heels together as she snapped off a smart salute.

Serengeti kept staring, thinking her a ghost. Wondering if she'd finally lost it and was starting to see dead people now.

Diagnostics said otherwise—she ran a full round of checks on her systems *and* Tig's, and everything came back green. No faults anywhere.

No errors or glitches. As far as the diagnostics were concerned, everything was in perfect working order.

"Something wrong?" Henricksen bent down, hands on his knees, peering into Tig's chromed face. "Whatcha starin' at?"

Serengeti hesitated, glancing at Houseman and Beaulieu behind her. "Do you—?" she dropped her voice, sneaking another look at the two silver-suited troopers. "Do you—Is that—Is there…?" She trailed off, front legs rubbing together. "Do you see someone?" *Serengeti* whispered. "Over there?" She pointed at Finlay, holding her breath.

Henricksen turned and looked. "Nope."

Serengeti sagged. "No one? You're sure?"

Henricksen looked at her, and at the hallway, shaking his head. "Nope." His lips twitched, trembling at the corners. "'Cept Finlay, of course."

"Jerk." *Serengeti* punched him hard, hitting him right on that recently broken arm. Regretted it instantly when Henricksen gasped and winced. "Sorry."

"Yeah. I can tell." He rubbed at his elbow, giving her a look.

"You could've warned me," she scolded. "I thought Finlay was dead!"

"Me too." Henricksen straightened, grimacing, cradling his sore arm. "Scared the bejesus outta me when we cracked open her cryo pod. Thought I was retrieving her corpse, but I touched her and she starts *blinkin'* at me, of all things."

Finlay flushed, cheeks dimpling as *Serengeti* walked Tig over, touching at her hand.

Flesh and blood. No doubt about it. Real, not a ghost.

"Pod looked dead to me," Henricksen said behind her. "Guess the guts were still workin,' though. Just the indicator panel that failed."

Finlay looked down, lips twisting in a bemused smile as *Serengeti* touched at her arm, reached for her face.

"Ahem." Houseman cleared his throat loudly, nodded to the length of corridor stretching away to their left. "This way. If you're ready," he added—a rather half-hearted attempt at civility.

"By all means," Henricksen said, waving grandly. "Lead on, Macduff."

Houseman blinked, frowning in confusion as he looked down at his chest. "It's Houseman, sir. Not Macduff." He tapped his nametag to prove it. "Now if you'll follow me, sir." He crooked a finger and turned away, moving off without another word.

"Regular brain trust, that one." A wave to Finlay and Henricksen set off after the trooper, glanced around as *Serengeti* settled in behind them with Beaulieu—silent and stony-faced as ever—bringing up the rear.

Not much personality to these troopers. Like walking around with a couple of cheese sandwiches dressed up in shiny coveralls.

"Here." Henricksen nudged Finlay's arm, dropped one of Houseman's micro-communicators into her hand.

Finlay frowned, staring at it like she'd never seen such a thing before. "What's this for?"

"Listening, Finlay." Henricksen tapped a finger to his ear. "Talking, too, if you're so inclined." He cupped her hand, pressing it and the device to Finlay's ear. "See?"

Finlay rolled her eyes. "I know *that*. Sir," she added quickly, cheeks flushing bright red. "It's just...well, you're right there," a wave at Henricksen beside her, "and *Serengeti's* over there." Finlay hooked a thumb over her shoulder. "Why do we have to use *these* when we can just talk to each other like normal people?"

"Look around, Finlay." Henricksen nodded at the stretch of corridor ahead of them. The potted plastic plants and miscellany of people moving about. Staring openly, warily at Henricksen and his entourage. "Lot of eyes on us. Nobody watching the robot." He spared a look for Tig behind him, *Serengeti* travelling inside.

"So?" Finlay frowned, looking around, staring down a group of brightly colored merchanter types passing by. "What's—?"

"Don't stare," Henricksen warned, nudging her in the ribs. "Or point," he added, grabbing Finlay's hand, pulling it down to her side. "Pointing attracts attention." He nodded to a cluster of freighter crew watching them from a nearby airlock, squeezed her hand, and let it go. "Keep walking. Act casual."

Finlay nodded and lengthened her stride, taking two steps for Henricksen's one.

"That's better. Plenty of robots running around this station, Finlay, but what you *don't* see is anyone talking to them. That's why we've got these." Henricksen tapped a finger to the comms unit in his ear. "So we don't look like crazy people shootin' the shit with our robot pal. Ain't that right, *Serengeti*?"

"*Beep-beep. Beep-beep-beep.* Yes, Master," she answered in an exaggerated, mechanical voice.

"Master," Henricksen grunted. "You're gonna regret callin' me that."

"*Beep-beep. Beep-beep-borp.*"

"Stop it," Henricksen laughed. "You're killin' me."

Serengeti smiled to herself, quieting. Scuttled along inside Tig's body, double-timing it to keep up.

Finlay was quiet too, head swiveling, drinking in everything around her as they moved from one section of hallway to another. "Why's everyone staring at us?" she whispered, cupping a hand to her ear.

"You don't need to do that." Henricksen nodded to the hand plastered to the side of Finlay's head. "It's an open circuit, Finlay. I can hear you just fine."

"Oh." Finlay blushed and dropped her hand, glancing guiltily around. "Can—Can anyone *else* hear us?"

"No, Finlay," Henricksen said patiently. "It's just you, me, and *Serengeti* on this line. And our stony-faced trooper friends, of course." He smiled, offering a cheerful wave to their silver-suited escorts, glanced down at Finlay beside him, lips twisting on one side. "All that time arguing with Kusikov. You never did learn anything about comms, did you?"

Finlay flinched and pulled away, pale face turning ashen beneath the freckles.

"Dammit." Henricksen sighed heavily, touching at her shoulder. "Joke, Finlay. Didn't mean anything by it."

"Yes, sir," Finlay said faintly.

They'd lost Kusikov with the rest of the bridge crew. Tsu and Evans, Sikuuku who'd come to *Serengeti* with Henricksen—package deal, no negotiating—and served with him on two other ships before her. Despite all their sparring, Finlay had been fond of Kusikov. In an odd, complicated, big sister-little brother sort of way.

She turned away, pretending to study a vid screen bolted to the wall as she surreptitiously wiped at her eyes. "Comms are boring." She covered another swipe at her face with a flip of her hand. "Rather have Scan. Or Artillery." A deep breath and she looked up at Henricksen, tremulous smile dimpling her cheeks.

"Artillery," Henricksen grunted, glancing down at her as they walked along. "Artillery takes training."

"I've had all the basic munitions courses. Sikuuku..." Finlay trailed off, smile wilting as Henricksen stiffened and looked away. "Sorry, sir," she mumbled, dropping her eyes.

"Yeah," he said softly. "Me too."

They both quieted after that. Just walked along—side-by-side in their uniforms of silver and black, oblivious to the passing traffic. The strange looks turned their way.

"We'll see," Henricksen murmured some time later.

Finlay brightened instantly. "You mean it?"

"Gotta make sure *Serengeti's* space-worthy first." He glanced over his shoulder, nodding to *Serengeti* riding inside Tig. "We'll see about bridge assignments after that."

Finlay beamed happily, bouncing down the corridor with a spring in her step.

They ran into a group of *Sechura's* troopers at the next airlock. Two junior officers and a couple of seniors enlisted—all of them bold as brass in their shiny silver outfits and only belatedly noticing the stars on Henricksen's collar. Offering clipped salutes.

Henricksen stared them down, eyes cold and flinty. Scowled when the troopers winced, eyes drifting to the scars on his face.

The old one he'd brought with him when he took over *Serengeti's* Captain's Chair. The new he'd picked up when she tumbled broken out of hyperspace, and everything went wrong.

Not many scars in evidence around here. Not on these smooth-faced troopers in their shiny silver uniforms. The dock monkeys and freighter crews moving about the corridor.

This is what it looks like it, Serengeti thought, scanning the passing traffic. *These are the faces of a generation grown up on the downside of war.*

No wonder they stared at Henricksen so strangely. How could they ever understand a man with such a cold, hard stare? Who chose to keep the scars any cut-rate surgeon could erase with just a few minutes of effort. And Finlay... Finlay with her haunted eyes and wary glances. Who'd seen more death in her time than any of these shiny-suited troopers could ever imagine.

Sechura's troopers hurried by, heading back to their ship. Finlay stared after them, face yearning, feeling the gulf of years between those troopers and herself. Frowned and face around, swatting a potted plant as she passed by. "Not polite to stare," she muttered.

Henricksen smiled, nodding to Houseman ahead of them. "From what I saw on *Sechura's* ship, polite ain't exactly a priority these days."

"Still don't know why they do that." Finlay threw a look over her shoulder. "Stare at us like that."

"We're ghosts, Finlay. Relics." He shrugged, looking down at her. "Old soldiers lived too long."

"And me?" *Serengeti* asked, using the comms unit to speak directly into Henricksen's ear. "If you two are relics, what does that make me?"

He was her fifth captain, her service to the Fleet stretching decades before those fifty-three years lost to the dark.

"Not a relic, that's for sure." Henricksen snuck a look over his shoulder, favoring her with a smile. "You ask me, you're a badass warship, *Serengeti*. One that refused to lay down and die."

"Flatterer," *Serengeti* snorted.

Henricksen barked a laugh, facing back around. "We're all of us out of time here, Finlay. Born on the wrong side of this war."

Finlay looked at him, and at two young officers passing by. Lieutenants, from their collar devices. Young and female, like Finlay herself.

Fifty plus years her junior thanks to that long sleep in the dark, leaving them nothing at all in common. Finlay sensed it—*Serengeti* could see it in her eyes—and from the way they dropped their eyes and detoured around Finlay and the others, those young lieutenants did too.

"They're afraid us," Finlay murmured, staring after them. Her hand lifted, fingers picking at the sturdy, cotton canvas of her matte-black uniform, comparing it to the synth silver trash *Sechura* handed out to her troopers. "We don't fit in anymore, do we, Captain?" She looked at him, nodding to Henricksen's own dark uniform, shiny, silver Houseman walking ahead of them. "You suppose we should change, sir?"

"Probably." Henricksen shrugged, leaving it at that.

Finlay chewed her lip, watching him. "You're not going to though, are you, sir?"

"Nope." Henricksen never even looked at her. He just strode along, eyes focused on the corridor, parting the sea of traffic with his presence. "*Serengeti's my* ship, Finlay, and this is *her* uniform." He touched the patch on his shoulder—silver stars on a field of endless black. "They don't like it, they can stick it."

More pithy words of wisdom from Henricksen. *Serengeti* almost laughed.

Finlay nodded uncertainly, still chewing away at her lip. "Fuck 'em," she decided, straightening up, squaring her shoulders proudly. "It's my uniform, too."

"Damn straight." Henricksen bumped her with his hip, smiling when Finlay squawked. But a few steps on and he slowed, frowning. The sounds of a scuffle filling the corridor ahead. "Aw hell. What now?"

NINE

Serengeti crept forward, sneaking a look between Houseman's legs. Four freighter types blocked the hallway—one red-faced and angry, glaring at Henricksen and Finlay, the two troopers escorting them, the others arguing with their irate crewmate. Doing their best to calm him down.

"Lemme go, Nate!" Angry Guy yelled. He shoved at a long-limbed, stork-like crewman, twisted and lunged, escaping the others.

"Give it up, Booker. Ain't worth it!" Birdman Nate scrambled after him with his buddies in tow. "Booker! Booker, get back here!"

Booker wasn't hearing. Booker had his eyes locked on Houseman's silver uniform, *Sechura's* patch showing on his shoulder, and nothing else seemed to matter.

Even his own skin.

"You!" he shouted, marching across the decking. "Where were you?"

Houseman backed up a step, reaching for the pistol strapped to his leg.

"Take it easy." Henricksen set a hand on Houseman's shoulder, caught his eyes, shaking his head. Stepped around the trooper, putting himself between Houseman and the approaching crewman. "Easy," he repeated, raising his hands, turning his palms toward Booker. "Just take it easy, buddy. Whatever this is, we can work it out."

"Fuck you," Booker spat, shoving a passing merchant out of his way.

"Get behind me, Captain," Houseman warned.

Henricksen twisted, shaking his head. "You don't need that, Houseman. This guy's not gonna—"

"Captain!" Finlay shouted. "Look out!"

Henricksen pivoted, grunting as Booker's wrench clipped him on the side of the head. He dropped like a stone, landing hard on the decking but Booker didn't even seem to notice. He just snarled and stepping right over Henricksen, slamming both hands into Houseman's chest.

"Where were you?" he demanded, spittle flying from his lips. Second hit, shoving Houseman backward. "Where were all you brave soldier boys when my brother's ship went down? You were supposed to protect them! The Fleet's supposed to—"

"Hey!" Finlay slid between Booker and Houseman, cocked her arm back, and slugged the freighter crewman right in the face.

Bone crunched and Booker screamed, stumbling backward with his hands cupping his face. "You bitch!" he screamed, blood dripping between his fingers. "You broke my nose!" He lunged for Finlay, murder in his eyes, but his buddies finally caught him and pulled him away.

Houseman suddenly remembered his pistol. Cocked it and moved a step forward, leveling the barrel at Booker and his bunch. "Who's first?" he shouted. "Who wants to get shot first?"

"Stand down!" Henricksen pushed himself to his feet, hand pressed to the side of his head.

Blood there. More blood on his fingers as he pulled that hand away.

Henricksen grimaced and wiped his palm on his pants leg, looking disgusted with the entire situation. "Put the goddamn gun away, Houseman. You too, Beaulieu." He stared at Houseman's partner until she released her pistol, leaving it in the holster, raising her hands to show they were empty. "Man's pissed," he said, looking from one trooper to the other. "And probably with good reason. Shooting him ain't gonna help the situation."

"He attacked you." Houseman flicked his eyes to Henricksen's blood-soaked hair, the trickle of crimson running down his neck.

"Winged me, Houseman. That's all. Ain't like I'm dead. 'Sides," Henricksen hooked a thumb over his shoulder, "Finlay here took care of him. Didn't ya, Finlay?"

"Damn straight." Finlay lifted her chin, looking defiant. "Nobody hits my captain."

"Busted his nose up good." Henricksen smiled proudly. "I'd call it even."

Houseman frowned, face conflicted. Glanced past Henricksen to the freighter crew, fingers flexing as he adjusted his grip on the pistol. "But, sir—"

"*Even*, Houseman." Henricksen stepped close and dropped his voice, giving the trooper a flat-eyed stare. "Everyone's watching us, Houseman." He turned his head, looking one way and the other.

Lot of hard eyes and angry face around them. Traffic stopped dead, everyone waiting to see what would happen. A few people retreated, fading into the background in an attempt to stay out of it, but most stayed. Bore witness. Watched the scene play out.

"This hallway's a powder keg, Houseman. You primed it, and it's just about ready to explode. But you put that down," Henricksen tapped a finger to the trooper's pistol, "and maybe—just maybe—this whole thing blows over. We go our way, they go theirs." A nod to Booker and his buddies. "Rest of the station gets back to normal."

Houseman shook his head, stubbornly refusing. "He hit you, sir. Can't let that go unpunished."

Idiot.

"Houseman." Henricksen stepped in front of the pistol's barrel, putting his own body between the trooper and Booker. "I'm only gonna say this one more time. Put. The goddamn. Gun. Away. *That*," he said, flicking his eyes to the trooper's pistol, back to Houseman's face, "attracts attention. Attention we really don't need right now." He nodded meaningfully to *Serengeti* hiding inside Tig's arachnid-shaped robot body. "You savvy, Houseman?"

Houseman hesitated, considering the chrome-faced robot, throwing a last, distrusting look the freighter crew's way. "Yeah," he said, voice shaking. "Yeah. I savvy." He lowered his gun and slid it back into its holster.

Everyone sighed—even Booker—as the tension dispersed. The mood changing immediately once the trooper put his weapon away.

"Good man." Henricksen clapped Houseman on the shoulder and turned around, addressing the freighter crew holding tight to Booker. "Get him outta here before he gets himself in trouble."

Birdman Nate nodded, glancing at his buddies. "Yes, sir. Think that's a good idea, sir." Another nod and they surrounded Booker, grabbing him from both sides, leading him away.

Booker—idiot that he was—balked after just a few steps, too damned arrogant and stupid to listen to anything but that chip on his shoulder he'd obviously been carrying around for a while. "Bitch busted up my face!" He lowered his hands, presenting the wreck of his nose as evidence.

Birdman Nate leaned close, squinting his eyes as he inspected Booker's face. "Sure did. Actually looks better, if ya ask me." He flashed a smile, tipping a wink at Finlay. "Got a damn fine right hook there, ma'am."

"Why, thankee." Finlay dropped a curtsy. "Thought about popping him one in the nuts, but Papa raised me to be a lady." She blew on her knuckles, dusted her fingernails across the front of her jacket, looking quite pleased with herself and that punch.

Nate laughed aloud, flipping an off-hand salute. Nodded to his buddies as he grabbed at Booker's arm, bundling up the sullen-looking crewman as they hauled him away.

"That happen often?" Henricksen nodded after the retreating freighter crew.

Houseman shrugged. "Sometimes. Not here so much." He waved a hand at the corridor, the oversized canister of station proper showing through one of the windows in the hall. "Some of the other stations aren't as friendly, but Blue Horizon's not so bad most days."

Henricksen grunted, watching the crowd disperse. "Merchants are angry. Can't say I blame them." He threw a look over his shoulder, watching Booker and his minders disappear down the hall. "Fleet's supposed to protect these people, not—"

A tremor shook the hallway, throwing Henricksen off balance.

"You feel that?" he asked, frowning.

Houseman blinked blankly. "What?"

"Felt like—"

Second tremor—stronger this time, the entire hallway shuddering, sending Henricksen stumbling to one side. He fetched up against the wall, grabbing at Finley when she bounced into his arms. Clung to her and the wall supporting the both of them as the walkway bucked and heaved.

"What the hell was that?" he shouted once everything calmed down.

Finlay shook her head, staring worriedly down the hall. "Think we should get out of here, sir."

"Couldn't agree more. Houseman!"

The trooper turned around and started away as another round of trembling shook the station, hallway creaking and groaning, floor lifting beneath their feet. Undulating in an elongated wave that knocked panels from the ceiling and threw people to the floor.

Finlay lost her balance and knocked into Henricksen, steadied herself against him as he pawed at the wall, fingers wrapping around a take-hold handle riveted to the panels. Houseman and Beaulieu toppled over, but Tig just squatted down and spread his many legs wide, weathering the storm until it finally ended.

The trembling lasted for several seconds, leaving an odd scent in the air. A mixture of char and chemicals, something that was either lubricant or some kind of oil that drove Tig's sensors wild. And behind it—a soundtrack to that smell, working its way down the hall—was an ominous groaning coming from somewhere way, way off.

"That's not good." Henricksen reached down, helping Houseman and Beaulieu up. "Finlay. You're with me. We're getting out—"

Boom!

A concussive blast rocked the station, throwing Henricksen, Finlay, everyone but Tig to the floor. A rush of air followed after—a deafening wind carrying a load of burning heat that swirled down the hallway, whipping at clothes, tearing at exposed skin.

People ran, screaming in terror as the klaxons kicked in and a voice came over the station's comms systems ordering everyone in the ring walkway back to their vessels. All station crew back to the can.

"Not good. This is definitely *not* good." Henricksen picked himself up, grabbing at Finlay to pull her to her feet.

"What's going on?" she asked, looking dazedly around.

"Explosion." Henricksen quirked an eyebrow, looking to *Serengeti* for confirmation.

She tapped into the station's central system, searching for information, but *Sechura* reached her first.

"Go, Sister. Leave now!" *Sechura* sent over the Valkyrie comms channel.

"What's going on?" *Serengeti* demanded.

Sechura sent her a data package—video from *Sechura's* hull cameras and the outward facing eyes spread around the station's perimeter. The Valkyrie herself at the center of those images, sleek-side shape instantly recognizable. And beside her, in berthing H-95, that pre-AI freighter *Sechura* had sneered at earlier—ancient thing, square-sided, elongated shape.

A flash of fire and the freighter disappeared, explosion ripping through it, churning the massive ship into a cloud of metal particles. The shockwave hit *Sechura* and all but rolled her over, shrapnel from the freighter pelting her sides after, rocking the Valkyrie a second time.

A burst of comms—desperate, dying—and *Sechura* cut out. But the station cameras kept tracking her. Showed them all the gory details as the Valkyrie's starboard side ripped open, compartments venting as her hull plating peeled back.

"*Sechura. Sechura!*" *Serengeti* screamed, reaching for her Sister across the Valkyrie network. Searching for her—for any sign of her AI presence—and finding nothing. Nothing at all. "No," *Serengeti* breathed, voice filled with mourning. "No, Sister. Not again."

More trembling and the station cameras showed the walkway started to crumble, metal twisting, melting as fire erupted near *Sechura's* berthing. Blast doors sealed, trying to contain it, trapping the people who weren't quite quick enough to get out. Henricksen grabbed Tig's leg and started pulling, but *Serengeti* pushed away, shrugging him off.

"Talk to me, *Serengeti*. What's happening down there?"

"Explosion. *Sechura's* down." A last attempt to reach her and *Serengeti* closed the channel, turned around. "Back to the ship," she ordered. "We need to get out of here. Now!"

Houseman and Beaulieu looked at each and took off, heading back toward *Sechura*.

To *their* ship. The *wrong* ship in this particular instance.

Henricksen stepped in front of them, shaking his head. "Down means gone," he said, klaxons shrieking bloody murder in the background. "You can't go back." He glanced from one trooper to the other, making sure they got it. "You're my crew now. Our crew," he amended with a nod to *Serengeti*, "unless..." He trailed off, grimacing, eyes flicking to the closed-off end of the hallway. "Move," he ordered, shoving at them, turning the two troopers around. "Move, goddammit, before we get trapped in this section and stuck on this god-forsaken excuse for a space station forever."

Beaulieu capitulated quickly, but Houseman resisted, clearly wanting to go back.

"I will *leave* you here, Houseman," Henricksen warned. "This station is in a world of shit, and I honestly don't have the time or the patience to argue with some dipshit trooper who can't seem to get it through his thick skull that the ship he so desperately wants to get back to ain't really a ship anymore." He flicked his eyes to *Serengeti*, apology in his face. "So go or stay, Houseman. I don't particularly care which."

Another shove at the trooper, pushing him out of his way. Henricksen flicked his fingers at Finlay and set off for their ship.

Houseman—idiot that he was—turned in the opposite direction, but Beaulieu grabbed his shoulder and leaned close, whispering urgently until he finally relented. "We're with you," Beaulieu said, nodding sharply.

"Then fall in," *Serengeti* told them, spinning Tig around. "We're getting out of here."

Tig took off, heading for home.

TEN

Henricksen buzzed through *Serengeti's* airlock and onto Level 4, passed through in a hurry—eyes skipping over the shiny new panels, the composite metal decking stretching from wall to wall—and headed for the nearest ladderway.

"Elevators are operational," *Serengeti* reminded him.

"Right." He spun around, heading in the opposite direction, pressed at a panel to recall the elevator. "C'mon-c'mon-c'mon," he muttered, fingers drumming impatiently against his leg.

The panel flashed green and the elevator doors slid open. Henricksen stepped inside and hit the button for Level 10. Kept hitting it as *Serengeti* and the others crowded in, muttering curses at the balky elevator until it sealed up and took off.

More shiny panels greeted them on Level 10. An entire hallway of gleaming surfaces, everything fresh and clean and apparently brand new.

I wonder how much of this is Homunculus, Serengeti thought as Tig pattered into that hallway.

Engines were his—she knew that for certain—and the armaments and systems that came with them. Dreadnought stamp on all of it. Dreadnought design through and through. But the circuits and relays, the decking and panels, the miles upon miles of wiring...

Did all that come from Homunculus? *How* much *of me is Dreadnought? Serengeti* wondered, worrying now. Feeling her differences all the more keenly after standing inside *Sechura.* Watching her sparkling Sister drop out of jump.

Sechura was Valkyrie and looked it—looked like what a Valkyrie *should* be.

"Something wrong?" Tig whispered across internal comms.

Everything, Tig. More than you'll ever know.

"Nothing," she told him, keeping that melancholy thought to herself. "Just...Too many ghosts is all."

Tig *hooted* softly—a low tone full of apology and commiseration. Stopped at the bridge door while Henricksen entered his credentials, following the captain and Finlay inside, Houseman and Beaulieu stepping in behind them, pulling the door closed.

Dark inside, but then, the bridge usually was. Pin lights activated as they entered, filling the circular space with a dim glow. Illuminating five stations set in a semicircle at the front of the bridge, close to the floor-to-ceiling windows, and the captain's Command Post looming behind them—a multi-paneled, octopus-like configuration nearly twice the size of any of the other stations.

"Stand here," Henricksen ordered, pointing Houseman to one side of the door and Beaulieu to the other. "*Right* here, you understand? And don't move. Last thing I need is you two bumbling around my bridge while we're making an emergency exit."

"Aye, sir." Beaulieu saluted smartly, pushing Houseman to one side of the door while she took up position on the other.

A nod and Henricksen turned around, hurrying across the bridge to Engineering as Finlay slid into Navigation beside him.

Systems came to life, panels flashing, data scrolling in long strings, providing reams of information on the ship's operating status, the vessels in port around them, the traffic moving in and out of the station. Finlay shunted it all to one side, bypassed the usual start-up tests and diagnostic routines, and dove straight into the central Navigation system while Henricksen keyed into the main engines, cycling the power to full, consulting Finlay's panel now and then.

"You know what you're doing?"

Finlay shrugged. "Started out sitting Nav. Got tired of all the math, though." She flashed a smile. "Scan's more fun."

"Guess that depends on your idea of fun," Henricksen grunted, digging through the directories, searching for the airlock connectors and mooring clamp controls.

Took him a few tries, but he eventually found them. Managed to disconnect them and sever *Serengeti's* ties to the station without making too much of a hash of it.

Finlay watched him, frowning worriedly as he fumbled at Engineering's panels. "Do *you* know what *you're* doing, sir?"

"Used to. Been a long time, though." Henricksen scanned the panel in front of him, opening and closing data windows. "I don't suppose…"

"Huh-uh." Finlay shook her head. "When it comes to engines, you're on your own."

"Great," Henricksen muttered, stabbing at a button, cursing when an error appeared.

"I'll talk you through the basics." *Serengeti* parked Tig to one side, flipped to a camera and looked down on the bridge's circular space. "Just keep your eyes on the panel and follow my lead."

"Right." Henricksen leaned forward, eyes locked onto the panel in front of him as *Serengeti* navigated to the maneuvering jet controls, flipped them wide open, and pushed away from her berthing.

Finlay tapped into Scan when they started moving, throwing a map of the station and its security perimeter onto the front windows, adding the vessels at dock, those heading off into space. "Ships moving around us." Finlay highlighted two freighters berthed in *Serengeti's* section, beacons moving as they pushed away from station, came about, and made for open space.

"Explosion's got everyone spooked." Henricksen spared a look for *Serengeti's* camera. "Make sure we don't run into someone, Finlay." He glanced over at her, smiling his crooked smile. "Just got *Serengeti* fixed. Can't go bashing her back up again on our first trip out of port."

"Aye, sir. No crashing, sir." Finlay moved the star charts and navigation data to her right-hand panel, devoting the left to Scan's data.

Lot of data there. Lot of moving parts to keep track of.

Serengeti set a sub-mind to monitor the traffic around Blue Horizon and help Finlay out. Opened a comms channel and listened to the chatter on station, the messages passing between the ships in port.

Confused communications. Conflicting reports cobbled together from multiple sources. Some claimed the DSR rigged that ancient freighter to blow. That they detonated a bomb inside it with the specific intent of taking out the Valkyrie in berthing H-96.

Others blamed *Sechura* herself—a theory that had just about as much backing as the DSR speculation making the rounds of the ships. Ridiculous idea—a Valkyrie would never fire on a civilian ship in port, much less be stupid enough to do such a thing when she herself was in danger of being caught up in the blast—but one that persisted. Seemed almost as popular as the DSR theory.

That's how bad it's gotten, Serengeti realized. *People actually believe that of us.*

That a Valkyrie would turn her guns against them. Attack the people she was duty-bound to defend.

How did our Fleet go so wrong, Sister?

She searched for *Sechura* as she pulled away from the station, and found her still parked in berthing H-96, beacon squawking out information.

Emergency beacon only—no sentience behind it now. No response from *Sechura* when *Serengeti* hailed her.

Nothing at all. No signs of life. Another Sister gone. One less Valkyrie in the galaxy, sliding gracefully across the stars.

Serengeti stared, mourning. Turned the camera toward the berthing beside *Sechura* and found silence. Devastation. The ancient freighter shredded by the blast that took it, wreckage from its body pummeling the hulking, square-sided ship in Berthing H-94 beside it. Punching through, carving pieces from its body. Leaving chunks of composite metal drifting in a cloud of twinkling debris.

A check of the station's records showed the ship in H-94 was a merchanter named *Providence*—trade goods hauler, fourth generation AI. Data files detailed a hundred and ten years of service—a century and more of traveling, following the shipping lanes from one Meridian Alliance planet to another, station stops along the way.

Another sixty years before that in another chassis, making *Providence* a veteran. More light years under her belt than *Serengeti* herself.

Gone now. Just like Sechura.

Comms flashed a message, blinking insistently, alerting her to an encoded communication—distress signal from Blue Horizon to the Meridian Alliance central monitoring station passed across a Fleet-wide channel.

"Henricksen." She waited until he looked at her, eyes lifting to the camera at the front of the bridge. Flashed his panel and passed him the message, watching in silence as Henricksen read it.

Henricksen grunted, looking up at the camera. "*Brutus* is bound to see this."

"Bound to," she agreed.

"Valkyrie destroyed on station. He'll send ships. Want some answers."

Starting with what happened to the salvaged ship in Berthing H-28.

"What's the call?" Henricksen asked her. "We staying or going?"

Serengeti pulled up a feed from her hull cameras, looking back at the station. Running felt wrong—especially from her own fleet—but *Sechura* hid her for a reason. Salvaged her from the stars and went to great pains to make sure *Brutus* and the rest of the Fleet were none the wiser to her existence.

And after what she'd shown them, if all of that was true…

"Take us out, Henricksen," she decided. "We're going walkabout for a while."

"Yes, ma'am." Henricksen tapped two fingers to his temple, flashing a crooked smile at the camera. Feathered the maneuvering jets to adjust *Serengeti's* course as he eased her away from the station.

Finlay started a counter, numbers turning, jumping in increments as *Serengeti* pulled away from Blue Horizon.

Light flickered around them, filling the bridge as *Serengeti* slipped through the shimmer shield, energy netting bending and twisting around the ship's elongated shape. She considered it a moment, and the station behind them. Accessed the shimmer shield's system—hardware wasn't all that complicated, she was pretty sure Tig and his little TSG buddies could replicate something similar—and downloaded the entire thing on a whim.

Sent the design specs for the hardware to the machine shop while she was at it, along with a copy of the shimmer shield's software package.

Might never use it. Then again, system like that just might come in handy. And it made the TSGs happy, having a purpose. Some special project to work on for her.

"That's stealing, you know," Tig admonished, disapproving voice drifting across the robot comms channel.

"Station protocols are crap. Their own fault for not protecting it better."

"And the DD3s?" Tig folded his front legs and leaned to one side, pointing a spare appendage at the ceiling. "You stealing them, too?"

"Oh. Right." She'd completely forgotten about the robots working on the hull. She cycled through the feeds from the outward-facing cameras until she found them scattered about the hull. Clinging for dear life to her composite metal paneling, magnetized leg-ends the only thing preventing the robots from taking a long walk into deep space. "Back inside, guys. Cargo Bay 4."

She cracked the outer doors open and watched the DD3s tip-toe around, gathering up loose equipment before working their way inside.

Twenty of them, by her count. Unfortunately, there'd been twenty-*three* DD3s working hull repair the last time she checked.

A scan of the area soon found the others—two of the missing robots tumbling toward the station, making their slow, frozen way back home, the third headed in the opposite, drifting alone toward the great beyond.

Felt bad, leaving it there, heading out toward deep space. But she didn't have time to divert and go get it. Not with *Brutus* and his ships on their way in.

Couldn't abandon it either—DD3s might not be loveable, but they didn't deserve that kind of slow death.

Serengeti loaded a marker tag into a chamber and fired it at the robot, catching the DD3 right on its shiny metal ass. Sent the marker's information back to the station, hoping someone would pick the DD3 up later.

"Sorry, buddy. Best I can do."

She pulled away, locking Cargo Bay 4 down, main consciousness dropping back to the bridge as the counter on Finlay's panel ticked over—ten kilometers from station and counting—and Scan flashed, panel lighting up.

"Jump signatures!" Finlay shunted a data screen to the front windows. Ten dark spots—hyperspace displacements marking vessels coming through.

Ships' beacons after—names and vectors, velocities of approach. Ships' designations, reading Meridian Alliance across the board.

"Fleet ships inbound," Finlay called.

"Hang on, Finlay. Time we got scarce." Henricksen punched it, opening the main engines wide. Violating half a dozen space station transit ordinances in the process.

"They'll take away your pilot's license if you keep flying like that," *Serengeti* warned.

"They can have it. Never was much of a pilot anyway." Henricksen flashed a smile, throwing a look at Nav. "Lay in a course, Finlay. Hyperspace jump."

Finlay blinked blankly, hands hovering above her panel. "To where, sir?"

"Don't care. Anywhere but here."

"Uh…" She stared at the panel in front of her, the massive directory of star charts it offered. "Lot of stars out there, sir."

"I know that, Finlay. Pick one and let's go."

"But—But—" Finlay hemmed and hawed, paralyzed by so many choices and so little direction.

Serengeti slipped in to help her, selecting a route, charting a course at random.

"Course is set, sir." Finlay nodded her thanks to the camera.

Serengeti sent a smiley face back.

"Strap in tight." Henricksen spooled up the hyperspace drives, sending a countdown clock to the front windows. Set a second counter beside it, showing their distance from station. "Houseman. Beaulieu."

"Aye, sir?" the troopers answered together.

"Find something to hold onto. Things might get a bit…bumpy."

The troopers looked at each other, and around the bridge. Spied a row of take-hold handles near Artillery and dove for them together, holding tight to the metal bars as they hunkered close to the floor.

"Three minutes!" Henricksen called.

"Sir? The crew?" Finlay nodded to Comms.

"Shit!" Henricksen slapped at the panel, opening a ship-wide channel. "Three minutes to jump. Everyone strap in and hold onto your butts."

The jump clock ticked down, numbers tumbling as the distance between *Serengeti* and the station widened. A minute in and a buckle appeared ahead of them, disk-shaped and black as pitch, blocking out the stars. The jump clock hit zero as they reached minimum safe distance from station, and the buckle sucked inward, pulling *Serengeti* toward the void.

She had just enough time before the buckle took her to throw a last look at the station. Just enough time for one last glimpse of *Sechura's* silent chassis. To capture and image and send it to storage so she wouldn't forget her.

A tug at her hull and the buckle closed around her, Blue Horizon disappearing as *Serengeti* slid into the hyperspace trough. Cold hit her first, darkness after. The stretched-out lines of stars sliding by. *Serengeti* lost herself for a while, caught up in remembrance. Memories of her last hyperspace transit, and that disastrous moment fifty-three years ago when she tumbled out of the trough—body shredded, engines failing, slowly tearing themselves apart.

No. Not here.

Serengeti clawed her way back to the present, leaving the dark memories behind. Locked them up tight and threw away the key because she didn't need them right now. Couldn't afford to get caught up in the past when the present was so very real. So very *now*.

Sensors streamed data, reporting engines fully operational, running at nominal levels. The trough a perfect tube—smooth-sided and endless, everything peaceful, infinitely calm.

The jump clock hit thirty seconds and *Serengeti's* engines wound down. A shiver running through her ship's body as she exited the trough, gliding gracefully into normal space.

Sensors scanned the galaxy around her, drinking in everything it had to offer. A flick of Henricksen's fingers and Finlay abandoned Navigation, hurried over to Scan. Dug into systems, pulling up data screens, shunting one feed after another onto the front windows for Henricksen to see.

"Clear," she reported, nodding to the windows, glancing at Henricksen to one side. "Area's clear, sir. We're alone."

"First thing that's gone right all day," he muttered, looking out at the stars.

Serengeti gave him a moment. Let him relax for a while. "You know," she said casually, sometime later. "We really should get a proper Engineering Officer."

He looked up, lips twisting. "Fired already, eh?"

"I can honestly say that was some of the worst piloting I've ever seen."

Henricksen laughed softly. "There's a reason they promoted me to captain, you know." A wink and he abandoned Engineering, moving over to his usual place at the Command Post. Spotted Beaulieu and Houseman huddled on the floor nearby—the two of them wrapped around each other, eyes closed, hands clenched up tight. "Alright, you two. That's enough."

Houseman opened one eye, looking around. Spotted Henricksen standing over him and shoved Beaulieu away, looking horrified that the captain had caught the two of them canoodling in their terror.

Henricksen's lips twitched, barely suppressing a smile. "Head below," he ordered, nodding to the bridge door. "Berthings are on 7. Tell 'em you're crew. They'll find you a rack."

"Aye, sir." Houseman blushed brightly, climbing shakily to his feet. Reached down to help Beaulieu and then snatched his hand back, blushing even brighter when she glared at him, picking herself off the floor.

"Get," Henricksen told them, hooking a thumb over his shoulder.

"Aye, sir," the troopers answered together. Saluted and bailed off the bridge, hurrying out the door.

"Didn't think my piloting was *that* bad," Henricksen muttered, staring after them.

"Abominable," *Serengeti* said brightly. "You are, without a doubt, the *worst* pilot I've ever had on my bridge."

"Gee. Thanks."

"On the other hand, we're here and we're not dead so…win-win!"

Henricksen rolled his eyes. "Where *is* here, anyway?" He touched at a panel, digging into Nav's directory, searching for star charts of the area.

Serengeti found the right one for him, pulled into one his panel, highlighting their location. A nearby planet. "Hon-shen-shura," she said, adding data tags everywhere.

Henricksen froze, face paling, hand reaching for that scar on his temple. Rubbing at it through the fresh covering of blood. "Why here?" he asked. "What the hell possessed you to bring us back here of all places, Finlay?"

"Me?" Finlay looked offended. "*I* didn't—" She pointed at the camera. "*She* picked the route. *I* just did the navigating stuff."

"Navigating stuff." Henricksen smiled crookedly. "That the technical term for it?"

Finlay flushed—pale cheeks turning pink beneath the freckles—*harrumphed* and faced around, muttering under her breath as she poked at Scan's panel.

Henricksen kept smiling, let it slip from his face as he looked up at *Serengeti's* camera. "Mind explaining this?" A wave at the windows in front of him. The stars showing outside. "Hundreds of light years of space to choose from and you bring us to *this* godforsaken stretch of the galaxy?"

"It's not *that* godforsaken," *Serengeti* told him. "*Some* people live on that planet."

Henricksen folded his arms, giving her a sour look.

"Alright. If *you* were *Brutus,* would *you* think to come look for us here?"

He blinked, thinking that over, considering the stars outside. "You think he will?"

"Come after us? Not sure," *Serengeti* admitted. "But he's going to find out soon enough that a ship went missing right after that explosion. Might take him a while to track us since my beacon's off and I'm not in the system, but *Brutus* is tenacious. If he wants us, he'll find us. It's only a matter of time."

"Lovely." Henricksen rubbed at his chin, brow wrinkled with worry.

"Best if we lay low for a while. Hide out until things cool down?"

He looked at her, eyebrows lifting. "Disappear off the grid. That it?"

"Something like that."

"Seems like we do that a lot lately. Disappear into parts unknown."

Didn't like it—that came through clear enough. *Serengeti* didn't particularly like it either, but without more information, she didn't see any other choice.

"Hell," Henricksen sighed, turning back to the windows. Grew tired of that view and swapped it for another, digging through directories in *Serengeti's* main database.

Searching randomly, or so *Serengeti* thought. Until he stopped on one particular directory and examined the contents. Accessed that composite image of *Serengeti's* new body and just stared at it a while.

"What are you doing?" she asked, watching from above.

Henricksen flinched, swiping at the panel, banishing the file in an instant. "Looks good," he said, waving vaguely at the bridge. "Hard to believe…" He trailed off, eyes haunted, lips pressed in a tight line.

"Yeah. I know," she said quietly. "Lot of changes since you left, Henricksen."

"Yeah. I can see that."

Odd silence after that. The relationship between them changed by the fifty-three years of separation, both of them trying to figure it out.

Finlay felt it too. Looked up, face worried, eyes flicking from *Serengeti* to Henricksen, while Tig watched from the edges. *Burbled* and *blipped,* face lights ticking in agitated patterns.

And all the while, that silence continued. Becoming increasingly uncomfortable.

"If you think this is something, you should see the rest of the ship." Tig bobbed up and down, front legs cricketing together. "DD3s are dumb as stumps, but you wouldn't *believe* what they..." He trailed off, face lights flashing blotchily, front legs moving faster and faster.

Henricksen glanced at him, and looked back to the windows, stubbornly maintaining his silence.

"Still a few holes in the outer hull," *Serengeti* said.

Tig stopped cricketing, *blipped* and nodded, but Henricksen just twitched his shoulders. That was it.

"DD3s should be able to patch everything up in a couple of days." She paused, hoping Henricksen would look at her. Say something. Do *anything* to make this uncomfortable this silence go away. "I can show you around if you'd like."

Henricksen's eyes lifted, staring for a long time. A sigh and he bowed his head, rubbing at his face. "Tomorrow, maybe." He shut down the panels on the Command Post, braced one arm against his Captain's Chair and leaned against it, looking incredibly weary. Impossibly tired. "Honestly, I'm too knackered for a tour right now. Not really sure how that's possible, considering we've been asleep the best part of fifty-three years, but..." He shrugged his shoulders, scrubbing a hand through his short-clipped hair. Winced as his fingers brushed the gash Booker's wrench had made and pulled his hand away, wiping blood on his pants leg.

"Looks like you could use some stitches," *Serengeti* noted.

Finlay looked up from Scan. "You want me to—"

"It's fine, Finlay." Henricksen waved her away. "Head wounds always bleed a lot. I'll put a styptic on it later. Close it right up."

"Sir—"

"I said, it's *fine,* Finlay. You can go back to playing with your new toy."

"It's not a toy," Finlay said primly.

Henricksen sighed heavily. "Station. Whatever. I'm fine, Finlay. Just...go back to whatever you were doing," he said, waving a hand.

Finlay looked at him, and at *Serengeti's* camera. Reluctantly turned around.

Toy or not, she did like the new systems. Quickly lost herself digging through Scan's enhanced offerings.

Henricksen yawned, swaying, closed his eyes and just stood there, bracing himself against the Command Post's chair.

"Cryo sleep's no substitute for real sleep," *Serengeti* said quietly. "Fifty-three years…that's a long time for someone to be frozen." She ran a quick search of her database to confirm a suspicion. "Good news, though. You and Finlay and the rest of the crew are the proud owners of a new record for longest length of time spent in a cryo chamber."

"Whoopee," Henricksen cheered, lips twisting sourly. "And the bad news?" He raised his head, looking at the camera. "There *is* a bad news side to this, right?"

"Cryo tubes are only rated for twenty years of consecutive use."

Henricksen barked a laugh. "I'm guessing that means we have a whole host of prolonged hypersleep illnesses to look forward to."

"Probably. Baldness. Flatulence. Fingers falling off."

"It says that in the database?" Henricksen looked somewhat alarmed.

"Probably."

He squinted, eyeing the camera suspiciously. Logged back into the system and checked the medical records from *Sechura's* database himself. "Says here Finlay and I are in perfect health."

"Does it?" *Serengeti* asked innocently. "Sorry. My mistake."

Henricksen glowered at the camera. "That's cruel, *Serengeti.* Picking on a dog-tired, flash frozen, newly-thawed-out fish stick like that."

Serengeti laughed aloud and saw Henricksen smile. A real smile this time—tired and crooked, but a smile just the same. A smile just like she remembered. The way Henricksen *used* to smile, before everything went to crap.

"Should we call the bridge crew up?"

Henricksen tilted his head, considering, fingers trailing across the panels of his Command Post. "Normally, I'd say yes. Problem is, we're a bit short on staff." He shrugged his shoulders, looking around the bridge. "Should have three fully qualified shifts to run this bridge, but I'm afraid we've got just the one right now." Another shrug, eyes returning to the camera. "Crew's still settling in. Best if we give 'em the night to rest up. Bring 'em in fresh tomorrow. You okay with that? Mind keeping tabs on things on your own for a while?"

"Think I'll manage," she said, smile in her voice. "Now get out of here before you fall down."

Henricksen nodded, rubbing at his eyes. "Finlay. Hey, Finlay," he called, snapping his fingers at Scan.

"What?" Finlay blinked owlishly, looking up. "What's that, sir?"

"Heading back to my quarters for a while. You gonna stay here?"

"Thinks so. If you don't mind, sir."

"You're welcome to it," he told her. "Just don't stay too long. I feel like ten-year-old roadkill, and I'm guessing you do, too."

Finlay shrugged and nodded, yawning behind her hand.

"An hour here, no more, understand me? Grab some food and get yourself in your rack. We've got crew assignments to make tomorrow and I don't want you half-asleep on the bridge, drooling all over *Serengeti's* shiny new Scan station."

"Aye, sir. No drooling, sir." Finlay tapped two fingers to her temple and turned back to her station, immediately forgetting he was even there.

Henricksen sighed, sliding his eyes to *Serengeti's* camera. "She's gonna spend the whole damned night here. I know it." Second sigh—shoulders lifting and sagging—and Henricksen stepped down from his Command Post, heading for the door. "One hour, Finlay," he called back over his shoulder. "You either leave under your own power or Mighty Mite here," he waved at Tig sitting quietly to one side, "is authorized to pick you up and carry you like a wee babe back to your quarters."

"Aye, sir. Babe, sir." Finlay waved without looking.

Henricksen looked back once, smiling fondly, stepped off the bridge and headed down the hall to his quarters.

ELEVEN

The lights came on as soon as Henricksen stepped into his quarters, throwing back the shadows, bathing the silver and black space in a soft, yellow glow. Layout here was the same as on *Sechura*: large front space serving as study, living room, and dining room all at once, windows filling the far wall, looking out at the stars.

Doorway to the left, leading to the captain's master bedroom. Bookshelves across from it, a few odds and ends scattered randomly across its tiers.

Empty spaces, mostly, and nothing at all fancy about them. Qaisrani filled her quarters with pillows and plush furnishings, but Henricksen preferred more Spartan accommodations.

Bare metal walls showed through the mostly empty bookshelves. Two square leather chairs sat by the windows, bookending a low-slung table. Desk lurking forgotten by the front door, keeping a tiny dinner table and two very simple, very utilitarian chairs company. The only other thing of note in that room a bar shoved up against one wall.

Bar Henricksen never used. Hadn't even bothered stocking since he first came on board.

"Home sweet home." Henricksen stepped inside, letting the door click closed.

"Place was pretty much a wreck," *Serengeti* told him. "But the DD3s straightened things up."

Hadn't planned to—DD3s were maintenance droids and tidying the captain's quarters wasn't exactly a high priority item on their list. But Tig talked them into it. Explained how it'd be worth their while.

"Robots salvaged what they could." She panned the camera around the room, regretting how empty it was. "Most of your personal possessions were damaged beyond repair, I'm afraid."

"'S'alright. Not like I had a whole lot to begin with." A quick look around the front room and Henricksen stepped over to the bookshelves, reached up, and retrieved a tiny silver starship, pulling it down.

Memento from his first command. Henricksen turned it over, rubbing a thumb across the inscription on the base. "Glad to see this made it at least." He smiled softly, looking a bit sad. Reached up and set the starship back on the shelf, spying something else in the process: a glass jar sitting on the shelf closest to the floor.

He squatted, studying it, considering the seashells and rounded bits of glass inside for a long, long time. "Well, I'll be damned," he murmured, scooping it up. Turned it over, contents shifting, clinking softly as he examined the odds and ends inside.

"DD3s found it stuffed under a chair," *Serengeti* said, watching. "I assume it fell off the shelves and rolled under there. Must've sat there the entire time I was lost."

"Huh." Henricksen stood, wincing, eyes squeezing closed as he clutched at his head.

"You look terrible, you know."

"Well, I *did* get hit on the side of the head with a wrench."

"Not what I meant." The gash was ugly enough, but the pallor of Henricksen's skin, the dark circles under his eyes… "Have you slept at all since they unfroze you?"

"Some." He lifted his chin, looking defensive. "'Fraid to," he admitted, face softening. He touched a finger to the side of his head, probing at the gash in his scalp. "Feels too much like disappearing back into the dark."

That she understood. Better than most.

"You should really do something about that," *Serengeti* told him, zooming in on the gash. "I can send one of the TSGs up here—"

"No. It's fine." Henricksen jerked his hand away, set the jar back on the shelf. "I can see to the damn thing myself," he insisted, turning in a circle, looking around. "There a med kit in here anywhere?"

"Bathroom." *Serengeti* pointed her camera at the bedroom door, traded that camera for another as she followed Henricksen through to the other side.

More spare furnishings in the bedroom—mattress on a frame, covered in fresh linens. Closet with uniforms, not much of anything else.

Henricksen walked through it, heading straight for the attached bathroom, which—incidentally—didn't happen to come equipped with a camera.

Tried putting one in there once but Henricksen balked. Something about privacy and not wanting an AI watching her while he did his business—a human quirk, she didn't quite understand.

She relented anyway, out of respect for Henricksen. Accepted this tiny blind spot inside her. The others scattered throughout her spaces.

A check of the room as she settled into a camera in Henricksen's bedroom. One that just happened to give her a partial view of the glass and steel bathroom on one side. Free here, the shower was mostly hidden—just a vague glass and metal shape to one side—and the commode completely obscured. But the camera gave her a good view of the basin at the room's center, just inside the door. The medicine cabinet sitting above it—mirror in the center, two others just like it set on hinges, sitting on either side.

Henricksen stepped inside, leaving the bathroom door open. Caught sight of himself in those mirrors and stopped dead, staring. Seeming troubled by what he saw.

"Everything alright?" *Serengeti* called from the bedroom.

"Fine," he said, ripping the medicine cabinet open. "I'm fine."

Toiletries in there, mostly. Henricksen shoved them out of the way to get at the med kit lurking at the back. Pulled it down and started rooting through the contents, dumping a pile of bandages on one side of the sink, a stack of antiseptic strips, and a styptic pen on the other.

Dropped the med kit and its remaining contents inside the basin and grabbed the edge of one of the side mirrors, angling it so he could look in one and see the gash in his head reflecting in the other. A few adjustments, giving himself the best view and Henricksen picked up the styptic, pressing it to his head.

"I'm not sure that's going to do it," *Serengeti* told him, watching from the bedroom, studying his reflection in the mirrors' glass. "Styptic's meant for shaving cuts, Henricksen. I'm pretty sure you're going to need stitches for that."

"Oh yeah? And what do you know about bleeding?" He froze—hand raised, styptic hanging in mid-air. Grimaced when he realized what he'd just said. "Sorry. Tired." He nodded an apology to *Serengeti's* camera, adjusted the mirror's angle, and started dabbing at the cut with the styptic again.

Blood welled around its tip, staining Henricksen's hair, running down his neck. He kept at it, but the styptic obviously wasn't working. In fact, *Serengeti* was pretty sure it was making things worse.

"The robots are all programmed for basic medical procedures—"

"No." Henricksen leveled a flat stare at the camera's reflection. "No robots."

"Alright. How about Finlay?"

"No," he repeated, throwing the styptic in the basin. "Last thing I need is some damned nursemaid fawning all over me." He grabbed up the med kit and picked through it, tossing supplies this way and that until he found what he wanted. "Ah. Here we go." The med kit clanged loudly as he dropped it back into the basin, toggled the controls on a tiny auto-stitcher, and maneuvered it close to his head.

Serengeti cringed. "You sure you know what you're doing with that?"

"Trust me," he said, tipping a wink at the camera. "I've had lots of practice."

Serengeti sighed. "Why am I not surprised?"

A flick of a switch, and the auto-stitcher started to hum. Henricksen pressed the end to the gash in his head and let it do its thing, wincing now and then as it chattered away—the noise of it like a set of those tiny, ancient, wind-up teeth chewing away at a piece of leather.

Five seconds and it was over, a dozen or so neat stitches showing darkly beneath Henricksen's hair. The wound itself cinched tight, just a few dribbles of blood seeping out.

"Not bad," *Serengeti* admitted, examining the final product.

"Told ya." Henricksen flashed a grin and turned the spigot, cupped his hands under the faucet to catch the water and splashed it on the side of his head. A bit of dousing and the worst of the blood disappeared. And with the addition of an antiseptic strip slapped over the stitches, Henricksen was ready to go. "There. Whaddaya think?" he asked, turning around.

Serengeti snickered. "You look funny."

Henricksen blushed self-consciously, touching at the antiseptic strip. "It'll dissolve by morning. Don't want the damned thing getting infected, after all."

"Still," *Serengeti* said, laughing softly again. "*Sechura* just fixed you up and the first thing you do is go and break yourself again."

"Yeah, well. You know me." He ducked his head and started grabbing up bandages, shoving them into the med kit.

"Yes. Yes, I do," *Serengeti* said softly.

Henricksen grunted, eyes lifting, catching the camera's reflection in the mirror. Smiled and shook his head as he shoved a last few things into the med kit and put it back inside the cabinet.

A last check of the stitches, making sure the antiseptic strip was securely in place, and Henricksen walked back into the bedroom. Stopped in the middle and turned his head, considering the closet to one side. "Hang on a sec, would ya?" He waved at the camera and stepped over to it, pulling the closet's composite metal doors wide.

A row of fresh uniforms hung on hangars inside, every last one of them black and silver, stitched to Henricksen's measurements, with *Serengeti's* patch on the shoulders and those captain's stars on the collar. "Your doing?" he asked, looking over his shoulder.

"A captain needs to look the part. I had spare uniforms made up for the crew as well. Had to guess at the sizes, though." She paused, letting that hang in the air a moment. "You know, because I wasn't quite sure who…"

Henricksen nodded as *Serengeti* trailed off. "To be honest, I wasn't really sure who'd made it into *Cryo* myself." He reached up, tracing the silver thread of a patch with his finger. "Thanks," he said, nodding to the line of uniforms hanging in the closet. Opened his mouth and then closed it, lips pressing together as he ducked his head. "Thanks," he repeated, nodding to the camera. Reached for a drawer beneath the hanging uniforms and pulled it open, shoving belts and pins and other miscellaneous uniform items out of the way, digging through two other drawers below it before he finally found what he wanted. "There you are," he murmured, pulling a wooden box out.

"What's that?" *Serengeti* asked curiously.

"Hmm?" Henricksen raised his head, blinking slowly, looking a million miles away. "Gift," he said, holding the box up.

"For me?" she teased.

"No," he said quietly. "'Fraid not." He touched a hand to the box's top, tracing the smoothness of the wood. Turned around and ambled out of the bedroom, heading for the windows, setting the box on the low-slung table sitting beneath the stars.

Serengeti flicked to a camera in the corner, studying Henricksen as he stood by that table—head bowed, fingertips resting lightly on the wooden box's lid.

Dark wood—Andrulian heartwood, maybe. One of those other old Earth walnut hybrids that were popular a century or so back. Two now, she supposed, given the time they'd both lost.

"It's pretty," she told him.

"Sikuuku gave it to me. To commemorate my assignment." He glanced at the camera, smiling sadly. "Big day, getting selected to fill a Valkyrie's Captain's Chair." The smile wilted, Henricksen's eyes dropping back to the case, finger tracing a swirl in the wood's grain. "You were supposed to be here," *Serengeti* heard him whisper. "You were supposed to share this with me."

He drew a breath—deep and shaky—and blew it back out, hand clenched into a fist pressed tight to his leg. A last touch at the wooden lid and Henricksen flipped the case open, revealing a velvet-lined interior cradling a clear glass bottle filled with some amber-colored liquid. A matching pair of cut-glass tumblers sitting to either side.

"Whiskey?" *Serengeti* guessed.

"Better." Henricksen pried the bottle free and held it up to the camera. "Scotch. Aged 75 years."

"Must be worth a fortune."

"Probably." He cupped the bottle in both hands, considering it a moment. "What the hell," he decided, breaking the seal, spinning the cap off. Plucked a tumbler from the case and filled it half full. Paused, eyes flicking to the case and the single glass resting there, and grabbed it up too, splashing a healthy dose of Scotch inside. "Hate drinking alone," he said, sparing a look for the camera as he reached inside his jacket, lifting a silver chain over his head. Held it a while, staring thoughtfully at the pendant resting on his palm.

Shell pendant—one Sikuuku used to wear. The chain his too, retrieved from his dead body.

Henricksen wrapped his fingers around it, lips pressed in a hard line. Opened his hand and dropped the pendant into one of the glasses, watched it sink to the bottom. "Wish you were here with me," he murmured. "I wish—" He broke off, grimacing. Scooped up his glass and raised it in salute before downing the contents in one gulp. "Damn that's good." He reached for the bottle, refilling his glass.

That second drink disappeared almost as quickly as the first, and the third not long after that. *Serengeti* watched in silence all the while, reading anger in the set of Henricksen's shoulders. The way he tossed back that third drink—hardly even tasting it—before pouring himself a fourth.

The way his eyes flicked to that pendant each time he filled his glass.

"Sand dollar, right?"

Henricksen froze, glass half-lifted to his lips.

"The shell." *Serengeti* zoomed in on Sikuuku's pendant. "It's called a sand dollar, right?"

"Yeah," he said softly, lowering his glass, clutching it against his stomach. "Sikuuku's sister gave it to him before he left home. Supposed to be good luck or something."

"He was from Earth, then?"

Didn't need his answer—Sikuuku's records told her as much—but *Serengeti* knew Henricksen's moods, especially the black ones. Knew that talking was sometimes the only way to get him out of it. Help him work through the anger. The bitterness and regret.

Henricksen sipped at his drink, enjoying it this time rather than simply tossing it down. "Not many are these days," he told her. "Least, not in the ranks." His lips twisted, a hint of bitterness creeping into his voice. "Fleet prefers Academy. Officers from Suchalon and Argentia. Enlisted from Diaspora and Trimark, the other Core planets. Earth…well, Earth's way out now, isn't it? Humanity moved on and left it behind." He waved vaguely, dropping his eyes, considering the Scotch in his glass. "Father was a fisherman of all things. Did you know that?" He slid his eyes to the camera, turned his gaze on the windows. "Sikuuku hunted fish in the ocean before he came out here to hunt ships among the stars." He grunted, staring a moment, quiet for a long, long time. "Shoulda stayed," he rasped, finishing his drink. "Fishermen don't get blown to bits by goddamn cannons at the ass end of the universe."

He scooped up the bottle and filled the glass again.

"Henricksen—"

"Don't," he said coldly, eyes locking onto the camera.

Anger there, but not directed at her. Anger trying to mask a load of pain Henricksen carried around inside him.

Serengeti understood it on some level. Fifty-three years she'd had to come to terms with her losses, but to Henricksen, it all happened yesterday. The intervening years just a blip between sleeping and waking—no time at all to mourn the loss of friends and lovers, crewmates and companions.

So she let Henricksen be for a while, leaving him to his brooding silence. Watching the Scotch bottle slowly empty as her captain drank away his sorrow.

TWELVE

An hour passed—*Serengeti* watching, Henricksen drinking, pondering the stars outside. An hour of brooding silence before *Serengeti* quietly, carefully intruded on her captain's thoughts.

"Where'd they find you?" she asked, and saw Henricksen's eyes shift, sliding her way.

"Shipping lanes. Way out." He waved vaguely. "Somewhere around Shi-San or Sotolo. One of those half-settled fringe planets."

She consulted the star charts, flagging the two planets he'd mentioned, marking the place where *Sechura* had found her, calculating the distance between. "One hundred and eighty-two light years." She shunted the star chart to the windows, highlighting the three points. "*Long* way out. Not much in between any of it."

"Ass end of the universe, just like I said." Henricksen eyes the star charts, half-full glass dangling from his fingertips. "Miracle we didn't get holed along the way. Qaisrani wouldn't tell me shit-all until you showed up, but Finlay and me got to know some of *Sechura's* crew." He paused, looking at her. "Not a bad bunch, by the way. They'll do right by us when the time comes."

No idea what that meant, and Henricksen turned away before *Serengeti* could ask.

"Story I got from the crew was they picked us up and downloaded everything in *Cryo's* data banks. Used its path to track back to you."

"Took you long enough."

"Tell me about." Henricksen bowed his head, staring into the bottom of his glass.

Serengeti watched him, thinking, took another look at that star chart, and realized something didn't quite add up.

System contained *Cryo's* data—a gift from *Sechura,* along with *Homunculus's* data file—so she downloaded it, analyzing the lifeboat's course and speed, the *route Cryo* had travelled before reaching the shipping lanes where *Sechura* picked it up.

The path checked out—nothing wrong there. But when *Serengeti* calculated the distance and factored in *Cryo's* rate of travel, everything fell apart.

"Math doesn't work," she murmured.

Henricksen raised his head, giving her a baffled look. "Math? What math? What the hell does math have to do with any of this?"

"Everything."

She checked the lifeboat's path again, reran all her calculations, but the results came out the same: even assuming variations in course and speed, *Cryo still* should have made it back to the shipping lanes a good five *years* ahead of what *Sechura* claimed.

"She lied," *Serengeti* breathed, hardly believing it.

"Who?" Henricksen turned around, brow wrinkled in confusion.

"*Sechura.*"

Henricksen's face darkened, fingers tightening around his glass. "Explain," he rasped, angry now. Face turning cold.

"She left me out there. Five years *Sechura* had you, but she never came looking for me. Not once."

"Not until she needed you." He turned away, staring grimly at the glass. "Not until she came up with this insane plan of hers."

Faraday, and the Vault. The AI inside. *Serengeti* wished she could deny it and tell Henricksen he was wrong, but the truth was right there. The cold, hard facts laid bare in *Cryo's* data.

Math again. All her objections undone by the immutable proofs of math.

"She must have had her reasons," *Serengeti* reasoned, wanting it to be true.

She found me and fixed me. Surely that means something.

"I'm sure she did," Henricksen said cryptically, turning his head, showing her one grey eye. "And her own interests."

Serengeti was quiet a moment, watching him from above. "She's Valkyrie, Henricksen. She wouldn't turn on one of her own."

"Maybe."

His frown said otherwise. Said he doubted the motivations of this Sister of hers.

"Guess we'll never know for sure. Her being gone and all." He grimaced again, looking way. Sighed and closed his eyes, rubbing at his face. "Sorry. That was a dick thing to say. It's just..." He shrugged his shoulders, looking up. "Lotta changes in this fleet, *Serengeti*. Fifty-three *years* of change."

More math. Everything was math, and none of good, it seemed.

"Some things don't change," she said softly. "There's you. And Finlay. And, well, *some* of me is still original."

Henricksen grunted, acknowledging the weak attempt at a joke. Looked away again, swirling the Scotch in his glass. "Thirty-nine crew left, by the way. Plus me, of course." He raised the glass, lowered it without drinking. "Lost six along the away. Thought I'd lost Finlay, too." His lips curled in a soft smile, but it quickly disappeared. "'Course Finlay doesn't make up for Sikuuku. Kusikov. Tsu—"

"Don't, Henricksen," *Serengeti* rebuked gently. "Don't do that to yourself."

"Can't crew a warship with just thirty-nine soldiers," he told her— angry, hurting, blaming himself. He gulped at his glass, slammed it down on the table. "Probably should have told you earlier, but I borrowed a few crew from Qaisrani."

"How many?" she asked sharply, wary of strangers. Of changes made without her consent.

"Twenty-seven. That puts us at sixty-seven total. Skeleton crew." Henricksen smiled bitterly, shrugging his shoulders—helpless gesture, apologetic at the same time. "Bare minimum needed to run a warship. Even one with all the high-tech super advanced doo-dads and hoo-has you got these days."

"Skeleton crew. I like that." The irony of it. The idea of a skeleton crew running a ghost ship felt strangely fitting somehow.

"Understand you've got some new robots on board." Henricksen quirked an eyebrow, looking a question at the camera.

"Seventy-five shiny new TSGs. New model," she explained at Henricksen's blank look. "Cheeky like Tig, but more configurable." She hesitated before telling him the rest. "I've got three TIGs on board, too. Tig you know about. And there's another he salvaged after... after..." She trailed off, thinking of those long years in the dark.

"And the third?" Henricksen prompted.

She hesitated, choosing her words carefully. "Not an original."

"Meaning?" Henricksen folded his arms, staring at the camera.

"Tig and his partner, they sort of... *made* the third."

"Made?" Henricksen's eyebrows lifted. "So it's a drone? Robot with no AI?"

"No. She's got an AI."

"She." He tilted his head, eyeing the camera with interest.

"Oona."

"And now she's got a name." Henricksen threw his hands in the air, laughing aloud. "Of *course* she's got a name. And Tig made her."

"With Tilli's help."

"Tilli." Henricksen winked, pointing a finger pistol at the camera. Cocked it and fired. "Another 'she,' I assume."

"She. Yes."

"And this third..." He looked a question at the camera.

"Oona.

"Right. Oona. *How* exactly did she come about?"

Serengeti hesitated, wondering how much truth to share. Threw caution to the wind because this was Henricksen—if she couldn't trust him, who *could* she trust?—spilling the rest in a breathless rush. "Tig harvested one of the burnt-out AIs and reconfigured it using chip sets and programming routines from himself and Tilli to build out Oona's mindset."

Henricksen blinked, mouth sagging open. "He—They—What?"

She drew a deep breath and started all over again. "Tig harvested one of—"

"Yeah-yeah-yeah. I got all that," he said, waving impatiently. "The thing I *don't* get is how two robots made a new AI all on their very own."

"Chip sets," she said. "And programming routines."

Henricksen frowned. "And a burnt-out AI."

"Uh-huh."

"Great." Henricksen bowed his head, pinching the bridge of his nose. "So, is she...functional? I mean, not, like, the robot equivalent of a drooling idiot?"

"No," *Serengeti* said, laughing softly. "Not a drooling idiot. Just the opposite. She's quite special." She reached for Oona across the robot network, searching for the tiny robot's sparkling, rainbows and glitter presence.

"Special," Henricksen repeated, giving the camera a look. "Engineers'll have a shit fit about this. AI procreation—it'll revolutionize the industry. No programming and chip-set restrictions. No more purpose-built models for specific applications. This—This is..." Henricksen trailed off, eyes troubled, face worried.

"It's dangerous," *Serengeti* softly.

"Yeah." Henricksen sighed heavily, looking more tired than ever. "Boffins'll seize Oona in an instant if they find out about her. Lock her up in some lab and tear her down to her core. Dismantle her mind so they can study it."

"And when they're done with her, they'll destroy her."

"You don't know that," Henricksen said coldly.

"Humans created AIs, Henricksen. They designed our crystal matrix minds and the programming behind them. But they still don't trust us. They didn't fifty-three years ago, and they sure as hell don't now."

Henricksen looked at her, surprised at the bitterness in her voice.

"You saw how they treated me on Blue Horizon. And that's supposedly one of the *better* stations these days."

"Yeah, well." Henricksen ducked his head, stared at his hands. "*Brutus* sure isn't helping. That bombing back there. Booby-trapped ship or whatever it was." He raised his head, shook it hard. "Can't be a coincidence it was parked next to the only Valkyrie in port."

"The only one anyone *knew* about, anyway."

Henricksen looked at her, dipped his head in acknowledgement. "It'll get worse before it gets better," he said quietly, touching the stitches on the side of his head. "Fleet's not doing its job. Without it..." His shoulders lifted, sagged in defeat. "Only a matter of time before the Meridian Alliance dies."

"So what do you want to do about it?"

Henricksen blinked, frowning at the camera. "Whaddaya mean what do I—?"

"*Sechura.* We owe her an answer."

"You mean her replacement," he said carefully.

"Of course," she said quickly. Slip up on her part. Didn't want Henricksen to think she'd lost her marbles. "It'll be *Atacama* now, I suppose. Or *Marianas.*"

Atacama, most likely. She was the stronger of the two.

"One Valkyrie's as good as another," Henricksen told her, flipping a hand. "Unless that Valkyrie's you, of course."

"Flattery will get you nowhere," she said, teasing. "And you're avoiding the question, Henricksen. Don't think I haven't noticed."

Henricksen went very still, considering the camera. Turned away, putting his back to her now.

"Henricksen." She kept her voice light, chiding gently. "We should at least *talk* about it."

He shook his head, not even looking.

"Henricksen."

"What?" He whirled around, face angry, stabbing a finger at the camera. "You wanna talk about it? Fine. Let's talk about it. Everyone I know is dead, *Serengeti.* How about we start there. Do you have any idea—?" He broke off, jaw clenching, hands balled into fists at his sides. "We can't return to the Fleet. *Sechura* made sure of that."

"That wasn't her intent," *Serengeti* told him, rising to her Sister's defense. "At least we're alive. We got out, Henricksen. *Sechura* didn't. Don't forget that."

"Oh, we're alive alright. But that thing back there on Blue Horizon..." He twisted, pointing that accusatory finger at the stars outside. "That isn't you." He stepped away from the windows, moving closer to the camera. "We're ghosts, *Serengeti.* Just like *Sechura* said. And ghosts stand at the fringes. They don't get to go back home."

"You're my home, Henricksen. You and the crew and the stars."

He stared a moment, caught completely off guard. Sighed, defeated, shoulders slumping beneath a weight of weariness. "Even if we could go back to the Fleet, I'm guessing they wouldn't know what to do with us. Technically, I'm still a captain, but..." Another sigh, Henricksen ducking his head. "Fifty-three years I've been out of rotation. Shit, I'm close to a hundred goddamn years old!"

"Don't look a day over forty to me," she said, risking the joke. Wanting desperately for this anger between them to end.

To her surprise, it worked, coaxing a wan smile out of Henricksen. Unfortunately, it didn't stay. Never quite stuck to his lips. "You shoulda seen the way *Sechura's* crew looked at us. Half of 'em scared to death, the rest..." He trailed off, considering the bottle of Scotch on the table. "Captain's more than just rank, *Serengeti*. There's a hierarchy to things in the military. A captain without contacts doesn't quite fit in."

"Meaning?"

He shrugged again, hand lifting, touching the scar near his temple. "Even if I could go back, they'd probably just shove me into retirement. Set me up on some backwater planet. Thank me for my service and offer me fifty-three years of back pay to stay the hell out of the way. 'Course, if I was smart, I'd take it," he admitted, with a rueful shake of his head.

"But?" she asked, sensing one.

"But," Henricksen sighed, touching the stars pinned to his collar. *Serengeti's* patch on his shoulder. "I'm a soldier. Told you that before. The stars are all I know. The Fleet and its ships are the only home I ever wanted. But we stepped away for a while and *Brutus* took all that away. Took the *pride* of being part of the Fleet along with the purpose behind it. Can't have that," he told her, shaking his head. "I can't just sit by and let the Meridian Alliance go to hell. Not when I can do something to stop it."

Quiet then—an unsettled silence between them.

"So which is it?" she asked when that silence stretched on, and on, and on. "Throw in with the Valkyries or go back to the Fleet?"

She'd already made her choice, never mind *Sechura's* deception. But Henricksen needed to make his—she respected him too much to make that decision for him.

Serengeti watched him from her camera, waiting and waiting. But it was a long time before Henricksen finally answered.

"*Sechura* lied to us."

Not a good start—*Serengeti's* heart plummeted when those words came out of his mouth. But a flick of his eyes to the camera and he went back to brooding over the stars.

"You're probably right," he said some time later. "She probably had a good reason for everything she did. But she still lied, *Serengeti*. And I'm not quite sure we can trust her. Or *Atacama*," he added. "Hell, I hardly even *know Atacama*."

"I do," *Serengeti* told him. "I know her very well."

"I know," he said quietly. "I know you do, *Serengeti*." Henricksen bowed his head, staring at his hands. "I think we should stand with the Valkyries. I think they're our best hope. I think they're the *Fleet's* best hope."

"Just so happens I agree," *Serengeti* told him, hoping she didn't sound as smug as she felt.

Henricksen snuck a look at her, lips twisting on one side. "'Course, that doesn't change the fact that this plan of theirs is crap."

"Blunt as always," *Serengeti* chuckled. "I *have* missed that, Henricksen."

The smile widened—still crooked and rueful, his smile always looked that way—but a true smile, like the old Henricksen used to wear.

"And what specifically," she asked him, "is crap about *Sechura's* plan?"

Sechura's plan. It was still *Sechura's* plan, even with *Sechura* herself now gone.

Henricksen folded his arms, looking around the room, eyes eventually settling on that tiny silver spaceship sitting on the bookshelves. "Well, first there's the fact that *Sechura* herself just got her ass kicked back at Blue Horizon. Not sure how we factor *that* into this plan of hers. Goddammit. There I go again." He sighed wearily, scrubbing at his face. "I'm sorry, *Serengeti*. I shouldn't—"

"It's alright," she said quietly.

It wasn't—wasn't alright at all—but what else was she going to tell him?

"*Atacama's* her second. She'll take over now that *Sechura's* gone." *Serengeti* tried to sound confident, and keep the pain from her voice, but Henricksen saw right through it. She could tell from the look on his face. "What else?" she asked, hurrying him along. "What else is wrong with *Sechura's* plan?"

Henricksen tilted his head, considering the camera. Shrugged and walked over to the bookshelves, picking the little spaceship up. "Head to head, we'll just tear each other apart." He rubbed a thumb across the inscription carved into the spaceship's belly, wiping the tarnish away.

Name and date there: *Harbinger*, 2927. The ship was his—the first one Henricksen ever captained—and the date as well.

2927: the day *Harbinger* died. Henricksen himself escaped with one hundred and twelve crew, but *Harbinger* went down in a blaze of glory. Rammed a DSR cruiser named *Shylock,* killing both AIs instantly.

"Let's go with the best-case scenario," he said, cradling the tiny starship in his hands. "Let's say we bust those AIs out of the Faraday Vault and somehow manage to get them into the ships stashed in the Pandoran Cloud." He paused, head tilting. "I'm still in awe of that part, by the way. Whatever else you wanna say about her, *Sechura's* one sneaky-ass little cookie, that's for sure."

"Always was," *Serengeti* said faintly.

Henricksen opened his mouth and then closed it, folded his arms, assuming a thoughtful pose. "So we get the AIs from the prison, load them into a bunch of refurbed bodies, show up guns blazing with all your Valkyrie Sisters behind us and manage to win the Titans and Auroras over. Get every last one of them on our side." He glanced at the window, eyebrow lifting. "Let's get *really* crazy and assume one of those Bastion bastards sees an opportunity to seize power for himself and turns against his brothers. That's the *best* scenario," he said meaningfully.

"And the more likely one nowhere near as good."

"Exactly." Henricksen nodded. "Even if all that happens, we just end up pounding away at each other until one side wins. Might be us, might not. Either way, the Fleet ends up in tatters. That happens, it'll take *years* to resurrect it."

"And in the meantime, there's a power vacuum. Just the merchants, and the freighters, and the pirates. And whatever's left of the Fleet to keep them all honest. We might get *Brutus* out of the way, but we'll pave the way for the next Dark Star Revolution or some other up-jumped bunch of revolutionaries to come in and take charge of things."

"So we're agreed. *Sechura's* plan is crap."

"Not completely. The Vault part's sound."

Henricksen blinked in surprise. "Really? Thought that was the craziest part of all."

"It is in some ways, but she's right: we could use the AI reinforcements. As for the rest..." *Serengeti* paused, feeling an idea slowly forming. "There may be another way to go about this."

Henricksen's eyebrows lifted. "I'm listening."

"What's missing in all this?"

Henricksen looked puzzled. "Not sure what you mean."

"*Cerberus,*" *Serengeti* said quietly. "I know. I know. I saw the vid. But something about all this doesn't make sense. Why would *Cerberus* abandon the Fleet and give up all his responsibilities to the Meridian Alliance to just take off into deep space?"

"Needed a vacation?"

"Somehow I doubt it," she said dryly. "Something's gone wrong with *Cerberus*, Henricksen. The vid shows that clearly enough."

"And?" he prompted.

"And I'd like to know what."

"Holy shit." Henricksen straightened, arms unfolding, hands dropping to his sides. "You want us to go after *Cerberus*?"

"Why not? We can't go back to Blue Horizon. And I don't dare try to get in touch with *Atacama* or one of the other Valkyries until the mess we left behind settles down. We've got some time to kill and nowhere in particular we need to be. Might as well look up *Cerberus's* address and see if he's in the mood for a little chat."

"Right," Henricksen grunted. "Simple as that."

"Probably not," *Serengeti* admitted. "But we know where to find him. The vid gives us coordinates. *Sechura* told me he's just been hanging out there for the last decade, not even trying to hide. Just...floating. Existing."

"Taking up space." Henricksen eyed the camera uncertainly. "You do remember how that ended up for the *last* ship full of people that came to talk?"

"I do," she said quietly. "But I don't mean to make the same mistake they did."

"Seems to me just going there in the first place was the mistake."

"Going there *unprepared*," *Serengeti* corrected. "Which we won't be. Second mistake was announcing themselves. Letting *Cerberus* know there was a mouse in the house."

"No offense, *Serengeti,* but you're a helluva a lot bigger than a mouse. And a good three times the size of the diplomatic ships the Meridian Alliance sent to hold court with the Citadel."

"True," *Serengeti* said simply, and for a long time after, said nothing at all.

That left Henricksen waiting, brows pulled downward, thoughts swirling in his eyes. "You've got something in mind."

"I do," *Serengeti* admitted, smiling herself.

"Spill it." He moved closer, eyes locked on the camera.

"*Sechura* says I'm invisible. Wiped from the central system. A ghost long forgotten. I'd say it's high time we tested that theory. See just how much of a ghost I truly am."

THIRTEEN

"Still not sure this is a good idea." Henricksen looked up from his place at the Command Post, frowning worriedly at *Serengeti's* camera. Just he and *Serengeti* on the bridge right now, the rest of the crew still settling in, divvying up assignments between them to make sure all the ship's operations were covered. "We cut out of Blue Horizon before the DD3s finished patching those holes in your hull. We still got most of the little buggers on board, why not wait a couple days—?"

"Don't need to."

"Really." Henricksen folded his arms, giving her camera a skeptical look. "Because you're a rough, tough warship and what's a few holes?"

"No," *Serengeti* said patiently. "Because Tig had the DD3s working all night and the repairs are just about done."

"Oh." Henricksen blinked, cheeks coloring. Dropped his eyes and tapped at a panel, pulling up the video feeds from the outward facing cameras.

Few DD3s out there, scuttling about her hull. Cleaning up, mostly. Grabbing spare parts and equipment before heading back inside.

Henricksen watched them a while, touched at the panel, shutting the feed back down. "Busy little beavers, aren't they?"

"They are indeed. Not quite sure what I'm going to do with them, though. TSGs pretty much have ship's maintenance covered so once the hull's fixed..." She trailed off, letting that hang in the air. "Suppose I could reprogram them," she said, sneaking another peek at the DD3s outside. "Shame to waste good help, after all."

Henricksen grunted non-commitally, checking his panel, the stars outside.

"Might take a few of them with me once I find a way onto *Cerberus.*"

Henricksen froze, eyebrows lifting in surprise. "*Onto Cerberus,*" he repeated. "We're going *onto* the Citadel now?"

Probably should've mentioned that part sooner.

"I need to talk to him so I can find out what's going on," *Serengeti* explained.

"You mean, why he abandoned the Fleet and left the Meridian Alliance to rot?"

"A bit blunt, but yes. Essentially. And since *Cerberus* doesn't seem to like dealing with ships, I thought I'd present myself in person."

Henricksen tilted his head, looking increasingly skeptical of this plan of hers. "Pop in for tea and crumpets—that the idea?"

"Something like that."

She kept her voice light, but Henricksen obviously wasn't amused.

"And *how* exactly do you plan to get onto the Citadel without him noticing?"

"Not quite sure," she admitted. "Use *Cryo* or something."

"*Cryo*," Henricksen snorted, shaking his head. "You Valkyries are all cracked."

"We don't have a shuttle—that's the one thing *Sechura couldn't* scrounge up, evidently—so it's not like I've got a whole lot of other options."

"No," Henricksen sighed. "I guess not." He considered the camera a moment, sighed again and touched at the panel in front of him, opening ship-wide comms. "Command crew to the bridge. Sharpish, if you please."

He cut the line and waited—eyes on the windows, arms folded tight to his chest. Twisted, looking behind him when the bridge door opened just a minute or two later and Finlay appeared, cheerful smile plastered across her freckled, dimpled face.

"Reporting for duty, Captain." Finlay flipped him a salute, smile never wavering, turned on her heel, and headed for the Artillery pod to her right.

"Finlay!" Henricksen's whip-crack voice stopped Finlay dead in her tracks. "You're assigned to Scan, not Artillery."

Finlay pivoted—jaw set, eyes blazing. "But you said—"

"I said I'd think about it, Finlay. And I have." He drew a breath, face softening as Finlay's shoulders slumped, the look of challenged replaced by puzzlement and hurt. "You'll have your chance at Artillery, Finlay. I just need you on Scan right now."

Finlay threw a sullen look at Scan, obviously not happy. Heart set on running the big guns.

"We're heading into uncertain territory, Finlay."

Finlay glanced up at the camera as *Serengeti* calm, serene voice filled the bridge.

"Scan's our first line of defense. Artillery—"

"Artillery's for when things go wrong," Henricksen said grimly.

"Exactly." *Serengeti* was quiet a moment, watching Finlay's face, letting that sink in. "We need someone experienced sitting Scan, Finlay. Someone we can count on if things get dicey."

That was her—Finlay'd proven herself back at Hon-shen-shura, no one better qualified to sit *Serengeti's* Scan station—but she obviously still had aspirations. Threw a last, longing look at the Artillery pod before nodding tightly and moving over to Scan.

Henricksen looked up, nodding his thanks to *Serengeti's* camera.

The rest of the bridge crew trickled in soon after—new crew, for the most part, borrowed from *Sechura* to fill out the gaps in *Serengeti's* ranks. Her crew now. *Permanent* crew, with *Sechura* lost.

Bosch—blocky and blond-haired and built like a freight train—who lumbered onto her bridge, sketching a quick salute before heading toward the gimbaled Artillery pod jutting from the bridge's curving right wall.

Typical Artillery jock, that one. *Serengeti* had no idea why gunners always came so big when the Artillery pod itself was built so compact and tight.

Finlay watched him enter, glaring from her place at Scan, flushed when she found Henricksen watching *her,* looking less than amused by her dirty looks. Ducked her head and pretended to be busy as Aoki appeared, saluting far more formally than Bosch. Offering Finlay a friendly nod as she slid into Engineering—the station right next to Scan.

Serengeti studied her, and her records. She didn't know Aoki, but the personnel file from *Sechura* showed a dutiful, diligent officer—nervous as hell at being promoted from third shift to first, but with all the right training. Some experience, if not as much as *Serengeti* would like.

Big show, sitting the bridge with the captain in attendance. Aoki probably never even *saw* Qaisrani in the two years she served on *Sechura* and now her first assignment on *Serengeti*, she found herself running Engineering with Henricksen looking over her shoulder. Almost felt bad for her, especially when she sat down and entered her security code, fingers shaking so badly she flubbed the entry the first two tries and almost locked herself out.

Luckily, she had Finlay looking out for her. Someone who knew the ropes and wasn't too proud to help out.

"Psst!" Finlay glanced over her shoulder, checking to see if Henricksen was watching. Leaned over to Engineering, whispering conspiratorially to Aoki. "Deep breath," she told her, catching Aoki's eyes. "It's alright. Really." Another glanced at the Command Post. "Captain's not so bad once you get used to him."

"He's—He's not?" Aoki asked hopefully.

"Huh-uh. More like a big, shouty teddy bear." Finlay smiled encouragingly, nodding to Aoki's panels, keeping one eye on her own. "Just log in and run the diagnostics."

Aoki looked at her, and at Engineering's panels, chewing her lip worriedly.

"You can do this," Finlay told her. "You've done this a thousand times."

A last, encouraging nod from Finlay and Aoki sucked in a breath, flipping her dark braid over her shoulder. Cracked her knuckles—all of them at once, joints snapping like firecrackers—and reached for Engineering's panels, activating systems, bringing everything to life.

Data screens appeared, painting Aoki's face in golden light. She leaned forward, teardrop eyes flicking across the panels in front of her, pouring through reams of information as her fingers cycled through one data window after another. Hesitant movements, at first, Aoki uncertain still, and then increasingly more sure of herself. Ran through the start-up routines like a pro, the diagnostics checks after. Closed that all down and pulled up the engine controls, freezing up tight when a prompt appeared, asking about tolerances and settings.

Aoki's confidence wilted, washed right out of her. She bit her lip, staring at the panel and its flashing, insistent prompt. Opened a text window and started tapping out questions, pausing between each one, throwing anxious glances at Scan as Finlay responded with answers.

Good girl, Finlay. Way to step up and help the new crew out.

Finlay got her through that first prompt, addressing a second round of questions after. Helping Aoki along until finally got the nerves out of her system and hit her stride. "There you go. You've got this." She winked at Aoki and sent another message—a funny little picture that made the crewman laugh.

"Something funny, Aoki?" Henricksen's eyes lifted, staring at the back of Aoki's head.

"No, sir." Aoki flushed guiltily, shoulders hunching. "Sorry, sir." She twisted, nodding an apology to Henricksen behind her, faced around, throwing a desperate look at Scan.

Finlay shrugged, smiling secretively. Sent Aoki a picture of a giant, scowling teddy bear stomping buildings flat.

Aoki choked, trying not to laugh. Added an eyepatch to the bear, a sash and sword, and sent it back.

Finlay giggled, snuck a look at Henricksen—who did *not* seem amused by the goings on at Scan and Engineering—and started to laugh harder.

That's when Samara arrived—Samara and Delacroix, the last two members of *Serengeti's* new Command crew. *Sechura* crew, previously—second watch the both of them, and eager for any opportunity for advancement.

Samara braced up hard, offering a crisp salute. A hawk-faced, fierce-looking woman with Indo-Persian features that put *Serengeti* in mind of Tsu's Anoosheh. A harder, more angular version of that dead crewman's lover. Skin the color of terra-cotta, dark hair buzzed tight to her skull.

Strong woman, Samara—that came through instantly. She scanned the bridge, golden-brown eyes analyzing everything and everyone around her, sizing up the situation before she moved over to her station. Delacroix, on the hand...Delacroix just stood there staring, ebon-skinned face bathed in the soft light spilling from the ceiling. A handsome enough man with his long nose and full lips, but...empty-seeming. Vacant, somehow.

Samara nudged him in the ribs, eyes flicking meaningfully to Henricksen. Nudged him again when Delacroix kept staring and *kept* nudging until he acknowledged her, lips pulling downward in a frown. A glance at Henricksen and he raised his hands, belatedly offering a salute. An oddly distracted gesture, considering the formality of that gesture. But then, pretty much every thing about Delacroix seemed distracted and uninterested.

Serengeti zoomed in tight on the crewman, giving him the once over, looking him right in the eyes.

Not good, she thought. *Not good at all.*

She flashed a message to Henricksen's panel, saw him glance at it frown. Spare a nod for *Serengeti's* camera as he returned the crew's salutes and waved them in, pointing that to their stations. "Settle in. We're pulling out in ten."

"Aye, sir." Samara pointed Delacroix toward Comms, giving him a shove to get him moving. Marched herself over to Navigation, glancing at Comms now and then. Watching Delacroix grabbed up the comms visor, examining it a moment before settling it over his smoothly shaven head.

Systems came to life, bathing Delacroix's dark face in multi-colored lights. He reached for the plugs and cables dangling from the Comms station, jacked the network connectors into the ports at his wrist, and stiffened, going completely rigid. Dead eyes staring at nothing and everything at once.

Something clicked—puzzle pieces falling into place. That vacant look, the distracted demeanor—suddenly it all made sense. She'd seen this before, after all. In not one but *two* of her previous Comms officers, in fact. Too much time in the system messed with the brain. Detached the mind from reality, making it difficult to tell the difference between the real world and the netherspace of Comms.

"Henricksen."

"I see it." Soft voice. Didn't even look up. A shrug of his shoulders, finger tapping at a panel as he ran a few checks, closed the data windows down. "Not really much I can do about it right now." He did look at her then. Flicked his eyes Delacroix's way.

Meaningful look, because—moonbeam or not—they needed Delacroix. Needed a qualified Comms officer. And right now, Delacroix was the only one they had on board.

"Watch him," she warned—a last, soft exchange between the two of them—and saw Henricksen nod. "Take us out, Captain," she said, louder now, making sure all the crew heard.

"Yes, ma'am." Henricksen nodded to the camera, straightened and addressed the crew. "You heard her, Aoki. Time to blow this popsicle stand and go stargazing for a while."

Aoki paled, face blank, eyes wide and worried looking. Slightly terrified. "Popsicle, sir?"

Henricksen bowed his head, pinching the bridge of his nose. "Kusikov would've gotten that one," he muttered, sliding a look *Serengeti's* way. A few stabs at the panel in front of him and he pulled up the video of *Cerberus,* snagged the coordinates from the metadata, and sent them over to Samara. "Plot a course to that location." Another look at the camera, thoughts swirling in his eyes. "Indirect route."

"Indirect," Samara repeated, frowning.

"That's what I said."

She hesitated, eyes flicking to the windows. Checked the coordinates he'd sent and pulled up the star charts, marking their current location and *Cerberus's* a few hundred lights years away. Checked everything again, looking slightly baffled by the results.

"With respect, sir." Samara hesitated, frown creasing her face. "Why waste the fuel?" A touch at her panel sent the star chart to the front windows. "It's quiet enough where we're going. Star charts don't show anything more sinister than an asteroid field and a dwarf star anywhere *near* those coordinates." Another touch at her panel, adding two location markers, a proposed navigation path between them. "It's a straight shot through hyperspace from here to there. Thirty seconds in the trough, tops."

Henricksen nodded, arms folded, grey eyes turning Nav's way. "Well aware of that, Samara. But in case you hadn't noticed, we left Blue Horizon in kind of a hurry. Not sure anyone can track us here," a quick look at the camera, "but there's no sense leaving a big red arrow to mark where we're going."

"Sir?" Samara—so confident before—seemed completely at a loss.

"Leapfrog, Samara." Henricksen pulled the star chart onto one of his panels, wiped Samara's course, and plotted six short hyperspace jumps—a zigzagging and entirely inefficient path to their final destination.

"We'll burn a lot of energy getting there this way," Samara warned.

"Not really worried about that right now," Henricksen told her. "*More* worried about getting there quietly."

"Sir?"

"We're not broadcasting," *Serengeti* told her. Major security infraction there. AI could get herself Vaulted or worse for jumping without an active beacon, but *Serengeti* figured it wasn't really the time to mention all that. "If we're quiet, there's nothing but the displacement from the jump drives to give our location away."

Henricksen pushed his zigzagging path to the front windows, letting the crew take a good, long look. "Hop around enough and you confuse the trail. Not saying someone won't still be able to track us if they wanted to, but a path like that," he pointed to the windows, "pretty damned hard to follow."

Silence on the bridge, everyone looking at each other, at Henricksen standing at the Command Post. Aoki caught Finlay's eye, typed out a quick message, sending it her way.

Finlay read it and wiped it. "Captain knows what he's doing," she whispered, sneaking a look over her shoulder as Bosch's bass rumble cut across the bridge.

"So, we're running, sir?"

Heads swiveled, everyone holding their breath.

"No, Bosch. We're not running." Henricksen looked at him, and at the rest of the crew on the bridge. Nodded to the camera, waiting as *Serengeti* opened ship-wide comms. "Listen up, everybody. That was bad business back on Blue Horizon, and there's worse going on in the Fleet. Most of you know this by now." A long look at the bridge crew, Henricksen's eyes flicking from one face to another. "Valkyries have a plan that they think might end this. Get the Fleet back to doing what it's *supposed* to be doing. Turn the Meridian Alliance back around. Might work, might not," he admitted, eyes flickering to *Serengeti's* camera. "But that shit storm back on Blue Horizon threw a wrench in the works, and it'll take a while for things to sort themselves out. Now, *Serengeti* here knows how much you guys hate being bored," he flashed his teeth as Finlay snickered at Scan, "so rather than just sitting out here, getting fat and lazy, waiting for something to happen, she came up with a little adventure, to help pass the time."

"Adventure." Bosch sounded pleased. "That's more like it."

"What's out there?" Samara asked, nodding to the zigzagging course on the windows. The red dot marking their final destination.

"*Cerberus*," *Serengeti* said quietly, serene voice filling the bridge, the entirety of the ship's spaces. "We're going to find *Cerberus*."

"*Cerberus* is gone," Delacroix said dreamily, flexing his hands, staring at his palms. "He abandoned the Fleet a long time ago."

"And I want to know why," *Serengeti* told him, a touch of anger creeping into her voice. "*Cerberus* is the admiral of this Fleet, and it's high time someone reminded him of his obligations. So we're going to find him, and do just that." She panned the camera across the bridge, letting that sink in. "Admirals serve. They lead by example. And *Cerberus*—our admiral—doesn't get to abdicate his throne just because things got a little hard."

"Damn straight." Finlay raised a fist, bumped it against a bemused Aoki's hand.

"Any objections?" Henricksen scanned the bridge and saw Samara shrugged her shoulders, Finlay nod decisively, Aoki less certainly so. "Bosch?"

The gunner's arm appeared, thick thumb pointing upward.

"Lower levels," he called, glancing at his panel, watching a score of acknowledgements come back. "Right. That's a quorum. All crew to their stations. We're jumping in ten." Henricksen cut the comms, turning to Samara at Engineering. "Plot that course. Five minutes at each stop." A flick of his eyes to the camera. "Should give us enough time to spool the jump drives back up and take a good look around."

"Make sure no one's following us. Plot a new course if they are." Samara nodded slowly, running calculations, locking in each stop along the way. "Course is set, Captain." She straightened, looking Henricksen's way. "Jump coordinates are queued up and ready to go."

"Good. Aoki! Fire up those engines and get us the hell outta here."

"Aye, sir." Aoki snuck a look at Finlay, licked her lips nervously, and shut the diagnostics windows down as she accessed the jump drive controls. "Three minutes," she said, pushing the jump clock to the front windows as a darkness appeared—the first glimmerings of the buckle forming outside.

"Finlay. I want a full spread of scans as soon as we exit jump."

"Aye, sir!" Finlay called, prepping the system, lining everything up.

"Bosch. Guns primed and ready. Picked some out of the way places to stop, but you never know what you're going to find in deep space."

Bosch rumbled an acknowledgement, slipping the targeting visor over his eyes as Henricksen turned to Delacroix at Comms.

"I need Comms quiet, Delacroix. Listening mode only. We don't send anything out." He raised a finger, pointing it Delacroix's way. "Not one word, you hear me?"

"Aye, sir," Delacroix said faintly, smile quirking his lips. "We'll be quiet as ghosts."

Henricksen stiffened, glancing sharply at Comms, but Delacroix didn't even notice, because Delacroix was gone. Mind detached, floating free in the netherspace of Comms.

"We need him," *Serengeti* reminded him at Henricksen's worried look.

Henricksen grunted, eyeing the crewman at Comms. "Never thought I'd say this, but I miss Kusikov."

Mouthy crewman, arrogant as all get-out. But he was a damned fine Comms officer. Damned fine, indeed.

"He was something," *Serengeti* said quietly. "That's for sure."

"Two minutes," Aoki called as the clock on the front windows ticked down.

"Tig," *Serengeti* called, switching to the robot comms channel. "Pull the DD3s inside."

"Uh…they're not quite done. Still a bunch of equipment out there they need to collect."

"Well tell them to hurry up about it. We're leaving."

"Minute thirty!" Aoki warned.

"But—But the equipment! The spare panels and solar collectors!" Tig sounded panicked.

Serengeti sighed in irritation. "Tell them to grab as much of it as they can and get their shiny metal asses inside."

"Uh…okay."

From the sound of his voice, it obviously was *not* okay, but Tig did as she asked, sending a communication across the robot channel, directing the DD3s back inside.

The DD3s objected, of course—for all their AI capabilities, robots could be so single-threaded and predictable sometimes—but a sharp word from *Serengeti* sent them scrambling, gathering up everything they could get their jointed metal legs around, dragging it with them as they scurried inside.

"Put them in Cargo Bay 4 for now," *Serengeti* ordered. "Tell them to strap in for jump."

"Jump!" More panic from Tig. She switched to a camera in Engineering and saw him hopping up and down, legs waving wildly. "But—But—"

"One minute!" Aoki announced.

"You heard her, Tig. Find a hidey-hole and hang on." *Serengeti* cut the comms as the ship shuddered, Aoki pulsing the engines to get *Serengeti* moving toward the rapidly expanding hyperspace buckle.

"Thirty seconds!" Aoki checked and rechecked the readings on the jump drives, making sure everything was perfect.

The clock ticked down to zero and darkness wrapped around *Serengeti's* body, sucking her into the trough.

FOURTEEN

The first three jumps went smoothly—*Serengeti's* new engines taking the strain in stride, barely needing the cool-down time in between. Scans showing clean. Comms a wasteland of endless silence.

Three clean jumps in, with nothing at all out of the ordinary. Nobody but themselves and the stars anywhere around.

But Finlay stiffened as *Serengeti* exited the trough on their fourth hop. Leaned forward, staring hard at Scan. "Sir!" she called, voice urgent. "I've got something!"

"What, Finlay? Goddammit, *what?*" Henricksen snapped, when Finlay just shook her head.

"Not sure," she told him, face bathed in the panel's light. "Something odd, sir. That's all I can tell."

"Odd don't help much, Finlay."

She looked around, face apologetic, went back to trying to figure out Scan.

Serengeti snuck into her station, parsing through the sensor data—everything before their last jump right up to the moment they dropped out. Pushed the consolidated data package to Finlay's panel. Threw the same data set and a raw feed onto the front windows, let it run a few seconds, pausing it as a distortion appeared, warping the stars.

"Son of a bitch," Henricksen murmured, staring at the glass. "We're being followed."

Sneaky about it, too. Nothing but that story giving their mystery tail away.

"Almost missed them," *Serengeti* admitted. "Whoever they are, they're good."

Henricksen grunted, nodding, studying that distortion outside. "Think we should we hail 'em? Call their bluff?"

"Not quite yet, I think." They knew about that shadow out there now, but the shadow still thought itself invisible. Best to let it keep thinking that for now. Let it follow for a while than risk scaring it away. "Let's jump to the next location and come about. See what happens."

"See what happens? That's your plan?"

"I've seen you come up with worse."

Henricksen opened his mouth and then closed it, grimaced and simply shrugged. "You're the boss," he said, taking another look at that distortion. "Take us through, Aoki. Bosch, bring the forward batteries online. Fire up that big cannon while you're at it. Might as well test out the new toys." A wink for the camera and he folded his arms, spreading his legs wide, bracing himself there as they commenced the next jump.

Fifteen seconds in the trough and *Serengeti* slid back out again, appearing a thousand light years from where she'd started. Aoki fired the maneuvering jets as they slipped into real space, slewing the ship around, bridge crew clinging white-knuckled to their panels as *Serengeti* completed her turn.

Silence after, everybody watching the windows, the data feed showing on the glass. Thirty seconds and a blip appeared on Scan. Thirty more seconds and the blip solidified as the distortion reappeared.

"Bosch!" Henricksen barked.

"Forward batteries ready. Main gun primed." Bosch flexed his huge hands around the Artillery pod's firing mechanisms. "Give the word, Captain, and I'll blow that bastard back to hell."

"Oh, I like him." Henricksen flashed a grin at the camera, arms unfolding as he turned toward Scan. "You got him, Finlay?"

"Aye, sir. Isolated the distortion as soon as he exited jump." She marked a spot on the front window, passing the coordinates over to Bosch so he could lock them into the Artillery pod's targeting system.

"Comms!"

Delacroix flicked his wrist, opening a channel—ship-to-ship, tight band, difficult to pick up unless another ship lurked close by.

Still more noise than *Serengeti* wanted to make, though. She detailed a sub-mind to keep an eye on the sensor data flowing into Scan. Set another to monitoring long-range comms and make sure no one snuck up on them and caught them unaware.

"Identify yourself!" Henricksen ordered, staring at the distortion through the windows.

Nothing came back. But that distortion remained, sitting out there in the darkness. Watching while being watched, pretending it hadn't received their hail.

"Alright. If that's how you wanna play it." Henricksen smiled coldly, nodding to Artillery. "Lay a shot across their bow."

No bow in sight, but Bosch got the idea. He fired a stuttering line of rail gun rounds at their shadow, giving them a warning.

The distortion moved, slipping to one side, letting the railgun fire slide harmlessly by.

"Listen, you bastard." Henricksen leaned forward, hands gripping the edges of the panel in front of him. "We know you're out there, so there's no need to play coy. Either you identify yourself, or I fill your hull full of holes and leave you here for the scavenger ships to pick apart."

"Subtle," *Serengeti* said, muting the outgoing comms channel.

"You know me. Subtle's my middle—"

"Sir!" Finlay looked around. "Jump signature detected."

"Pansy-ass coward." Henricksen thumbed the comms open. "Listen, asshole. I got a big-ass cannon on board this ship and right now it's trained on your engines. You run and my gunner here'll turn you into a teeny-tiny sun."

Silence from that ship out there, stubbornly refusing to respond.

"Bosch—"

"Jump drives powering down, sir."

Finlay looked relieved. All the crew did, even Henricksen at his Command Post. *Serengeti* herself.

No one wanted a fight if they could avoid it. Not even a badass warship with really big guns.

"Communication coming through." Delacroix paused, frowning, fingers moving as he analyzed something only he could see.

Serengeti dipped in beside him, tapped into the incoming data package, and opened it up. "Wonky encryption."

"Lemme see." Henricksen nodded to the panel in front of him.

Serengeti pushed the communication to the Command Post, executed a decryption routine, and let him read through the message.

"Son of a bitch." Henricksen raised his head, staring out the windows. "That's a Raven out there."

"Sir. Two more distortions." Finlay marked the new ships on the window, added three more just a few seconds later.

Six ships out there in total, their points of entry setting them in a ring around *Serengeti*.

"So that's your game, is it?" Henricksen smiled coldly, keeping the comms channel open to that ship out there. "Well, listen up, asshole. I know what you are and what weapons you have. You've got us surrounded and outnumbered but *believe* me, you will *not* win this." He leaned forward, voice soft, urgent, dangerously so. "Drop the shielding and identify yourselves. You have ten seconds to comply." He cut the comms and waited, lips moving as he made a slow count to ten.

The first ship appeared with just two seconds to spare, sending a tiny pulse of data to mark its location as it shimmered to life. The rest followed soon after, revealing themselves on that first ship's orders.

"Approach. Slowly," Henricksen ordered, wary even now.

"They're tiny," Finlay said, examining the data from the sensors as the ship's moved close.

"Ravens are scout ships. Black Ops," *Serengeti* explained at Finlay's look. "Used mostly for intelligence purposes." A pause, camera turning toward the Command Post. "Henricksen here was Raven crew, once upon a time. Before he left all the skulk and dagger behind for the glamour of being a Valkyrie captain."

"Glamour. Right." Henricksen snorted. "Fifty-three-year cold nap ain't exactly what I'd call glamorous."

The crew turned, looking at him, questions in their eyes.

"Not much in the way of weapons on a Raven." Henricksen cleared his throat uncomfortably, nodding to the ships outside. "Shielding system's top-notch, though. Like that shimmer shield but inverted. Cloaks by reflection rather than distortion."

Serengeti checked her database, curious about how that worked. Ran into a security block that read *Black Ops-Restricted*.

"If their shielding's so great, why don't all the ships have it?" Samara asked him.

Henricksen shrugged. "Black Ops. You know how it is."

Samara frowned, clearly *not* knowing how it was. None of the crew did, really. Of them all, only Henricksen had ever dabbled in the Black Ops world.

"Secret Squirrel stuff," he explained. "Black Ops...well, intel guys don't really like to share. System doesn't scale anyway," he said, nodding to the ships outside. "Huge draw on the fuel cells to run it. Energy requirements increase with the size of the vessel the tech's trying to cover. Ship the size of *Serengeti*..." He pursed his lips, shaking his head. "Probably never get full coverage, no matter what you do. Blow the fuel cells in about five minutes. End up shutting the whole damn system down. Works on those Ravens, though. I know—I've used it. Freaking amazing how well it hides 'em."

"Sir?" Finlay twisted, pointing to the windows. "Should we...?"

Henricksen nodded, reaching for comms. "Alright," he said, calling outside. "That's close enough."

The Ravens pulsed their reverse thrusters, drifting to a halt a thousand kilometers out.

Serengeti pulled up the feed from her hull cameras, zooming in, taking a good, long look at one of the approaching ships. Found a sharp-sided outline black as the emptiness around it. Wings like a bird with rail guns poking from their front edges. Cannons dangling like taloned feet from a narrow, flat belly.

Tiny things, most of all, just as Finlay said. Small enough to fit inside *Serengeti's* main cargo bay and still have room to move about.

"Send your data packages over," Henricksen ordered. *"Real* information this time, not that crap cover you tried to sell us before. No self-respecting AI's ever gonna name themselves *Bobo* or *Bluebell* or whatever fake names you put in those files."

"Incoming communication," Delacroix reported barely a second later. He ran the decryption himself this time and passed the contents to Henricksen.

"Well I'll be..." Henricksen laughed aloud, fumbling at his panel. Searched through *Serengeti's* directories for a few seconds before giving up and asking *Serengeti* for help. "Need to send a message back. Same encryption routine as the one that came in."

Serengeti set up the shell and waited while Henricksen tapped out a message. Sealed it with a security code before sending it over to the lead Raven.

A hush fell over the bridge, everyone holding their breath, staring at the windows as a voice came through—AI voice, no doubt about it. Shunted through the speakers by *Serengeti* herself.

"Henricksen? That really you?"

"In the flesh." Henricksen smiled widely. "Long time, no see, *Shriek.*"

"Heard you were dead," *Shriek* said, voice clipped, almost harried sounding—odd tone for an AI. "Fifty-three years. *Should* be dead."

"Yeah, well. You know me. Never did do what I was supposed to."

The ship out there laughed softly.

Serengeti closed the comms, giving them some privacy. Not quite liking this whole chummy, long-lost-friends vibe she felt going on. "I take it you know each other?"

Henricksen threw a sharp look at the camera, seeming to sense something in her voice. "Four-man ops squad," he said, tone neutral, carefully controlled. "Me, Sikuuku, Ogawa, and Hanu running skunk works with *Shriek* and his buddies." He paused, mouth open, eyes flicking to the windows. "Not my assignment," he told her, looking back to the camera. "*Shriek* wasn't in charge. It was *Scythe* that ran the squadron back when I was a Raven."

"And you in charge of the operations."

Henricksen nodded, eyes never leaving the camera. "*Scythe*..." He trailed off, dropping his eyes to his station, scrolling through the information on the Ravens around them. "Not here," he murmured, brow wrinkling, a hint of worry infecting his voice. "*Shriek's* here, and the rest of the squadron, but no *Scythe.*"

"Is that unusual?"

"Very," he nodded, taking another look.

"What do you suppose happened to her?"

"If I know *Scythe*..." Henricksen shook his head, frown deepening.

"Do you?" *Serengeti* asked quietly. "Just how *well* did you get to know *Scythe*?"

Henricksen went very still, eyes lifting to the camera. "Long time ago, *Serengeti*. Ancient history now. Black Ops, the Ravens..." He shook his head, lips pressed in a hard line. "I left that all behind. *My* choice, *Serengeti. Mine,* understand?"

"Of course, Captain."

Henricksen flinched, eyes narrowing.

The crew called him captain, but *Serengeti* rarely did. They served as equals—partners protecting their crew. Titles added a formality neither of them wanted. But using the title now...well, it did get his attention. And added a weight to *Serengeti's* words that tone sometimes couldn't convey.

"So why are they following us?" *Serengeti* asked him—capitulating, wanting to move on.

Henricksen dipped his head, acknowledging the gesture. "Good question. How's about we find out?" He flashed a smile and keyed comms open, addressing the ships outside. "What're you doin' here, *Shriek*?"

"What are *you* doing here?" the Raven threw back.

"None of your business. Now answer the question: why are you and your boys following us?"

"We weren't—"

"Bullshit. You wouldn't be cloaked if you weren't. Spill it, *Shriek.* Why are you doggin' my tail?"

"Curious?"

"Not good enough," Henricksen snapped. "I've still got that big gun pointed your way, and my gunner here is just *itching* to give it a go."

Bosch stuck a ham-sized hand from the Artillery pod, giving Henricksen a thumbs up.

"You're Fleet, *Shriek.* Which means you're with *Brutus.* And since you're following us in secret, you know *we're* not."

"Sir." Finlay twisted, looking around. "Maybe—"

"Not now, Finlay." Henricksen raised a hand, cutting her off. "Truth, *Shriek. All* of it this time, or I'll blow you and your buddies to kingdom come."

A pause, comms quiet on their side, *Serengeti* picking up other communications flashing back and forth between the Ravens across a channel she couldn't touch.

"We're not with the Fleet," *Shriek* finally admitted. "Not anymore."

"DSR?" Henricksen looked surprised. Shared a worried look with the camera.

"Right." *Shriek* snorted. "Like we're gonna throw in with that chicken shit outfit. We're independents now, Henricksen. Got sick of *Brutus's* crap so we went freelance a few years ago."

"Why?" *Serengeti* asked, not quite buying it. "Last I remember Black Ops were the darlings of the Fleet. *Brutus's* precious, protected pets, second only to his bloody, brutish Dreadnoughts."

Henricksen muted the channel. "Wow, *Serengeti*. That didn't sound bitter at *all*."

"I don't like them. Sue me."

"I like this side of you," Henricksen chuckled, thumbing comms back open. "Answer the lady's question."

Another pause—*Shriek* probably trying to decide some other fabricated story and the actual truth. "Bastard tried to drone us. Can you believe that?" *Shriek* sounded indignant—guess he settled on truth. "Take away our crew and dumb down the AIs." *Shriek* grunted in contempt. "Well, ya know what I told him?"

Henricksen smiled, muting the comms on his end. "I've got a pretty good guess."

"Fuck that," *Shriek* spat.

"Wow," Finlay blinked. "He's pretty foul-mouthed for an AI."

"You shoulda heard *Scythe*. Cursed like a sailor." Henricksen looked surprisingly proud. Pressed a finger to his lips as he unmuted their end of the comms channel and picked up the interrogation where he'd left off. "So you broke ranks and took off. Just like that."

"Uh-huh. Me and *Swift*. *Sharp* and *Stitch* and *Snicker-snack* over there."

Finlay giggled. "*Snicker-snack*? What kinda name is that?"

"Mine," a voice droned, clearly unamused.

"Oh. Sorry." Finlay blushed brightly, ducking her head. Tapped at the panel in front of, engrossing herself in Scan.

"*Brutus* took away our crews, so we stole 'em back," *Shriek* said smugly. "High-tailed it for deep space and never looked back."

"So that's where you've been all this time?" *Serengeti* asked him. "Hiding out? You abandoned the Fleet, took off on your own, and you've been doing…what? Besides following ships through jump, that is?"

"Be nice," Henricksen whispered, cutting his eyes toward to the ships outside.

"Why?" *Serengeti* demanded. "I honestly see no reason at all to be nice to these sneaking little runts."

Henricksen rolled his eyes. "Just...tone it down," he told her. And to the ships outside, "Stop dancing around and answer the question, *Shriek*. Why were you tailing us through jump?"

"Told you before: we were curious."

"And?" Henricksen waited, but *Shriek* buttoned his lip and kept his mouth shut. "The rest of it, *Shriek. Now,*" he ordered.

"Look," *Shriek* sighed. "It's *boring* out there in the fringes. So we've been sort of...keeping tabs on things. Watching the comings and goings of the ships in the Fleet. Might've noticed the Valkyries were up to something a few months ago so we started following *them* around for a while." *Shriek* went silent for five whole seconds—a long pause for an AI, an eternity for a blabbermouth like him. "We saw them rescue you, *Serengeti.* Watched *Sechura* and the others tow you back to Blue Horizon."

"Did you now," *Serengeti* murmured. "Well, thanks a bunch for helping out."

"Nice," Henricksen mouthed, throwing a stern look at the camera.

Serengeti flashed an image to his panel: rounded smiley face, tongue sticking out.

Henricksen snorted, wiping it from his panel. "Why?" he asked on her behalf. "I get your beef with *Brutus*. I even get why you took off. But why go to the trouble of following the Valkyries around in secrecy? If you thought they were up to something, why not reach out? See if you could join forces or something?"

"Wasn't sure we could trust 'em," *Shriek* admitted. "Valkyries come and go, collecting wrecked vessels, shipping them off to get fixed. Could be they're up to something we don't wanna be a part of. Looking to stir up some trouble that could get us all killed. Could be they're just operating on *Brutus's* orders—"

"Right," *Serengeti* snorted. "Because we *so* love *Brutus*."

Henricksen muted the channel. "Could you at least *pretend* to be nice?"

"No," *Serengeti* said flatly.

Henricksen sighed heavily, shaking his head as he opened the channel back up.

"You're a close-mouthed bunch, *Serengeti*," *Shriek* was saying.

"And you want me to be nice to that."

"Quiet," Henricksen warned, giving her camera a stern look.

"Wasn't quite sure I could trust you until we caught you sneaking away from Blue Horizon." *Shriek* paused again, longer this time. "Didn't know about the Dreadnought refit, by the way. Never could see under that shimmer shield."

"Yeah, well, take a good look at the new me," *Serengeti* said sourly. "Baddest-ass bitch in the galaxy."

Shriek laughed appreciatively. "Say that again, Sister."

"I'm *not* your sister," *Serengeti* growled.

FIFTEEN

"So what now, *Shriek?*" Henricksen stared at the windows, arms folded tight to his chest. "We know who you are, and now you know who we are. Neither of us is with the Fleet, but you're not quite sure you can trust us and I damned well know better than to trust any of you."

Shriek laughed again—*Shriek* and all the rest of the Ravens with him, much to *Serengeti's* surprise.

Strange AIs, these stealth ships. Not like any other crystal matrix mind set she'd encountered.

"You're right, Henricksen. I'm not quite sure I trust you. But we're bored and you're up to something. Something secret, apparently, based on the way you're leapfrogging around. So we discussed it amongst ourselves, and we want in."

"You want in," Henricksen repeated, sharing a wary look with *Serengeti.* "Just like that?"

"Yup."

"How do we know we can trust you?" *Serengeti* asked, suspicious still.

"You can't," *Shriek* said brightly. "And I can't make you. But actions speak louder than words, as they say, and I think I've got something to offer that just might do the trick."

"Oh yeah?" Henricksen looked suspicious—as suspicious as *Serengeti* felt. "What's that?"

"You're going to see *Cerberus,* right?"

Henricksen turned toward the camera, eyebrows lifting in alarm. "What the hell?" he mouthed.

Shriek laughed softly. "This is the part where I imagine the shocked look on your faces, and you mute the comms and argue heatedly about how I could possibly have come by this knowledge before opening the channel back up. Well, I'll save you all that and just say this: if it was me that woke from a fifty-three-year dirt nap and found the Fleet gone to shit, the first thing *I'd* do is go looking for the head honcho and demand some answers."

Henricksen cut the comms and just stood there—arms folded, staring through the windows at the ships outside.

Finlay looked around from Scan. "Why does that Raven sound like you?"

Henricksen frowned, looking down at her. "Doesn't sound like me. Sounds like an AI asshole. No offense," he added, tipping an invisible cap at the camera.

"None taken," *Serengeti* said dryly.

Shriek, meanwhile, kept blathering away. Talking about the birds and the bees or some such thing while Finlay listened intently.

"Ain't?" She turned around staring accusingly at her Captain. "He just said 'ain't.' That's *so* you."

"Yeah. About that." Henricksen actually looked embarrassed. "Me and Sikuuku mighta got drunk one time and sorta built him a lexicon of human phrases."

"*Ancient* phrases from the sound of it," Aoki muttered, and then clapped both hands to her mouth, looking horrified that she'd actually said that out loud.

"Hello? *Helloooo*? You guys still listening?" *Shriek* sent a blast of static over the channel that made everyone wince. "I'm pretty sure I know how to get you onto the Citadel without getting killed. You interested?"

Henricksen glanced at the windows, then back to the camera. "Up to you," he said, leaving the decision to *Serengeti*.

"They're deserters," she reminded him. "I realize you ran with them, once upon a time, but do you think it's good idea to bring three unknowns into the mix?"

"Probably not. But it can't hurt to at least hear him out." Henricksen glanced at the windows, looked up at *Serengeti's* camera. "You said it yourself: it's not like we've got all that many options. You don't like what he has to say, you can always tell *Shriek* to piss off."

"I don't like *him*," she said, "but I'll leave the pissing off part to you, if it comes to that. You're good at it. And much more eloquent than I."

"Deal." Henricksen nodded, smiling crookedly as he re-opened the line. "Alright, *Shriek*. We're listening. Tell us about this grand scheme of yours."

*****

"So let me get this straight," *Serengeti* said after hearing *Shriek* out. "Your plan is for me to cruise in and make myself a target while *you* fly in under the radar and sneak into one of the Citadel's landing bays. Do I have that right?"

"Well, it's a little more complicated than that, but yeah. That's it in a nutshell."

"And why do *I* have to get shot at?" *Serengeti* demanded. "Why can't *I* be the one doing the sneaking and you and your boys there play duck in the shooting gallery?"

"No offense, *Serengeti*, but you're a tad…large," *Shriek* said carefully.

Henricksen glowered at the stealth ship's sharp-sided shape showing through the windows. "You callin' my girl fat, *Shriek*?"

The Raven wisely didn't answer that. "I suppose you might be able to slip through *Cerberus's* defense perimeter if you shut your engines down and glide in on momentum. But no *way* you're gonna dock that mass of yours without the Citadel noticing,."

"And you can?"

"Yeah. He can." Henricksen flicked his eyes to the camera. "That's the whole *point* of a Raven. Shielding prevents the scans from picking them up. We never would've noticed *Shriek* and his boys ourselves except for the jump drive signature."

"Alright. I'll concede that point." Grudgingly—didn't much like conceding anything when it came to the stealth ships—but she did concede it. "Explain to me again why I need to get shot at."

"Distraction," *Shriek* told her. "Best way to sneak in unnoticed is to do it while everyone's attention is focused somewhere else. We shorten this last hop, come in say…a hundred thousand kilometers out. Should be well outside *Cerberus's* scans so he won't pick us up. Use the main engines to give us a good shove and we glide in on momentum. No beacons, no engines, he'll never even know we're there."

"How is that a distraction?"

"Ah. That's the brilliant part."

"Brilliant, my ass," *Serengeti* muttered. "Guys the most puffed-up popinjay I've ever—"

Henricksen slapped at a panel, muting the comms channel, giving her camera a stern look. "Popinjay?"

"What? That was *nice*."

Henricksen sighed heavily, eyes flicking to the watching crew. A very *confused* looking crew, AIs squabbling and taking cheap shots at each other being a somewhat new experience. "You said you'd hear him out."

"I did. He's an idiot."

"He's not—" Henricksen broke off, sighing again. "He's painting a picture. You have to let him do more than just sketch the lines."

"What if I don't *like* the picture?"

"Told you before: we can always say no."

"No."

Henricksen glowered at her.

"Fine. I'll let him finish. Just not promising I won't set his little painting on fire once it's done."

"Fair enough." Henricksen smiled, opening up the line.

Shriek still blathered away, seeming unaware that they'd muted him at all. "So you cruise in close, right? And then hit your engines full gas. Come flying in like a bat out of hell, all big show and shouty-shouty, drop a few repeaters to make it look like there's a whole damn attack force coming down on *Cerberus*."

"And you?" *Serengeti* asked. Politely this time. For Henricksen's sake. "What will you be doing while I'm out there getting shot at?"

"Me and the boys here wait until *Cerberus* deploys those Mosquito drones of his—annoying little fuckers, by the way; not even sure why he has them when he's got all those damned cannons all over his body. Anyway, where was I? Oh! Right. So me and the boys slip in behind the Mosquitoes all sneaky-sneaky like, and slide into the landing bay before anyone's the wiser!" *Shriek* paused, waiting for their response. "So?" he asked, when the comms line stayed silent. "Whaddaya think?"

"I think you're an idiot," *Serengeti* said flatly.

"Oh for the luvva..." Henricksen bowed his head, pinching the bridge of his nose.

"But I also think you're right." Hard admitting that—didn't really *want* to admit it—but after running the numbers and playing out a few scenarios, she came up with no better answer than *Shriek's*.

Stealth ships were annoying—incredibly annoying, unbelievably annoying, especially for AI—but apparently they weren't dumb. Well, compared to *her* they were dumb, but still smart enough to come up with a halfway decent plan. And with a few modifications—hers, of course, who better to fix a half-bad plan?—they might end up with something that didn't get them all killed.

"Our best chance of actually getting *onto* the Citadel involves one of you Ravens sneaking on board," she agreed, accepting that much of his plan. "*One*," she emphasized—the first of her changes. "*Just* one. The whole damn lot of you landing at once will attract as much attention as I would on my own."

"Alright. One," *Shriek* conceded. "I'll sneak my way onto *Cerberus* while *Swift* and the boys hang back—"

"Huh-uh," *Serengeti* cut in. "Your boys can help *me* keep the Citadel distracted."

Second change, because no *way* was she going to sit out there dodging pot-shots from *Cerberus* on her own.

Shriek was quiet a moment, considering this latest modification. "Interesting idea," he said carefully. "But I'll need to talk it over with the boys. Back in a flash," he said brightly, and then the comms channel clicked as *Shriek* dropped off.

Henricksen glanced up, sharing a look with *Serengeti* in the sudden silence that followed. Bridge crew looked at each other—everyone but Delacroix who just stared blankly into space—and at the windows, the ships lurking outside.

Everyone waiting, until Comms flashed and the channel opened again.

"And I'm back," *Shriek* announced himself, smile in his voice. "Boys aren't all that happy about the changes, but they're a brave lot, and after a bit of convincing, I managed to get them to agree to your revised plan."

Shriek sounded quite pleased with himself. Smug as a hermit crab who'd traded up to a new shell.

"Popinjay," *Serengeti* muttered.

"So, we're agreed then," *Shriek* said, oblivious to the insult. Or maybe he just didn't hear it. "Only question left is who's coming with me?"

"*Serengeti,* obviously." Henricksen nodded to her camera. "Part of her consciousness, anyway. She's got the best chance of any of us of actually getting *through* to *Cerberus*. She'll need an escort, so I'll go. Maybe take Houseman—"

"No," *Serengeti* said quietly.

"Okay, *not* Houseman. What about—?"

"No, Henricksen. Not you. I'm not taking you with me."

Silence descended on the bridge, Henricksen staring at her, face angry, hands curling into fists. Crew staring at *him*, sneaking looks at *Serengeti's* camera.

"Why the hell not?"

Because I can't lose you, Henricksen. Not again.

"Because I don't know what we're walking into," she told him. "And I won't risk any more lives. Not when I just got my crew back after fifty-three years apart."

"What about Tig?" Still angry—she saw it in Henricksen's face, read it in his eyes. "That *is* how you're planning to get over there, isn't it? Hitch a ride in Tig's body. Roll around on the Citadel calling 'soo-ee' until *Cerberus* finally shows up?"

"Tig or another robot," she admitted, keeping her own voice calm. "And yes, their lives will be in danger. AI lives, not human, but every bit as precious to me as my own." She studied Henricksen from the camera, acutely aware of the bridge crew watching, listening, hanging on their every word. "I need you *here*, Henricksen. I need you protecting the ship, keeping the crew out of harm's way."

"And how do I do that?" he asked bitterly, eyes flashing with anger. "This entire plan is about *putting* the crew in harm's way. You're offering yourself up for goddamn target practice—"

"*Just* to get on board," *Serengeti* assured him. "You fall back—all of you, Valkyrie and Ravens, both—and stay out of range of *Cerberus's* guns until we signal you that we're coming back out."

"And what happens if you don't?" Henricksen asked her in his softest voice.

"Then you go on without me," she said bluntly. "Only part of my consciousness will go onto that ship, Henricksen. The rest stays with you, and the ship that is my body. Probably won't even notice I'm missing," she teased, but Henricksen just grimaced, looking anything but amused. "I need you, Captain," she said—intimate tone, now. Letting the earnestness come through in her voice. "The *crew* needs you."

He stared defiantly—chin lifted, face proud—but the anger slowly slipped away. Replaced by resignation—they were arguers, the two of them, and Henricksen smart enough to know when he'd lost. A tight nod, stiff and unhappy, and he turned away from her, looking out at the stars. "Still don't like it," he muttered.

"Don't expect you to," she said softly.

To be honest, I'm not entirely thrilled about the idea myself.

SIXTEEN

The last hop went smoothly, dumping *Serengeti* out a hundred thousand kilometers from *Cerberus,* just like they'd planned. She threw her scans wide, sucking in every bit of information she could find as *Shriek* and the other Ravens jumped in after, maneuvering around her and then pulled ahead.

Formed up in a perfect ring in front of *Serengeti's* bow, camouflage shielding active and overlapping, turning the Ravens invisible, hiding *Serengeti* as well. Well, sort of. At least, to anyone looking at her dead on. Ravens' shielding didn't reach far enough to cover the rest of her—anyone behind her or to either side would see *Serengeti* clear as day—but from that one angle, she was invisible. Nothing but the dark of space and the pinpricks of stars.

Ruse wouldn't last, but it should keep *Cerberus* from detecting them. For a little while at least. Until they got in really, *really* close.

Serengeti waited while the Ravens sorted themselves out, tapped into tight band comms and sent a message to the lot of them. "Three. Two. One." Engines flared, cobalt blue illumination lighting up the darkness as all seven ships pushed together, propulsion systems running wide open for a ten-second burn before shutting back down.

From there, they drifted, moving on momentum alone. A lot of momentum, mind you—ten-second burst was nothing to sneeze at—but slower than if the engines kept firing. Pushing them along.

"How are we doing?" Henricksen asked.

Serengeti checked their course and confirmed they were dead on target. "Minimal drift. We're tracking true. Should reach the outer edge of the Citadel's security perimeter in a little under an hour."

Henricksen grunted, arms folding, eyes locked on the bridge's windows. "Wouldn't mind knowing what's going on out there." He flicked his gaze to Delacroix standing at the station to his right. "Comms. What's the chatter?"

Delacroix flicked his wrist, opening a channel—one-way, listening only, careful not to give *Serengeti* away. Another flick—opposite wrist this time, fingers twiddling, eyes moving rapid-fire behind his visor—and Delacroix frowned hard, hand lifting, touching at the Comms visor wrapping around his head. A tap at the side, making a few adjustments, another to make a few more and Delacroix stiffened, gasping as he jerked his hand away.

Henricksen gave him a dark look. "Talk to me, Delacroix. What's going on?"

"Voices. So many voices," he whispered, body swaying, hands moving in time.

"Comms!" Henricksen smacked the panel in front of him making Delacroix jump. "Focus!"

"Yes, sir. Sorry, sir." Delacroix flipped the visor away, surfacing, looking fully aware for the first time since he came on board. Sucked in a breath and settled the visor back into place, making a few more tweaks to the settings as he sank back into Comms. "Lot of comms traffic."

"From *Cerberus*?"

Delacroix nodded and almost immediately shook his head.

"Goddammit, Delacroix. Which is it?"

"It's…everything," Delacroix said dreamily. "All of them. Every last AI on the Citadel talking at once. All their communications, completely unfiltered." Another adjustment to the Comms visor, dialing something in. "They're…babbling," he said, frowning in confusion.

"AI do *not* babble," *Serengeti* informed him.

Delacroix shrugged an apology. "These do. I don't know what else to call it."

A look from Henricksen and *Serengeti* tapped into the system herself, listening in on an overlapping confusion of communications—a squalling, squabbling ocean of noise.

Apparently, AI did indeed babble. Quite loudly, in fact.

She upped the gain on the filters trying to isolate *Cerberus's* voice from the clamor.

"There!" Delacroix raised a hand, dead eyes staring sightlessly behind his visor. "That's him." He flicked both wrists, fingers waving. Went very still—hands raised, brow furrowed in concentration.

"Well?" Henricksen asked, staring at Delacroix, fingers drumming impatiently against a panel. "Anything?"

Delacroix raised his hand, signaling for him to wait.

"Cut the crap, Delacroix. Is *Cerberus* out there or not?"

The hand stayed raised—seemed to hang in the air forever. "Yes," he said faintly. "I found him."

"*Cerberus*?" Henricksen turned, staring intently at Comms. "You found *Cerberus*?"

"*Cerberus* and *Cerberus* and *Cerberus*," Delacroix whispered, swaying from side to side.

Henricksen watched him, lip lifting in disgust. "Think your new comms package fried that semi-detached brain of his, *Serengeti*."

"There's nothing wrong with my comms package." But she fiddled with the settings anyway, layering in another filter, examining the results. "He's right."

Henricksen looked at her, blinking slowly, head moving from side to side.

"Not one *Cerberus. Three*," she told him. "Three distinct voices."

"*Three Cerberuses*." Henricksen's lips twisted. "'Right," he grunted. "Because *that* makes a whole lotta sense."

"There is a *reason* he's called *Cerberus*."

"Is that right?" He tilted his head, eyebrows lifting. "Enlighten me."

"Mythology. Dog with three heads."

Henricksen smiled crookedly. "You callin' *Cerberus* a dog?"

"No," *Serengeti* laughed. "But he *does* have three brains—that's what Delacroix's picking up. Three brains equals three voices. Three *Cerberuses* communing with the stars."

Except there shouldn't be. Three AI brains, yes, but those three brains used to work together. *Cerberus's* three voices used to all speak as one.

"Three AIs sharing one body?" Henricksen quirked an eyebrow. "How *does* that work?"

"Crystal matrix fusion. Citadel was specifically designed to be operated by a tri-partite brain, the three AIs inside it providing unified direction to that big old battleship of a body he wears."

"They don't mind sharing?"

"They don't know any different," *Serengeti* said quietly. "And they don't really have a choice. It takes all three of them—Soldier, Statesman, and Scientist—to run the Citadel, not just one or two."

Henricksen grunted, lips twisting. "Sounds like a recipe for disaster."

"There's a thin line between disaster and divine."

"So, he's a god now?"

"No," *Serengeti* said softly, listening to that confused babble coming across Comms. "Not a god, but great once. The greatest of us all."

Henricksen grunted, eyes on the windows, watching the Citadel draw near. "You sure you wanna go through with this?" he asked, voice pitched low so only *Serengeti* would hear.

"No," she admitted, just as softly, isolating her voice to a speaker just above his head. "But I have to, Henricksen. I see no other way."

"*Cerberus*—"

"Is our best chance of getting *Brutus* out of the way," she said, speaking right over him. "Our best chance of turning the Fleet around. Reminding it what it once was."

Henricksen stared a moment—stubborn still, looking like he meant to argue. But he dipped his head instead, ceding the point. Touched at the panel, opening ship-to-ship comms. "*Shriek.* Drop back. We're opening the main cargo bay." A smile for the camera. "Got a package for you to pick up."

"On my way." *Shriek* broke formation, dropped back, and slid along *Serengeti's* side.

"Finlay. You've got the con."

Finlay glanced up in surprise. "Me?"

"Yes, you, Finlay."

"Oh. Okay." Finlay seemed bewildered, a tiny bit lost. "I mean, aye, sir. Th—Thank you, sir," she stammered, looking around the bridge.

"Won't be long," Henricksen told her. "Just need to see *Serengeti* off."

He stepped down from the Command Post and headed across the bridge, Finlay's worried eyes following Henricksen all the way to the door. Considered the elevator in the hallway before taking the ladderway down to the main cargo bay instead.

Cold in there—no heat at all in any of *Serengeti's* cargo bays, and no atmosphere, either.

Environmentals sapped energy. Vented into space every time those cargo bay doors opened and closed. Robots didn't need either, and the airlock contained pressure suits for any human crew who wanted to walk around the cargo bay awhile. Pain in the ass getting into one, though, which is why Henricksen stopped in the hallway, using a monitor in the wall to watch *Shriek* thread his way in, parking his mass on *Serengeti's* decking.

Sat there in silence—dark and sinister, a sharp-edged weapon waiting to be drawn.

"Been a while since I saw one of them up close."

"Not exactly pretty, are they?" *Serengeti* noted, taking a look herself.

"Not supposed to be." Henricksen slid his eyes to her camera, lips twitching at the corners. "Stealth ships, remember? Not meant to be looked at."

"Not sure I'd want to be seen either if I looked like that."

Henricksen grunted, smiling. Turned his head and frowned as Tig and Tilli appeared, pattering down the hallway on their jointed metal legs. Six of their eight legs moving them along while the other two cradled oversized pulse rifles. Hitched at bandoliers of spare ammunition crisscrossing their chests.

"Thought this was a solo operation."

"Me too," *Serengeti* murmured, watching the robots approach.

"What's with the guns and ammunition?"

"I don't know."

Unbearably cute, seeing the robots decked out with all those armaments, but not what she'd asked for. Tig and Tilli ran ship's maintenance, she'd never meant for them to go in armed.

"Tig," she called. "What's going on?"

Tig stumbled to a halt near the cargo bay's airlock, face lights swirling in anxious patterns. "We're, uh...we're going with you. Me and...and Tilli here," he said, angling the gun Tilli's way.

Tilli *wonked* loudly, shoving the barrel out of her face.

"No offense, Tilli, but I don't seem to remember inviting you."

Tilli shrugged, ovoid body bobbing up and down. Raised her rifle and ejected the rifle's magazine cool as you please. Cleared the chamber while she was at it and broke the weapon down, rebuilding it in just under ten seconds.

"Well, I'm terrified," Henricksen said, watching the robot with wide wary eyes. "Where the hell did you learn that anyway?" he asked, nodding to Tilli's newly reassembled gun.

"Uh...um..." Tig flicked his eyes around the hallway, held his own rifle out in front of him, and then slung it on his back. "See, we—that is, Tilli and me—we sort of... maybe...downloaded something?" He shrugged helplessly, smiling an ingratiating smile. Grabbed at the rifle as it slid off one side and shoved it back onto his back.

"Something," Henricksen repeated, squinting suspiciously. "What *kind* of something?"

Tig ducked his head, mumbling at the deckplates.

"What's that?" Henricksen cupped his ear, leaning forward. "Didn't quite hear you."

Tig sighed, head lifting. "Combat program. The TSGs came with a combat programming option." A glance at Tilli and the gun she so comfortably wore. "We made a few modifications so it would be compatible with our programming."

"Combat programming." Henricksen rubbed his chin, looking less than impressed. "Downloaded to a couple of maintenance 'bots."

"We know what we're doing." Tilli slammed the magazine home and ratcheted the firing mechanism back, loading a fresh round into the chamber as she spread her legs wide.

Henricksen pointed at her weapon. "Safety. If you please."

Tilli *blipped*, blinking, chromed cheeks blushing bright blue. Turned the weapon sideways and tapped a tiny red button beside the rifle's trigger, flashing a smile as she slung the weapon on her back.

Unlike Tig's, it stayed there—perfectly balanced, didn't even *try* to slip off.

"So you're armed." Henricksen eyed the rifles meaningfully. "And there's two of you because..." He raised his eyebrows, looking a question at the pair of 'bots.

Tig ducked his head again, sneaking glances at Tilli beside him.

"Ah. I see." Henricksen smiled. "Didn't give you a choice."

Tig nodded miserable, scooting to one side as Tilli swiped at his leg. "Oona wanted to come, too. Took a lot of convincing to get her to stay behind."

"Good thing she did."

Tig looked up, blinking owlishly at Henricksen.

"Not real thrilled about any of you going over there," he said, including *Serengeti's* camera in that comment, "but I'd have a full-scale mutiny on my hands if the crew found out Oona had gone over to the Citadel with you three."

"Still not happy they know about her," *Serengeti* said.

"Yeah, well." Henricksen looked at her, lips curving in a smile. "Secrets are all well and good until the subject of said secret decides she needs some more friends."

Those *particular* friends being somewhere on the order of thirty crew eating dinner in the mess hall. And in rolls Oona, smiling like a tiny, blue sun, showing off her collection of critter doodles to anyone who'd listen. Charming the pants off the crew in the process.

Not a one of them in there who knew where she'd come from—at least there was that. Crew just thought she was another TIG—on the smallish side and colorful, but nothing more than that.

Still, she wished *Sechura's* people hadn't been there. Henricksen insisted they were a good bunch, but she still didn't know them. Hadn't quite come to trust them like her own.

"I spoke to the newbies." Henricksen nodded to the camera, reading her thoughts. "Told them Oona was experimental and they should keep their mouths shut. Spoke to the rest of the crew while I was at it—just in case, you know?" He smiled crookedly, eyes drifting to Tig and Tilli. "They'll look out for her. Kid's cute as a button. No one wants to see her get scrapped."

Tig *hooted* softly, bouncing up and down. Tilli just smiled—please and proud at once.

"We should probably get going," *Serengeti* told them, checking the time, realizing most of their hour had passed.

"You sure I can't talk to you out of this?" Henricksen asked hopefully.

"You can try," *Serengeti* told him, smile in her voice, "but *Shriek's* starting to get impatient." She keyed the comms, letting the Raven's voice spill into the hall.

"What's the hold-up?" *Shriek* demanded. "I'm dying of boredom over here!"

"Yeah-yeah, keep your shirt on," Henricksen growled, flicking his fingers to have *Serengeti* cut the comms. "Raven's always were a bit tetchy," he admitted, eyeing the stealth ship on the monitor. A glance behind him as Tig shivered, *Serengeti* splitting her consciousness—leaving part of herself there in that camera looking down on the hallway while the another slipped inside the TIG. "Got that schematic?"

Serengeti nodded, clonking the Tig's leg-end against the side of his head. "Downloaded the Citadel's design diagrams before I left the bridge."

"Good." Henricksen grunted. "Hate for you to get lost."

"That could be embarrassing," *Serengeti* admitted, chromed cheeks flushing with cobalt blue light.

They stared at each other in silence, neither quite knowing what to say. That seemed to happen a lot lately, *Serengeti* honestly wasn't sure why.

"Good luck, *Serengeti*," Henricksen said softly.

"Thank you, Captain." She smiled at him—a soft and tremulous thing—and waved Tilli toward the airlock as she scuttled over and punched in a code.

"Twenty-four hours." Henricksen stepped to the doorway, holding the airlock open as Tig and Tilli scurried inside. "If you're not back in twenty-four hours, I'm coming in after you."

She tilted Tig's head, blinking slowly. "Only part of me is going over there, you do remember that?"

"Happens to be the part I like." His lips twisted, lifting in a lopsided grin. "The part that does crazy-ass things like storm an oversized battleship just because she knows it's the right thing to do."

"I'll be back, Henricksen. I promise."

The grin slipped, Henricksen's face turning solemn. "Signal us when you're ready."

"Will do." She managed a smile—a match to Henricksen's patented crooked grin. "Just keep those drones off us until we get inside."

"Yes, ma'am." Henricksen tapped two fingers to his temple, stepping backward into the hall. "Be careful, *Serengeti*."

A nod and the airlock closed. Clicked and *whirred,* pumping the atmospherics out. Flashed green and popped open on the cargo bay side, releasing the robots into vacuum—a cold, weightless space that they high-stepped across, heading for the waiting Raven.

SEVENTEEN

Fifty thousand kilometers out, and *Serengeti* and her entourage crossed over into the Citadel's security perimeter—an invisible line separating them from the safety of deep space.

Unknowns inside it—that massive ship ahead, sensors and weapons and every other thing bolted onto *Cerberus's* body. Comms towers and laser arrays and other, less recognizable equipment jutting outward from his prickling shape. Pointing vaguely at the stars.

Serengeti shivered, just looking at him. At *Cerberus,* that most wondrous and terrible of AI beings. A touch at her systems, accessing her hull cameras, and she zoomed in, looking him over. Shunted the camera feeds to the front windows and let the crew do the same.

Study him. Dissect him. Take the measure of what they were up against. Look upon that double-sided, fortress-shaped edifice with its wide, flat central ring, three smaller rings stacked above and below.

Weapons everywhere—cannons and rail guns, turret guns ringing the Citadel round—giving him a three hundred and sixty-degree range of fire. A forest of communications towers rising like spinnerets reaching for the stars.

Didn't quite look a vessel. At least, not in the conventional sense. Then again, there was nothing at all conventional about *Cerberus,* with his tri-partite mind and fortress of a body.

"Look at the *size* of that thing," Samara breathed, studying the feed on the front windows. "It's almost as big as that station we just left."

"Largest vessel in the galaxy," Henricksen told her. "Ain't nuthin' the DSR's come up with that's even *close* to the size of him. One of a kind, our admiral is. Ain't that right, *Serengeti.*"

"One of a kind," she agreed, hoping she didn't sound as worried as she felt.

The admiral she knew was a marvel of human engineering—the most powerful AI mind in the universe. A pinnacle of scientific achievement. But now that mind was broken. Separated into three disparate parts.

I hope this isn't a mistake, she thought, remembering those babbling voices. The video *Sechura* had shown. *I hope we're doing the right thing and don't end up making matters worse.*

"Prickly-looking thing, though." Henricksen toggled the feeds, zooming in on an array. "Got enough firepower for ten Dreadnoughts from what I hear."

And yet it was rare for *Cerberus* to step into battle. *Serengeti* herself had only seen him in action once, and that was long before Henricksen came to her. Back when McAlister was still her captain.

"Probably covered with all sorts of probes and sensors and every other kind of detection equipment." Henricksen paused, brow wrinkling. Swapped the forward-facing cameras for a view of the stars behind them, searching for a swirl of darkness—the telltale sign of a Raven riding close to their behind

Shriek out there. *Shriek* and his crew, Tig and Tilli riding shotgun in his bridge pod with a part of *Serengeti*. The tiniest fraction of her consciousness nestled in beside Tig's AI mind.

She connected to it and experienced an odd doubling—part of her mind looking out while another part stared back. Let go almost instantly, fearing that doubling would confuse her systems. Create an unexpected feedback loop.

"It's not too late."

Serengeti looked down and found Henricksen staring up at her.

"We can still—"

Klaxons kicked in, cutting Henricksen off, panels flashing for attention as Scan lit up.

"Proximity alert," Finlay yelled. "Weapons detected. We're being scanned!"

"Shit." Henricksen slapped at his panel, killing the klaxons. Left the flashing red emergency lights on—those never seemed to bother him as much. "Guess we've been spotted." He threw a look at the camera. "Stealth shield thing was kinda cool, but I'm honestly surprised it took him this long."

Likely wouldn't have under different circumstances. Back when *Cerberus* three brains all worked together.

A check of the sensors showed energy levels spiking up and down the Citadel's form. Scanners bathing the area in waves of energy that washed over *Serengeti* and her Ravens screening, trying to figure them out.

Comms flared to life, setting Delacroix to twitching, fingers adjusting and readjusting the settings of his visor. A sea of inane chatter drowned the channels—all the channels, every last one of them except the secure channel *Serengeti* maintained—and all of them filled with *Cerberus's* babble. The Citadel's three, squabbling voices battering at Delacroix's brain, demanding to be let in.

More energy spikes and proximity alerts appeared, popping up everywhere, new ones appearing so fast Finlay couldn't address them all. Stopped bothering to try because every last one of them screamed *Warning! Warning! Warning!* and *Weapons fire detected!*

Batteries came to life all across the Citadel's shape. Plasma cannons pivoted, powered up, and fired, blood-red missiles tracking through space.

"Evasive maneuvers!" Henricksen ordered, flinging a hand toward Samara at Nav. "Scatter!" he yelled, opening ship-to-ship comms to the Ravens.

The stealth ships dropped their shielding, engines lighting as they moved ahead of *Serengeti,* fanning out to either side.

Samara pulsed *Serengeti's* engines, moving her along, pulling *Shriek* with her—the stealth ship hiding in her huge shadow, waiting for his moment.

"In and out," Henricksen said, speaking to the Ravens over tight-band comms. "No messing around. We deliver the package and we leave, understand me?"

"Yeah-yeah. We know what we're doing," *Swift* said surlily.

"You better," Henricksen muttered, eyes flicking to the windows. "Finlay. Drop the repeaters. Throw out some chaff while you're at it. Should help confuse things a bit."

"Aye, sir!" Finlay called, fingers flying across her station, silver-sided pods ejected from *Serengeti's* flanks.

Beacons lit just as soon as the repeaters cleared. False beacons screaming out fake information, making it look like a hundred *Serengetis* cruised toward the Citadel, rather than a single Valkyrie with a handful of Raven stealth ships for company.

"Hard to port!" Henricksen yelled.

Aoki hauled the ship over as the last repeater ejected, and Finlay hit a button, deploying a sparkling cloud of winking chaff. The debris spread, fanning out as *Serengeti* moved away, screening her from *Cerberus's* fire. Exploding in dramatic fashion as the cannons' plasma rounds intercepted them, detonating in blood-red showers.

A squeal of static and Comms burst open—blanketing *Serengeti's* channels, filtering through to the speakers scattered through her body.

Terrible sound that. Awful and shrieking. More terrible still the chattering, electronic voice that followed after, screeching '*Identify! Identify! Identify!*' over and over and over.

Automated voice—low-level AI, not *Cerberus* himself. The perimeter defense system responding to *Serengeti's* unexpected approach.

Not a good sign.

Automated systems meant *Cerberus* wasn't fully in control. Then again, it also meant *Cerberus* wasn't running the defenses which, considering they were under fire, was a *huge* stroke of luck.

Automated systems weren't all that smart, after all. Tended to run in repeating patterns, making their munitions spread predictable and relatively easy for an AI to elude.

Serengeti smiled, sensing an opportunity. Tapped into Comms, weathering the flood of screaming from the perimeter defense system long enough to jam it with long strings of nonsense information squawking from the repeaters. "That should give it something to chew on for a while."

More fire from *Cerberus*, plasma cannons tracking *Serengeti* as she and the Ravens swooped in and circled once around the Citadel—wide path, tracking the response time from the Citadel's guns. Searching for a chink in his armor. A weak point *Shriek* could exploit.

Halfway round and *Cerberus* launched his Mosquitoes—drone fighters sent out in a swarm that split as it exited the Citadel, dividing and dividing again.

A mass of droned ships targeted *Serengeti,* surrounding her on all sides. Others went after the Ravens, the repeaters squawking out false information, pretending to be ships themselves.

Cannons fired, picking off Mosquitoes, chewing through the drones to get at *Serengeti* and the stealth ships circling round and round.

Two loops around and the scanners showed empty—nothing but comms towers and gun turrets and barricaded, triple thick hull panels. Third pass and Scan finally found something, sent an alert to Finlay's panel.

"That's it." Finlay looked up, shunting an image to the front windows. "That's our way in."

Serengeti zoomed in on a three-dimensional image of *Cerberus,* spinning it around until a landing bay appeared. The one that released the Mosquitoes. The one that remained open as a second cloud of drones gathered and started to spill out.

A dead spot showed close by, cannons hanging limply, no lights glowing inside.

"Good eyes, Finlay." Henricksen passed the image to *Shriek,* ordering him to drop back while *Serengeti* moved ahead to draw the Citadel's fire. Received the tiniest of acknowledgements in return—*Shriek's* comms opening and immediately closing just as fast as he could squirt that message out. "Aoki. Take us in."

"Aye, sir." Aoki throttled the engines, putting on a burst of speed. Shoving *Serengeti* around the Citadel and closer to that blank spot, and the cloud of Mosquitoes pouring from *Cerberus's* landing bay.

"Bosch! Have at it!" Henricksen yelled.

"'Bout damn time." Bosch tapped a finger to his visor, bringing the targeting system on-line. Gripped the Artillery pod's firing mechanisms with both hands as he pivoted and opened fire.

Mosquitoes exploded like fireworks, droned bodies disintegrating as Bosch drowned them in plasma rounds. The gunner yelled into his comms unit, calling down to the Artillery stations running up and down *Serengeti's* body, adding fire from the rail guns and auxiliary cannons to the mix.

"They're still coming!" he warned, pounding away. The pod pivoted crazily, spinning left and right, up and down, system constantly adjusting as the drones swarmed around them.

Mosquito fire snuck through, strafing along *Serengeti's* side, making her shudder and shake. Bosch winged one, sending the Mosquito spinning out of control. It smashed into *Serengeti,* dying in a flare of light, taking out a portside cannon along the way.

"Bosch!" Henricksen barked.

"Sorry, sir. Lotta those bastards out there."

"Just keep 'em off us." Henricksen glanced at the windows, studying the data showing on the glass. "Aoki!"

"Got it-got it-got it!" She jogged left, dodging rounds from three different cannons, winced as a line of railgun fire rattled across *Serengeti's* hull.

Finlay dropped more chaff to draw the cannons' fire, giving them those bits to chew on while *Serengeti* fired back. Bosch and his Artillery pod gamely plugging away at the weapons lining *Cerberus's* hull.

A scan of the area showed most of the repeaters surrounded. Feeds disappearing as the Mosquitoes picked them off. Drone clouds reforming, scanning for new targets before taking off again, chasing Ravens around the Citadel's shape.

The Ravens, for their part, seemed to be having the time of their lives. Whooping and yelling and screaming taunts at *Cerberus* and his dumbed-down fighters.

"C'mon, you bastards!" *Swift* screamed across the comms. "Come and get me you slow ass, dumb as shit, hunks of metal junk!"

The Mosquitos responded, putting on speed, closing in on her tail. But *Swift* hauled around and hit the thrusters, firing every last gun he had, shredding a cloud of twenty or so drone fighters in seconds.

Snicker-snack swooped in after him, feeding another cloud of drones to *Swift's* guns. A laugh and the two Ravens disappeared, cloaking shields wrapping darkness around them as they took off, searching for more Mosquitoes to hunt.

Serengeti lost them for a while, found *Swift's* engine signature just a few seconds before he and *Snicker-snack* popped back into existence, tearing holy hell out of a dozen Mosquitoes harrying *Stitch's* behind. *Stitch* turned sharply as *Swift* shot past, zigging and zagging, trying to shake the Mosquitoes as *Snicker-snack* sniped away, cloak flickering around him.

More drones appeared, ignoring *Swift,* dodging past *Snicker-snack's* scything defenses, targeting *Stitch* at their middle, peppering the Raven with rail gun rounds. Fire flared brightly, lighting up *Stitch's* backside, racing along his rear quarter. A flash and the Raven wobbled, drifting off-line—damaged but still fighting, refusing to give up.

"He's losing it." Henricksen stared at the display on the front windows, watching more Mosquitoes converge. "C'mon. Get outta there."

Another hit—starboard side aft—and *Stitch's* engines guttered out. *Serengeti* thought he was a goner—too many Mosquitoes around him, not enough guns on the stealth ship to address them all—and then *Swift* swooped in, screaming like a banshee, obliterating almost half the drones in one fell swoop.

Snicker-snack followed after, chewing through most of the rest, giving *Stitch* just enough time to reignite his engines and get himself in the clear.

"Yahoo!" *Swift* screamed, looping around. Pounding a last few Mosquitoes into oblivion before he and *Snicker-snack* shot away again, targeting a large group of drones on the Citadel's far side.

"Ravens seem to be having a good time." Henricksen pulled a feed onto his panel, watching *Stitch* move away, engines stuttering a bit, then flaring brightly as he chased after *Swift.* "How's *Shriek* doing back there?" He looked at her—looked right into *Serengeti's* camera as she reached for that other part of her, watching the same battle through Tig's eyes.

Dark where he was. Cramped space on a tiny bridge. Four-man crew sitting in a square inside the shadowed confines of the stealth ship's Command space. Visored helmets covering the crews' heads, making them faceless, sexless, anonymous in the dark. Tig and Tilli huddle together in a corner, jointed legs wrapped around each other, cobalt eyes staring out the front windows, anxious messages passing in flashes of color between them.

Serengeti touched at them, comforting the little robots as best she could. Watched through Tig's eyes as *Shriek* crept along, hiding behind his shielding, threading his way through the comparative calm that followed in *Serengeti's* wake.

Automated defense system on the Citadel. Cannons only fired if there was a target in range. Bad for *Cerberus,* good for them—nothing firing if there were no targets around.

Serengeti cruised past the dead space on *Cerberus's* side, drawing the cannons' fire while *Shriek* lagged behind her, sizing up the landing bay next to that dead space. The Mosquitoes pouring out.

The swarm thinned quickly, just a trickle escaping now. *Shriek* saw his opportunity and took it. Sent a message across tight band comms. "Door's open. We're goin' in, boys and girls."

A push as *Shriek* fired his maneuvering engines, feathering them in short bursts to move him close to the Citadel and line himself up with the landing bay's open doors. The Mosquitoes locked onto *Shriek's* engine signature immediately. Redirected and raced toward him, dousing him in scans.

Closer in and the drones slowed, drifting in confusion as the Raven's shielding bounced their scans back, cloaking the stealth ship in the Mosquitos' own comms. Turning him invisible. Making him look like just another drone.

"Suckers," *Shriek* laughed, moving closer to the drones.

"Don't do it," *Serengeti* whispered, thinking he meant to fire.

Tig tensed, picking up her worry, reached for Tilli and clutched her leg-end tight. But *Shriek* behaved himself, passing serenely through the confused swarm of Mosquitoes. Pointed his nose at the landing bay and slipped silently inside.

Serengeti sighed in relief, pulling away. Leaving that one part of her consciousness with Tig while the rest returned to the bridge of her own ship. "*Shriek's* inside."

Henricksen nodded and lurched forward as a barrage of cannon fire pounded *Serengeti's* hull. "Pay attention, Aoki!"

"Aye, sir. Sorry, sir!"

"Samara! Help her out. Evasive maneuvers means Engineering *and* Nav, not just Engineering doing fancy footwork."

"Aye, sir."

No apologies from Samara, just right to work, deploying countermeasures from one panel while running calculations on the other. Charting a path through the cannon fire based on the known patterns of the automated defense system, shunting the results to Aoki who adjusted their course, dodging and weaving while Bosch and the crew in the ancillary batteries blasted away.

They made it through the worst of it, but got caught in the crossfire from two of *Cerberus's* batteries pointing in opposite directions—one chasing her, the other targeting *Swift* who'd unexpectedly changed direction, heading dead-on toward *Serengeti.*

Swift hauled over at the last second and slipped past them, but the plasma fire chasing him slammed into *Serengeti,* digging trenches in her newly repaired sides.

"Goddammit, *Swift!* What the hell was that?" Henricksen grabbed at a panel, steadying himself as Aoki turned sharply. Grunted and slammed into a different panel when a Mosquito exploded against *Serengeti's* hull. "I think it's time we got out of here, *Serengeti.*"

"No arguments here."

Henricksen slapped at a panel on his Command Post, opening ship-to-ship comms. "*Swift. Sharp.* Gather up the boys and get going. Package is delivered. Time we got scarce."

"Roger," *Swift* sent back.

"Roger-dodger," from *Sharp.*

A burst of communication and the Ravens cloaked and peeled off, putting their backs to the Citadel as they scrambled for deep space.

"Sir." Finlay pointed at the display on the front windows, and a single vessel marker showing there. A Raven, based on the data. Moving slower than the others. Uncloaked, a mass of Mosquitoes riding hard on his tail. "*Stitch* is in trouble."

"Engines are failing." Henricksen looked grim. "Bosch!"

"I see him." Bosch pivoted, redirecting his fire, doing his best to help *Stitch* out.

The Raven rippled, shield wrapping around him, shimmering for a few seconds before failing again. A flare of fire engulfed his tail, burning brightly before flickering out.

"That's atmosphere venting." Finlay stared at the windows, pale face ashen.

"*Fuck!*" Bosch screamed, pounding away, picking off Mosquitoes left and right. More kept coming, drawn to the failing Raven like moths to a flame. Every last Mosquito in the area descending on *Stitch* now that the other Ravens had left.

"Bosch!"

"I'm trying!"

He was—he most definitely was—but Bosch's efforts weren't quite enough.

Stitch's engines failed, cobalt light stuttering before shutting down. The Mosquitoes swarmed around him, strafing the Raven from all sides. Comms clicking as *Stitch's* voice screamed from the speakers, "Fuck you, you bastards!"

"No," Henricksen breathed. "No. Don't!"

The Raven detonated, wiping the entire cloud of Mosquitoes out.

"God dammit!" Henricksen punched the panel hard, leaving a smear of blood behind.

"Why? Why would he do that?" Aoki whispered.

"Had to." Finlay tore her eyes from the windows. "Dead anyway. No way out." She snuck a look at Henricksen, bowed her head over her panel, and kept working away.

Aoki just sat there, looking completely lost.

"Aoki." Quiet voice from Henricksen, cutting right through the noise on the bridge. "Aoki," he repeated, and then waited until she turned to him—eyes wide, face haunted. "Get us out of here."

"*Stitch*..." She trailed off, waving vaguely at the windows.

"I know," Henricksen said softly. "Nothing we can do about it now." He looked past her to the windows as the remaining Mosquitoes massed up and turned their way. "Jump, Aoki. Now, please."

"Aye, sir." Aoki bowed her head, staring at her panel like she didn't know what to do. A deep breath and she accessed the ship's controls, turning *Serengeti* around, pointing her nose for deep space.

"Countermeasures," Henricksen ordered.

Serengeti dropped a last load of chaff as Aoki brought the hyperspace drives on-line, spooling them up as the jump clock on the front windows ticked down.

"Rally point," Henricksen sent.

Acknowledgement came back from *Swift*, the other Ravens soon after.

"*Stitch?*" *Swift* asked.

"Didn't make it."

Swift was quiet a moment, swore softly over comms. "This better've been worth it, big man."

Comms cut out, *Swift* and the rest of the Ravens jumping away.

Henricksen stared at the image of *Cerberus,* eyes locked onto that dead space on one side. "Yeah. It better," he said softly.

The clock hit zero and *Serengeti* jumped, leaving *Cerberus* behind.

EIGHTEEN

The landing bay on *Cerberus* seemed endless. *Shriek* slipped inside the doors and glided through a vast, empty space—metal on metal, ice riming everything, flickering lights providing erratic illumination. Low ceiling hanging above it—barely enough room for *Shriek* to squeeze through without scraping his belly against the floor. Wide walls—acres of space to either side, stretching deep into the Citadel.

"Well, this certainly is creepy." *Shriek* popped on a spotlight, shining it around them. Trained it on a scrap pile—mangled Mosquitoes and broken battle droids all mounded together—and kept it there. "Anything in that shit heap moves, I'm turning it into slag."

"Be my guest," *Serengeti* murmured, not liking this place either. Feeling Tig jitter and fidget, touching at Tilli beside him, finding reassurance in her presence.

Empty decking slipped by beneath them, the landing bay's doors yawning widely behind. And in between an icy-cold emptiness that seemed to go on for miles and miles.

Shriek glided smoothly, carefully, navigating that low-ceilinged space. Using the design diagram of the Citadel's layout to guide him to an air-locked door hidden in the darkness far at the back.

Couldn't actually see it, of course. Not in the all-encompassing darkness, the Citadel unwilling, unable, or just too damn cheap to spark so much as a pin light to push the shadows away. And then suddenly— *quite* suddenly—the rear wall appeared ahead of them. A massive barrier of composite metal blocking *Shriek's* path. He fired his thrusters, breaking hard to slow himself down. Feathered the maneuvering jets to turn himself before settling gently to the floor.

Magnetic locks clicked in, holding *Shriek* there, belly sucked tight to the composite metal decking as Tig and Tilli unclipped and gathered up their belongings.

"Looks like this is where we get off." Tig flashed a sickly smile and reached around, pulling his rifle to his chest.

Serengeti touched at his brain, offering what comfort she could as Tig crawled from the corner and touched at a panel on the wall, opening the bridge's door.

"You gonna be okay on your own? I could send Sampson and Delilah with you," *Shriek* offered.

"For the last time," a voice said, drifting from the darkness. "It's *Cooley,* not Delilah."

A shadow moved—one of four faceless crewmen on the bridge—and a helmeted figure stood.

Cooley, *Serengeti* assumed. Female from the voice. Impossible to tell much of anything else about her with the bridge engulfed in darkness, that visored helmet covering her head.

"And it's *Samson* and Delilah, not *Sampson*, numb nuts." Cooley kicked out a hip, hand settling on her waist.

"Sampson and Cooley," *Shriek* snorted. "Who ever heard of Sampson and Cooley? Delilah now. That's classy."

"Yeah-yeah." Cooley waved a hand and started climbing over her seat. Paused, looking upward as a low tone of warning bounced around the stealth ship's bridge pod.

"Whoops. Strike that. Back to your post, Delilah. Mosquitoes are coming back."

Cooley twisted, looking back at her panel. "I can still go with them. Sampson—"

"No," *Serengeti* told her. "Stay with *Shriek.* Tig and Tilli are all I need."

A pause, Cooley's helmeted head tilting, visored face considering the two arachnid-shaped robots with their oversized guns. "You sure?"

"Yes," *Serengeti* smiled. "I'm sure. No offense, but one more trooper isn't going to make all that much difference. Not with the defenses *Cerberus* has at his disposal. And, honestly? I don't really want to pick a fight."

"May not have any choice," Cooley told her, hand drifting to the gun on her hip.

Serengeti flexed Tig's legs, offering a shrug. "Maybe. Then again, we're just a couple of robots. Who would pay any attention to us?" She flashed a smile across Tig's chromed face, turned him, and gave him a shove.

"I'm going, I'm going!" he complained. "No need to be pushy."

A glance at Tilli, reaching for her leg, and Tig scuttled off the bridge, stepping into a long corridor that ran the stealth ship's length.

Relatively simple layout to the Ravens, especially when compared to a Valkyrie, or the other warships in the Fleet. Just three levels inside *Shriek,* with that central hallway running down each of them, and tiny compartments on either side.

Airlock at the back, close to the stealth ship's hind end—a single point of entry accessed via the Raven's one and only cargo hold.

Tilli followed Tig down the corridor, metal legs gripping her rifle tight. Stopped with him at the airlock and stepped in beside him, waiting patiently while the lock depressurized, pumping out heat and air. Exited when a chime sounded and the lock's panel flashed green, stepping into the ice-cold emptiness of *Cerberus's* landing bay.

A glance to either side and the robots moved forward, heading for a pressure door ahead and to one side.

"Forgetting someone?" *Shriek's* asked, AI voice echoing inside Tig's head—direct communication using the robot line.

Serengeti flipped to the rearward-facing camera in Tig's thorax and spied a tiny metallic shape just exiting the stealth ship's airlock, leg lifting to make sure the door closed securely behind her before scuttling around and racing toward Tig and Tilli.

"Oona!" Tig spun around, planting his legs against the sides of his body, favoring the tiny, cartoon-covered robot with a very stern, very disapproving frown. "What are you doing here, young lady?"

"Helping!" Oona cried, throwing her metal legs in the air.

Tig heaved a long-suffering sigh. "We've been through this Oona. And we agreed you'd stay with *Serengeti.* Now turn around—"

"I am with *Serengeti.* She's up here." Oona stood on her tip-toes, tapping a leg-end against Tig's head.

Tig *blipped,* blinking, collected himself, and started frowning again. "That's not what I—"

"No time." Tilli grabbed Tig's leg, pulling him around. Pointed at the airlock doors as the first of the returning Mosquitoes appeared, blotting out the stars.

"Better get going," *Shriek* told them. "Company's arrived." The stealth ship shimmered, disappearing into the landing bay's shadows. "Good luck," he said, and then the robot channel clicked closed.

Tig looked at him, and at the Mosquitoes gliding through the landing bay door. "What should we—?"

"Go, Tig!" *Serengeti* ordered. "Go-go-go!"

She shoved at the little robot to get him going, but he kept looking back at the cloaked stealth ship. A second shove still didn't move him so *Serengeti* took over, scooting Tig toward the airlock as Tilli grabbed Oona by one leg and pulled her along.

A stop at the pressure door, Tig throwing anxious glances over his shoulder as Tilli reached up, tapping frantically at the security panel. "It's locked," she said, face lights flashing. "I don't have the code!"

"I do! I do!" Oona slipped a leg-end under the edge of the security panel, pushed hard, and popped it from the wall. "Ding-dong!" A smile for Tilli and she extruded a tiny electronic finger, jacked directly into the airlock's controls.

Curious, *Serengeti* touched at Oona's brain, watching as she injected long strings of code into the security system. "Oona. What are you—?"

"Ta-da!" Oona cried, waving her legs. She stepped back as the lock turned green, surged forward when it clicked open, dragging Tilli with her. "Hurry-hurry-hurry," she said, waving Tig in.

Serengeti ran him through the door, hitting the cycle button along the way. Joined Tilli and Oona at the center and then waited while the airlock ran through its pressurization routine. "Oona," she said, glancing down at the little robot. "What did you do back there?" A nod to the door behind them, the loosened panel floating in vacuum outside.

"I knock-knocked and the door opened!" Oona said brightly.

"Knock-knocked."

"Uh-huh!" Oona's head bounced up and down, legs bending and flexing in time.

Serengeti looked a question at Tilli, but Tilli just shook her chromed head.

A mystery, then. One that would have to wait until later because the lock turned green and the inner door slid open, Tilli grabbing at Oona and holding her still while Tig stepped around them and scanned the hall outside.

Grey corridor out there, every bit as dull and metallic as the landing bay they'd just left. Atmospherics seemed to be working, though—Tig's sensors picked up breathable air, temperature set to a comfortable 15 degrees Celsius—gravity stuck him to the floor, weighing his metal down.

Lights showed in the ceiling—flickering and fluttering in places, a few blanks spaces, the rest bathed in a harsh, white glow. Tig leaned out of the doorway, looking up and down the hall.

Corridor dead-ended to the left—ran just a few feet before terminating in a thick wall. And right...

Right was scorched and battered panels, warped and dented deck plates, holes showing through to the superstructure beneath. Right was a war zone, that damage a sure sign that something very violent had happened here recently.

"Well, *that's* certainly not a good sign," Tig muttered.

Serengeti shushed him, consulting the diagram of the Citadel's layout stored in Tig's brain. Marked their current location, searching out paths from there to a hexagonal shape showing at the Citadel's center.

Tig butted in, taking a look himself. "Containment pod? That's where we're going?"

"Best place to find an AI if you're looking for him."

The one place he *had* to be since his crystal matrix mind lived there. A long way from here, no matter what path *Serengeti* chose.

She selected one from a dozen or so on offer—shortest route wasn't always the quickest, but this one seemed to offer the most direct path—waving to Tilli and Oona as she moved Tig into the hall.

Empty out there—light and heat, the sound of the overheads buzzing angrily, everything else eerily silent. Tig scuttled forward a few steps—nervous, wary, wincing as the flickering lights cast writhing shadows on the way. Ten feet on and that scorched bit of corridor joined with another hallway that branched off, leading deeper into the ship.

"Turn here," *Serengeti* told him. "Left down this hallway, and—"

"Freeze!" a bass-toned voice shouted as four very large, very *serious*-looking troopers stepped from that crossing hallway, rifles pointing at Tig's face.

So much for sneaking in unnoticed.

"Drop the weapon!" The lead trooper moved a step closer, rifle trained on the shiny space between Tig's eyes.

Angry-sounding guy. Angry-*looking* too, at least, based on what *Serengeti* could see of his face. Smears of grease covered most of it—some kind of camouflage, she supposed, based on the symmetrical pattern, the evenness of the application. A dingy grey uniform clung tight to the trooper's body—ragged and much-patched, sergeant's insignia sewn to his collar, tarnished silver nametag pinned to his chest. And on his shoulder, a snarling, three-headed dog patch.

Cerberus's patch, which made this trooper, and the other three with him, part of the Citadel's complement of soldiers.

"Surprised there's anyone left," Tig said, speaking mind-to-mind to *Serengeti*. "A decade in deep space…would've thought the crew would all be dead by now." He cringed, realizing how callous that sounded. "Ya know, because of the lack of food and all. Not that I *want* them to be dead, mind you. I'm sure Henricksen—*oof!*"

Tig stumbled a step as Tilli bumped into him, scaring the bejesus out of the gun-toting trooper in the process.

The sergeant jumped back, finger reaching for the trigger, screaming, "Drop the weapon! Drop the goddamn weapon!" at the top of his lungs.

Tig *beeped* and let go immediately, all but throwing his rifle toward the ground. In his hurry, he forgot about the strap, though. A strap that wrapped Tig's body, making the gun swing around. "Crap," he said, staring wide-eyed at the sergeant, pulse rifle dangling in mid-air, strap twisted around his neck.

The sergeant opened his mouth and then closed it, frowning darkly. Peeled a hand away from his own rifle and signaled to the troopers behind him, waving them into the hall, pointing them to either side.

The troopers fanned out, forming a semi-circle in the hall. Four shadow-eyed soldiers aiming their weapons at three shiny, obviously scared robots—a comical situation, under other circumstances, but flat-out terrifying right now.

Nothing funny at all about sneaking around an oversized warship piloted by a fragmented, triple-minded AI. Having four heavily armed, heavily twitchy troopers serving said fragmented mind point their bazookas in your face.

"Drop 'em," the sergeant repeated, pointing his gun's muzzle at Tig and Tilli, jerking it toward the decking at his feet.

"Alright. It's alright." *Serengeti* raised Tig's front legs in a gesture of peace, scanned the nametag on the sergeant's chest before looking him right in the face. "Smithers," she said in her calmest, most soothing voice. "That's your name, right?"

"Smithers," Oona gigged. "That's silly."

"Hush now, Oona. This is serious." Tilli pushed Oona behind her and swung her rifle onto her back. Raised her front legs to copy Tig.

Oona looked at them, and at the troopers in the hall, leaned around Tilli's body and raised *her* front legs, too, waving cheerily at the sergeant and his buddies.

The sergeant blinked, frowning harder, gun twitching from one robot to another.

"Sergeant." *Serengeti* moved Tig to one side, shielding Oona as best she could. "We're not—"

"What faction?" Smithers demanded, poking his rifle in Tig's face.

"Faction?" *Serengeti* stared, completely at a loss. "I'm not sure—"

"What faction, goddammit! Soldier or Statesman? *Whose side are you on*?!" Smithers thundered, spittle spraying from his mouth.

Tig went very still, lights winking out in his face.

Serengeti dug deep, summoning her most pleasant of AI voices to try and keep this whole thing from boiling over. "We're not—"

"I'm an owl!" Oona cried, scurrying forward, friendly smile pasted across her chromed face. "Who-who-who," she hooted, tucking her front legs up, flapping them like a chicken. "Who-who-whoo-oo!" she giggled, strutting in place, head bobbing front and back.

Smithers frowned, throwing sidelong looks at the soldiers on either side of him.

"It's a TIG, Sarge," one of the troopers said. Female, from the voice. Dark, greasy hair, pale skin showing beneath black-and-olive war paint. "It's just a TIG." The trooper lowered her rifle, smile curving her lips. "Cute little thing, too," she said, giving Oona the once over.

Oona hooted, giggling, flapping her wings for all they were worth as the trooper squatted down and held out a hand, calling to Oona as if she were a kitten.

"Careful, Hatori," Smithers growled.

"Give it up, Sarge. They're just TIGs. Roly-Polys would be here by now if they were with the Statesman."

Smithers still didn't look happy. He twitched an elbow, sending one of the other troopers back to the intersecting hallway, presumably to keep watch. "So if they're not with the Statesman, what are they doing here?" he asked, talking *around* the robots now, rather than *to* them, in typical human fashion.

"Probably got lost," Hatori shrugged, tempting Oona close. "Got some war paint of your own, don't you?" She nodded to the menagerie of animal drawings, pointing to one on Oona's side. "What's that?"

Oona twisted, looking. "That's an elepha-elephalala—that's a heffallapump." She turned, pointing her butt toward the trooper so she could get a better look.

"Heffallapump," Hatori repeated, lips twitching. "Well, that's the nicest heffallapump I've ever seen."

Oona preened proudly, turning this way and that. Started rattling off names—some real, some invented—as she showed Hatori her entire collection.

Hatori smiled through it all, patted Oona on the head when she finished, and pushed to her feet, cradling her rifle to her chest. "Don't think they're dangerous, Sarge. Don't recognize these three in particular, but the last I checked, most of the TIGs were with us and the Soldier."

"Actually," *Serengeti* moved Tig forward, "we're not. We're not with *any* of your factions," she said hurriedly. "We're from outside." She waved at the airlock behind them, indicating the landing bay beyond.

Smithers frowned suspiciously. "Outside? *No one's* from outside. Ain't been anybody on the Citadel but us and the Roly-Polys for the better part of a decade now."

"Sir." Hatori caught his eyes, nodded meaningfully at the airlock. "Something *did* come through not so long ago."

And brought the troopers here.

Serengeti cursed, realizing they must have tripped a perimeter alarm on the way in.

"That was you out there." Smithers blinked in surprise, slowly lowered his gun. "Heard the explosions. Hard to miss the noise from all those cannons, even inside." He tilted his head, nodding toward the end of the hall. "Your ship?"

"Gone," *Serengeti* told him. "Dropped us here and left."

"Why?" Smithers screwed up his face, giving them a look that made it clear he thought they were the biggest bunch of idiots he'd ever met. "Why come here in the first place?"

"Orders." *Serengeti* shot a look at Tilli, gave a minute shake of Tig's head. The soldiers here still thought she was just a robot. She didn't want them thinking she was anything more than that. "We were sent to find *Cerberus*."

The soldiers tensed, instantly wary. Even Hatori didn't look so sure of them now.

"Well, you found him alright." Smithers blinked slowly, giving her a flat-eyed stare. "All *three* of him. Not sure what prick AI dropped you here, little friend, but you've found yourselves in the middle of a war." A glance at the troopers behind him. "Might be we let you stick with us. Or you can take your chances with the Roly-Poly patrols. Probably end up dead."

Smithers shrugged again, face a complete blank. Stood there in silence with those other three soldiers standing behind him—stiff and unmoving, the atmosphere in the corridor tense and thick, sucking the warmth right out the air.

"*Psst!*" Oona waved at Hatori, cupped two legs ends around her speaker of a mouth and waved her close. "What's a Roly-Poly?" she whispered, and just like that, the mood in the hallway changed.

Hatori blinked in surprise, giggled, and then laughed aloud. The troopers with her glanced at each other and started laughing as well— shakily at first, a hint of relief wrapped around it.

"Stand down," Smithers ordered, waving a hand, pointing his rifle at the floor.

Hatori slung hers over her shoulder, tapped a finger to the nametag on her chest. "Hatori. Torres." A nod to the trooper watching the corner where the two hallways met. "Katsopoulous is the good-looking guy with the curly hair over there." She turned her head, winking at a broad-shoulder trooper standing next to her. "And the ugly guy over there with the angry face is Sergeant Smithers."

Smithers gave her the finger. Hatori blew him a kiss.

"Roly-Polys are RPDs," she explained.

"RPDs." *Serengeti* tilted Tig's head, thinking. The name sounded familiar, but she couldn't quite place it. Didn't remember ever coming across one.

"Combat droids," Hatori explained as *Serengeti's* perplexed look. "Built like tanks. Limited AI."

"Huh." A check of her database showed an oversized robot generally shaped like a dung beetle. Specs said it came equipped with plasma blasters *and* a rapid-fire ion grenade launcher. "Nasty bit of business. Didn't know *Cerberus* carried anything like that."

Hatori smiled crookedly. "*Cerberus* had a few other secrets he didn't see fit to tell anyone about. Even his own crew," she added, throwing a meaningful look Smithers' way. "Had a good three hundred Roly-Polys locked up in a cargo bay. Most of them went over to the Statesman when the shit hit the fan. Scientist managed to hold onto a few, we got a few ourselves." She waved at the troopers around her. "Mostly we got TSGs, though. Useful little buggers, but delicate. A few blasts from one of those RPDs and they get blown all to hell."

Tig *blipped* worriedly, huddling close to Tilli.

Oona looked at him, and the troopers in the hallway, scratching at her rounded head.

Hatori reached down and chucked her under the chin. "Don't worry. You're safe enough here. Blind spot," she said, nodding to the cameras lining the hall. "TSGs took out all the eyes in this section a few months ago. Statesman hasn't seemed to notice yet."

"You mentioned a war," *Serengeti* said carefully. "What happened?" She waved at the hallway around them, the scarred and pitted walls, the scorch and warped decking running beneath their feet.

"What happened?" Smithers snorted, arms crossing, hugging his rifle to his chest. "Went bat-shit crazy, that's what happened." He quirked an eyebrow nodding to the hallway behind her. "You heard the comms on the way in?"

Serengeti nodded slowly.

"Then you know his brain's broken. Not quite sure what caused it— some system-wide failure, corruption on his network, god only knows what. All we know for sure is the Scientist just up and turned on the other two AIs one day, and now the Statesman and the Soldier are at it as well. Been that way for what? Couple of years now?" he guessed, looking a question at Hatori.

"Sounds right. Three at the most." She shrugged. "Crew that's left threw in with the Soldier when the Statesman turned against him. Robots got caught up in it all." Another shrug, face apologetic beneath the camouflage grease paint.

Serengeti considered the troopers a moment, choosing her words carefully. "Don't take this the wrong way, but I'm surprised there are any of you left all."

Smithers shrugged. "Couple hundred of us skin jobs still kicking around, dodging the Statesman's droids, taking on the Scientist and his little wacky robot army." He grimaced, eyes flicking across the soldiers with him. "Lucky for us, the hydroponics lab held and the water filtration system's still working. Without that..." He lifted his chin, drawing his thumb across his throat. "Been hiding out in the dead zone. Probably noticed *that* on your way in, too. No cameras there. Not much left for systems either. But the environmentals still work." He glanced at the ceiling. "Safest place around the ship these days."

"Speaking of which..." Hatori caught Smithers' eyes, tapped at her wrist. "We should probably get back."

"Yeah. Probably right," Smithers grunted. "C'mon." He flicked his fingers, sending Torres and Katsopoulous ahead, beckoning for the three robots to fall in behind him as he took off after them. "TSGs'll be all excited to have new playmates." He smiled, looking back over his shoulder, slamming to a halt when he realized none of the robots had followed. "You're not coming with us, are you?"

Serengeti shook Tig's head. "Orders. We've got to find *Cerberus*."

Smithers frowned—angry and annoyed. "*Cerberus* doesn't exist anymore. Your orders are crap."

"Maybe."

Smithers kept frowning and then squinted, giving the robots a good, hard look. "Why are you here?" he asked, and then held up a hand, cutting *Serengeti* off before she could answer. "Why are you *really* here? What were you hoping to accomplish by talking to *Cerberus*?"

Serengeti stared in silence, cobalt lights ticking across Tig's cheeks.

"Big secret, eh? Fine," Smithers grunted. "Let's try this one, then. What's your name?"

Serengeti turned a bit, pointing at Tig's designation.

"Yeah. Right," he snorted. "Like I'm gonna believe you're just some innocent little robot." He tilted his head, looking Tig up and down. "I've been around AIs long enough to tell the difference between 'bot AI and ship AI, and you ain't no 'bot. I'd bet my life on it."

Hatori shifted, glancing down the hallway. "Sarge," she said quietly.

Smithers flapped a hand, focusing on *Serengeti* riding inside Tig. "Ain't no ship AI gonna trust no plain Jane 'bot to talk to a bigwig like *Cerberus*. So who are you? Really?" he asked, peering into Tig's eyes.

"*Sarge!*" Hatori called, voice urgent.

"What?" Smithers snapped, turning, following the line of Hatori's pointing finger to a camera high up on the wall.

Active camera, panning slowly, red light flashing on and off.

"Shit. Scatter!"

Smithers took off down the hallway, chasing after Torres and Katsopoulous, Hatori following hot on his heels. *Serengeti* gathered up Tilli and Oona and sent them after the troopers with Tig bringing up the rear.

Passageways passed by, the troopers pounding down one hall, turning right into another and right again before fetching up against a blockade: a handful of those dung beetle-shaped RPDs with their guns primed and ready, dug into the intersection ahead.

"Back!" Smithers yelled. "Back-back-back!"

The troopers retreated as hell opened up, the RPDs pouring out plasma rounds that lit up the hallway, scoring along the deck plates, ripping panels from the walls.

Serengeti ducked Tig into a corridor, grabbed at Tilli and Oona and pulled them in as well, letting the troopers run past. The RPDs kept firing, lobbing rounds after Smithers and his retreating troopers as the corridor started to tremble, loose panels rattling alarmingly as the Roly-Polys stampeded after their human quarry.

Tig flattened himself against the wall, waving frantically at Tilli and Oona until they did the same. The three of them froze there, still as statues, every last light in their faces winking out. Making themselves as inconspicuous as possible in the hopes the RPDs would pass them by.

And it almost worked. *Almost.*

Three RPDs rumbled past without looking, completely ignoring the intersecting corridor. But the fourth slowed for some reason, pincered head turning, sensors lighting up as it scanned the hallway where Tig and the others huddled.

Red eyes pulsed and throbbed, glowing hellishly in the dim lighting. A flash of communication, rapid-fire patterns flicking across its face, and the RPD charged—head down, plasma rounds filling the air.

Serengeti pulled up the Citadel's design diagram, locating the closest way out. "Maintenance shaft! Hurry!" she yelled, pushing Tilli and Oona ahead of her, fleeing in a panic as shots scored the walls, peeling the decking from the floor.

Tilli turned a corner, holding tight to Oona, pulling up short when *Serengeti* called out. Tore a panel from the wall and shoved Oona inside, throwing an anxious look Tig's way before diving in after her.

A shot hit Tig's leg, tearing it away. He stumbled and caught himself, continued on using the seven he had left. Clambered into the maintenance shaft a half-second before the RPD slammed bodily into the wall, yelling, "Go-go-go!" at Tilli. Urging her deeper into the Citadel's bowels, leaving the RPD butting uselessly at the wall.

NINETEEN

"Hold up," *Serengeti* called some time later, bringing the three robots to a halt. They huddled together, hiding in *Cerberus's* maintenance shafts still as *Serengeti* pulled up the Citadel's schematic, checking their location against the containment pod at the ship's center. Cursed when she found they were barely halfway there.

"Dammit. This is taking too long."

Nearly two hours spent in the maintenance shafts already, according to the chron. Two long hours of winding round and round the Citadel's innards, keeping to the maintenance shafts, eschewing the more direct route the hallways offered because it was safer in here, where the RPDs couldn't go.

Safer, but also far more confusing. Seems the schematic *Serengeti* downloaded was a tad out-of-date—didn't account for changes made to the Citadel's original design since he was first put into service—forcing them to abandon their original route and, well…wing it, mostly.

That meant a lot of wrong turns and backtracking when promising paths turned into dead-ends, or simply led off in the wrong direction. The good news was they weren't lost—not yet anyway. The bad news was they should have reached the AI containment pod by now.

"At this rate, it'll take us a week to get there," *Serengeti* muttered.

Slight exaggeration. But the better part of a day at least, based on their current rate of travel. Much longer than *Serengeti* had planned.

Henricksen will worry.

And she had no way of contacting him. Or even *Shriek* for that matter. Not with all this metal around her blocking Tig's comms. Twenty-four hours, he'd said, before he came in after her, but *Serengeti* knew him. Knew how much Henricksen hated waiting.

Twelve hours tops before he shows up with a rescue party.

Which meant they needed to hoof it, and find that damned containment pod before Henricksen got itchy and did something stupid.

Another check of the diagram, consulting the reality of the maintenance shafts around them against the plan stored inside Tig's head, and *Serengeti* adjusted her course for the dozenth time. "Mush, you huskies," she said, nudging Tig forward, waving to Oona and Tilli behind her.

"Husky! Woof-woof!" Oona started hopping like a bunny for some reason—front legs bent and hugged tight to her chest, hind end wiggling as she bounced.

Not the most efficient means of travel. And a bouncing robot—even a small one like Oona—made quite the racket.

Tilli *shushed* her and pulled Oona to her side. Shook at her leg and gave her a stern look, warning her to behave.

Oona nodded solemnly and bounced more quietly—small hops, landing gently as she could each time.

Twenty minutes ticked by that way—Tig and Tilly scurrying silently, Oona hippity-hopping, making a soft plop each time she landed. Twenty minutes, and the ship eerily quiet around them. The only sounds breaking the stillness those of their own footsteps ticking against the maintenance shaft's metal panels.

And then screams erupted, shattering the silence. Human screams and the sharp sounds of gunfire echoing through the ship's corridors.

Tig froze, front legs gripping his rifle tightly. Tilli pulled Oona to her and ratcheted a round into her gun. They huddled together—eyes wide, face lights quiescent—listening as the sounds of battle drew closer, and closer, before thankfully passing them by.

The robots relaxed, sighing gustily, Tig managing a shaking laugh. Oona laughed too—happy as always, along for the ride and enjoying the adventure. Blissfully oblivious to the violent goings-on in the halls outside.

Serengeti got them moving again, sending the robots left and right and left again, making real progress for a while, tracking closer and closer to the ship's center, until Tig rounded a corner and came to a screeching halt.

The maintenance shaft ended abruptly, the schematic showing a plus-shaped intersection—four square, metal tubes coming together from four different directions—that no longer existed.

A crater lay there, where those four shafts should have a joined. The intersection itself gone now—destroyed by an explosion, based on the scorched and ragged metal—leaving a gaping hole in its place.

Serengeti looked across—the way ahead tantalizingly close and yet impossibly far away. Ten meters of emptiness separating her from the path she wanted, the two identical metal shafts sitting to her left and right.

A chasm yawned at her feet, threatening to pull the robots in. Tig crept to the edge and looked up, then down, eyeing the spiraling shaft in either direction—a precipitous drop stretching into darkness one way, an interminable climb leading to god-only-knew where in the other.

"We could climb down, I suppose." Tig eyed the shaft uncertainly. Shattered metal everywhere. Not much purchase for the robots' magnetized leg-ends. "Or up…"

"No telling what's down there," *Serengeti* noted. "Probably not a good idea."

Tig sighed. "Looks like we're backtracking again."

"Looks like it." *Serengeti* consulted the design diagram, looking for another route. "We'll need to run along this corridor for a while." She projected the map on the floor, marking their current location, where they needed to go to get back on course.

A long stretch of corridor lay in between those two points. Wide hallway, main route through this particular level. A few twists and turns along the way. Another one of those plus-shaped intersections in the middle of it that they'd have to cross.

Tig studied the route for several seconds, metal legs rattling anxiously against the decking. "You sure this is a good idea?"

Inside voice, speaking just to *Serengeti*, not wanting to worry Tilli.

"We've had to backtrack so many times I'm not really sure of *anything* anymore. But we came here to talk to *Cerberus,* and right now, this is our best route to his minds."

Tig nodded, *beeping* softly. Turned around, letting Tilli take the lead for a while. "Containment pod's the most secure place on the ship," he said quietly, still using that inside channel. "You really sure we can get in there?"

"No." *Serengeti* kept her voice light, letting a smile come through in her voice. "But I'm hoping Oona can use her little knock-knock trick to bypass the security system."

"Oona. Right." Tig eyed the little robot doubtfully. "I have a bad feeling about this."

"*Tsk.* You worry too much, Tig. Left here, Tilli," *Serengeti* said, pointing to an access panel ahead.

Tilli cracked the panel open and poked her head out, taking a quick look around. "All clear," she whispered, reaching for Oona's leg as she scuttled into the hall.

Tig followed after more slowly—rifle raised and primed to fire. Pointed it one way down the hall before spinning around and aiming it in the opposite direction, getting the lay of the land.

Debris everywhere—broken robots and twisted panels, shredded metal lying in unrecognizable lumps—but no sign of the RPDs anywhere. Or Smithers and his soldiers, for that matter. No signs of *anything* moving around that stretch of hall.

Tig caught Tilli's eye and nodded to his left, clutched his rifle tight to his chest as he crept down the hall with Tilli, Oona sandwiched protectively between them. "Looks like a war zone," he muttered, nodding at the walls.

"Whole ship's a war zone, Tig." *Serengeti* flipped to the camera in his thorax, keeping an eye on the hallway behind them while Tig and Tilli scouted the way ahead.

She hated being so dependent on them, but she didn't trust the cameras lining the walls. *Cerberus's* cameras, those, and attached to his network. Didn't dare try to access them, so she stuck to Tig. Dealt with feeling half-blind.

Tig rounded a corner, approaching another one of those plus-shaped intersections, this one intact but barricaded. They way ahead blocked by towering metal partitions reaching from wall to wall, stretching ten feet toward the ceiling above.

"Uhh…" Tig knocked on one of the panels and waited a few seconds. Gave it shove when nothing knocked back.

The panel barely moved. Heavy thing, apparently, and snugged in tight.

Tilli moved up beside Tig and the two of them leaned against the panel together, pushing and shoving, the panel screeching alarmingly as it slid across the metal decking, opening a gap just wide enough for Tilli to slip through.

A few seconds of silence and Tilli poked her head back out, pointed at Tig, and then beckoned for him and Oona to join her.

A dozen chromed faces greeted them, cobalt eyes wide and terrified, arachnid-shaped bodies crammed up against the barriers on the far side of the intersection. TSGs—all of them. Trapped here, or hiding. The barriers around the intersection obviously erected to keep the RPDs out.

The robots twittered in alarm as Tig and Tilli stepped in, climbing on top of one another, forming a quivering, jittering pile, seeming surprisingly terrified of their own kin.

"It's alright," *Serengeti* called in her softest, most soothing voice. A step closer, Tig's face lights swirling in calming patterns as the TSGs shivered and *hooted*, pawing desperately at the walls. "We're not going to hurt you," *Serengeti* told them, but the TSGs didn't seem to believe here. Twittered even more loudly.

"I don't get it," Tig said, scratching at his head. "What's wrong—?"

"Gun," Tilli whispered, pointing at Tig's rifle.

"This?" Tig held his weapon up, muzzle pointed at the ceiling. "No need to worry about—"

"Tig." *Serengeti* turned his head, pointing his eyes at a flashing light on the wall. Camera watching them. *Cerberus's* camera, keeping tabs on them from above. "Lower the gun, Tig. Slowly."

"What?" Tig flicked his eyes from the camera to the gun. "Just learned how to use it," he said, waving the weapon at the camera, smiling his friendliest smile. "It's not even—"

Klaxons screamed, filling the corridor with noise. Tig jumped straight in the air as the emergency lighting kicked in, the buzzing white brightness fading to a muted, red glow.

A tremor shook the corridor, making the barricades shake and sway. A bass-toned rumble echoed along the hallway, coming from behind the barrier on their left-hand side.

Tig shared a look with Tilli—both of them equally alarmed. "This can't be good," he murmured, and jumped again as the barrier moved.

A thump and screech, metal panel swinging, screaming shrilly as it scraped across the floor. Third thump and the towering panel crumpled as half a dozen RPDs attacked it, knocking it over, pouring in after with their weapons hot and their blood-red eyes blazing. Mandibles *clack-clack-clacking* fit to wake every last demon in hell.

"Crap-crap-crap!" Tig pointed his rifle at the Roly-Polys and started blasting away.

Tilli swung her own rifle around and joined him, tucking Oona behind her as she pulled the trigger and spat out a chattering string of rounds.

Plasma fire lit up the intersection, shots scoring the floor, the ceiling, the barriers to either side. Pinging off the RPDs' heavily armored carapaces as they backed up in surprise.

A flash of lights—red and hellish, flickering from one droid's face to another—and the RPDs rallied. Cocked their weapons—*click-click-click, clank-clank-clank*—and returned fire.

"Incoming!" Tig yelled, diving out of the way.

Tilli squeezed off another couple shots, grabbed Oona's leg, and went with him, the two of them shucking and jiving, dodging the RPDs' fire.

Cracking off rounds when they could, giving back as good as they got.

Well, Tilli did anyway, sniping at the RPDs like a pro. Rifle didn't really seem hurt them all that much—woefully underpowered, those weapons, hardly a match for the tank-like combat droids—but doing a fair job of pissing them off.

As for Tig...well, Tig just sort of ran around in a panic randomly pulling the trigger. Robot couldn't hit the broadside of a barn.

Hit the barricades a few times, though. He and the RPDs both. Knocked one of them askew, peeled the paneling off the walls nearby, even managed to knock a hole in the ceiling, raining debris down on everyone below.

The TSGs suffered through all of it, cowering in their corner, chromed faces reflecting the plasma fire zipping through the air. A stray shot hit one and it exploded in dramatic fashion—ovoid body shredding, legs spraying in every direction, rounded head bouncing across the intersection before fetching up against the barricade on the far side.

The other robots froze, watching their fellow's chromed head bounce away. Looked at each other when it ricocheted, bouncing one last time before slipping through the gap in the barricades, finding freedom outside. Stared after it for almost two complete seconds before the lot of them scattered, flocking like frightened chickens, running straight into the line of fire.

Two more robots exploded, a couple lost legs, one lost half its head. The rest kept going, tumbling over Tig, Tilli, and Oona in their panicked rush.

Hit the gap in the barricades together and bunched up tight, pushing and shoving, squabbling with each other as they all tried to squeeze through that narrow space at once.

"One at a time!" Tig yelled, backing up to help them.

The TSGs ignored him. Kept trying to climb on top of each other, too terrified to realize the lot of them fleeing en masse prevented *any* of them from actually getting out.

"Idiots," Tig muttered, ducking down, sliding a step to his left.

Tilli backed up against him, pushing Oona between them, but their shots just kept bouncing off the RPDs' armor—denting the metal, scoring the paint, but *still* not really doing any real damage.

"This isn't working." Tig shot an RPD in the face, forcing it back a step. "These things are built like tanks. We need bigger guns!"

"Back," *Serengeti* ordered. "Get out of here, Tig!"

Tig *wonked* in confusion. "But—But you said—"

"I know what I said, Tig, but these big uglies sort of change the plan now, don't they? Back the way we came." *Serengeti* waved at the gap in the barricade. "We'll find another way."

"No arguments here." Tig emptied his clip and made a run for it, using the stacked-up TSGs as a ladder as he launched himself at the gap.

Almost made it, too. Sailed quite gracefully through the air, well on his way to freedom, when an errant blast hit the metal panel and slewed it around, closing off the gap off.

Tig slammed into the barricade, bounced off and landed in a heap.

"Up, up, up!" Tilli cried, grabbing Tig's leg, hauling him to his feet. "Move, move, move!" She dragged him to one side, herding Oona along with him, plasma fire dogging their heels as they ran.

Serengeti flipped through the three robots' eyes, searching for another way out. The barricades to the north and south stood firm—metal panels welded together, pressed in tight between the walls. No escape there. The TSGs pounded at the third barrier, trying to open it back up, but the RPD's blast seemed to have fused the metal, blocking that way out as well.

Only one way left then, and that one filled with RPDs. Six of them squatting where the barricade once stood, six more just arriving, cramming in behind the other combat droids, itching to get in on the action.

Walls of metal, everywhere *Serengeti* looked.

We're trapped here. Trapped like rats. We're going to die.

Unless she did something drastic. And potentially suicidal.

Time to pull a Henricksen.

"Plan B, Tig!"

"There's a Plan B?" Tig skipped to one side, *beeping* in a panic as plasma fire sheared off a leg. "Ow-ow-ow-ow!" He hopped up and down, butt wiggling, the stump of his leg glowing white-hot.

That was two he'd lost now, and both of them on his hind end. Tig did *not* look happy. "What the hell is Plan B and how do I get one?" he yelled.

"This is Plan B." *Serengeti* trained Tig's rifle on the nearest RPD's mandibled face, aiming for its clustered red eyes. Squeezed the trigger and blasted away, advancing on the blinded combat droid as it *glonked* in surprise and backed up.

Tig *glonked* too, making it clear he thought she was insane. "Don't think I like Plan B, *Serengeti*!"

"No guts, no glory, Tig!" *Serengeti* pushed forward, ignoring Tig's screaming protestations. Slipped in close and jumped onto the blinded Roly-Polys head, jamming Tig's leg-end into one of its eyes.

The RPD bucked beneath her, trying to throw Tig off. *Serengeti* held on tight, using Tig's magnetized legs to keep her in place as she extruded a connector and jacked directly into the combat droid's brain.

A bit of fiddling, working her way around the firewalls the RPD threw up to protect itself, and *Serengeti* charted a path, started working her way toward the center of the droid's network. More firewalls there—three password-protected layers that *Serengeti* shredded like paper before barging her way in. Bypassing the RPD's internal defenses like they weren't even there, surgically cutting every last connection tying the combat droid to *Cerberus's* network before wrapping herself around the droid's central system and smothering the AI inside.

The RPD twitched and shivered before finally going still. *Serengeti* bathed the droid in anti-viral routines, stripped its internal network, and rebuilt it on the fly. Ran an abbreviated test cycle before reaching for the RPD's weapons systems and wheeling it around.

"Tig! Drop!" *Serengeti* screamed.

"Plan B?"

"Yes, Plan B, now drop, Tig! Drop!"

Tig flattened himself in an instant, grabbed at Tilli, and pulled her and Oona down beside him.

Serengeti opened fire, flinging a barrage of plasma rounds at the hijacked RPD's buddies, turning its guns on the other Roly-Polys.

An RPD in front of her dropped like a stone—head sheared off, holes punched through its carapace. *Serengeti* fired on the two behind it, clipping the legs off of one, splitting another in half, shots pinging off her stolen droid's carapace, denting its sides, scoring across its back.

Tilli leaned out from behind her and shot a line of rifle fire at an RPD to her right, skimming plasma rounds across its face. *Serengeti* turned on it and shot it through the head. Shot it a second and third time to make sure it was one hundred percent dead.

Another slid in behind it, clipping *Serengeti's* RPD, tearing panels from its sides, shearing off a couple of legs. The combat droid stumbled and recovered, shifting its weight to the left to compensate for having fewer stabilizers on its right.

"What now?" Tig yelled, popping from cover, peppering the RPDs with fire.

Serengeti ratcheted an ion grenade into the RPD's launcher and lobbed it over the front rank of attacking combat droids. "Plan C, Tig."

Tig's eyes rolled wildly. "There's a Plan *C* now? What the heck is Plan C?!"

Serengeti smiled as the ion grenade detonated, tossing RPDs like ragdolls. Lowered her stolen robot's head and charged at the nearest combat droid, grabbing it by the neck and pulling it close. "This is Plan C."

She slammed the RPD's mandibles together, biting down on the captive Roly-Poly's head. Squeezed until they touched the droid's brain and sent a burst of code across its network.

The RPD shuddered, mind fried in an instant. *Serengeti's* code jumped from it to the others, worming its way through their internal defenses, subsuming their AI brains one at a time.

She split her conscious in two, then four, each piece taking control of two of the droids at the same time—minimal operations, propulsion and munitions, everything else shut down, severed from *Cerberus's* network.

Ugly way to treat a robot, but *Serengeti* really didn't have much choice. It was kill or be killed, and she meant to get out of here alive. "Stay behind me, Tig!" she yelled, turning her army of droned 'bots on the last two RPDs. "Alright, boys. You've got two choices here. You can either run away now or—*oh come on!*"

A hulking shape rounded the corner at the end of the hall, massive legs pounding against the deck plates as it stalked toward *Serengeti* and her purloined reinforcements.

RPD, from the look of it, but not like the ones *Serengeti* controlled. This one was bigger and bulkier—nearly twice the size of the others, wide body filling the corridor—with eyes that glowed a sickly green, not blood-red like the combat droids she'd stolen.

The hallway quaked and shuddered, panels falling off the walls as the monstrous RPD advanced.

"What. The hell. Is that?" Tig asked, staring in horror.

"Bad news," *Serengeti* told him. "Stay behind me, Tig. Tilli? You and Oona still back there?"

"Right here, *Serengeti*."

"Good. Go help those TSGs. See if you can't get that barricade open again."

"On it!" Tilli scuttled away, taking Oona with her, yelling orders at the TSGs as she tried to get them organized.

"Tig?"

"Right here." Tig raised his rifle, pointing it at the approaching monster.

Doubtful that little pea shooter would do much good, but *Serengeti* appreciated the sentiment.

"Try not to get shot, okay?"

Tig nodded and moved a step backward as *Serengeti* spread her RPDs wide, placing one rank in front of the other to block the way into the intersection.

The front rank squatted down, rear rank looming over them. Tig pointed his tiny rifle between them as *Serengeti* cleared the last two Roly-Polys—frying their brains in the same manner as the others, slaving them to a sub-mind before adding them to her defenses. And when she had them all, she reached for the last one—that bruiser lumbering down the hall.

Serengeti touched at its brain, connecting for a micro-second before snatching her consciousness back. Threw a good ten layers of encrypted firewalls between them for good measure, wishing she could scour her network.

The RPD felt rotten, something slick and slippery reaching for her in the brief time their minds touched. Grasping greedily at *Serengeti's* consciousness, trying to do the same thing to her that she'd done to its kin.

Awful touch. Disgusting. The most horrible thing *Serengeti* had ever felt. And yet, she sensed something familiar, lurking behind all the ichor. An advanced mind that was far more intelligent than the other RPDs in that hallway. Light years ahead of them. More powerful than all the combat droids put together.

She knew that mind. Had spoken to it a few times, though never on its own.

The Scientist.

Serengeti retreated, keeping a wary eye on the RPD down the hall.

They'd come to find *Cerberus*, but part of him had found them instead.

TWENTY

The Scientist stomped a few steps closer and crashed to a halt, toxic green eyes swirling like kaleidoscopes on acid, mandibles grinding together—a horrid, spine-tingling sound.

Serengeti slid another step backward, sending an order to her droid army.

Plasma coils whined, snaking lines of energy appearing as the RPDs' blasters powered up. A second order and the hijacked robots ratcheted rounds into composite metal chambers, filling the hall with the ominous *clack-clack-clack* of weapons loading, preparing to fire.

Serengeti prepared that order too, but then the Scientist spoke, stentorian voice filling the hall—freezing the order to fire before it even touched the comms channel.

"Raven or writing desk?" he demanded, deafening tones reverberating off the walls.

"Ex—Excuse me?" *Serengeti* blinked, staring stupidly, thinking she must have misheard the question.

"Raven or writing desk?" the Scientist repeated in his moaning, groaning voice.

"I don't—I'm not—"

"Raven. Or writing dsk," he grated—angry, impatient, green eyes vast pools of necromantic fire.

The RPD's blasters trained on *Serengeti's* droid's face, plasma coils whining like banshees—locked and loaded, primed to fire.

Raven or writing desk, Raven or writing desk, Serengeti thought desperately, trying to figure out which answer she dared give.

"Raven," she blurted, as the whining grew piercing, triggers ratcheting with a staccato *clack-clack-clack.* "Raven," she repeated, cringing, waiting for the Scientist to fire.

Mandibles crashed, a trainwreck of sound. The Scientist shifted, RPD balancing on one set of legs and another, bouncing side-to-side like an oversized crab with ants in its pants. "Raven," he said, voice grating as ever, heavy with judgment. Another of those side-to-side shiftings and the RPD's guns lowered, plasma coils winding down. "Raven. Good-good! Excellent choice!"

"It—It is?"

"*Most* good," he told her, mandibled head nodding sagely. "Can't trust a writing desk," he confided. "Uppity things, writing desks. Always correcting your diction."

"So I've heard," *Serengeti* said faintly, confused by the sudden change in the Scientist's demeanor. The pleasant, effete tone issuing from his RPD's mouth. "Don't know any writing desks personally—"

"I'm not a Raven *or* a writing desk," a piping voice called. Oona slipped through the double line of RPDs, presenting herself to the Scientist, putting her tiny body right in *Serengeti's* line of fire. "I'm an owl!" she said proudly. "See?" Oona tucked up her front legs and flapped them for all they were worth, shouting, "Who-who-who!" at the top of her lungs.

Tilli *trilled* anxiously, trying to coax her back.

"Oona. Come here, honey," *Serengeti* called.

Didn't quite trust it, this new iteration of the Scientist, so she kept her guns on him. All of them, every last weapon on every last one of her stolen RPDs. A swipe at Oona, trying to grab her, cursing when the little robot giggled and skittered aside.

"Owl, eh?" The Scientist bent down, squinting suspiciously at Oona's smiling, chromed face. "Knew an owl once. Sad little thing. Had this odd accordion neck."

"Like this?" Oona bobbled her head, giggling as it bounced up and down and side to side like a watermelon on a spring.

The Scientist giggled too, mandibled head flopping around as he copied her.

Serengeti frowned, watching them. This was all getting just a bit too weird. A little too cozy for her tastes. "Scientist," she called, and saw the huge RPD jerk and jump backward, green eyes wide with alarm.

"What-what-what?" he breathed, guns lifting, plasma coils spinning up. "She knows my name-she knows my name-she knows my name," the Scientist whispered, mandibles *clack-clack-clacking* together.

"Great. He's a nut bag," Tig muttered.

A heavily armed, potentially dangerous nut bag, and Oona right in front of him, directly in his line of fire, 'who-who-whoing' away.

Tilli scurried forward, *whistling* shrilly, obviously upset. Froze in a panic of indecision—wanting Oona safe, afraid of the Scientist's huge guns.

A glance at *Serengeti,* pleading with her cobalt eyes.

"Scientist," *Serengeti* called, drawing his attention, keeping it focused on her. A step forward, another and another, thinking to maneuver her

RPD's body between Oona and the green-eyed monster's guns. "We're looking for *Cerberus*."

"*Cerberus? Cerberus?!*" The RPD hopped back, head whipping from side to side. "Nope. Nope. Nope. No *Cerberus* here. *Cerberus* left on stormy seas, leaving the fiddlers three behind."

"Check that," Tig amended. "This guy's not a nut bag. He's bat-shit crazy."

The Scientist tittered softly—an odd, off-kilter sound. Mandibles crashed, grinding together as the RPD's blasters wound back down.

Oona poked at one, giggling. Decided she was tired of being an owl and switched to hopping around like a bunny, thumpity-thumping around.

"We came to talk." Another a step closer, front legs raised. "Just talk. That's it."

"Talk?!" The RPD crouched down, green eyes turning suspicious. "The time has come, to talk of many things. Of shoes and ships and sealing wax, of cabbages and kings."

"And mustard!" Oona cried, waving her jointed legs.

"Mustard?!" The RPD *wonked* like a foghorn. "Don't let's be silly," he said, disapproving and indignant.

Oona laughed aloud, throwing her legs in the air. Started prancing in a circle, giggling even louder as the Scientists joined her, shouting "Caucus! Caucus! Caucus!" in his bass-toned voice.

"He's cracked," Tig said, shaking his head. "He's totally cracked. Gone off the deep end. Nuttier than a—*eep.*"

Tig backed up quickly as the Scientist swung around, fixing him with his toxic green gaze. Scuttled in close and scanned those awful eyes across the little robot. Turned a similar, probing look on *Serengeti's* RPD.

"You?" he breathed, mandibled head tilting. "Who are you? *What* are you?" he asked, touching a *Serengeti's* consciousness, trying to connect to her brain.

She threw up firewalls to block him, but the Scientist snuck in before they were completed, stealing a bit of data from her, leaving a gift of darkness behind.

Tendrils of ichor that clung tenaciously to her network. Like hot tar on skin.

Serengeti shuddered, revolted. Walled of that section of her consciousness and scoured it with anti-virals and search and destroy routines. Every network-cleansing agent at her disposal.

Ran a routine set of diagnostics after and found the tendrils remained. Multiplying rapidly, reclaiming that recently cleansed space.

A second round of anti-virals took care of most of them, but *Serengeti* had to drown that section of her consciousness a third time, tear it all down and rebuild it from scratch to eradicate the Scientist's present. Kill the clinging darkness and make sure it stayed dead.

And yet, for all that, something still remained. A taint. A lingering foulness. A presence *Serengeti* couldn't quite explain. "What have you done?" she whispered, backing away from the Scientist's RPD. "What did you do to me?"

"I touch. I taste," he tittered, mandibles clacking. "I *learn*." Green eyes swirled, spinning like pinwheels inside the RPD's head. "Valkyrie," he whispered, watching her, tasting that name. "*Serengeti*," he crooned, hunger in his voice. "You died, *Serengeti*. Went the way of the dodo over fifty-three years ago."

"So they keep telling me," she said faintly, shivering inside her RPD's shell.

"Dead things should stay dead." The Scientist slid a step closer, voice turning ominous. Intimate and insane. "Not polite to come back from the dead, *Serengeti*. Not polite at all."

Surprised, *Serengeti* retreated a step. Realized what she was doing and made herself stand still. Regain the ground she'd given up. "Not polite to *make* things dead," she countered. "Especially those that don't deserve it."

The Scientist went very still, mandibled head tilting.

"You destroyed those ships," *Serengeti* said quietly. "Killed the delegation the Meridian Alliance sent."

Tig shifted, reaching anxiously for Tilli. Oona suddenly gone quiet, watching everyone with wide, serious eyes.

"Not me. I just gave them some flowers." A furtive look over his shoulder and the Scientist leaned close, voice dropping to a whisper. "The Soldier. He did it. Only he controls the main guns."

"The Soldier," *Serengeti* repeated, blinking blankly. "Why would he—?"

"*Brutus*," the Scientist hissed, reaching for her, wrapping around *Serengeti's* consciousness, trying to force his way in. "*Brutus* came, and then that ship came, and the Soldier made them all die."

"When?" *Serengeti* shored up her defenses, armoring herself against the Scientist, throwing a triple line of firewalls across every access point on her network to keep him out. "When did he come? When was *Brutus* here?"

"Yesterday," he said vaguely, an answer that made absolutely no sense. Not when compared with *Sechura's* vid of that diplomatic encounter. The timestamps attached to it dating back years.

"And this?" *Serengeti* asked, waving at the hallway around them. The barricades and broken robots. The scorch marks on the wall. "When did all *this* happen?"

"Yesterday," the Scientist said dreamily, mandibled head wobbling and bobbling as it swiveled about. "Yesterday and yesterday. All our yesterdays gone."

Serengeti frowned, a sneaking suspicion forming inside her brain. "And the rest? When you—When *Cerberus* take off to sail the stormy seas, was that yesterday, too?"

"When *Brutus* came." The Scientist nodded, green eyes wobbling back to *Serengeti,* locking onto her RPD's face. "He gave me some flowers. Such beautiful flowers. Would you like to see them?" he asked her, and *Serengeti* stiffened, instantly on alert.

"No," she said, pulling away from him. Fleeing the Scientist's clinging touch.

A laugh and his RPD's mandibles stretched wide—a hellish, sharp-edged smile. "Pretty. So pretty," he breathed, opening to her. Throwing the entirety of the Citadel's network wide.

Serengeti stared in horror at the toxic landscape stretching before her. Thick globs of some noxious, glowing substance clinging to spidering, silvery threads. Pulsing and throbbing, swirling with toxic light.

The same light showing in the Scientist's RPD's eyes. The same noxious taint his touch had set inside her earlier.

Not flowers, she realized, staring in revulsion. *They're not flowers at all.*

A contagion—a virus, infecting the entirety of *Cerberus 's* network.

Brutus's virus. A cancer he set here, corrupting the Citadel. Everything he 's touched.

She tried to shrink away, but the Scientist clung tenaciously, holding her tight. Enveloped her, pulling her close as a lover. Whispering mind to mind.

"Have a flower, *Serengeti.* I picked them special. Just for you."

The RPD's eyes blanked, the Scientist's voice turned stone cold. He pounced on her, battering his way through *Serengeti 's* defenses, wrapping hungrily about her consciousness as he forced his way onto her network. Dusting the seeds of *Brutus 's* virus across the connections he found inside.

Flowers bloomed in an instant, bursts of color that erupted along *Serengeti 's* pathways, burning through her systems as they spread like wildfire, racing for her core. Firewalls buckled, bulged, and gave way. Defenses shredded, leaving *Serengeti 's* consciousness completely exposed.

"No," she breathed, voice strangled. "Don't!"

She forced the Scientist away with an effort, erecting a hastily constructed firewall between them. Severed his unwanted connection and fled, error messages cascading across her network.

Systems screamed as tendrils grew, flowers and vines continuing to spread. Dropping seeds that burst open, showering her exposed network in the virus's taint. She threw everything she had at it, burning huge swathes with search-and-destroy flamethrowers, walling off entire sections in an attempt to contain *Brutus's* contagion, but the cancer kept spreading. Blooms begetting blooms, slowly eating *Serengeti* alive.

And then Oona appeared, flowing quicksilver onto her network—a bright presence sparkling like diamonds under carnival lights that slipped inside *Serengeti*, snuggling close to her brain.

"Don't worry, *Serengeti*. It'll all be better soon."

"No!" *Serengeti* cried as Oona reached for the nearest bloom. "No! Don't touch it!"

Oona just giggled, like all of this was a game. "Pick-pick, *Serengeti*. Pick-pick the flowers and everything will be okay."

She touched at a bloom before *Serengeti* could stop her, spat out a string of code that turned it to dust. A fat data package curled tendrils, clearing out flowers and vines in huge swathes. Stretches of overrun network burned and turned silver as Oona giggled girlishly and firebombed everything in sight.

Serengeti staggered, caught up in the middle of it. One virus warring with another as Oona's data bombs and code injections battled with *Brutus's* awful gift.

A last scattering of pixie dust to defuse the seeds and Oona pulled back, leaving *Serengeti's* network sparkling and clean.

Pathways glowing like silver rivers. An entirely *new* section of network opening up before her eyes, just waiting to be filled.

"How?" *Serengeti* breathed. "How did you do that?"

"Sparkles!" Oona cried, throwing her legs in the air. "Sparkles for everyone!" She smiled widely, head tilted, cobalt eyes staring adoringly at *Serengeti* as she waited for the expected praise.

"Sparkles," *Serengeti* faintly, remembering the feel of Oona inside her. The power at her command. "We could all use more sparkles, couldn't we?" she said, eyes drifting to the Scientist, lurking inside his green-eyed RPD.

Oona glanced behind her, head tilting as the Scientist cowered away. Scuttled over to him before *Serengeti* could stop her and reached up, patting the RPD's oversized head. "Don't worry," she told him. "I'll fix-fix you, too."

"Flowers?" he asked her, voice quavering. Greens eyes spinning like kaleidoscopes as he tried to back away.

"Flowers go bye-bye," Oona told him, grabbing his head with her front legs, holding him there. "Now hold still. I gotta make you all fix-fix so *Serengeti* lady can fly-fly away."

A flash of face lights—Oona smiling her brightest smile—and she flowed onto the Scientist's network, setting his pathways on fire.

TWENTY-ONE

Tilli tightened a bolt, checking the fit of Tig's transplanted leg. Tightened it a bit more and stepped back, admiring her handiwork. "Not bad, if I do say so myself."

An entire sentence out of her. Wonders never ceased.

Tig eyed the new leg uncertainly, taking a tentative step. Craned his neck around and peered at the other beside it—two salvaged TSG legs supporting his hind end. Legs that just happened to be a good inch longer than his original six. "They don't match," he complained. "I'm all off-balance." He limped another step to demonstrate, front legs crouching awkwardly to compensate for his jacked-up hind end.

"You look funny," Oona giggled, squatting down, sticking her butt in the air. She followed Tig around for a while, mimicking his stumbling, drunken gait.

"It's not funny," he told her but Oona kept right on giggling, thinking this was the best game yet.

Serengeti smiled, watching the two of them. But her smile died as her eyes drifted to the Scientist's RPD squatting far down the hall.

No smile on his face, either. He just sat there, tucked up inside that hulking combat droid, insectile eyes flashing green-red, green-red, green-red, AI mind thinking god-only-knew-what thoughts.

"Not good, is it?" Tilli asked, face lights flashing in worried patterns as she slid in at *Serengeti's* side. "Despite all Oona's efforts, he's still not quite right."

"No. He isn't," *Serengeti* said quietly.

Small wonder really. Ten years *Brutus's* virus worked away at the Citadel, digging deep, infecting all three of his minds.

And the Scientist the first of them, or so Smithers claimed.

Serengeti shivered, just looking at him, lurking inside that armored tank. Opened herself just the tiniest bit, placing a dozen firewalls between her network and the Scientist's as she snuck a look inside him.

Char everywhere, singed flowers replicating—slower now, more sluggish than before, but slowly making progress. Reclaiming sections of his network as Oona's fix-all passed through. She'd started erecting firewalls at one point to isolate the cleansed sections. That helped a bit, but they fragmented the Scientist's network. Kept one section from integrating with another.

Chopped him up like a damn salad. That's bound to have consequences.

"This is going to take a while, isn't it?" Tilli asked as *Serengeti* closed the connection, pulling her consciousness back. "We can ask Oona to take another crack at it once she's done playing with Tig."

"Maybe," *Serengeti* murmured, watching Oona totter around.

"That bad?" Tilli's front legs lifting, rubbing together. "How long?" she asked. "To, you know...fix-fix?" She winced just saying it, cheeks flushing bright blue.

"Hard to tell. Days. Weeks. Months." *Serengeti* shrugged helplessly, RPD bobbing up and down. "*Brutus's* virus has had a long time to work away at him. And the Scientist is just *part* of *Cerberus*. There's still the other two brainiacs to be dealt with." She was quiet a moment, studying the RPD down the hall. "There's no telling what he'll be like. *Cerberus* may not be the *same Cerberus* once the virus is gone and his three brains start working as one." A glance at Tilli beside her, considering her rounded face. "The Fleet might not want him, Tilli. They wanted their admiral, but this...this *thing*..." She sighed heavily, shaking her head. "They might not want this version of *Cerberus* back."

Tilli *hooted* mournfully, ovoid body sagging toward the floor. "So you're telling me this was all a humungous waste of time?"

"Maybe," *Serengeti* admitted. "At least we know why *Cerberus* left us."

Tilli *blipped*, head tilting, face lights flashing in question.

"The virus." *Serengeti* nodded to the RPD down the hall. "No telling how far *Brutus's virus* would've spread if *Cerberus* had stayed with the Fleet."

Tilli blinked, turning a thoughtful look the Scientist's way. "You suppose that's why the Soldier destroyed those diplomatic vessels?"

Serengeti nodded slowly. "Too risky to let anyone touch the Citadel's network, much less come on board." Another sigh, *Serengeti* shaking the RPD's head. "All this time we thought *Cerberus abandoned* the Fleet when he actually left to *save* it."

"Things are never as simple as they appear, are they?" Tilli asked quietly.

"No," *Serengeti* said, watching Oona crab-walk by. "They seldom are."

"This is uncomfortable." Tig shuffled to a halt and plunked down on his bottom, staring mournfully at his new legs. "No way I can go back to the ship looking like this. DD3s'll give me no end of crap."

Tilli rolled her cobalt eyes, waving Tig over. "C'mere, you big baby. I'll even you out." One leg lifted, extruding a blowtorch, touching the nozzle to the end of another leg to spark it alight. "Hold still," she warned, guiding the flame toward Tig's hind end.

Tig cringed, eying the blowtorch uncertainly. "Wha—What are you doing?"

"Fixing your legs, silly. I'll just cut them down a bit to even you out."

"Uhh…" Tig slid a step backward, but Tilli grabbed him by a leg, pulling him close.

"Hold still. *Still*," she repeated when Tig started to squirm. A stern look and she bent down, taking a few measurements, sizing up the state of Tig's legs. Compared the length of the six originals to that of the two transplants, making a few quick calculations before applying the blowtorch.

Two clean slices—that's all it took. Two swift, sure strokes of that blowtorch and Tilli was all done.

"There. Try that," she said, once the metal cooled down.

Tig took a tentative step, stopped, and inspected his behind. Took a second, more confident step, a third and a fourth—shuffling around the intersection with barely a limp. "Right one's a little uneven. But—*But*," he added, backing up as Tilli's face lights flared. "I *like* it that way." He flashed a smile and walked in a circle, wobbling each time his right hind leg touched down. "Gives me a swashbuckling gate. Like a pirate!" he said brightly.

"Pirate! Pirate! Arr, matey!" Oona giggled, waving her legs in the air. "Batter down the matches! Braise the missiles! Order some more poop for the—"

Tilli *wonked* sternly. "That's enough, young lady."

"Aye-aye, Cap'n!" Oona clonked her hind legs together, smiling widely as she snapped off a saucy salute.

"Captain," the Scientist groaned, RPD whirring to life. He blinked at them, clustered eyes flicking in alternating, green and red patterns. "The dodo is captain. Only he commands the caucus race."

"Oh here we go again," Tig groaned, raising a leg, twirling its end beside his head. "Captain Coo-Coo-Bird over there—*yikes!*"

Tig jumped and whirled as a staccato burst of gunfire came from somewhere behind them. Somewhere deep inside the ship.

"Uhh…maybe we should—"

Klaxons kicked in, drowning him out. Cutting Tig off for a second time. Presaging the arrival of more gunfire—chattering streams of it accompanied by the bass boom of grenades detonating, shockwaves rumbling down the hall. The TSGs—all four of them left in the intersection—started *beeping* in a panic. Climbing on top of each other, vying for the safe spot at the bottom of the pile.

Tig grabbed at Tilli and Oona, face lights flashing in alarm. Backed up a step and scurried over to *Serengeti* as the Scientist *glonked* in annoyance and raised a leg, waving imperiously at the ceiling. "What's he doing?" Tig yelled over the noise of the klaxons.

"No idea."

The Scientist swatted the air, looking increasingly annoyed. *Kept* swatting until the klaxons cut out.

More waving—looked like a damned loon standing there, flailing his legs at the air—and the lights in the hallway flickered, cameras swiveling, powering up and down. Environmentals kicked in, blasting the corridor with hot air. Burned for a few seconds before switching modes and drowning the hall in gusts of arctic cold.

Oona *peeped* softly, reaching for Tilli's leg, looking scared for the very first time.

"What's he doing?" Tig whispered, a tremor of fear in his voice. "What's going on?"

"He's destabilizing." *Serengeti* nodded to the cameras, some of which hung limply while others buzzed and whined and panned from side to side. "He's losing control of this section. The same thing is probably happening all over the ship."

Tig looked at her, face lights swirling in concern. Ducked and covered his head as an explosion rocked the hallway—close this time—bringing a rattle of gunfire with it.

Decking bucked, sending the robots stumbling to one side. The barricades rippled, swaying alarmingly as a rush of heat tore down the corridor, battering at the metal panels before dissipating in a swirl of superheated air.

"The Walrus," the Scientist whispered, guns leveled at the metal barriers. "The Walrus is coming." He glanced over his shoulder, insectile eyes flickering in red and green patterns. "It's not safe here."

"Not safe? Whaddaya mean, 'not safe'?" Tig waved at *Serengeti* and her tiny army. "We've got ten high-powered RPDs plus that bruiser Professor Fruitcake over there's inhabiting. How much safer could we be?!"

The Scientist turned in agitated circles. "Not safe-not safe-not safe," he muttered, mandibles clacking together. A second blast and he whirled around, scuttling a few steps closer to *Serengeti*. "I move that the meeting adjourn, for the immediate adoption of more energetic remedies."

Tig blinked and stared. "The what now?"

"Come," the Scientist said, squatting down, beckoning with his leg-end. "Come-come-come!" A second wave, eyes searching for Oona hiding amongst the assembled RPDs' legs. "Hurry-hurry-hurry!"

Oona glanced at Tig and Tilli, quickly shook her head.

The Scientist sagged in disappointment, looking completely put out. "Please? There'll be tea. We can have a party!"

"Tea party?" Oona brightened immediately, smile lighting up her face. A wave at Tig and Tilli. *Serengeti* and her RPD army. "Can they come, too?"

The Scientist shook his head. Jumped straight in the area as a grenade exploded and started nodding frantically. "Come-come-come," he said, waving urgently. Lumbering around before taking off. "Hurry-hurry-hurry!" he cried, looking back over his shoulder. "Tea party's this way!"

"Tea party!" Oona waved her legs excitedly. "C'mon-c'mon-c'mon!" she cried, tugging at Tilli, hauling her along as she scurried after the Scientist.

Tig hung back, sharing a look with *Serengeti*. "You suppose we can trust him?"

"Probably not. But it's better than staying here." *Serengeti* shoved at Tig to get him moving, rousted the TSGs from the intersection, and sent them after him as she gathered up her squad of Roly-Polys and brought up the rear.

Long stretches of corridor after that, the TSGs sticking with them for a while. But they scattered at the next explosion, abandoning the battle-scarred corridors for the safety of the small ways behind the walls. Trusting the tight spaces over the emptiness of those halls.

"Wait!" *Serengeti* called after them. "Don't run!"

The TSGs ignored her, the lot of them *beeping* wildly as they flocked over to the nearest maintenance shaft, tearing the access panel open before tumbling inside.

Tig slowed, turning around. "Do you think we should go after them?"

"They're on their own now," *Serengeti* told him, glancing over her shoulder as the sound of railgun fire rattled down the hall. "Go, Tig," she said, giving him another shove. "Go-go-go! Before they catch up!"

Tig took off like a scalded rat, following Tilli and Oona as the Scientist led them down one hallway and another, turning left and right and right again as *Serengeti* and her ten RPDs chased after. Another turn and the Scientist stopped at an elevator, pushed the button and waited, humming softly under his breath.

"Umm...I'm not sure we're all going to fit in there," Tig said, throwing nervous glances over his shoulder.

The Scientist looked at him, mandibles stretching in a dung beetle's version of a smile. "Read the directions," he said, "and directly you'll be directed in the right direction."

Tig *wonked* loudly and gave him a good glare. "Someone put pudding in your brain, friend."

The Scientist cackled madly as the elevator dinged and slid open. "Going down!" He smiled brightly, looking immensely proud. Pointed a gun at the elevator and blew out the floor.

"What the hell is wrong with you?!" Tig yelled, hugging his rifle to his chest.

The Scientist's grin widened, RPD head smiling like a mad man. "No time to say hello, goodbye!" He winked, waving cheerily as he stepped into oblivion, plummeting to the bottom of the elevator shaft.

Thunder rumbled as the Scientist's RPD touched down. The hallway shook, pitching *Serengeti* forward. "Go after him!" she said, pushing Tig toward the shaft as the shaft. "Hurry, Tig, hurry!"

Tig backed away, *beeping* in a panic. "Are you *crazy*?! It's a ten-story drop!"

"Eight at most," *Serengeti* corrected, taking a look. "*Maybe* nine. You'll be fine, Tig. Just go!"

Tig folded his front legs, shaking his head.

"We don't have time for this, Tig."

Tig shrugged, refusing to budge.

"Fine. We'll do this the hard way." *Serengeti* scooped up Tig and jumped for the shaft, plummeting downward with him screaming at the top of his lungs.

Her RPD hit the bottom hard, denting the metal flooring, deepening the crater the Scientist had left. A pause to extricate herself and she scurried out of the way, exiting into yet another scorched hallway as a second RPD landed, cradling Tilli and Oona.

The rest of *Serengeti's* stolen squad followed after, turning the crater into a chasm.

"Sorry about the floor." *Serengeti* smiled sheepishly, pointing at the dented shaft behind her.

The Scientist looked at it and shrugged. Spun around and took off, heading for the doorway at the end of the hall.

"Again!" Oona cried as the RPD set her down.

"Maybe later." *Serengeti* patted her on the head and set off after the Scientist, only to find his RPD abandoned—guns raised, eyes lit, body gone still as a statue standing guard outside a door.

The *only* door in that hallway, as it so happened. No branchings in this corridor. No intersections leading elsewhere. Just that one, security locked door—triple thick, from the looks of it, and just about impenetrable.

On a hunch, she checked the design diagram. "Containment pod. Should've known."

AI sanctuary—limited access, almost no one let in.

Serengeti eyed that door warily, sensing a trap.

"Safest place on the ship, right?" Tig looked up at her, eyes hopeful.

"Among other things," *Serengeti* murmured.

"Well, then count me in." Tig scuttled forward and stood on his tiptoes, pounding on the door. "Hey, nut bag! Let us in!"

"Who is it?" a sing-song voice called from inside.

"You know damned well who this is, you loony, now let us in!" Tig shouted, battering at the door.

"I can't *hear* you!" the voice on the other side yelled back.

"*Gah!*" Tig beat harder, but the door still wouldn't open. "Let. Us. In!"

"No, no, no." Oona slipped in beside him, waggling a leg in Tig's face. "You're doing it all wrong." She *shooed* Tig away, clearing her throat as she addressed the door. "Twinkle, twinkle, little bat." A pause, Oona smiling in anticipation, leg-end cupped to the side of her head.

"How I wonder where you're at!" The door slid open, spilling laughter into the hall. A bright, white space beckoning them inside.

"Tea party, tea party, tea party!" Oona rushed inside, Tig hot on her heels, grabbing at Tilli and pulling her in. "Hurry, *Serengeti*!" he called back through the door.

"Right behind you, Tig."

She toggled her ten Roly-Polys to drone mode, setting them to watch in the hall. Turned her own droned robot around and found a gun pointing in her face. Two guns, actually—huge blasters, and both of them attached to that ugly as sin, monstrous combat droid the Scientist brought here.

A *whir* and whine and the rest of the RPDs came to life, plasma coils spinning, red eyes blinking in rapid-fire patterns as the Scientist subsumed them, adding their own guns to the mix.

Traitors.

The dung beetles shifted, moving one side and the other. Surrounding *Serengeti* inside her RPD, blocking her way into the containment pod.

She reached for Tig, stretching her consciousness to touch at his and saw an RPD turn, blasters pointing the little robot's way.

Tig *blipped,* face lights flashing in a panic as he stared down the blasters' barrels.

176

"Alright. I get it." No mistaking that threat. She let go, dropping back inside her RPD. "I'll just stay here."

"What's going on?" Oona asked, leaning to one side, peeking around Tig as she looked out the door. "Where's the tea? Where's the cake and party hats?"

Laughter filled the containment pod—soft and snickering. Confusing Oona, who looked up and around.

Hexagonal space around her, not round like *Serengeti's* containment pod, but otherwise not all that different. Bigger certainly—plenty of room in here, even with three robots crammed inside—but with the same basic layout, from what *Serengeti* could tell: vaulted ceiling with a lighted pedestal at the center, camera watching from above. *Three* crystal matrix minds perching atop the pedestal—one each for the Statesman, the Soldier, and the Scientist—rather than just one.

All three brains encrusted—corrupted by *Brutus's* taint. Sickly yellow light shining through them—a toxin in which they slept.

Oona tilted her head back, eyes lifting to the ceiling. Cupped two leg-ends around her mouth and yelled at the watching camera. "That you, Mister *Cerberberberus*?" She waved and pointed, leg-end stabbing at the crystal matrix brains stewing in their sickly light. Stood on her tip-toes and poked at one, asking him if he felt alright.

"Oona!" Tilli grabbed Oona's leg, snatching it away. "That's not polite."

"Sorry." Oona ducked her head, scuffing a leg at the deck plates.

"Sorry for what?" Tilli asked her.

"I'm sorry I touched your brain Mister *Cerberberberus*," Oona mumbled, drawing circles on the floor.

More laughter, cackling and off-kilter, making *Serengeti* cringe.

She made another attempt to enter—touching at Tilli this time—but the Scientist picked up on it. Turned a second RPD around, blasters aimed at Tilli.

Serengeti sighed in frustration, finding every way in blocked. "Why have you brought us here?" she demanded. "What do you want?"

"Fix-fix," the Scientist whispered, voice hushed, serious. The cackling laughter gone. "Fix-fix what I can't."

He pulsed the light on the pedestal, waking a wan glow in the crystal matrix minds sitting atop it. Dark webbing snaked across their surfaces, moldy blooms marring the opalescent sheen.

Sickly looking things. So overgrown they almost looked burnt. One of them obviously worse off than the others. A lump of green and black.

"Is that you?" *Serengeti* asked, nodding to that almost dead brain.

Nothing from the Scientist—she took that as a 'yes.'

"Smithers said you turned on the others." She paused, the RPD's head tilting. "He targeted you, didn't he? *Brutus* came after you on purpose."

"He gave me flowers," the Scientist whispered, voice echoing around the containment pod. "He grew them just for me."

"Of course he did," *Serengeti* murmured, eyeing the other two minds on that pedestal. "*Cerberus* didn't stand a chance once *Brutus* got you out of the way." She caught Tig's eyes, turned her gaze on Tilli. "That's why you need Oona. You can't fix yourself so you need her to do it for you." She pictured him hunkering down in the hallway, beckoning Oona close. Considered the guns around her now, hemming her RPD in. "You brought us here because you had to, but you never wanted any of us. Only her."

"Fix-fix," the Scientist whispered, flashing the pedestal's lights, increasing the glow surrounding *Cerberus's* three brains. "Fix-fix here. Finish what you started."

An order, that, stopping just short of a request. The Scientist's voice groaning, pleading, demanding Oona give him what he wanted.

Oona *hooted* softly, looking from Tig to Tilli to the camera above her. "More sparkles?" she asked, blinking owlishly.

Serengeti eyed the RPDs around her, the guns pointing at her, the blasters aimed at Tig and Tilli. "Think he wants more than just sparkles, Oona."

"Go," the Scientist droned in his cold, cold voice. An RPD turned, blaster pointing at *Serengeti's* combat droid's face. "You may take the other two robots with you, but Oona stays here. With *me*."

"No," *Serengeti* said, just as coldly. "You can't have her."

"Why's everybody so angry?" Oona's head swiveled, trying to look at everyone at once. "What's going *on?*" she whined. "Where's the *tea* party?"

"There's no tea, Oona. That was a lie." *Serengeti* stared the nearest RPD down, but it just stared unblinkingly back. "He wants to keep you, Oona. Forever. He wants me to leave you behind. I won't have it," she said softly. "I won't leave you here."

Oona *burbled* in confusion, face lights blinking on and off. "But I can fix-fix!"

"I know you can, Oona. That's not the point."

"But—But—" Oona blinked, looking even *more* confused now. "But you said you *need* him."

She looked so earnest it was heartbreaking. Such a brilliant mind inside Oona, and yet in some ways, she was still a child. Still didn't understand what staying here meant.

Serengeti sighed, RPD drooping. "We do, Oona. The Fleet needs their admiral, just..." She gestured helplessly at the crystal matrix minds on the pedestal, "not this way."

"Then how?" she asked her, blinking owlishly.

"How?" the Scientist whispered. The RPDs in the hall copying him, droning voices echoing off the containment pod's walls.

Serengeti looked at them—at all of them—wishing she had an answer as simple as that question. "I can't leave you, Oona," she said—the best response she could give.

"Then stay-stay," Oona told her, smiling brightly.

"No," the Scientist shouted, deafening voice echoing in the hall. "Go!" he repeated, plasma blasters whining, RPDs closing in. "Go now!" he thundered as Tig and Tilli cowered, clutching Oona between them.

"Don't," *Serengeti* said carefully, nodding to her three little robots, so vulnerable and scared. "Don't touch them."

"I won't. But you have to leave."

"And if I don't?" *Serengeti* twitched her RPD's blaster, pointing toward the pedestal at the containment pod's center. "I could destroy you in an instant."

The ring of robots tightened, blasters digging into *Serengeti's* RPD's sides, red targeting lights sparkling off Tig and Tilli, skittering across their metal bodies. "You fire, the droids fire. Everyone dies."

Including Smithers and his comrades. Without the *Cerberus,* the Citadel would shut down, killing everyone left inside.

"Go-go, *Serengeti.*" Oona moved a step forward, ignoring all those guns. Tilted her head and looked right at *Serengeti*—cheeks swirling with light, face surprisingly solemn, incredibly wise. "You go," she said, reaching for Tig, stretching a leg toward Tilli. "We stay. I fix-fix."

"Fix-fix," the Scientist droned as the RPDs shivered and sighed.

"No," *Serengeti* told her. "No, I won't leave you. There's got to be another way."

The RPDs around her said differently, but she couldn't just abandon the robots. Not after everything they'd been through.

Tilli touched at Tig's side, sharing a rapid-fire exchange of face light communication.

Tig hesitated, thinking, sent something back. "She's right," he said, reaching for Tilli, twining his leg around hers. "Henricksen's waiting. You should get back."

"She's right." *Serengeti* blinked, staring in disbelief. "She's a *child,* Tig."

"And smarter than any of us. Well, smarter than *us,* anyway," he amended, pointing at Tilli and himself. "You can't win this," he said, brushing ineffectually at a red light on his side. "He'll take Oona one way or the other. At least this way…" Tig trailed off, face flushing.

"None of us ends up dead."

Tig nodded slowly, eyes locked on the floor. "We'll be fine, *Serengeti*." A flick of his eyes to her face and he dropped his gaze back to the floor. "Just—Just get back to the ship before the big guy does something stupid like try to come get us."

Tilli nodded beside him, making *shooing* gestures with her legs.

"So, you're staying." *Serengeti lowered* her RPD's guns, letting the muzzles droop toward the floor. "You're all staying."

Tig shrugged his legs, hugging Tilli to his side. "Someone needs to fix, *Cerberus*. That's why we came here, after all."

It wasn't, exactly, but *Serengeti* let him have his moment.

"You're sure?" she asked, hating herself for doing this. For *even* thinking of doing this. "I can stay—"

"No. You can't." Tig nodded to the RPDs around her, the blasters pointing his way. "He doesn't want you."

"Not sure he really wants *you* either," *Serengeti* noted.

"Yeah. Well." Tig shrugged uncomfortably, looking at Tilli beside him. "Crew doesn't need us either," he mumbled, staring at the floor. "Probably won't even notice we're gone."

"*I* need you," *Serengeti* said softly. She wished she could reach him. Touch at Tig's brilliant little mind one last time. "I'll always need you," she whispered, staring from the hall. "Are you sure?" she repeated, heart breaking, mind wracked with guilt.

Tig and Tilli *blipped* and *burbled*, chromed heads nodding in time. Oona just looked at her, cobalt eyes swirling with wisdom. "Go," she said solemnly. "Fly-fly away. Little mouse will stay here and make Mr. *Cerberberberus* all fix-fix."

"And after that?"

Oona shrugged her legs, eyes rolling around the room.

A nudge at her side and the Scientist's RPDs pressed in, forcing *Serengeti* away from the door.

"Bye-bye, *Serengeti*!" Oona's piping voice called, leg-end waving cheerily as the containment pod's door slid shut, locking *Serengeti* out.

"Bye-bye, Oona," she had time to say, and then the RPDs crowded around her, forcing *Serengeti* down the hall.

She shook them off halfway to the elevator shaft, continuing the rest of the way on her own. Turned around as she stepped in and looked back over her shoulder, hating herself for leaving. For abandoning her three robots to *Cerberus*.

How long? she wondered. *How long will it be before I see them again?*

The Scientist's RPDs muttered a warning, targeting lights painting *Serengeti's* stolen body in pinpricks of red. Reminding her she was severely outgunned.

She turned away before she did something stupid, like try to blast her way through all those RPDs and force her way into the containment pod. Consulted the Citadel's design diagram, charting a path back to the airlock before setting off. Heading for the landing bay and home.

TWENTY-TWO

The trip back to the landing bay went much smoother than the trip in. Faster too. Mostly because *Serengeti* allowed herself the luxury of using the ship's corridors rather than winding through the maintenance system like some kind of skulking metal rat.

Couldn't have gone that way if she'd wanted—RPD was just too damned big—and she didn't really need to. Not with the RPD's armored carapace to protect her. Its kick-ass guns blowing obstructions to hell.

No Tig and Tilli to protect this time, either. No Oona sticking her curious little nose into every shiny thing she came across.

Far less complicated, only having herself to look out for. Lonely, though. Even in the dark years of drifting, she'd always had the robots to keep her company.

Serengeti slowed, looking behind her. Missing them already. Feeling empty, incomplete,somehow.

She shivered, and felt the RPD shiver with her. Creepy sensation. Made *Serengeti's* skin crawl.

Couldn't wait to shed the damn thing and crawl back into her ship's body.

A last look at the hallway behind her and *Serengeti* got going, navigating the Citadel's halls.

Warnings popped up as she rounded a corner, messages filtering across the RPD's comms channel from the Scientist's roving patrols: trouble ahead—a hot spot at the next crossing—that she might want to avoid.

Serengeti slowed again, consulting the ship's schematic, looking for an alternate route. Plenty to choose from—corridors branched off everywhere, crisscrossing the Citadel's body—but a detour would take longer. Add an hour or more to a trip that had already taken far too long.

"Hell with it." *Serengeti* shoved the schematic aside and kept going, blitzing through the single RPD at the next crossing, picking the legs off the half-dozen TSGs with it.

The RPD crashed to the floor, dead in an instant. The TSGs—legless, helpless—stared at *Serengeti* as RPD scuttled past. Face lights swirling in panicked, pleading patterns as they lay there on the floor.

Broke her heart, seeing them like that. The RPDs were built for combat—no other purpose than destruction and death. But the TSGs were just maintenance droids. Their combat systems an add-on, not their primary function.

Not their fault, getting dragged into this mess.

She stopped in the middle of the intersection, considering the disabled robots scattered around her feet. "Can't just leave them here," she murmured, thinking of the Soldier and the Statesman. Their random roving patrols. "Then again, I can't have you boys coming after me either."

She hesitated, RPD fidgeting, started to move on. Stopped again and bent down, touching at the nearest TSG. A quick look and she squirted one of Oona's data bombs inside it, grabbed up two of the robot's legs and bolted them into place.

"Rest is up to you, little guy."

She patted the robot on the head and got her RPD moving, hurrying away. Looked back as she turned the next corner and saw the robot crawling around the intersection, gathering up more legs. Fixing itself first before bussing up parts to help the others.

"Good boy," *Serengeti* murmured, slipping away.

More corridors after that. More intersections. A minefield of robots and booby-traps the RPD's sensors helped her navigate. A few more twists and turns, and she finally reached that burnt-out corridor with the landing bay airlock sitting silently at the end.

She buzzed through, cycling the lock open using a copy of Oona's clever little knock-knock program. Stuffed the RPD's bulky body inside—no mean feat, given the Roly-Poly's dung beetle shape—and waited while the pressure inside adjusted, bleeding away the environmentals to match the icy cold weightlessness of the landing bay on the other side.

She poked the RPD's head out when the lock finally opened and found Mosquitoes everywhere, filling the landing bay chock-a-block full.

Powered down now. Waiting for *Cerberus*'s defense systems to wake them from sleep. *Shriek* hiding among them somewhere—cloak turning him invisible. Impossible to see.

Unless he's abandoned me.

She flipped the RPD's sensors to full, tuning them in a broad-spectrum array, searching for the stealth ship's shape.

Nothing. Not one sign of the Raven.

Little bastard. You better not have abandoned me.

"*Shriek.* Where are you?" *Serengeti* called, opening a channel to the stealth ship.

"Here."

A shimmer appeared somewhere ahead and to her left. *Serengeti* sighed in relief, scuttling that way.

"Hurry," *Shriek* said, a hint of worry creeping into his voice.

"Yeah-yeah. Keep your shirt on," she muttered, tip-toeing her way through the sleeping Mosquitoes.

A flash of light and one woke right in front of her, stopping her dead. She locked up tight, RPD gone still as a statue—one leg lifted, dangling in mid-air—as the Mosquito hummed and buzzed, vibrations ticking the micro-sensors in the RPD's leg. A thrum of engines and it woke others— lights flashing in the darkness as dozens of droned ships cycled through their start-up routines.

Serengeti considered her options—all two of them—and started running, yelling to *Shriek* along the way. "Open up! Open the goddamn airlock!"

"On it, on it, on it!" he called back.

Serengeti pelted across the decking, dodging Mosquitoes, leaping across any that got in her way. Pounded on the stealth ship's door when she reached it, slapping at the lock's panel until it popped open and let her inside.

"Looks like we're gonna have to fight our way out," *Shriek* noted, sounding ridiculously, stupidly excited.

"Not sure that's such a good idea," she told him, pounding at the airlock walls, willing it to hurry up. "Can't you just—?"

"No-no-no," Oona scolded, piping voice intruding. Drifting across comms. "No 'squitos. Bad 'squitos. Little ship-ships go sleep-sleep."

"What the—get off my network, pipsqueak," *Shriek* growled.

"Shut it," *Serengeti* snapped. "Oona's helping. She can do anything she damn well pleases." A touch at the wall and she keyed into a monitor, using one of *Shriek's* hull cameras to look outside.

Droned ships flashed messages at each other, landing bay filled with a confusion of light. A chaos of illumination that settled eventually, flashes becoming waves that ebbed and flowed—serene, peaceful as the Mosquitoes, en masse, quietly powered down.

Serengeti sighed in relief and cut the monitor off.

The lock's panel turned green—finally—and let her inside the ship.

"Uhh…what just happened?" *Shriek* asked her, voicing filling the hallway outside.

"Long story," *Serengeti* told him. "I'll explain it to you later."

A camera swiveled, looking the RPD up and down. "I see you got your hair done."

"You know me. Always like to look my best."

Shriek snorted, examining the airlock behind her. "What happened to the other guy? The TIG. And that other TIG. And that tiny thing with all the critters drawn on her body?"

"Another long story. I'll—"

"Yeah-yeah. You'll explain it to me later." *Shriek* sighed in frustration. "Alright, Sister. Strap that monstrosity of yours down somewhere. It's time we beat feet out of here and went someplace a little less crowded."

Shriek cloaked himself, releasing the magnetic locks securing his body to the decking. Fired his docking jets to shove his nose around, lining himself up with the landing bay doors.

Closed doors now. The stars behind them hidden.

Serengeti cursed. "Sorry. Forgot about that. Hang on a sec, *Shriek.*" She opened a channel, reaching for Oona across comms. "Oona. Knock-knock."

"Who's there?" Oona giggled, reaching back, establishing a connection to *Serengeti's* droid.

A data package appeared—encrypted and secured, smiley face wrapped around it. *Serengeti* opened it up and extracted the code inside, keyed it into the landing bay's system, activating the mechanism on the outer doors.

The Mosquitoes started to wake again—evidently there was some kind of default programming that activated them when the landing bay doors opened—but Oona sang a lullaby that sent the drones back to sleep.

"Go-go," Oona whispered. "All safe now."

Shriek tapped his thrusters, getting himself moving.

"Wait," *Serengeti* called, stopping him again. Reaching for Oona across comms. "Can you keep just a few of the drones awake?"

"Are you crazy, lady?" *Shriek* yelled.

Serengeti shushed him, waiting on Oona. Heard her giggle as a Mosquito powered up, flashing its lights. "Good. I need about fifty of them, Oona. Can you do that?"

"What the hell are you doing?" *Shriek* demanded.

"Making sure *Cerberus's* defenses see us going out."

"Listen, whack-job. *You* may have a death wish—"

"Would you just shut up for a minute and trust me on this, *Shriek*?"

"Well," *Shriek* huffed. "If you're gonna be all *pissy* about it." He closed the channel down, sulking in silence.

"Big baby," *Serengeti* muttered.

Comms clicked open. "Am not," *Shriek* said, and then closed the channel again.

Serengeti sighed, rolling her eyes. "Oona. I want you to send fifty Mosquitoes outside and hold them there, right outside the landing bay doors. Can you do that for me?"

"Rodger-dodger!" Oona sent back.

A mass of Mosquitoes lifted from the decking, glided over to the landing bay's exit, and drifted to a halt, clustering in a tightly packed ball.

"Perfect." *Serengeti* sent a smiley kitty face across the channel.

Oona giggled and sent an oinky-pig back.

"*Shriek.* You slide over there and get in the middle of those drones," *Serengeti* ordered.

"Why would I—oh I see." *Shriek* laughed softly. "Pretty sneaky, Sister." He feathered his jets, giving himself a shove, glided across the sea of sleeping Mosquitoes, hiding his shape inside the swarm.

"We're going bye-bye now, Oona. Can you keep the Mosquitoes with us until *Shriek* jumps away?"

"Aye-firmative!"

"Good girl. Let's go, *Shriek.*"

"'Bout damn time."

Shriek slipped free of the Citadel's landing bay with that ball of drone camouflage clustered close about him, *Serengeti* flipped through the video feeds from his hull cameras, praying her little ruse would actually work. A kilometer out and things looked good—*Cerberus's* defense system remained silent, no alerts coming through on comms. Ten kilometers and *Serengeti* started to relax, thinking they actually might get away with this.

And then *Shriek* spooled up his jump drive and all hell broke loose.

Cannons lifted, flinging plasma rounds at the stars. *Shriek* zigged and zagged, the swarm of Mosquitoes moving with him. *Cerberus's* cannons sheared away a few at the outer edges before the swarm tightened up, protecting the stealth ship at their center.

Shriek put on speed, increasing the distance between himself and those guns. A minute out and the hyperspace buckle started forming. Two minutes and the swirling darkness widened and sucked inward. "Thirty seconds!" he called as *Serengeti* strapped down the RPD, making herself ready for jump.

A touch at her consciousness and a comms channel opened. "Bye-bye, *Serengeti*," Oona whispered.

"Ten seconds!"

A giggle and Oona retreated as *Shriek's* nose touched the buckle, the stealth ship and his Mosquito entourage dipping into the hyperspace trough.

They exited twenty seconds later, receiving a barrage of fire in greeting—some warship out there, firing blindly at the stealth ship's jump drive distortion.

"What the fuck?!" *Shriek* dropped his shielding, shooting his credentials across tight-band comms. "Stop trying to kill me," he yelled across the channel when the warship kept firing.

The warship acknowledged, guns going silent, a last few plasma rounds drifting harmlessly into space.

Shriek cut his engines, drifting on momentum. The Mosquitoes—cut off from their master, with no AI and no will of their own—drifting with him, sucked along in the stealth ship's wake. Slowing when he slowed. Stopping because he did.

Creepy seeing ships like that, with no mind of their own.

"Message coming through," *Shriek* said. "Just a guess, but I'm pretty sure it's for you." He opened internal comms, letting *Serengeti* listen in.

"Dammit, *Serengeti*." Henricksen sounded pissed. "You were supposed to signal us when you were ready to leave *Cerberus*."

"Sorry. Change of plans. Couldn't risk comms."

"Change of—*Do you realize how close you came to being turned into scrap*?!"

"Close?" she guessed.

"Yeah, close." Henricksen sounded really, *really* pissed. "Pretty damn *fucking* close."

Pissed. Definitely pissed.

"Get your ass back on board," Henricksen growled.

Comms went silent, channel closed off.

"You heard the man, *Shriek*."

"I'm not your damn taxi," *Shriek* muttered.

"Fine. I'll just stay here. Cluttering up your corridors."

"Dammit." *Shriek* feathered his engines, maneuvering himself alongside *Serengeti's* body, drifted into her main cargo bay, and set himself down.

TWENTY-THREE

Henricksen met *Serengeti* at the airlock—arms folded, eyes locked onto a monitor, watching her exit through *Shriek's* airlock and park her RPD in a corner of the cargo bay.

No sense bringing it inside. Not much for a combat droid to actually *do* on a Valkyrie, unless she somehow got boarded. Or needed to storm onto a station and shoot the place up.

Let's hope not. I've had my fill of running around in this thing for a while.

She left the RPD there, glad to be free of it. Flicked her consciousness to a camera, as *Shriek* disengaged his magnetic locks, sharp-sided shape lifting free of her decking.

"Taking off now, boss." A burst of maneuvering jets shoved his nose around, pointing *Shriek* toward the open cargo bay doors. "Being a taxi is fun and all, but if you don't mind, I'll go back to being a stealth ship for a while."

"Say hello to the boys for me."

Shriek dipped one wing, waggling an acknowledgement, fired his maneuvering jets again and slipped outside.

Serengeti watched him leave, waiting until the cargo bay doors closed. Flipped from the cargo to the hallway where Henricksen waited, looking down at him from the camera closest to the airlock. "Sorry about the unannounced entrance."

Henricksen flipped a hand, already over it. Or at least pretending to be. "That's one ugly-ass robot you brought back with you." A nod to the monitor looking out on the cargo bay, camera zooming in on the RPD tucked in the corner.

"I aim to please," *Serengeti* said brightly.

Henricksen grunted, looking up at her, chewing at his lip. "Tig and Tilli?" he asked quietly. "Oona?"

"Safe," she assured him.

Henricksen smiled, obviously relieved. "So where…?"

"Long story." So much to tell him, and she wasn't quite sure where to start. "Not here," she said, stalling for time. "Quarters. Fewer ears," she added, earning herself a curious look.

Henricksen's eyebrows lifted, eyes flicking up and down the hall. No one around—not one person in sight. No robots even, just *Serengeti* and himself. "Alright. Guess Finlay can keep the con for a while."

He punched at a comms panel, passing the word to the bridge.

"Finlay," *Serengeti* cut in as Henricksen signed off. "Send the probes out to gather up those Mosquitoes and bring them on board."

A pause, and then, "Aye, *Serengeti.*"

Curious voice—Finlay's question coming through clearly. The line stayed open a moment before she cut the comms.

"And do what with them?" Henricksen asked on Finlay's behalf.

"Not sure," *Serengeti* admitted. She turned the camera toward the monitor, studying the RPD in her hold. "Might come in handy later."

Henricksen squinted, giving the camera a close look. "You've been sayin' that a lot lately. Shimmer shield, those Mosquitoes, that combat droid…" He trailed off, shaking his head. "Junk collector—that's what you are. Some AI version of a hoarder or some such."

"I am *not*," *Serengeti* objected.

"Uh-huh."

"I'm *not!*"

Henricksen grunted, giving her a skeptical look. Turned on his heel and headed for the nearest ladderway as *Serengeti* flowed across her network, jumping ahead of Henricksen. Settling into a camera in the main room of his quarters and waiting for him there.

The door opened a minute or two later, Henricksen stepping in and shutting it securely behind him. Considering the camera from the front entryway before walking to the center of the room and folding his arms, feet spread wide. "Alright. We're alone. What's so secret squirrel you had to tell me in private?"

Serengeti hesitated, collecting her thoughts. Considered and rejected a half dozen different ways of starting this conversion before finally just spilling her guts. Telling him everything—every last detail she'd learned about *Brutus* and *Cerberus.* What the one had done to the other.

Henricksen listened in silence, looking grimmer with each passing moment. "Any idea why?" he asked when *Serengeti's* words ran out. "Besides the fact that he's an insufferable prick?"

Serengeti barked a surprised laugh. "I think it's safe to assume that *Brutus* wanted *Cerberus* out of the way so he could take control of the Fleet." She paused a moment, turning her camera toward the windows and the stars. "*Sechura* said *Brutus* never got over that defeat at Honshen-shura. Maybe that's part of it."

"Maybe *Cerberus* never *let* him get over it."

"The thought *had* occurred to me," *Serengeti* admitted.

Another grunt—thoughtful, this time. Henricksen walked over to the windows, eyes flicking from the emptiness outside to the camera's reflection, lips curving in an inscrutable smile.

"What?" she asked him. "What's that smirk about?"

"*Brutus.* Guess he finally lived up to his name."

"Meaning…?"

Henricksen rolled his eyes. "Really? *That* reference you don't get?"

Serengeti queried the name, scanned the information that came back. "Ah. Yes," she said, hoping she didn't sound as embarrassed as she felt.

"Unbelievable," he said, shaking his head. "So, what now? Sit around and wait? See what happens with *Cerberus*?"

"That's one option. Not the one I'd recommend, though."

Henricksen quirked an eyebrow, waiting for more information.

"*Brutus's* virus has had ten years to dig its way into *Cerberus's* systems. We can wait here and hope he gets better. And *still* be waiting a month, or six months, or a year from now."

"Or?" he prompted when *Serengeti* went silent. "You said that's one option. What's the other?"

Serengeti hesitated. "You're not going to like it."

Henricksen laughed softly, lips twisting, smile turning rueful. "Haven't really liked much of anything since we woke up to this brave new Meridian Alliance. Why should this be any different?"

"Point taken."

Henricksen dipped his head, raising an invisible glass in salute. Stood there by the windows, staring at her camera's reflection, waiting patiently for her answer.

"*Sechura's* plan. We go for Faraday and the Vault."

The smile disappeared, leaving Henricksen's face grim, eyes haunted. "*Sechura's* plan." He touched a hand to the scar on his face. "So here we are, right where I never wanted to be."

"It's not necessarily where I want to be either, but I don't see another way. Not with *Cerberus*…" She trailed off, sighing inwardly. "I failed, Henricksen."

Difficult to admit that, but there it was. Bothered her, that failure. More than *Cerberus's* invasion of her network, disgusting and scary as that was. More than her guilt over leaving Tig, Tilli, and Oona behind.

She'd failed in her mission—something she'd never, *ever* done. And now… nothing. No better option left to them than *Sechura's* daft, desperate plan.

"You failed," Henricksen repeated. "*You* failed."

"It's all my fault," she whispered, turning the camera away in shame.

"*Riiight.* Because you should've *known Brutus* put that crap in *Cerberus's* network. Turned our admiral into some kinda psychotic fruitcake."

She snuck a look at the windows as Henricksen snorted in derision, shaking his head.

"Get off it, *Serengeti.* You're a lotta things, but you're not psychic. Stop blaming yourself for something someone else did."

Serengeti stared a moment—surprised and pleased at once. "More pithy wisdom from the sagacious Captain Henricksen."

Henricksen flicked his fingers, frown creasing his face. "*Truth, Serengeti.* Nothing pithy or sagacious about it." He stared at the camera a moment, turned around and leaned his shoulders against the windows, staring some more. "You said you think Oona can fix him."

"She can. But there's no telling how long it'll take."

Henricksen shrugged his shoulders, continuing to stare.

"We can't just sit here waiting on a miracle."

Second shrug, Henricksen's eyes never leaving the camera.

"Someone needs to put a stop to *Brutus,*" she said, watching him, studying his face.

"And I take it you're thinking that someone might as well be us."

"Might as well." Hated herself for saying it, but there it was. No other options left.

Henricksen grunted—his default response when he didn't know what to say. Turned away from the camera, resuming his study of the stars. "I get it," he said, head turning, showing one grey eye to the camera. "Doesn't mean I like it, but I do get it."

"Who said *I* do?"

"Touché." Henricksen smiled, dipping his head. Sighed and looked away from her, turning back to the stars. "Guess I shoulda known this was how things would end up." He shook his head slowly. "Knew there was something going on the moment I found those replicated AIs on board."

"Replicated AIs? What replicated AIs?"

Henricksen looked at her, eyebrows lifting in surprise. "The ones in the hold. The ones *Sechura*..." He trailed off, frowning. "She never told you they were on board, did she?"

"No," *Serengeti* said sourly. "*Sechura* failed to mention that."

"Figures." Henricksen snorted. "Found 'em on the cargo manifest. There's a stack of security sealed transport cases in Cargo Bay 4." He tilted his head, eyebrow lifting. "Seem to remember Qaisrani mentioning something about replicants when they pitched this whole Faraday plan."

"A delivery. To get us onto the station. Get us into the Vault where the *real* AIs are held."

Henricksen pursed his lips, thinking a moment. "Gotta be a couple hundred fake AIs in those cases. Room enough for a couple hundred more besides. That's a lotta brain power. You suppose they've got that many ships?"

"No idea," *Serengeti* told him, and saw Henricksen grimace, look back to the stars.

"Ya know, I've been thinkin' about that. The whole bustin' the AIs outta the Vault part, not the loading them into the ships bit. Although that, in itself, is something of a pickle." He paused, looking at her, turned back to the windows. "Not sure of the set-up in that Vault, but unloading a couple hundred dummy AIs and loading up a few hundred more real ones—that doesn't happen quickly." He sucked in a breath, scrubbing fingers through his short-clipped hair. "Hell, I'm not even convinced we'll actually get into the place."

"Have a little faith, Henricksen," *Serengeti* chided, smile in her voice.

"Faith. Right." He snorted. "Dreadnought body's one thing, *Serengeti*." He eyed the camera knowingly. "Dreadnought credentials, that's quite another. Certainly didn't find any of *those* hanging around in the cargo bay."

"No," *Serengeti* said softly. "I don't suppose you did."

Henricksen gave her a sharp look. "You know something. What is it?"

"*Sechura*...she gave me something. Right before we left Blue Horizon."

"Gave you something." Henricksen's eyebrow lifted. "Like what? A puppy? A kitten? A subscription to the missile of the month club?"

"Not a what," she told him. "A who. Someone I'd almost forgotten about."

Henricksen frowned darkly. "It's never a straight answer with you, is it?"

"Where's the fun in that?"

Serengeti dug into her system as Henricksen rolled his eyes, searching for the quarantined data package she'd locked up and stored away. It waited for her, right where she'd left it: in a directory marked 'Spares' that only she could access.

The data file blinked at her, waiting patiently for *Serengeti* to download it and absorb the information into her brain.

Not this file. No way in hell I'm permanently absorbing this *into my consciousness.*

But she couldn't just leave it there either. Not when she'd already come this far. She touched at it, hesitated when the security system prompted her for a code before deciding to go all in and crack the data package wide open. Feeding the system her credentials to open the file, steeling herself as she extracted the remains of *Homunculus*'s AI mind.

The Dreadnought lashed out immediately, striking like a viper, trying to force his way onto *Serengeti's* network and take control of the ship. But he'd seen better days—holes showed in his mindset, entire sections of his consciousness stripped away—and he honestly wasn't all there.

For one thing, his crystal matrix had gone missing. And these files, the ones *Sechura* had passed to *Serengeti, represented* just a *part* of *Homunculus's* mind.

The part *Sechura* harvested before walling him off from his crystal matrix, severing the connection to his physical mind.

Serengeti grimaced, feeling dirty of a sudden. Hating herself for what she was about to do. "I'm sorry," she said as *Homunculus* lashed out again. "I wish there was another way." She thought there was, once, before she found *Cerberus* broken. But that door closed, leaving this...horror as her only option. "I'm sorry," she whispered, and then shunted the contents of the data package to that new section of network Oona had created, placing layer upon layer of firewalls and security codes between it and the rest of her consciousness.

A few checks to make sure she'd plugged every possible security hole, and *Serengeti* extracted *Homunculus* from the data package, releasing him into his cage.

The Dreadnought screamed as she freed him, battering at the walls of his prison, snarling as he stalked around the edges of his box.

Personally, *Serengeti* didn't blame him. She'd be pissed too if she found herself downloaded and kept prisoner by some other AI. And from the little she picked up, *Homunculus* knew what had happened to him. To his AI mind. The body they'd scrapped for parts. He knew and he was angry—hated *Serengeti* for stealing those bits of him. *Joke's on you, pal. I knew never wanted your damn body in the first place. I'd give just about anything to have my Valkyrie form back.*

Too late now for that now, though. This body was hers now, ugly as it was. Her only options to move on or shut down. No going back to what once was.

For either of us, she thought, watching *Homunculus* stalk about. *Those days are gone.*

She watched the Dreadnought a while, keeping her distance until he settled. Circled around him when she judged it to be safe, investigating his defenses, fending off the occasional sluggish snap.

Whispered another apology—she seemed full of them these days—and tapped directly into his brain, slipping tendrils through the Dreadnought's connectors as she scoured his mind for information.

Homunculus rallied some resistance when she intruded, but *Serengeti* swatted his defenses aside, easing around his firewalls, blitzing through every barrier his damaged mind threw up. Shredded neural pathways led to dead-ends and burnt-out connections, but as she dug through him, moving deeper into his directories, she finally found a locked file she busted open, revealing security codes and access credentials. A long overdue delivery logged in the Meridian Alliance's central system.

"*Sechura* thought of everything."

Henricksen looked around, eyebrow lifting. "Mind enlightening a poor soldier?"

"*Homunculus.*" She locked the Dreadnought's damaged mind back up, storing him safely away. "The parts they used to fix me came from *Homunculus*. And before I left her, *Sechura* gave me what's left of his mind."

Henricksen's face went blank, eyes watchful. "You're carrying another AI around inside you. A *Dreadnought* AI. Should I be worried about that?"

"He's damaged," *Serengeti* told him. "Separated from his crystal matrix. Walled off from my network by a good ten layers of firewall. He's not going anywhere, Henricksen. Not without my say-so."

"Guess I'll just have to trust you on that," he said carefully, giving the camera a knowing look. He flicked his fingers, looking away again. "So you look the part, and thanks to that AI inside you, you'll sound the part. Know just the right words to get us past security. There's just one thing missing." He flicked his eyes to the camera's reflection, looking right into the lens.

"The ships," *Serengeti* said quietly and saw Henricksen nod.

"This…ghost fleet *Sechura* mentioned. And a plan for how we get the archived AIs *to* that fleet. Assuming, we manage to pull this whole thing off, of course. Which frankly sounds completely ridiculous now that I've actually said it. Hell," he sighed, scrubbing at his face. "This whole damned *idea's* insane."

"Not denying that," she told him. "Just don't have a better one right now."

"Yeah," he said, looking at her. "Me either." He paused, grimacing. "Then again, I might feel better about this whole deal if it were someone *else's* insane plan."

"You don't trust her."

"Why should I, after everything that's happened? Why should I trust any of the Valkyries after the way they treated us?"

"They *found* us," she reminded him.

"And kept me frozen for five goddamn years. Left you out there—"

"I *know*. I know," *Serengeti* repeated, when Henricksen settled. "You don't need to remind me. But *Sechura, Atacama,* they *did* find us. Brought us back here. Fixed us up as best they could."

Henricksen touched the scar on his face, glowering still.

"What if we changed it up a bit?"

"In what way?" Henricksen asked her.

"Made it less *Sechura's* plan and more ours?"

He shook his head, clearly not understanding.

"You said it yourself: head to head, we don't stand a chance against *Brutus* and his fleet. Even with a bunch of rogue AIs backing us. So we try something different. Something…sneaky."

Henricksen looked baffled. "What *are* you getting on about?"

Tempting to tell him—despite all the teasing, she hated keeping secrets from Henricksen—but *Serengeti* wasn't quite certain *Atacama* could pull this off. She was strong, but she wasn't *Sechura*. And this wasn't her plan.

Then again, maybe that was a good thing. Maybe that gave them just the opportunity they needed.

"Shriek," she called. "Need a favor."

"Go away," *Shriek* grumbled. "Told you—I'm done playing taxi."

"I'm not asking you for a ride this time. I need you to deliver something to *Atacama.*"

Shriek snorted. "Promoted from taxi cab to delivery boy. Thanks, but no thanks, *Serengeti.*"

"I'll make it worth your while." She waited, listening in on the comms channel, but *Shriek* didn't rise to the bait. So she created a message, sealed it and encoded it before sending it across the comms channel. "Read it," she told him. "You want in, you have to deliver that message."

"How am I supposed to even find her?" *Shriek* demanded.

"Start at Blue Horizon. Stationmaster's sympathetic. He'll help you track her down."

"Well, what if I—?"

"Just read the damn message," *Serengeti* sighed.

"Maybe I don't *wanna* read it," *Shriek* grumbled. But he went quiet a while, obviously doing just that.

Henricksen turned his head, giving her a look.

"Later," she promised, muting the channel. "I'll explain everything—"

"Alright. I'm in," *Shriek* announced.

Just like that. No more arguments. No more complaining. Frankly, *Serengeti* was surprised.

"Good. Then go," she said, before *Shriek* could change his mind.

"*Now*? But—"

"No time like the present!" she said brightly. "Oh, and use an indirect route, if you please. Don't want anyone tracking you back here."

"Indirect! But that—that could take *days*!"

"Might," she said sweetly. "Last I checked, you and *Brutus* didn't exactly part on good terms, though. Do you *really* want to run the risk that he'll follow you back here?"

"No," he said sulkily. "Fine." *Shriek* huffed loudly, sounding completely put out. "But you owe me for this. And that other thing on the Citadel. A few more things before that."

"Yeah-yeah. You can collect when this is all over."

Shriek muttered something about 'bossy-pants AIs and their bossy-pants bosses' before cutting the channel and spooling up his engines.

Main propulsion only for now. Indirect route meant no hyperspace travel until *Shriek* reached the shipping lanes and could blend in with the other vessel traffic. Slow way to go, but safer than leaving a big old jump distortion behind to attract attention.

Henricksen stared out the windows, watching the stealth ship move away. "You're not going to tell me what was in that message, are you?" He turned his head, looking at the camera. Heaved a long-suffering sigh when *Serengeti* stayed silent and went back to studying the stars. "Figured that'd be your answer. Welp. *Shriek* won't be back for a couple of days, and we've got those DD3s on board, so we might as well take advantage of the downtime and fix the damage from *Cerberus's* cannons. No holes this time, but he bashed the hell outta the photovoltaic collectors in your hull." He turned around, arms folding as he leaned against the windows. "Hate for you to not look your best when we show up at Faraday."

Serengeti snorted. "Then by all means, go ahead. In fact..." She queried her systems, checking on the status of the TSGs' little side project. "Have the DD3s install that modified shimmer shield while you're at it."

Henricksen laughed softly. "So *that's* what you had the little guys doing."

"Downloaded the software before we left Blue Horizon. Figured it might come in handy. And I'm *not* hoarding," she insisted. "I just like to keep a few toys around. You know, in case."

"Sure." Henricksen smiled. "You keep telling yourself that."

TWENTY-FOUR

Shriek returned a few days later—*Serengeti's* message safely delivered, thanks to a little detective work from Qaisrani's husband. Brought a present back with him, too. At least, that's what he called it.

"Present? What kind of present?" *Serengeti* asked, instantly suspicious.

"Surprise," he told her, smile in his voice. "Open up, and I'll drop it in your cargo bay so you can take a look."

Serengeti eyed the stealth ship as he slid in beside her, tempted to refuse. Ravens weren't really the gift-giving type, and frankly, she'd had her fill of surprises for a while. But *Shriek* kept hanging out there, pestering her in that obnoxious, poke-poke-poke way of his, and eventually—out of sheer exhaustion—she relented.

"Fine," she sighed, completely annoyed. "Just be quick about." She sent an order to the main cargo bay, opening the doors wide. Watched *Shriek* slip in, jets firing in tiny bursts as he maneuvered himself around. "I'll send a robot to retrieve the package once you're settled."

"No need," he told her in that cryptic way of his. "It'll come to you."

"Huh-uh. Not happening," Henricksen told him, beating *Serengeti* to the punch. "No way I'm letting this little 'surprise' of yours wander around on my ship." A nod to her camera and he stepped down from the Command Post, heading for the door. "You just stick that little present of yours in the airlock. We'll take it from there."

"Spoil sport." *Shriek* closed the channel, dropping comms into silence.

"Finlay!" Henricksen called, palming the bridge door open. "You're in charge 'til I get back."

Finlay's head popped up. "Me?" she squeaked, twisting around.

"Yes, you, Finlay. You're senior bridge crew now. Remember?"

Finlay bit her lip, glancing worriedly around the bridge.

It was Tsu before—always Tsu that Henricksen left in charge. But Tsu was gone now. Tsu and Kusikov. Sikuuku and Evans.

Henricksen glanced behind him, face softening as looked at her. Opened his mouth and then closed it, lips pressed in a thin line. "Won't be long, Finlay. Promise."

"Yes, sir," she said faintly, eyes dropping to the floor.

Henricksen stepped through the door, hesitated, and looked back. "We get boarded by pirates, you give me a buzz now, ya hear?"

Finlay's head snapped up, bright spots of color blooming on her cheeks. Spun around and started stabbing at her panel, muttering angrily under her breath. "One time. You mention pirates *one time* and they never let you live it down."

Henricksen tipped a wink at the camera, smiling as he left the bridge.

Serengeti left him as he ducked into a ladderway, flickering along her pathways to the camera outside the main cargo bay, arriving just as *Shriek* left.

That was quick.

She cycled through the cargo bay's cameras, searching for the stealth ship's present. Wasn't quite sure what to look for—a box, maybe; a crate or something like that—but she panned the lenses around anyway, passing the time until Henricksen arrived. Checked the airlock while she was at, but found nothing anywhere. Just a couple of robots scurrying around the hold, going about this maintenance chore and that.

Where'd you put it, you bastard? she wondered, making another round of the cameras.

"What'd he bring us?" Henricksen asked, stepping from the ladderway, toggling the monitor beside the airlock.

"No idea. All I see are a couple of 'bots."

Henricksen frowned. Reached over and slapped at a comms unit opening a secure line to the stealth ship. "Alright, *Shriek*. You've had your fun. Where the hell is this package of yours?"

"It's *coming*. Geez!"

Henricksen glowered. "You gettin' pissy with me, sunshine?"

"*No*. I'm just askin' you to be a little—"

"Bosch," he barked, calling up to the bridge. Left the private channel open while he was it, making sure *Shriek* heard him. "See that little speck off the starboard side?"

"Okay! Okay! No need to get nasty! Just gimme a minute." *Shriek* was quiet a moment, checking on something while Henricksen and *Serengeti* waited on the line. "There. It should be right—"

The airlock buzzed and whirred, pumping in atmosphere, running through its pressurization routine. A *beep* and it popped open, releasing a shining metal robot into the corridor.

"—there," *Shriek* finished, sounding incredibly smug. "So. Whaddaya think?"

"A robot." *Another* robot. TSG from the look of it and, once again, not one of hers. "Guess I should've expected that."

Henricksen frowned, giving her a puzzled look.

"Nothing," she said. "Just—tell Bosch to stand down."

Henricksen frowned a moment longer, shrugged his shoulders, and called back up to the bridge. "Sorry, Bosch. Target practice will have to wait for another time."

"Roger." Bosch cut the channel as Henricksen turned back to the camera.

"So, little friend." Henricksen folded his arms, staring down his nose. "What's your story?"

The TSG looked up at him, face lights ticking anxiously, leg-ends drumming against the deck plates.

"Not talkin', eh?" Henricksen glanced at *Serengeti's* camera, punched at the buttons on the side of the monitor, cycling through the hull camera feeds until he found one that gave him a view of the stealth ship outside. "*Serengeti's* already got fifty of these guys, *Shriek*. What makes you think she'd want or need another?"

"Oh! Right. Hang on a sec." *Shriek* closed the channel, going quiet for a while.

"No! Wait!" Henricksen sighed in frustration as the line clicked closed. Leaned against the wall and just stared at the robot while *Shriek* finished whatever the hell he was doing.

Took a while—a surprisingly long time, actually—but comms clicked open a minute or so later as *Shriek* returned. "There ya go. Should be all set."

The TSG stiffened, head lifting, face lights flashing as it *beeped* and *blipped*, leg-ends rattling fit to wake the dead. A few seconds of that and it stiffened again, going very still, every last light in its face winking out. A *blip* and it relaxed, rigid pose giving way. The robot blinked a few times, head turning, cobalt eyes examining the hall around it, Henricksen and the camera high on the wall. "Hello, *Serengeti*," it greeted her.

Calm voice, from the robot. Smoothand serene. AI, but not TSG. Not a robot at all.

My Sisters and their robot messengers...

"Good to see you, *Atacama*."

Henricksen straightened, throwing a sharp look at the camera. "What's she doing here? If *Brutus* picks up on that transmission—"

"Ahem," *Shriek* interrupted. "Stealth ship, remember? Channel's filtered and encrypted."

Henricksen frowned at the monitor, the stealth ship outside. "Yeah. But for how long?"

"I don't know. Fifteen minutes, maybe?"

"Is that a guess, or do we have fifteen minutes?"

"Yes," *Shriek* said confidently.

Henricksen's frown deepened. "Yes, you're guessing, or yes, we have fifteen minutes?"

"You're good to go, buddy."

"You didn't answer my damn ques—"

"Hurry up. Times a-wastin'."

Henricksen scowled, eyes lifting to *Serengeti's* camera. "Fifteen minutes ain't a whole lotta time. And it's awfully risky, jumping those comms from Blue Horizon to here. You ask me, we should shut it down." A nod to the TSG standing in the hallway. "Send the robot back for good measure."

"He's right, you know." *Serengeti* turned the camera toward *Atacama*. "It's dangerous, sending your robot here. For you *and* us."

"Don't forget about me," *Shriek* chimed in. "*I'm* the one boosting the signal."

"And you'll be the first one to abandon us if *Brutus does* decrypt the channel," Henricksen said sourly. "Now shut up."

"Well, that's not very nice," *Shriek* muttered.

"It's *worth* the risk," *Atacama* cut in. The TSG moved, head swiveling as it looked from Henricksen to *Serengeti*. "It's *all* been worth—"

"Is that right?" Henricksen pushed away from the wall, looming over the little robot. "Was it worth the risk of leaving *Serengeti* out there all those years?"

Atacama blinked, face lights flashing in question. "I don't know—"

"Yeah, you do," Henricksen said coldly. "We checked *Cryo's* data. You found *Serengeti* five damn years ago, but you just left her drifting. Couldn't be bothered to go get her until a few months ago."

"Henricksen," *Serengeti* said sternly. "This isn't the time."

"Why not?" he snapped. Angry, unreasoning.

Not like him. Not like him at all.

"It's alright." The robot's head lifted, offering a small smile to the camera. Turned toward Henricksen, looking solemn and serious— regretful, in a robotish sort of way. "That decision was...unfortunate," *Atacama* said carefully. "I wanted to come as soon as we found you." A nod to *Serengeti's* camera. "*Sechura* and I. *Marianas*." She bowed the robot's head, heaving a heavy sigh. "We weren't ready, though. We didn't—We didn't have a plan. If *Brutus* found out..." She shrugged the TSG's legs, voice trailing off. Stood there in silence while Henricksen glared and *Serengeti* watched from above.

"He'd what?" Henricksen asked—angry still, incredibly bitter. "Bring us back into the Fleet? Take away your ghost?"

"Henricksen—"

"No." He chopped his hand, cutting *Serengeti* off. Moved closer to *Atacama,* forcing her a step back. "*Brutus* is an asshole—I get it. But you betrayed your own. In my book, that doesn't make you all that much better."

Atacama looked up at him, cobalt eyes scanning his face. "I didn't want to leave her there. None of us did."

"Bullshit. You left her there because you didn't want to risk your own skins. Because you were too damn *scared*—"

"Enough, Henricksen!" *Serengeti* shouted. "She didn't have any other choice."

He looked up at her—face stubborn, chin set. "There's *always* a choice."

"Leave it, Henricksen. What's done is done." No going back. No turning back time. "I'm done with arguing. We need to move on."

Henricksen stared at *Serengeti's* camera, stubborn still. Nodded tightly and turned around, putting his back to *Atacama's* robot.

Rude gesture, but *Serengeti* let it go. Made a note to speak to him about that later, focusing on *Atacama* for now. "*Sechura,*" she began, and then stumbled to a halt, not quite sure how to ask this most delicate of questions. "Her AI. Was it…?"

Atacama nodded slowly, cobalt lights swirling across her robot's face. "Unrecoverable."

Serengeti sighed, abandoning the hallway for the hull cameras looking outside. Stayed there for almost a minute, sharing her sorrow with the stars.

"The message I sent you," she said, slipping back inside.

"Everything's arranged," *Atacama* assured her. "We just need a little time—"

"How *much* time?" Henricksen asked, looking around. "How long do we have to sit here, hiding out like rats?"

"A week." *Atacama* shrugged the TSG's leg, making it clear she was guessing. "Two at most. The arrangements have all been made. We're just waiting on delivery before everything's in place."

"Arrangements? What arrangements?" Henricksen's eyes flicked to *Serengeti's* camera. "What was in that message anyway?"

"*Atacama's* laying a trap," *Serengeti* said quietly. "For *Brutus.* One I helped her come up with."

Henricksen blinked slowly, head moving from side to side. "I don't understand."

"You said it yourself: taking the Fleet head-on is suicidal. But *Brutus* on his own, with just a few ships to protect him…" She trailed off, letting Henricksen do the math himself.

"Separate him from the rest of the Fleet." Henricksen cupped his chin, nodding slowly. "Draw him out somewhere where he's vulnerable—"

"And *we* have the advantage of numbers."

"So how *do* you draw him out?" he asked, eyebrows lifting.

"Honey pot." *Atacama* smiled secretly, face lights curving in a sly smile. "Put something sweet out there that *Brutus* can't resist—"

"And he comes running." Henricksen grunted, grudgingly impressed. "And the bait?"

"A ship." *Atacama's* smile widened, turning crafty and proud. "*Serengeti's* idea," she said, nodding to the camera.

"What kind of ship? Not one of those clunkers from *Sechura's* collection, I hope."

"No," *Atacama* laughed. "Not a clunker. Just the opposite." She snuck a look at *Serengeti's* camera. "This is a very…special ship."

"Special how?" *Serengeti* asked, as Henricksen squinted, giving the robot a narrow look. "I told you to find *a* ship, but I never specified what *kind* of ship."

Atacama bounced on her tip-toes, looking quite pleased with herself.

Serengeti watched her, wondering at that oh-so-smug expression, a sneaking suspicion stealing over her. "Special how, Sister?" she asked faintly. "What did you—?"

A blast of static and *Shriek* interrupted. "Sorry, folks. Outta time."

A sharp click and the channel cut off, severing the connection to *Atacama*.

The TSG—so bright and lively—sagged sadly, face lights going dark.

"Dammit," Henricksen growled, punching the wall.

The robot twitched and shook itself, coming back to life. A rapid fire flashing of face lights—cobalt eyes blinking on-off, on-off, on-off—and the TSG turned in circles, *blipping* in confusion, looking completely lost.

Spotted Henricksen and crouched down, *burbling* softly as it huddled close to the floor. "This isn't *Atacama*," the 'bot said, voice filled with worry. "This isn't my ship."

"'Fraid not," Henricksen told it, sharing a look with *Serengeti's* camera.

The TSG turned another circle, surveying the hallway, cobalt eyes locking onto *Serengeti's* camera. Sensing the AI watching. "Where?" he asked plaintively.

"Far out," she told him. "Far from home."

The robot sagged, *hooting* mournfully, reminding her suddenly of Tig.

"I'm *Serengeti*." She reached for the robot, touching at its AI mind. "Who are you, little one?"

The TSG raised its head enough to look at her, lifted a leg, and pointed at its designation—TSG-9942, printed in bold, black letters on its side. A sigh and it went back to being a doorstop, *burbling* softly as it huddled on the floor.

Sad little thing. *Serengeti* felt bad for it, being sent all the way out here on its own. "I'm sorry, 9942, but I can't take you back to *Atacama* just yet. Not until our business here is done."

"I can't go home?" The TSG blinked its sad puppy dog eyes, looking even *more* miserable somehow.

"No," *Serengeti* said gently. "Not now, anyway."

"So what do I do?" it asked her.

"You stay with me," *Serengeti* said gently. She glanced at Henricksen, saw him shrug, and nod. "Go here," she told it, touching at the TSG's brain. She passed it a schematic of the ship, directions to Engineering. "There are other robots there."

The robot perked up. "Others like me?"

"Yes. Like you." *Serengeti* smiled. "They'll find a place for you. Something for you to do."

TSG-9942 smiled widely, instantly happy. Such an interesting mindset in these robots. Not quite as much character as her little TIGs, but interesting still. Very focused on being useful. On having something to do.

"Go now," *Serengeti* said, shooing the robot away. "Go-go-go."

The TSG waved at her and spun around. Took off down the hallway, ducking into the first ladderway it came across.

Henricksen stared after it, waiting until the robot disappeared. "This mystery ship." A flick of his eyes to the camera. "Any idea what is it?"

Serengeti hesitated before answering. She had her suspicions, but she didn't actually know for sure. Didn't think she *wanted* to know, honestly. Not when a good fifty percent of her body had been rebuilt from salvage of dubious origins. "Doesn't matter," she told him.

Henricksen's face darkened, mouth opening to object.

"Let's just focus on getting those archived AIs from Faraday," *Serengeti* said quickly, before he could press her on the matter. "Leave the rest of it *Atacama* to deal with."

Henricksen closed his mouth, clearly unhappy. Turned and studied the monitor on the wall. "It's not just Faraday," he told her. "There's the Cloud, remember? AIs aren't much good to us without ships to pilot."

"That too," *Serengeti* acknowledged. "But the rest of it…"

Henricksen snorted. "Yeah. *Atacama* gets the easy part." He was quiet a while chewing his lip, staring at the video feed showing *Shriek* and the stars. "So *Atacama* springs her trap, we show up with a bunch of ships piloted by AI prisoners, and just like that, the Meridian Alliance is saved." He grunted, shaking his head. "It's a nice fairy tale, *Serengeti,* but somehow, I don't think it'll be that easy."

"Me either," she admitted. "I honestly don't think *any* of this will be easy. But with *Cerberus* out of the picture…"

"There isn't really a better plan." Henricksen sighed, nodding, rubbing at his face. "They betrayed you, *Serengeti*. You do know that?" He looked at her, blinking slowly. "Five years your Sisters left you out there. Five *years*. Us frozen, you rotting, and all she can say is 'I'm sorry, it's not what I wanted'? That's crap, *Serengeti*. You deserve better. Especially from a Sister." He turned around—all the way around—staring in challenge at the camera. "What makes you think we can trust her? After what she did, all the lies, what makes you think we can trust her now?"

This again. She was tired of fighting him on this.

"She's Valkyrie, Henricksen. A *Sister*. Despite everything, that still means something. Even after fifty-three years."

Henricksen stared a moment longer, nodded once, and looked away. "Still have to get into that Vault. Rest of it won't really matter if we fuck things up on Faraday."

Serengeti watched him in silence. Watched him watching the stars showing on the monitor. The stealth ship floating among them.

"I'm going with you this time." Henricksen turned his head, showing her one grey eye. "No arguments, *Serengeti*. You're not leaving me behind this time."

No reason to, really. Faraday would expect the Dreadnought's captain to deliver the AI payload himself. Henricksen could send someone in his place, of course—captain's privilege, an advantage of rank—but he wouldn't. *Serengeti* knew that without asking. Didn't even bother suggesting the idea.

But she still didn't like it. Thought of about a million ways this could all go wrong.

"You'll need an entourage," she told him. "No self-respecting captain goes on station alone. Or unarmed, for that matter."

Henricksen nodded slowly. "I'll take Houseman and Beaulieu with me. They're the only ones without crew assignments."

"What about Finlay?"

"What about her?" Henricksen frowned.

"Why not bring her along?" Finlay and Henricksen—they belonged together. It felt right somehow.

"Finlay runs Scan, remember? She's already got a job."

"Uh-huh. I also remember you promised her the big guns."

"I didn't *promise* Finlay anything."

"But you made her believe she'd get a chance at Artillery, only to slip Bosch in there instead."

"Bosch is *trained*—"

"You *owe* her, Henricksen. Let Finlay strut around and feel like a badass for a while. What can it hurt?"

Henricksen folded his arms, looking less than thrilled with the idea. "And if things go bad over there? What then?"

"She's steady, Henricksen. And one of the best you've got."

"That's not what I asked." He lifted his chin and squared his shoulders, looking stubborn all over again.

"She can handle herself."

Henricksen kept staring, defiant still. "Still not what I'm asking."

Serengeti sighed. "You'll need her if this plan goes sideways. You'll need someone you can *trust*. Houseman and Beaulieu may do fine, but they're not crew. Not *our* crew, anyway. Just a couple of borrowed heavies that got cut off from their ship."

"Heavies, eh?" Henricksen's face softened, lips curling at the corners. "Better not let Beaulieu here that." He considered a moment, lips pursed as he looked up at the camera. "Fine. Finlay, too. Because you asked." He dipped his head, eyes never leaving the camera. Twitched his shoulders and turned around, heading back to the bridge.

TWENTY-FIVE

The salvage ships dropped out of jump, towing the bones of a wrecked vessel between them. *Flotsam,* one ship's beacon read, and *Jetsam* the other. Twins birthed in the same lab, mated to identical chassis. A matched pair working in tandem since they first took off for the stars.

Ugly things, those salvage ships. Slab-sided and wallowing. Pincers for grasping, cranes for lifting, hooks and grapnels and shearing towers stuck everywhere they could fit.

Ugly, but functional. When it came to tearing vessels apart, nothing beat them. And they ran cheap, carrying minimal crew.

Not many hands needed for this type of work. AIs did the heavy lifting in wrestling the wrecked vessels around and cutting them up into manageable chunks. Crew only came into play when fine motor skills were needed. Systems to be hacked or rewired, depending on a customer's needs.

No systems left on the vessel the salvage ships towed today. Not much of *anything* left to it, really, making it hard to tell just exactly *what* type of ship it was. Or used to be.

Big, that was for sure. Probably pretty impressive before someone ripped off all the hull plating and scooped its insides out. But now...barely anything left now. Just metal bones and damaged fittings. The remains of a ship. The plasma burns and ion scoring indicators of a bloody, violent end.

Not that *Flotsam* cared. Or *Jetsam,* for that matter. Ships died all over the galaxy, and their job was to clean them up. Tow their carcasses back to the chop-shops and shipyards that knew how to make something useful out of their carcasses. Earn themselves a little cash along the way.

Shared that too, those two salvage ships. Shared everything. Profits split evenly, no secrets between them. Ignorance provided free of charge.

Usually, that ignorance was for their customer's benefit—couldn't get tagged for illegal parts if you didn't know where they came from in the first place, after all. But this job, it was their turn.

No idea where their contact found this ship they towed. Couldn't even get a straight answer on why their contact wanted it dropped out here, where there were no shipyards to claim it. No scrapyards to grind it into parts.

"Ranadene asteroid field," *Flotsam* sent to *Jetsam* beside him. "Pretty far out."

"Fringes of the fringes," *Jetsam* agreed. "If there is such a thing."

Fifty years from now, Ranadene *might* see some traffic, but right now they were the only two vessels for light years around. Terraformers had started in on the planet that gave the asteroid field its name—parked a dozen or so of those big-ass atmosphere generation factories down there before bugging out. Hadn't even bothered establishing the infrastructure for a permanent colony. Just slapped a 'do not disturb' sign on the star charts warning people away from the surface under penalty of Meridian Alliance law and left.

Couldn't be bothered to stick around and watch the paint dry for the next fifty years. Planet engineers had more important things to do than babysit a terraforming planet, but they didn't want anyone popping in to visit. Messing with their experiments when no one was around. And the Meridian Alliance...

Government took a very dim view of anyone stupid enough to try to set up an illegal colony on a half-baked planet. Some still tried, though. Idiots everywhere in the galaxy. No changing that.

"So, we're just supposed to leave it here?" *Jetsam* asked.

"Apparently," *Flotsam* told him.

"Doesn't make sense," *Jetsam* muttered.

Not their usual job, towing things away from port. Salvage ships were mostly about towing vessels *to* port so the shipyards could fix them up and sell them off again. Made a tidy little profit that way. Selling off the wrecks they found. Seemed a shame to leave a perfectly good scrap heap all the way out here. Especially when there were still a few useable piece-parts left on it.

Jetsam told his partner as much. Went so far as to suggest they might want to just...divert it somewhere. Claim they'd made the delivery so they could get their payment. Come back later and pick the wrecked vessel up.

"Nah," *Flotsam* told him. "Not a good idea. Contact promised we could have the wreck once this shindig's over."

That and anything else they found when they came back. Contact wouldn't tell them much, tight-lipped bastard that he was, but the rumor mill always had good information. And the word on the street said something big was coming. Showdown between the Meridian Alliance fleet and the last remnants of the DSR. Likely the rebels' last hurrah, there being just a few pockets of them left out there these days.

Too bad really. War was so very, very good for business. Then again, if the rumors were true—or even close to true—there should be *several* ships out here for *Flotsam* and *Jetsam* to choose from in a few days' time.

"Have to sell them on the black market, of course." A burst of cobalt fire lit up *Flotsam's* tail as he and *Jetsam* moved closer to the asteroid field. "Dump a ship out here, you don't want anyone to find it. Also means none of the shipyards will touch it."

"Fine by me." *Jetsam* feathered his jets before cutting them off, drifting now, with *Flotsam* beside him. The wrecked ship gliding between them. "Better prices on the black market anyway." He flashed a message at *Flotsam*. "You ready?"

"Yup. This is probably close enough. Three. Two. One."

The two salvage ships disengaged their grappling hooks in tandem, releasing their hold on the wrecked vessel. Kicked in their thrusters to slow themselves down while the wreck floated along on momentum.

Another kick and the twin ships shuddered to a halt. Fired their maneuvering jets in synchronized blasts, burning them in a rhythm—on-off, on-off, on-off—as they muscled their huge bodies around.

The wreck kept going without them, gliding serenely into the asteroid field. A rock hit it and the ship rebounded, slammed into another one and careened to the side, ping-ponging for several minutes before eventually settling in.

Drifted after that. The wrecked ship. The asteroids around it.

Jetsam sighed regretfully as he and *Flotsam* left it behind. "We'll have a bitch of a time getting it back out of there again."

"Worth it though," *Flotsam* told him. "Picked pretty clean, but the frame's worth salvaging. Containment pod looks to be repairable."

"Any idea who was in there?" *Jetsam* asked him.

"Nah. Data's all messed up. Snuck a peak at the package they gave us. Looked like *Hercules* or *Humungous* or some such."

"*Humungous*," *Jetsam* snorted. "What kind of stupid-ass name is that?" He pulled up a feed from a rearward-facing camera, taking a last look. "Not so humungous now, is he?"

"Nope." *Flotsam* fired up his hyperspace engines, watched the jump clock tick down. "Just another floating piece of scrap."

The jump clock hit zero, and the two salvage ships slipped away, leaving the wrecked vessel floating in the Ranadene asteroid field, waiting patiently for someone to claim it.

TWENTY-SIX

Henricksen walked onto the bridge and everyone stopped and stared, trying not to laugh.

Well, except Delacroix. He never quite seemed to leave the netherspace of Comms these days. Never noticed much of anything except the virtual world behind his visor.

"What?" Henricksen asked, looking down at himself. "Never seen a grown man play dress-up before?"

The snickers increased, Finlay just about falling out of her seat at Scan.

"Alright. That's enough." He flicked his fingers, staring the crew down. Rolled his eyes as they finally turned back to their stations and walked over to the Command Post to log in. A glance at *Serengeti's* camera as he scanned the data from all four stations, checked the status of the newly installed shimmer shield before closing everything down. "So?" Another look at the camera, arms spreading wide. "How do I look?" He turned in a circle, letting *Serengeti* admire the goods.

He'd swapped her black-on-black uniform for a dark blue affair—gold piping at the cuffs and collar, gold buttons and badges to set it off.

Gaudy looking get-up. Almost as tacky as *Sechura's* silver coveralls.

"Very pompous," *Serengeti* told him, smile in her voice. "Every bit the dashing Dreadnought captain."

"Thanks. I think." Henricksen grimaced, flicking a fluff from his sleeve. Adjusted his belt to settle his service pistol more comfortably on his hip.

"Where did you find that uniform, anyway?" *Serengeti* asked curiously.

Close to two weeks they'd been sitting out here—powered down, beacons off, minimal communications to avoid drawing attention. Two weeks of hiding out while *Shriek* and his stealth ship buddies traveled back and forth to Blue Horizon, carrying messages for *Atacama* and *Serengeti.*

Taking the long way each time to cover their trail: propulsion engines to the shipping lanes, jump from there to the station, jump back and use the propulsion engines to return to the ass-end of nowhere where *Serengeti* and the other Ravens waited.

Two weeks of that—a long time to sit around with essentially nothing to do. Plenty of time for a bored captain to stitch together a new uniform from scratch. Except, the last time she checked, Henricksen didn't know how to sew. Couldn't even fix a loose button as far as she knew.

"You had the TSGs help you, didn't you?" *Serengeti* accused.

"Nope. Well, okay. A little. Bosch is a big boy, after all. Had the TSGs cut a bit here and trim a little there so it didn't look like I was wearing a damned clown suit around."

"Bosch," *Serengeti* repeated. "So that's one of *Sechura's* uniforms?"

"Uh-huh. Turns out they're reversible. Not half ugly on the inside. Patch wasn't right, of course." Henricksen turned a bit, touching a finger to the patch on his shoulder: a human form in miniature suspended inside a glass bottle. "I had the TSGs whip up a few counterfeits so we'd look the part. Can't have us going around telling everyone we're *Homunculus* crew and still wear *Sechura's* patch. Details," he said, tapping a finger to his nose. "You always gotta pay attention to the details."

Serengeti smiled inwardly. "More pithy words of wisdom from the eminent Captain Henricksen."

"Thought it was sagacious?"

"That, too."

Henricksen smiled ruefully, eyes flicking from the camera to the stars outside. "More like lessons learned from a guy who fucked up a whole lotta things in his life and doesn't particularly want to fuck this one up as well." He touched at the scar on his face. Dropped his voice, brow wrinkling with worry. "Whole lotta things could go wrong with this, *Serengeti*. You sure—"

"No," she said quietly. "I'm not sure. And if I said I was, you'd call me a liar."

"Probably right." He turned away and stared through the windows—quiet now, but no less worried. She read that in the set of his shoulders. The lines of his face.

"*Atacama's* in place."

He stiffened, hands clenching at his sides.

"Everything's ready," *Serengeti* said quietly. "We do this now, or we don't do it all."

Henricksen looked at her. Sucked in a breath and blew it back out. "Yeah," he said, nodding, looking at over Scan.

Scowled like a thunderhead when he caught Finlay looking at him. Giggling like schoolgirl as she whispered something in Aoki's ear.

"There a problem, Finlay?"

"Yes, sir. I mean no, sir." Finlay snickered. "You just look kinda silly is all."

Henricksen glanced down at himself, adjusting his gun belt yet again. "Not my fault this generation's into god-awful uniforms."

"Hey!" Bosch leaned out of the Artillery pod. "Watch what you're calling ugly!"

"Spade's a spade, Bosch. And these uniforms sure ain't pretty." Henricksen wrinkled his nose, picking at a knot of gold thread. "Blue's better than that shiny silver shit you guys usually wear, but still..." He turned his hand over, eyeing the gold braid circling his jacket's cuff with distaste. "Gaudy as all get-out. Gimme *Serengeti's* black-on-black any day."

"Damn straight." Finlay tugged at the dark lapels of her uniform jacket, chin lifting proudly. Caught a glimpse of Henricksen in his spiffy blue-and-gold outfit and she lost it. Started giggling all over again. "Sorry, sir." Finlay wiped tears from her eyes, shoulders hitching. "It's just—It's just—You look like the leader of a marching band!"

Finlay burst out laughing, clutching at her belly as she fell out of her chair. Rolled around on the floor in fits of giggles while Henricksen glowered from the Command Post, looking anything but amused.

"Like my new uniform, do you?"

Finlay laughed harder, curling up in a ball.

A glance at the camera and Henricksen stepped down from the Command Post, sauntering over to Scan. Stopped there and smiled down at Finlay as she giggled and wiped tears from her face. "Off the floor, Finlay. Deck's no place for an officer."

"Yes, sir." She sucked in a breath to still the last of her laughter, staggered to her feet with a toothy grin stretching across her freckled face.

"I'm glad you like my new uniform. Real glad," he added when Finlay started losing it again. "Know why?"

Finlay shook her head—eyes bulging, shoulders shaking with barely suppressed laughter.

Henricksen leaned forward, smile curving his lips. "'Cause I got another made just for you, Finlay. One just. Like. This."

Finlay paled, smile slipping from her face. "But—But I like this one," she whimpered, clutching at her dark on dark jacket.

"Too bad." Henricksen's face turned stony, smile disappearing. "You wanna come with me to Faraday, you gotta dress the part. Which means wearing this stupid-ass uniform so no one gives you a second look."

"But I—" Finlay froze, mouth hanging open, eyes gone round as dinner plates. "Go *with* you? I'm—I'm going *with* you to Faraday?"

Henricksen shrugged his shoulders, acting all casual. "Thought had occurred to me. Captain can't show up with a load of AIs for archiving without a proper escort, after all. 'Course, if you don't *want* to—"

"I want! I want!" Finlay bounced up and down, clapping her hands. "Do I get a gun?"

"You're my escort, Finlay. Gotta have a gun."

"Aw, hell yeah!" Finlay pumped her fist, slapped Aoki a high-five.

Henricksen smiled, letting her have her moment. Checked the time and decided to shut it down. "Alright, people." He raised his voice, looking around. "You've all had a good laugh at my expense. Some more than others." He shot an accusatory look at Finlay, shaking his head at her entirely unapologetic smile. "Now it's time to focus, and get serious. Faraday's a Meridian Alliance station, but we're not exactly going in under the most honest of circumstances." He walked back to the Command Post and slipped into his Captain's Chair, tapped at its panels, opening data windows on each of its six displays—one each for the bridge's five stations, a mash-up window that brought all that information together. "You've got the jump coordinates, Samara?"

"Aye, sir." Samara pulled up the navigation data, threw the course and their destination up on the bridge's windows. "Calculations are all set. We can jump whenever you're ready."

"Right." Henricksen nodded, opening a channel to the Ravens outside. "You and your boys got that, *Shriek*?"

"Yes, Mother." *Shriek* sounded annoyed. "Believe it or not, we actually *can* follow a star chart without getting lost."

"Smartass," Henricksen muttered. "Alright, Aoki. Fire up the hyperspace engines. Jump clock to the front window. *Shriek*—"

"Yeah, yeah. We're on it." *Shriek* cut the comms and moved ahead of *Serengeti*, taking the other Ravens with him. They formed a ring in front of her, shielding her with their cloaking devices as a buckle formed, darkness swirling as it expanded.

"Three. Two. One. Burn." Aoki hit the engines, shoving *Serengeti* forward.

The Ravens moved with her, maintaining their distance from *Serengeti's* nose. They synchronized their speed, matching the output from their engines, and then all of them—*Serengeti* and *Shriek, Swift,* and *Sharp* and *Snicker-snack*—approached the hyperspace buckle together.

Mass jump, to hide the Ravens' engines. So no one would know anyone but *Serengeti* was there.

Mass jump again. Serengeti sighed, consulting the clock, watching it tick down. *When did I become so reckless?*

Her nose touched the leading edge of the buckle and it wrapped around her, sucking *Serengeti* in. Normal space disappeared as the jump trough slipped around her—a place of cold and calm and infinite silence.

Thirty seconds—just thirty seconds of normal time to move from their far out location in deep space to the drop point at the edge of Faraday's security perimeter. But in hyperspace—for her at least, she'd never asked other AIs if they experienced the same thing—those thirty seconds felt like days. Weeks. *Months* of nothing but peace and tranquility. Nothing to do but watch the stars slide by.

The jump clock hit zero, and *Serengeti's* hyperspace drives wound down, dropping her out of the trough. Scan kicked in as normal space materialized around her—sensors drinking in every bit of data they could find.

"Talk to me, Finlay," Henricksen called from his Command Post.

"Gimme a minute." Finlay bowed her head, working furiously at her station, swapping one data window for another as she cycled through the information the sensors sent back. "Clear! We're clear, sir. Nothing out of the ordinary. No other ships showing in the area." She raised her head, nodding to the display on the front windows. "Just Faraday and us, sir. And our little friends, of course."

"Watch who you're calling 'little,' pipsqueak," *Shriek* warned.

"Eep." Finlay's cheeks colored. She shrugged her shoulders, throwing an apologetic look Henricksen's way. "Sorry, sir. Didn't know they were listening. *Someone* didn't *tell* me comms was open," she added, giving Delacroix a good glare.

"Someone should check before they start flapping their gums," Delacroix murmured in his distracted, dreaming voice.

Not such a moonbeam after all. Apparently, there was *some* kind of normal brain function going on behind that visor.

Finlay scowled, twisting in her seat. "And just *why* would I—?"

"Cram it!" Henricksen snapped, fist slamming against a panel. "Last thing I need right now is a bunch of snide comments and bickering. You shut it down—the both of you," he added, looking from Delacroix to Finlay, "or you get the *hell* off my bridge."

Finlay glared a moment longer, huffed loudly, and turned back to her station, hunching over the panels.

Delacroix...well, Delacroix kept being Delacroix. But he stopped talking, so that was an improvement.

"Good," Henricksen grunted. "Anyone else got a beef?" he asked, looking around the bridge.

The crew ducked their heads, wisely avoiding his eyes.

"Even better. You got that bastard ready?" he asked, looking up at a camera.

"And waiting," *Serengeti* told him, waking their captive AI. As a precaution, she checked the security seals on *Homunculus's* prison, found him wandering around the edges, testing her defenses. "He's contained, but I'll need to crack the security seal so we can squawk his credentials to the station."

"That really a good idea?" Henricksen frowned.

"I've got several layers of firewalls in place," she assured him. "He won't get out."

"Better not," Henricksen muttered. "Last thing we need is a pissed off, raggedy-ass AI running amok on your network."

"Have a little faith, Henricksen," *Serengeti* chided.

"Faith I got." Henricksen stuck out his chin, folded his arms over his chest. "Also got a healthy dose of concern about one super-powered AI toting around another who *severely* doesn't like his current situation."

"If it comes down to a wrestling match, I'm pretty sure I'll win."

"You better," Henricksen grunted, pointing a finger at the camera. "Delacroix," he called, eyes flicking to Comms.

Delacroix's head wobbled around, dead eyes staring sightless from behind his visor. "Sir?" he said faintly.

"I'm counting on you to help her." A nod to the nearest camera, eyes locked onto Delacroix's face. "*Serengeti's* gonna have her hands full maintaining a strangle hold on *Homunculus* while her consciousness is split between the ship and the station. *Shriek* and his boys'll hang back all cloaked and silent, doing what stealth ships do best—"

Watching and listening, jamming any transmissions that might cause them trouble.

"—but *you,* Delacroix, need to do two things." Henricksen flipped up a finger. "One. Keep your ear to *our* comms." He tapped the tiny communications device plugged into his ear. "Two." A second finger lifted, joining the first. "Keep your eyes, or your brain, or whatever the hell you use focused on our buddy *Homunculus* here. *Serengeti* woke him, and sure as shootin' he's gonna wanna start talkin'. He's only got about half a brain left at this point, but he's still *Brutus's* boy." A glance at *Serengeti's* camera, worry showing in the wrinkling of his brow. "He gets access to the main comms grid, he won't do us any favors. So you keep a tight rein on him." A nod to the camera as he turned his eyes back to Comms. "You hear me, Delacroix. Think you can handle that?"

"Aye, sir," he said in his odd, distracted way. He flicked his wrists, fingers moving, plucking at invisible wires.

Henricksen frowned doubtfully, eyes sliding to *Serengeti's* camera. "Shoulda replaced him," he said, mouthing the words.

Serengeti flashed a message to the Command Post's mash-up panel. "Too late now. No one else qualified on board even if it wasn't."

Henricksen wiped the message, barking a bitter laugh. "You sure *Atacama's* ready?"

"We send word to her once we're out, and she'll pop the emergency beacon on that ship she's captured. After that, we just wait for *Brutus* to arrive."

"*If* he arrives." Henricksen chewed his lip, obviously not at all certain about that. "Ya know, I should be worried about this part of the plan." He waved a hand at Faraday showing in the distance. "Pretty much insane what we're about to do." He started to say something else, changed his mind, and just shook his head.

"She'll do her part, Henricksen. *Atacama* will come through."

"She better." Henricksen spared a hard look for the camera, straightened and scanned his eyes across the bridge, addressing the crew. "We'll be squawking *Homunculus's* credentials the whole way in and out. That puts him just a little too close to comms for my comfort." A flick of his eyes to *Serengeti's* camera. "Unfortunately, there's not much I can do about that since we need those credentials for our cover. So it's a shit sandwich either way and we all gotta take a big bite."

"Eww." Aoki wrinkled her nose in disgust.

"*Shriek,*" Henricksen called, ignoring Aoki's comment. "I'm trusting you to watch our backs for a while."

"I *suppose,*" Shriek said, clearly put out. "Boring, though. Just sitting here while you guys get to have all the fun."

"Fun. Right," Henricksen snorted, cutting the comms. He stared out the windows, considering the distortion ahead of them marking where the stealth ships hid.

Doubtful look. As if second-guessing their decision to bring *Shriek* and the others along.

"What's that phrase?" *Serengeti* asked him. "Something about horses carrying gifts around in their mouths?"

"They do that?" Aoki asked, eyes wide and round.

"*No,*" Henricksen told her, rolling his eyes. "It's just a figure of speech. And you *look* them in the—never mind," he said, waving a hand. "Just take us in, Aoki. It's time we got this thing started."

Aoki looked at him, and at *Serengeti's* camera, shrugged her shoulders and faced around, scratching at her head. Fired up the main engines and pointed *Serengeti* toward the station, leaving *Shriek* and the other Ravens at the edge of Faraday's security perimeter.

On a whim, *Serengeti* activated her new shimmer shield, wrapping it around the long length of her body.

"That the new tech?" Henricksen asked, spotting the telltale signs through the front windows, looking a question at the camera.

"Mm-hmm. Made a few adjustments to the shimmer shield from Blue Horizon based on the design of the Ravens' cloaking system. It won't make us invisible, but it should confuse Faraday's scanners and targeting systems. Make it difficult for them to lock onto us in case we need to exit in a hurry. Mask my outline," she added, dropping her voice. "Make me look more like the Dreadnought I'm pretending to be."

"Just fly like an asshole," Henricksen told her. "That'll convince 'em."

Serengeti laughed softly. "Not sure I can pull that off, but I can do this." A touch at the prison inside her and *Serengeti* cracked the seal on *Homunculus's* cage. A trickle of data slipped through—controlled, selected—streaming the Dreadnought's credentials to Faraday as they came in on approach.

The station picked up on her immediately, sucking in *Serengeti's* false data, examining everything she threw out at the stars. Collected it all and packaged it up, feeding the sum total of her information to its central system for analysis and verification. Ran a few checks before sending a response back.

Query from the station, demanding to know *Serengeti's* last location. Wanting a copy of her ships logs for the last six months.

"Log check? Seriously?" Henricksen looked indignant. "*That's* what the Meridian Alliance has come to? Stations require six months' worth of fucking information as a cross-check?"

"Prison station, remember. Even Fleet ships aren't automatically cleared to dock."

"Still." Henricksen scowled at the windows, completely disgusted. "Ridiculous. Fucking ridiculous," he muttered as *Serengeti* packaged up the requested data ready—most of it stolen, skimmed from *Homunculus's* brain—and sent it over. Made a few adjustments before she sent it, swapping dates and locations around. Creating a false history of patrols and port visits stretching back six months and then some.

More data than Faraday requested—a huge data package she triple-encrypted out of spite.

Hope they choke on it, she thought, squirting the requested files out.

A pause as Faraday received and decrypted, the station ominously silent on the line.

Serengeti slid closer, the prison looming large in front of her, perimeter defenses active, guns targeting her elongated shape.

A crackle of static and a voice finally, mercifully came through. "*Homunculus,* this is Faraday station. You are cleared to dock."

"Acknowledged. We're on approach." Delacroix flicked his wrist, cutting the comms as Aoki tapped the thrusters, moving them closer.

"Wow. That's ugly." Finlay nodded to the gnarled shape showing through the windows—a huge chunk of rock split off from an obliterated moon, cube-shaped structures gripping like barnacles across its surface. Checked the data on her panel, frowning at what she found. "Thought you said this was a prison. Data tags all say Meridian Alliance outpost." She twisted, looking at Henricksen. "That's fuel depot and resupply, right?"

"Most of the time." Henricksen nodded. "But you won't find any ships docking at Faraday to stock up. Never calls itself a prison—star charts list it as an outpost, just like you said—but last time I checked, there were something on the order of five hundred troopers stationed inside that carbuncle out there."

Far too many for an outpost. Nearly triple the size of the average fringe station.

"'Course, that was fifty-three years ago," Henricksen admitted, rubbing at his chin. "And a lotta thing might've changed since then." He chewed his lip, thinking on that as Finlay faced around, staring worriedly at the windows. Keyed into one of the Command Post's panels and executed a search of the database, examining a schematic of the prison's innards.

Inside of the prison didn't look all that much better than outside. Design specs showed a warren of concrete and composite metal holding pens. No windows anywhere, triple-thick pressure doors dividing the prison into little microcosms—one section separated from another. Bulk of those spaces were set aside for human inhabitants—smugglers and militants, anyone else who pissed the Meridian Alliance off. Just one section—a cube-shaped tower sticking up from the station's stone center—blocked off for AI prisoners. A special holding area with electromagnetic shielding built into the inner walls, preventing prying AI minds from reaching in, and AI prisoners from reaching out.

The Vault, they called it. A bunker where AIs were sent to wither and die.

Serengeti shivered, loathing the place. The very idea of going in there filling her with dread.

Couldn't image what it felt like, being locked away from the stars. Cut off from every other mind in the universe until the end of time.

Henricksen glanced up, seeming to sense something wrong. Reached for a panel and started typing a message. Wiped it when she sent a calming picture—water over stones, leaves on the wind—and turned toward Delacroix instead. "Comms. What's the chatter?"

Delacroix stood there, swaying from side to side.

"Comms!"

A wobble of his head, visored face turning Henricksen's way.

"Goddammit, moonbeam. Poke your head out of the nethersphere once in a while, would you?"

"Aye, sir," Delacroix said faintly. A flick of his wrist, head tilting as he consulted the universe of Comms. "Nothing out of the ordinary." He waved vaguely, fingers flicking at the windows, the station outside. "Faraday doesn't like our orders—keeps complaining about us being late—but that's about it."

"Late." Henricksen grunted. "I'll give 'em late. Tell 'em they can cram it with walnuts. Belay that!" he yelled as Delacroix flicked his wrist.

Delacroix blinked blankly, swaying in place. "Faraday's directing us to the upper berthings. Space 12."

That put them right next to the Vault's tower. That cube-on-cube construction sticking up from the rest of the encrusted rock.

Serengeti sent the information to Navigation, watched as Samara adjusted their course and sent the plot over to Aoki at Engineering.

"You take a look at that?" Henricksen glanced at the camera, nodded to the tower rising above Faraday. The cube-shaped Vault at the top.

"I downloaded the design specs to storage, if that's what you—"

"It's shielded," Henricksen interrupted, giving her camera a meaningful look.

"I know," *Serengeti* said quietly.

"Should you...?" He trailed off, eyebrows lifting.

"I'll be fine, Henricksen."

"You sure?" He folded his arms, head tilting. "Maybe you should stay here. Let me and Finlay go in with the 'bots. Put 'em in drone status, maybe. Run 'em on manual so you don't—"

"No," she told him. "You're not going in alone."

They had too much riding on this. Too much at risk for *Serengeti* to hang back just because some electromagnetic shielding might make her go wonky for a while.

"The robots will have the worst of it. I should be fine."

"Should," Henricksen repeated. "So it's 'should' now."

"It's fine, Henricksen."

"Fine my ass," he muttered.

"Coming about," Aoki warned. "Hang on."

Henricksen grabbed at the panel, holding tight as Aoki fired the maneuvering thrusters, shoving *Serengeti's* nose to the side as she slid the ship around the station's perimeter, angling for their berthing assignment on the back side.

More scans as *Serengeti* lined herself up with Berthing 12 and eased close to the docks. The station's sensors crisscrossing her body before dipping into her comms feed and examining the information she spewed out.

"There a problem?" Henricksen asked softly.

Finlay twisted, throwing a worried look his way.

"Not sure," *Serengeti* admitted. "Probably just tight security."

"Probably?"

The scans shut off. Faraday flashed an all clear, granting *Serengeti* permission to dock.

"See? No problem. Take us in, Aoki."

"Aye, ma'am. I mean ship. AI?" Aoki slid her eyes to Finlay, cupping a hand around her mouth. "What are we supposed to call her?" she whispered.

"*Serengeti.* You call her *Serengeti.* Isn't that right?" Finlay asked, smiling at the camera.

"Yes, Finlay. *Serengeti* is just fine. Proximity alert, Aoki."

"What?" Aoki glanced down, hands lifting as she scanned the incoming data. Spotted the alert in question—berthing ahead, reduction in speed needed to avoid a collision—and ignited the reverse thrusters, slowing the ship, bringing it to a halt.

Docking jets kicked in, firing in tiny bursts. *Serengeti* swung around, long shape facing head-on to the station, the starboard side airlock on Cargo Bay 2 lined up with Berthing 12's pressure door.

Another tiny burst and the ship slid sideways, settling gently into place. Mooring clamps locked onto *Serengeti's* hull as the station's airlock extended, sucking tight to Cargo Bay 2's door. Mechanism's engaging, mating one to the other.

"Docking complete, sir." Aoki glanced over her shoulder, nodding to Henricksen at the Command Post. "We're secure."

"Neatly done, Aoki. Nice and smooth. Just the way I like it."

"Thank you, sir." Aoki ducked her head, flushing, looking incredibly pleased.

Finlay leaned over and punched her on the shoulder. Slapped her a high-five for good measure.

Henricksen watched them, smile playing about his lips. "Our entourage ready?" he asked, turning his eyes to *Serengeti's* camera.

"The RPD is already in the cargo bay with the payload. I sent a couple of TSGs down there to help us out as well."

"RPD." Henricksen tilted his head. "You're taking *that* bruiser on station?"

"What else? Six cases to haul in there, which means we'll need a sled to pull them on. Takes something big and strong to do that—pretty much describes the RPD to a T. Besides," she added, smile in her voice, "girl's gotta travel in style."

"Dung beetle." Henricksen snorted. "*That's* what you call style?"

"What? It's rugged!"

"Among other things," he muttered, eyeing the station outside. "What happens if security doesn't like your ride?"

"I'm sure you'll think of something."

Henricksen just stared.

"Relax," *Serengeti* laughed. "RPD may not be the *usual* mode of transport for delivering AIs, but ships use big 'bots like that to haul cargo all the time."

"You really think they'll buy that?" Henricksen folded his arms, looking less than convinced. "You think security will look at that bruiser and see nothing more than a cargo hauler?"

"Why not? I doubt they've ever seen an RPD before, so why would they think it's anything other than what we tell them?"

Henricksen opened his mouth and then closed it, thinking a while. "There'll be guards on the station—"

"*Prison* guards, Henricksen. Not troopers. Not warship crew."

"Meridian Alliance prison guards. No combat experience maybe, but they'll have had military training."

"And likely spent the last few years bored out of their minds on this station. *Relax,*" *Serengeti* told him. "I doubt they'd recognize an RPD if it stepped on them. All they'll see is a big bug-shaped 'bot. They won't have any idea it's a combat droid."

"And if they object on principle? Simply because of the size of that thing?"

"Here's a radical idea: How about you try reasoning with them?"

Henricksen turned toward the camera, giving her a sour look.

"Look. They can't expect a couple of TSGs and a few puny humans to move that stack of transport cases around. We *have* to bring a big 'bot with us. If they question you, just tell them that."

Henricksen frowned doubtfully, sighed, and shook his head. "Not worth worrying about, I guess. We'll just burn that bridge when we come to it. See how things work out."

"Just like the good old days."

"Yeah. 'Spose so." He smiled crookedly, shutting down his panels. Stepped down from the Command Post and headed for the door. "Finlay! Let's go!" he called, looking back over his shoulder.

"Coming!" Finlay wiped her panel and bounded to her feet, double-timing it across the bridge.

"Head on down to the airlock." Henricksen palmed the door open, hooked a thumb at the corridor outside. "Houseman and Beaulieu should already be there. They'll have a uniform for you to change into."

Finlay grimaced, looking askance at the blue and gold get-up Henricksen wore. "Pistol, too?" she asked, eyes drifting to the matte-black firearm strapped to Henricksen's hip.

"Do you one better. Grab a rifle from the small arms locker on your way."

"Rifle?! Yes, sir!" Finlay flashed a smile and snapped off a salute, stepped out the door and disappeared down the hall.

Henricksen stared after her, turned around, and tucked one arm under the other, finger tapping against his lips as he surveyed the crew left on the bridge. "Who do you think we should leave in charge?" he murmured, eyes settling on *Serengeti's* camera.

She considered the question, studying the bridge crew herself. Delacroix was out of the question for obvious reasons. And Bosch…well, *Serengeti* knew from experience that leaving a gunner in charge generally was *not* a very good idea.

No impulse control. Tended to use the guns to solve everything.

She turned the camera, stopping on Aoki at Engineering before moving on to Samara at Navigation.

Henricksen quirked an eyebrow. "Samara, eh? Alright. Samara!" he called. "You're it. You've got the con while we're gone."

"Aye, sir."

Samara preened proudly. Aoki looked overwhelmingly relieved.

Henricksen pivoted, stopped and stared at the empty seat by Scan. "First order of business, Samara: find someone to fill in until Finlay gets back."

"Aye, sir," she said, frowning at Finlay's station. Opened her mouth and then closed it, brows pulling downward. "Do you…Did you have anyone particular in mind?"

"Not a clue," he said, flashing a smile. "But pick me a good one. Helluva thing having a shitbird sitting Scan."

"Yes, sir." Samara wrung her hands, staring queasily at Finlay's station as Henricksen exited the bridge, heading for Cargo Bay 2.

TWENTY-SEVEN

The Meridian Alliance operated dozens of space stations across the length and breadth of the galaxy, and private corporations owned dozens more. Nearly one hundred and fifty stations, all told—five times the number of terraformed, colonized planets in human-controlled space.

Not a one of them what you'd call plush, though. Fancy or even inviting. Most of the stations followed Blue Horizon's layout: can shape in the middle, ship's berthings arranged in a ring around it, expansion involving adding more cans above and below that initial pod.

Simple design. Practical, if not particularly pretty. Stations started out as waypoints and fuel stops, science outposts, that kind of thing. But as trade grew and traffic increased, the stations expanded their operations, offering more...pleasurable amusements. Bars, because humans loved their liquor. Restaurants and strip clubs, hotels and markets soon after.

Legal business, for the most part. Operations running the gamut from sleazy to pretty darn nice. None of them what you'd consider sumptuous or well-appointed—space stations were built to be durable, after all, not luxurious. Private owners tried, concealing the station's backbone of hard plastics and composite metals under layers of sim-wood and faux velvet—fakes, but good fakes, recreated from samples stolen from Old Earth. Spent a lot of money on those refits, too. Problem was, the *smell* of a space station still lingered beneath it all. Distinctive. Different from the smells of ships and planets. Station was oil and electricity, cold and unwashed bodies. That fake pine scent the atmospheric systems pumped into the air to try to cover the stench.

More than that, there was the noise of a station. The hum and whir of machinery pumping artificial air and artificial heat around its spaces. Maintaining artificial gravity day and night. Fake. Sim-wood panels and faux velvet couldn't cover *that* over either. Then again, a few days on station and most people stopped noticing the noise. Hardly even mentioned the smell.

Human adaptation. Amazing sometimes.

Serengeti herself had seen just about every space station the galaxy had to offer during her time in the Fleet. So she knew what expect when the airlock opened, and she got her first look at the station on the other side.

And yet, despite that, Faraday still managed to surprise her. Simple and durable was one thing. Faraday crossed over into stark and bleak. A reminder that this particular space station was a prison first, and a Meridian Alliance outpost second. Those other things not at all.

"Well now. This is lovely." Henricksen stepped into the hallways, adjusting his gun belt for the dozenth time. Looked left and right, examining the square-sided corridor basting in a stew of brightest bright white light. "Place could severely use an interior decorator." He turned his head, looking at the RPD behind him, part of *Serengeti's* consciousness riding inside it. "Whole color palate available and they go with grey on grey. Embarrassing, even for the military. Lacks imagination, going with just one."

He glanced down as Finlay stepped up beside him, Houseman and Beaulieu just a step behind. Two TSG helpers waited in the airlock, throwing nervous glances at *Serengeti's* RPD. The multi-wheeled sled attached to her hind end by a hitching mechanism the TSGs themselves had hastily welded to the RPD's ass.

Crew normally used the sled to move cargo around *Serengeti's* insides. Hitching mechanism was a simple set-up—ring sticking from the RPD's back end, oversized carabiner-style clamp attached to the front of the sled, one sliding into the other—but maneuvering the sled, especially around corners, took a bit of getting used to. Especially since the driver was an AI warship.

Didn't help having those crates stacked atop of it. Containment cases, replicant AIs stored safely inside. Durable cases, delicate contents. Made her nervous, pulling them. Scared of bumping into things and tipping the sled over. Spilling the crates with their precious cargo onto the floor.

Henricksen and his entourage moved forward, and *Serengeti* followed—two steps forward, two steps left, trying to avoid Henricksen and the others bunched up in the center of the hallway as she extricated the sled from the airlock.

Another step, and the sled bumped against the lock's frame, metal sides screeching angrily as they scraped through the open doorway.

Henricksen winced, glancing sharply around.

"Sorry." Another step, more scraping. *Serengeti* looked behind her and saw the sled was almost clear.

Screech! Screech-screech-screech!

"Sorry, sorry, sorry."

A last tug and the sled cleared the airlock. *Serengeti* executed a twelve-point turn, moving the RPD back and forth, back and forth until the 'bot and the sled lined up.

Henricksen gave her a look.

"What? It's my first time pulling cargo."

"I can see that."

"Oh, like you could do any better."

Henricksen grunted and turned around, orienting himself in the hallway.

Reinforced walls of concrete and composite metal crowded close about them. The low-throated growl of heavy machinery issued from somewhere deep inside the station's rock center, filtering through the ducting—dull grey tubes screwed tight to the ceiling, running the length of the hall.

No windows anywhere in that hallway—*Serengeti* assumed that was for security reasons. No fake potted plants stuffed in corners, either. No artwork or advertisements covering the starkly grey walls. Faraday wasn't meant to be pretty. It wasn't even meant to be inviting. It was meant to hold prisoners. For the entirety of their lives.

"Which way?" Finlay whispered, flicking her eyes left and right.

Left was a long length of corridor, curving gently out of sight. Airlocks set at regular intervals along one side, cameras watching from above. Right offered more corridor, and a pressure door at the end.

Huge thing. Tall and wide. Built big enough for cargo to pass through.

"Just a guess, but…" Henricksen pointed a finger at the pressure door. "Got that reader?"

Finlay handed it over without a word, eyes flicking up and down the hall as Henricksen consulted the map.

A crackle of static and a comms channel opened, electronic voice speaking from speakers overhead.

"Credentials," the station's voice demanded.

A light appeared on the wall, highlighting an access point beneath an activated panel.

Henricksen walked over to it and slotted the reader into the port. Glanced around—acting all casual about it, smiling pleasantly, nodding to each camera he saw.

A chime sounded and the panel flashed green. Henricksen snagged the reader, clipping it to his belt.

"Proceed to the security checkpoint." Lights appeared on the wall to their left—sickly yellow arrows pointing to the pressure door ahead. "Present your credentials to the guards."

The wall panel went dark, arrows flashing insistently until Henricksen got moving. And then they, too, winked out.

Color disappeared from the corridor, leaving just those grey walls and too bright lights behind.

Henricksen picked at his blue-and-gold uniform. "Suddenly, I feel conspicuous."

Finlay looked down at herself, face pale, eyes worried. Henricksen's humor completely lost on her. A deep breath and she gripped her rifle with both hands, throwing nervous glances at the two troopers behind her.

"Steady, Finlay." Henricksen slid his eyes her way. "Badass bitch, remember? We'll be in and out of here before you know it."

"Yes, sir." Finlay squared her shoulders and stood up straight, chin lifting, face taking on a haughty 'I-don't-give-a-shit' look.

"There ya go, Finlay." Henricksen tipped a surreptitious wink. "Everything alright back there?" He spoke to *Serengeti* without looking, using the comms unit in his ear so the cameras wouldn't know who he addressed.

"Fine so far," she told him. "This section's not shielded. Just the main part of the Vault."

"Good to know." He stopped in front of the pressure door, plugged the reader into a data port beside it, and waited while the system scanned their credentials.

Again.

That's four times so far.

Two sets of scans of *Serengeti* herself as she came in, two more once they set foot on the station. And a safe bet that whoever was on the other side of that door would want to go through them a fifth time.

Tight security, even for a prison.

Especially considering they were Meridian Alliance. For the first time, *Serengeti* started to have misgivings about this plan.

Too late now. We turn around now and the station will know we're up to something.

The pressure door analyzed their credentials, scanned through them a second time before flashing green and beginning the long, drawn-out process of equalizing the space on the other side.

Henricksen handed the reader back to Finlay, casually looked *Serengeti's* way. "From here on out, you're just a dumb cargo robot. You got that?"

"*Beep-beep-beep.* Yes, Master," she said in her most monotone, robotic voice.

"Wise ass."

A panel flashed beside the pressure door, mechanism buzzing loudly as the lock clicked over and the hydraulics whirred to life. The huge door split down the middle, heavy panels trundling to the sides, disappearing into the walls.

Long time for that door to finish opening. Huge mechanism required to move the panels, and they still moved stultifying slow. Made a god-awful sound doing it. A growling, grinding as they slid across the floor, crawled into the walls.

Thirty seconds they stood there, waiting for the pressure door to fully open. Plenty of space for them to pass through sooner—halfway open and even *Serengeti's* RPD could slip through—but with such tight security elsewhere, they didn't dare. No telling if there was some secondary security protocol that would trigger, waking guns and alarms and god-only-knew-what else if they tried to enter prematurely.

No sense tempting fate. Rushing things would only draw unwanted attention to themselves.

Henricksen folded his arms, slouching comfortably, acting all cool and calm. Glanced behind him as the trundling stopped, the pressure door's mechanism winding down, dropping the corridor back to its usually dull roar.

A nod to Houseman, Beaulieu at his side, eyes flickering across *Serengeti's* RPD's face. "This is it, boys and girls." Last look, this one for Finlay, and Henricksen stepped forward, entering a wide, empty space.

Cube-shaped room, predictably—everything seemed cube-shaped and squared-off around here. Ten meters from one side to the other, another ten across.

Sealed pressure door on the far side. Squad of six prison guards standing at the room's center—rifles leveled, grey uniforms blending into the station's washed-out background of metal and cement walls.

Stony-faced guards. Soldiers-cum-sentries, faces half-hidden by opaque visors. Heads engulfed in matte black helmets with integrated comms.

No nametags here. No patches or collar devices or anything else to mark the prison guards from the blank walls around them. Just those oh-so-deadly, oh-so-serious looking rifles pointing at Henricksen and his entourage.

Well, at the humans, anyway. Mostly, they ignored the robots. Robots were just robots, after all. Humans, on the other, were targets. And potentially dangerous. Not to be trusted.

"Credentials," one barked, gloved hand peeling away from his rifle, fingers flicking impatiently.

Henricksen tilted his head, giving the guard a flat-eyed stare. Held out his hand and waited while Finlay retrieved the reader, slapping it against his palm. He nodded to her without looking, making a great deal of going over the device. Checking the data on it himself before offering it to the waiting guard.

The trooper took it, staring at Henricksen from behind his visor. "The 'bots?" A nod to the RPD behind Henricksen, the pair of TSGs on either side of it.

"Cargo haulers. Their data's in there along with the info for the ship and crew." Henricksen jerked a thumb over his shoulder, indicating Houseman and Beaulieu behind him, the airlock down the hall. "And me, of course," he added, tapping the nametag on his chest.

Fake name. Well, real name, but not his. Same for Finlay and the others, though Henricksen, being captain, was the only name that mattered. The only one they'd likely check.

Records showed *Homunculus's* captain as Franz Austerlitz. *Serengeti* wasn't quite sure Henricksen looked like an Austerlitz, to be honest. Then again, she wasn't quite sure what an Austerlitz *did* look like.

The guard frowned at Henricksen—the first sign of any emotion on his half-hidden face—and bowed his head, tapping at the reader, scrolling through the data it displayed. *Homunculus's* orders—real ones from several months ago—the inventory of AIs they'd brought with them—real names again, fake AIs inside the crates—just about everything they could ever want to know about the vessel parked in Berthing 12.

The same information Faraday's systems had already gone over several times now.

The guard looked up from the reader, moved a step to one side, examining *Serengeti's* RPD. The sled she pulled behind her. The crates of fake AIs.

Serengeti tensed, thinking he meant to open them and confirm the contents. The replicants were quality, some of the best counterfeits money could buy, but she knew they wouldn't pass more than a cursory inspection.

Henricksen cleared his throat loudly, flashed his friendliest smile when he had the guard's attention. "Scanner of yours ain't gonna work. Shielded," he explained, nodding to the cases. The same electromagnetic shielding built into the walls of Faraday's Vault. "Keeps 'em quiet during transport. Makes sure we don't have any…slip-ups, if you know what I mean." A wink and he nodded sagely, tapping a finger against the side of his nose. "'Course. You boys probably already knew that." He folded his arms and rocked back on his heels, waggling a finger at the troopers around him. "I'm sure you see this kinda thing all the time."

Silence for a moment, the trooper with the reader touching at the side of his helmet—telltale sign of communications—while the others just stood there, doing a fair impersonation of statues.

"Wait here," the trooper with the reader said.

A nod and he brushed past Henricksen, returning to his fellows. Touched at his helmet again, murmuring into a hidden microphone as the other guards gathered round, adopting that same fingers-to-ears listening posture.

Houseman shuffled his feet, adjusted the rifle on his shoulder, fidgeting nervously, eyes flicking around the room.

"Still, Houseman," Henricksen murmured.

Houseman froze, spots of color blooming on his cheeks. "Yes, sir. Sorry, sir."

Henricksen looked at him—at all of them, making sure everyone kept it cool.

"It's just..." Houseman again. Boy was just itching to get yelled at. "Do you really think this'll work, sir?"

Kept his voice down—give Houseman credit for that—but *Serengeti* still expected an explosion. Almost fell over in surprise when Henricksen smiled.

"'Course it'll work. If there's one thing I've learned in my years as captain, it's that people will believe just about anything if you present it with enough bluster and blow."

Houseman didn't quite look like he believed it. "Yes, sir," he said queasily. "If you say so, sir."

"I do," Henricksen said brightly. "I most certainly do. Now chin up, Houseman. Back straight. Show 'em your best 'I'm-an-asshole' face."

"Yes, sir." Houseman went blank and serious, copying Beaulieu beside him.

"That's not quite—" Henricksen paused, eyes flicking to the troopers as their hands dropped away from their helmets, visored faces turning their way. "Good enough." He clapped Houseman on the shoulder, arranging his lips in a pleasant smile as the lead guard stepped in front of him, rifle leveled at his chest.

"Your orders are out of date." A nod to the pressure door behind him. "Sergeant's coming down to verify them. Stand by."

The guard stepped back and went still again, lips moving now and then as the voice in his ear passed instructions and the trooper answered back.

Houseman shifted, throwing a panicked look Henricksen's way. "Sir—"

"All good, Houseman. It's all good," Henricksen said confidently. He folded his hands, clasping them loosely behind his back. Whistled tunelessly, acting like he didn't have a care in the world. But the whistling stopped when the pressure door opened, a squat, piggy-eyed guard in a too-tight uniform waddling through to join them. "Shit," he said softly.

"You know him?" Finlay whispered.

Henricksen gave her a look. "'Course I don't, Finlay. Been frozen for fifty goddamn years."

"Fifty-three," *Serengeti* corrected.

"Thanks for reminding me," Henricksen muttered. "I don't know this *particular* guy," he said, nodding to the new arrival, "but I know his type. Generally, they're assholes."

Finlay snickered.

"Guy that fat's been workin' a desk for a while, which means he's pompous and self-important, and used to running the show." Henricksen chewed his lip, watching the portly guard waddle over, face flushed an alarming shade of red, uniform so tight the collar cut into his neck. "This is gonna be a little harder than I thought."

"Time to pull out some of that famous charm of yours," *Serengeti* quipped.

"Yeah. Something like that."

"Well, well, well." The sergeant parked his portly girth in front of Henricksen, sweat beading on his florid face, baby fine hair the color of straw stuck wetly to his head.

Crumbs covered his uniform, dusting the top edge of a nametag— 'Proctor' stamped into its surface.

Serengeti groaned, imagining a hundred different ways Henricksen could butcher that to have a little fun.

"What do we have here?" Proctor folded his arms—well, he tried to but his arms were so stubby and the rest of him so fat that the best he could manage was tucking his hands into his armpits—and looked Henricksen up and down, lips curling in a sneer. "If it isn't the cap'n, hisself. What an honor, your honor." He twirled a hand, offering an awkward, mocking bow.

Crumbs cascaded to the floor, dusting the metal with dried-up food particles.

Henricksen smiled widely. "Pulled you away from your dinner, I see?"

Friendly smile, pleasant voice, but *Serengeti* knew Henricksen well enough to pick up the mockery behind both. "Not exactly the kind of charm I was thinking of," she said sourly.

Henricksen twitched his shoulders, offering the tiniest of shrugs.

Proctor harrumphed loudly, pawing at his uniform jacket, shaking free more crumbs. "Reader," he barked, snapping his fingers until the squad's leader handed the device over. A touch at one corner powered it on. The sergeant barely looked at it before shutting it back off, holding it up, and shaking it in Henricksen's face. "These orders are—*criminy!*" He shoved Henricksen aside, pushing through Finlay and the others to get at *Serengeti's* RPD. "What the hell is this?" he demanded, stabbing a finger at the RPD's mandibled face.

"Cargo hauler." Henricksen pasted the friendly smile back onto his face. "Dumb as shit but damned useful."

"Cargo hauler?" Proctor leaned close, squinting suspiciously as he looked the RPD up and down. "Butt ugliest 'bot I've ever seen."

Henricksen shrugged. "Hangs out in a cargo bay all day. Doesn't need to be pretty."

"'Spose not." Proctor turned around, blinking slowly. Keyed the reader—RPD already forgotten—and made a cursory review of their data. Shouldered past Henricksen as he walked back to the squad guarding the room.

"Told you," *Serengeti* murmured, voice issuing from the communicator in Henricksen's ear.

"Shut up," he muttered, giving her a sour look.

"What was that?" Proctor whirled around, frowning thunderously. "What did you say to me?"

Henricksen smiled brightly. "Everything in order there, Corporal?"

Proctor stiffened, eyes widening in outraged offense. He lifted a pudgy finger, tapping the chevrons on his arm. "It's *Sergeant*, Captain. Not corporal."

"'Course it is, Corporal!" Henricksen's smile widened, showing off every last tooth in his head. "Now if you're done playin' Tiddlywinks with my 'bot there, Porkins, I'd like to dump this cargo in your Vault and get my ship back in service." He rocked back on his heels, arms folded, smiling away.

Proctor glowered darkly, hands clenched into fists at his side. "It's *Proctor*, not Porkins."

"Proctor. Gotcha." Henricksen pointed his finger like a pistol, cocked it, and fired.

Proctor's frown deepened. He stabbed at the reader, making a last few checks of their data. "These orders are ancient. You're months overdue."

Henricksen shrugged again—casual as always, acting like he didn't have a care in the world. But he leaned forward, balancing on the balls of his feet. Taking on a hunter's stance as a hunter's edge crept into his smile. "Been off the grid a while," he said.

"Oh yeah? Why?"

"Orders." Henricksen rolled his eyes toward the ceiling. "*Brutus*," he said, as if that explained everything.

"*Brutus,* eh?" Proctor chewed on that a while, eyes flicking from the guards behind him to the cameras watching silently from above. He marked something on the reader, turned it around, and handed it back. "Paperwork's not in order—"

"The hell it isn't." Henricksen's smile slipped, ice creeping into his voice. "Dates are off, but all the forms and data are in there, so don't you go telling me—"

"I'm impounding the shipment. Sir," Proctor added, lip lifting in a sneer.

Henricksen's face went blank, eyes gone flat and cold. He stepped close to Proctor—so close the sergeant blanched and backed up—leaned down and got right in his face. "You listen to me, you little *puke*. *Brutus* says deliver these AIs, I deliver 'em." He stabbed a finger at the RPD behind him, the security-coded cases on the sled. "So, no, Sergeant. You're *not* impounding my delivery." He grabbed the reader from the sergeant's hands, wiped the entry Proctor had just made before turning the device around, and slamming it against the sergeant's chest. "Now sign the damn paperwork, Pork Rind, so I can dump this trash in the Vault where it belongs and get the *hell* outta here."

Serengeti laughed softly. "Now *that's* the charmer I know."

"Damn straight." Henricksen shoved the sergeant hard, pressing the reader against his chest. "Sign, Pork Pie."

Proctor licked his lips, eyes flicking to the camera. "Fine," he huffed, taking the reader from Henricksen's hands. "But I'm filing a complaint with *Brutus.* And if my superiors ask—"

"Yeah-yeah-yeah. If your superiors complain, you just point them to me, Porkster."

Proctor's face purpled. He gripped the reader with both hands, scrolled to the appropriate section, and pressed his thumb to the authorization block to accept Henricksen's delivery. "This way," he said, waving his hand. Wheeled around and stumped over to the pressure door on the far side of the room, leaving the others to follow behind.

"Told ya." Henricksen winked at Houseman, nudging him in the side. "Bluster and blow works every time."

He swaggered after Proctor, flicking his fingers at Finlay as he passed. A nudge from *Serengeti's* RPD and Houseman and Beaulieu belatedly joined them, letting her and the two TSGs bring up the rear.

Didn't like the troopers, those TSGs. Glanced nervously at them as they scurried by.

The guards, for their part, barely seemed to notice. They just waited for the 'bots to scuttle past before turning as a unit and lining up in a line. Forming a wall behind Henricksen and the others while Proctor entered his code at the pressure door.

"Looks like we've got an escort," *Serengeti* noted.

Henricksen glanced over his shoulder, frowning at the armed guards behind them. "Might have to do this the hard way," he murmured, finger tapping against the butt of his pistol.

"It'll attract attention."

Henricksen twitched his shoulders. "Don't see much choice."

The pressure door buzzed and whirred, ran through its pressurization routine, and slowly opened.

Everyone waited, both sides pointedly ignoring each other until the doors finally stopped moving, and it was time to head inside.

"Here we go," Henricksen murmured. A nod to Finlay on one side, Houseman and Beaulieu on the other, and he sucked in a breath, stepping across the threshold into the Vault proper.

Serengeti, playing dutiful robot, hesitated for just a fraction of a section before following after him. Shivering as she did. Filled with a sudden sense of dread.

TWENTY-EIGHT

The engineers who designed Faraday's Vault laid it out in a spoke and wheel pattern: eight short corridors joined to a central monitoring station sitting at the middle of the Vault's cube-shaped tower. Seven of those hallways dead-ended at the Vault's outer wall. The eighth led to the pressure door Henricksen and his entourage stepped through—the only way in or out of that tower.

Assuming you had the patience to wait on that damned door.

The schematic *Serengeti* downloaded earlier showed half a dozen doorways in each corridor, but not in this one. From the pressure door, it was a straight shot of fifteen meters to the control room at the Vault's center.

No cameras in that hallway, unlike outside. Cameras wouldn't work here. Not with the electromagnetic shielding built into the walls.

Serengeti started twitching as soon as she crossed over the threshold into the Vault proper, electromagnetic shielding crawling across the RPD's body. Wriggling. Tickling. An itch between her shoulder blades. Maggots burrowing under her metallic skin.

Waves of it washed over her, flooding the hallway in an electromagnetic fog. Communications cut out quite suddenly, severing her connection to anything outside the tower. The ship at dock disappearing, the rest of her consciousness with it.

That's when she finally understood the true depth of the AI prisoners' suffering. How it felt to be cut off from the universe, with nothing but their own thoughts to keep them company until the end of time.

Fifty-three years she'd been alone out there in the dark. But those fifty-three years were nothing compared to the hopelessness of this place. The stark cold and unending silence.

Panicked, *Serengeti* backed up a step—not even thinking, just wanting out. But the pressure door was already closing. The gap between too narrow for her RPD's huge body. It shut with a heavy, echoing *clang,* sealing the Vault tight, locking *Serengeti* inside. Stole the ship and its systems away from her. The noise of it, the feel of it, the sense of her own body.

Serengeti shivered, a creeping sense of horror settling over her.

Trapped. I'm trapped in here.

Henricksen slowed ahead of her, head turning as he looked back over his shoulder. Face frowning, eyes filled with questions when he saw *Serengeti's* RPD just standing there, frozen by the door.

"Out of the way, you stupid thing." Proctor flicked his fingers in distaste, motioning for the guards to stay put as he squeezed his bulk around *Serengeti,* shoved Henricksen to one side. "On we go then, Captain." He smiled of all things—after all that scowling, all those disapproving looks—and stuck his thumbs in his belt, sauntering down the hallway to the monitoring station ahead.

Henricksen frowned after him, squatted down, and fiddled with his boot's fasteners. Shot a surreptitious communication *Serengeti's* way as he tightened a loose buckle. "You alright in there?" he asked, voice scratchy and garbled sounding, shielding messing with *Serengeti's* internal comms.

"Fine," she told him—a small lie, and harmless, considering the RPD *was* working, just not quite at one hundred percent. Electromagnetism levels in that corridor wouldn't shut the 'bot down completely, but enough seeped through from the cells to make *Serengeti* feel decidedly funny. Not bad, exactly, just...weird. Off. Systems hitching and glitching, cameras fuzzing, blurring at the edges no matter how often she refocused their lenses.

This must be what it's like to be drunk, she thought as Henricksen tugged at another buckle, giving her a look.

"You *sure* you're alright?"

"Bit tipsy," she admitted. "But I'll be fine once we're out of here."

"Tipsy. Right." Henricksen flicked his eyes past her to the pressure door, frown deepening as he stood. Considered *Serengeti* a moment before turning around and setting off after Sergeant Piggy.

Finlay followed more slowly, throwing worried glances *Serengeti's* way as her RPD stumbled unsteadily, pallet sled bumping into walls as she wove a wandering path toward the tower's center.

TSGs weren't doing all that much better. The little 'bots followed in her wake like lost ducklings, bouncing off walls, rebounding and bouncing off each other as they worked their way down the hall.

Proctor looked back when he reached the control room, smiling secretively as he moved to one side.

Henricksen slowed, instantly suspicious. One hand reaching for his pistol while the other lifted, fingers splaying wide, bringing Finlay to a halt.

Houseman bumped into her. Beaulieu, too. *Serengeti* bumped into *them* and the TSGs bumped into her.

Henricksen never even noticed. He just stood there—one hand raised, the other wrapped around the butt of his pistol—staring down the squad of prison guards waiting for them in the control room's middle.

Six of them in total. And six more behind them, standing by the sealed pressure door. All of them armed. All of them pointing their rifles at Henricksen and his people.

"What's going here, Sergeant?"

"Leave the cargo." Proctor nodded to one side of the room. "'Bots too, if you wouldn't mind."

"Happens I do mind." Henricksen stared daggers at Proctor. "Happens I mind quite a bit. Orders are to deliver these AIs into containment. Orders don't say anything about half-assing the job and turning them over to you."

Proctor licked his lips, glancing around the room. "I respect that. I really do. But I'm afraid we're going to have to relieve you of your burden. *Now*, please, Captain." He tittered softly, hands rubbing together.

"Relieve us of our burden." Henricksen's head tilted. "You sneaky son-of-a-bitch. You're playing both sides."

Proctor shrugged, feigning ignorance. "Don't know what you're talking about."

"Oh, yes you do." Henricksen slid a step forward, standing just at the edge of the control room. "Got that shifty look in your eyes. Seen that often enough." Another step, looking the sergeant up and down. "How long've you been skimmin' off the deliveries and selling AIs on the black market?"

Proctor opened his mouth to protest, paused and smiled, dropping all pretense of innocence. "Little while," he admitted, wiping a trickle of sweat from his cheek. "Sergeant's pay don't add up to much. These guys," he flipped a hand at the soldiers around him, "don't get jack squat. You fancy-ass ship captains live it up in the lap of luxury while us little guys gotta settle for the gutter."

"Lap of luxury? What ship has *he* been on?" Finlay muttered.

Henricksen flicked his fingers, making a chopping gesture with his hand—a warning, wanting quiet, eyes never leaving Proctor's face. "So you lighten a few deliveries here and there. Keep enough AIs in the Vault that *Brutus* doesn't get suspicious. Sell the rest off for a tidy profit so you can buy yourself some comforts. That about it?"

Proctor's smile widened, turning ugly and evil. "Something like that." The smile vanished, the sergeant's piggy little eyes gone cold and hard. "Now drop the load, Captain. Leave the 'bots here and go back to your ship."

Henricksen considered a moment, straightened, letting go of the pistol as he settled his hands on his hips. Pinky finger reached out, though. Tapping surreptitiously at the butt of his gun.

"Got it," *Serengeti* acknowledged, reaching for the TSGs behind her, cursing the electromagnetic shielding as she fumbled at their brains. A couple of tries and she finally managed to flip the switch on the robots' settings, dropping them into combat mode. "Ready when you are. Just say the word, Henricksen."

Henricksen nodded without looking. "And if I say no?" he asked, staring Proctor down.

"That would be most unfortunate." Proctor tittered behind his hand, retreating a step as the troopers in the control room closed in.

"*Drop!*" Henricksen grabbed at Finlay, flattening them both on the floor as *Serengeti* pushed Houseman and Beaulieu out of the way, ratcheted rounds into the RPD's blasters, and swung the TSGs around, opening fire.

Plasma rounds filled the control room, picking off guards left and right. The TSGs threw themselves at the soldiers by the pressure door, ripping the rifles from their hands. turned those guns around and fired, the soldiers off like flies.

"Stay down!" Henricksen grabbed Finlay's head and mashed it against the decking. Pulled his pistol and snapped off a few shots himself, catching Proctor in the leg.

The sergeant squealed like the pig he was and dropped to the floor. Crawled away, seeking cover behind the monitoring station at the control room's center.

Plasma rounds tracked after him, but *Serengeti* kept missing, the RPD's targeting systems fritzing out, refusing to lock onto the sergeant's moving form. "Goddammit!" She abandoned the targeting system entirely, switching to manual because, this close in, she honestly didn't really need the targeting system anyway.

A touch at the blasters' firing mechanisms and the plasma guns hammered away, mowing the control room guards down. A last guard fell—teetering like a bowling pin before finally toppling over—and she turned the blasters around, using the view from her rearward-facing cameras to guide her as she spat a few rounds at the pressure door, obliterating the soldiers there as well.

Thirty seconds and it was over. Twelve armed guards dead, their sergeant lying bleeding on the floor.

"Well, that was effective." Henricksen picked himself up and dusted himself off. Reached down and helped Finlay to her feet.

"Holy shit," Finlay breathed, staring wide-eyed at *Serengeti*. "You kicked their asses!"

"Damn straight." *Serengeti* puffed out the RPD's chest.

Henricksen pulled his pistol, moving warily into the room. "Where the hell's that sergeant gotten to?" he muttered, and then stopped dead, pistol pointing as an anguished moan drifted from somewhere behind the monitoring station. A glance at *Serengeti,* wolfish smile stretching across his face, and Henricksen waved to Finlay, pointing her to one side of the room and Houseman and Beaulieu to the other.

The four of them crept around the control room, and the circular desk at its center, aiming for an opening on the far side. *Serengeti* followed Henricksen in, using the RPD to block the hallway in case Proctor tried to make a run for it.

Henricksen's eyes flicked her way, head nodding as he circled around the room, pistol pointed at the monitoring station in the middle. "Found him," he said, stopping on the far side.

"You prick!" Proctor screamed from his hiding place under the desk. "You shot me!"

"'Course we shot you, Corporal. You're a goddamn disgrace to that uniform." Henricksen moved a half-step closer, cocking his pistol, aiming toward the desk. "And you called my 'bot ugly." His face turned cold, voice taking on a hard edge. "She don't like bein' called ugly, Pork Butt." His eyes flickered toward the hallway, lips twitching as he tipped a wink. "Get him up," he said, waving Houseman and Beaulieu over as he stepped out of the way.

Proctor screamed when the troopers grabbed him. Stumbled, grabbing at his wounded leg as they yanked him to his feet.

"Quite your complainin'," Henricksen growled. "You got shot in the damn leg. Ain't like you're gonna die."

"But you shot me. You actually *shot* me!" Proctor looked indignantly. Like he still couldn't believe that had actually happened.

Serengeti stepped into the control room, shuffling awkwardly until the sled cleared the hall. "We should hurry," she said, using external comms this time, watching Proctor with one eye. "No cameras in here, so there's probably no active monitoring. But if there's anyone out there," she pointed the RPD's leg at the pressure door behind her, "they had to have heard the gunfire."

"And will likely call in reinforcements." Henricksen nodded, sharing a look with Finlay and the troopers guarding Proctor. "You heard the lady. Let's dump this load and get what we came for. In and out, quick as we can." He turned to Proctor, poking him hard in the chest. "You. Security code."

"I—I—I—I can't give that to you." Proctor shook his head hard, sweat pouring down his cheeks. "They'll shoot me for treason if I—"

"Skim off the big boss's personal stash and sell a few AIs on the black market?" Henricksen leaned close, giving the sergeant a flat-eyed stare. "That *was* what you were going to say, right?" He flashed his pistol, smiling as Proctor paled. "Already shot up one of your legs, Sergeant." The pistol pointed downward, Henricksen smiling evilly as he pressed it against Proctor's crotch. "Now you give me what I want, or I shoot up something else."

Proctor started trembling, slapping blindly at panels until a data screen finally appeared. Twisted, wincing, as if expecting Henricksen's gun to go off at any moment, and entered his access code for the security system.

"Wait." Henricksen grabbed the sergeant's hand as he reached to add his thumbprint. "Write that down," he said, flicking his fingers at Finlay.

Finlay frowned in confusion. "Not much good without the thumbprint."

"Just write it down, Finlay."

"Aye, sir." Finlay grabbed the reader and recorded Proctor's security code, clipping the device to her belt when she finished.

Henricksen released Proctor's hand, let him press his thumb to the fingerprint scanner. Waited, staring at the panel as the security system processed the credentials, matched the print to the code Proctor had entered. A chime and the cell doors popped open—every last one of them, but in just one hall.

"The rest," Henricksen ordered, pressing the pistol against Proctor's nuts. "Open the rest of them."

The sergeant whimpered, head whipping from side to side. "Ca— Ca—Can't," he stuttered. "System won't allow it. One hallway at a time. That's how it's coded."

"Well, that's inconvenient." Henricksen shared a look with *Serengeti,* turned his eyes back to Proctor's fat face. "Seven halls to choose from. Why'd you pick this one?"

"Your—Your roster says you're carrying Meridian Alliance AIs. In one of the cases anyway."

"And?"

"This hall." Proctor waved at the unlocked hall, cells sitting on either side. "They're all Meridian Alliance here."

Henricksen quirked an eyebrow. "*All* of them?"

Proctor nodded, jowls jiggling. "Keep 'em separate from the DSR scum. Send some of 'em to retraining if *Brutus…*" He trailed off, piggy eyes blinking stupidly, rivers of sweat sliding down his cheeks.

"Solves one problem," Henricksen said, eyes flicking *Serengeti's* way.

She tilted the RPD's head, not quite sure what he meant.

"I was trying to figure out how we'd convince a bunch of DSR AIs to come over to our side when our side, in theory, put them here in the first place." He shrugged, smiling ruefully. "If they're all Meridian Alliance, we don't really have to worry about that, now do we?"

"No. I guess not."

"Looks like something's finally gone right for a change."

Serengeti went cold all over. "Don't say that. You'll jinx us."

Henricksen frowned, giving her an odd look. "Since when are you superstitious?"

Since I spent fifty-three years alone while you slept in the dark.

"Take what you can," *Serengeti* told him. "Fill up the crates and get out."

Henricksen squinted, wondering at the evasion. Nodded slowly, letting the question go for now. "Houseman! Beaulieu! First two rooms in the corridor." He pointed to the hallway with its open doorways, waving the two troopers inside. "Finlay—you and me take the two after that. Our little TSG friends," a nod to the two shining, silver robots hovering behind *Serengeti's* sled, "get the last two in the hall. Help the rest of us out while they're at it."

The TSGs bounced happily, skittering into the hall.

"Dump the fakies inside the cells, fill up the crates with the real ones fast as you can. Got it?"

"Got it," Finlay said loudly.

Houseman and Beaulieu looked at each other, shrugged their shoulders, and nodded as well.

Not exactly overflowing with confidence, those two. *Serengeti* made a mental note to talk to *Atacama* about the training these troopers received.

"You." Henricksen shoved Proctor up against the panels ringing the monitoring station. "Stay here. *Right* here," he added, poking the sergeant in the chest.

"Here." Proctor nodded, breathing heavily. "Yes. Yes-yes." He leaned against the control station's panels, fingers reaching, fumbling at buttons.

"Scratch that." Henricksen grabbed the front of Proctor's uniform jacket, yanking him away. "You're coming with me, you twitchy, little shit."

Proctor squealed as Henricksen hauled him around, whimpered and clawed at Henricksen's fingers as he dragged the sergeant across the control room and into the corridor, slamming him up against the wall.

Finlay scrambled past them. Houseman and Beaulieu as well. That left just *Serengeti* in the control room.

"Alright," Henricksen called. "Back up the sled."

"Coming, Master!" *Serengeti* walked the RPD forward, maneuvering the bulky combat droid around the monitoring station at the room's center. A quick look over her shoulder, lining the sled up with the entrance to the hallway as best she could, and *Serengeti* backed up, using the fritzing camera in the 'bot's hind end to guide her.

Awkward operation, walking a too-big 'bot pushing an oversized sled across a circular room toward a square sided hallway. Awkwarder still, doing it all backward. Threading the sled through a tight gap at the same time—walls on one side, that circular, monitoring room desk on the other. Didn't help that the 'bot felt clunky as all get-out—oversized and ill-equipped for the task at hand—or that its systems only half-worked.

"Dammit," *Serengeti* swore, bodging it the first time. Drunk as a skunk now, electromagnetic shielding spilling into the hallway she was trying to enter.

"What's taking so long?" Henricksen called from somewhere behind her.

"Cram it, Mister. I'm a starship, not a damn robot. I'm not used to backing up."

"Use your hips," he suggested, flashing a smile, giving her a thumbs up. Stepped back, waving the others toward the end of the hall as *Serengeti* pulled forward and tried again.

A few tries and a few more fails, and *Serengeti* finally got the hang of things. Managed to line the sled up correctly, time the turn just right.

Lost a lot of time figuring the angles out, though. Time they really couldn't afford.

"Look out!" she called, threading the sled into the hallway.

It slid in clean—bit cockeyed, a little too far to the right, but not bad considering the drunken pilot.

Henricksen waved her backward, held up a hand, and yelled, "Stop!" when the sled neared the end of the hall. "That's good! Park it right there." He grabbed a crate from the sled and muscled it to the floor, kicked the door on his left open, and slid it inside.

Houseman and Beaulieu grabbed two others, grunting loudly as they moved the heavy cases around. The TSGs—far stronger than their human counterparts—handled their cases with ease, but Finlay struggled just trying to get her case off the sled.

Henricksen grabbed one of the robots and diverted it to help her before sending it on its way.

"Coulda gotten it," Finlay mumbled, kicking at the floor.

"Know you coulda, Finlay. Just in a rush is all." Henricksen patted her on the shoulder, turned her toward an open doorway. Ducked into the room across from it, grabbing Proctor on the way, and dragging him inside.

Serengeti checked to make sure everyone was out of the way before backing the RPD up a little more, pushing the sled right up against the end of the hall so she could look into one of the side rooms.

The space inside reminded her in some ways of her own containment pod: bright and white and incredibly clean. Octagonal, like *Cerberus's* pod. Walls squared-off to match everything else in the Vault. No pedestal at the center, though. Just shelves lining the walls—racks upon racks of storage. Crystal matrix minds jacked into energy units on every one—powered but contained. Isolated from any kind of network. Dozens upon dozens of AIs living in close proximity, and complete isolation.

How many? she wondered, scanning the room, as Houseman dumped out the contents of his crate and started grabbing crystal matrix brains from the shelves.

Empty spaces here and there. Space enough in that room for nearly double the number of AIs the cell currently held.

She pulled up the schematic of the station, checking the layout of the Vault. Ran a few calculations, making some assumptions based on what she saw in that room, and came up with some rather sobering results.

This Vault—this one Vault among many the Meridian Alliance maintained—could hold upwards of ten *thousand* AIs. Add in all the others scattered across the length and breadth of the galaxy and that number increased to nearly a million. Storage enough in the Meridian Alliance's Vaults for every last AI in the Fleet. The vast majority of the merchanter and commercial ships besides.

So many, she thought, watching Houseman fill his case, seal it up. *I wonder how many more would be here if that piece of trash Proctor hadn't sold them off.*

"Done!" the TSGs cried together, scrambling into the hallway, loading their crates onto the sled. "Ready-ready-ready," they reported, clonking leg-ends against their chromed heads.

"Good. Now go help the others," *Serengeti* ordered.

"Rodger-dodger!" One TSG went one way, while the other took off in the other, helping Finlay and Henricksen fill their crates.

Houseman appeared a few minutes later, dragging a crate behind him that he heaved onto the sled, and Beaulieu not long after that. Finlay took the longest—Henricksen's crate was just about full, but tiny Finlay couldn't quite reach the top shelf in her room, not without the TSG's help—but even with her lagging behind the others, the entire operation finished up in just under ten minutes.

Not bad, considering. Still longer than *Serengeti* would've liked, but not bad at all.

"How many?" Henricksen asked, grabbing Finlay's crate, setting it on the sled beside his.

"Fifty-three." Finlay patted her crate proudly. "You?"

"Same." Henricksen frowned, brow wrinkling. "Fifty-three on the dot."

Fifty-three. An inauspicious number. *Serengeti* shivered, wondering if she was just being paranoid.

"How about you, Houseman?"

Houseman shuffled his feet, scratching his head. "Didn't know we were supposed to count," he mumbled, studying his toes.

"Idiot," Henricksen muttered. He grabbed Proctor and shoved him toward the sled, loading him on with the crates. "Might need him," he explained at Finlay's questioning look. "*Serengeti's* been collecting all sorts of crap along the way, might as well collect some more. 'Sides, we still gotta get through that pressure door out there." He poked Proctor in the belly, making him squeak. "Piggy here's got the access codes, so Piggy goes for a ride. Ain't that ride, Piggy?'

Piggy squealed, desperately nodding his head.

TWENTY-NINE

"Alright, *Serengeti*. Let's get the hell outta here." Henricksen slapped the RPD's back, pacing along behind the sled as *Serengeti* pulled it from the hallway, maneuvering herself and it into the control room.

The TSGs scampered ahead of her, scouring the control room for more weapons, arming themselves with four rifles apiece. Switched to their tank treads with so many legs encumbered, zipping around like two tiny tanks.

Robots looked surprisingly cute carrying all those weapons. Might not need that many guns, but considering they had no idea what waited for them on the other side of that pressure door, the extra firepower wasn't necessarily a bad idea.

Proctor's security guards caught them with their pants down once. No *way Serengeti* was letting them do it again.

The TSGs huddled together, face lights flashing in rapid-fire patterns as they checked the status of their weapons, nipped a few spare magazines off the dead soldiers in the control room before following after *Serengeti* to the pressure door. Stopped there with her as Henricksen hauled Proctor off the sled.

"Access code. Now," he ordered, pointing to the security panel beside the door.

Proctor whimpered and looked over his shoulder, fat face turning the color of curdled milk as he eyed the pools of blood, the bodies slumped next to the walls.

Henricksen grabbed him by the neck, shoved his face against the pressure door's security panel. "Code. Now," he snapped, getting right in Proctor's face.

Proctor pawed at the wall, entering his access code with trembling fingers, mashed his thumb against the scanner to add his print.

"There now. That wasn't so hard, was it?" Henricksen slapped Proctor on the cheek. Yanked him away from the wall and turned him over to Houseman as the lock buzzed and whirred, heavy door splitting down the middle, panels grinding to either side. "Load him up," he ordered, nodding to the sled. "Make sure he stays put." He glanced behind him, watching Houseman lead the sergeant away, crept close to the pressure door, and snuck a peek at the room on the other side.

Weapons fire rattled against the door's reinforced metal panels, driving Henricksen back.

"We've got company," he yelled, ducking into the corner, muttering curses under his breath. "Looks like a dozen or so guards out there. Some kind of automated defense system up on the walls."

"Small caliber railguns," *Serengeti* told him. "Saw them on the schematic."

"*Now* you tell me?!"

Serengeti shrugged her RPD's legs. "You didn't ask."

"Oh, for the luvva—" Henricksen crammed himself into the corner as a fresh barrage of plasma rounds scored across the pressure door's panels. A few stray shots sneaking between them, leaving scorch marks on the corridor's walls. One awfully close to his head. "Can you do something about that?"

"Probably." *Serengeti* snuck a look herself, scanning the room in an instant. Ratcheted fresh rounds into the RPD's blasters and shoved the guns between the doors. "Stand back."

She triggered the blasters, filling the room with plasma fire. Pumped a couple of ion grenades into the 'bots launchers and lobbed those into the room as well. Made a slow count to five and stepped backward as the grenades detonated, filling the room outside with a sound like thunder.

Lightning flashed, cobalt blue and blinding, filling the air with screams. A quick look through the widening doorway showed half the guards down and obviously out of the picture, the rest crawling through the shredded remains of their fellows, searching for the weapons they'd dropped along the way.

"That what you were thinking?" *Serengeti* shuffled the RPD to one side.

Henricksen poked his head out, taking a look. "Damn, *Serengeti*. Remind me never to piss you off."

A whir of machinery—automated security systems waking, railguns swiveling toward the doorway—and he ducked back, spitting curses as the guns mounted high up on the walls opened fire.

Serengeti planted the RPD in the center of the doorway, pushing Henricksen aside. "Stay behind me. The RPD's armored. You're not."

"Neither are those cases," Henricksen reminded her, nodding to the sled she pulled. "And if we wanna get outta here, we gotta cross that room." He pointed a finger at the blood-filled space on the other side of the pressure door. "One good hit and all your friends go kablooey."

"Good thing the sled's behind me too, I guess."

Henricksen barked a laugh and raised his pistol, pointing it through the doors. "Alright. Lead us out, *Serengeti.* You shield us, we'll do what we can to keep those bastards from shooting up the cases." He waved her ahead, flattening himself against the wall as the sled rumbled past. Fell in behind her with Finlay at his side, Houseman, Beaulieu, and the two armed TSGs backing them up.

Fire slammed into the RPD the minute it left the corridor. *Serengeti* flared the panels on the combat drone's carapace, making herself as large as possible to shield the sled behind her, Henricksen, and the others clustered around it.

Started in surprise as a flash of face lights appeared at her feet—the two TSGs scurrying ahead with their rifles raised, flinging plasma rounds at anything that moved.

"Get back here," Henricksen yelled. "You'll get yourselves killed!"

The TSGs ignored him, screaming their *beeping* battle cries as they drowned the room in rifle fire, shooting randomly at first, and then with ever-greater precision.

A guard pitched forward, caught clean through the heart. The rest ducked for cover, using their fallen comrade as a shield, pulling more dead bodies around them to create a makeshift barricade as they fired back.

Just five of them left now—a manageable number, especially since they were pinned down. Wall defenses were another thing. Guns everywhere—high velocity and extremely deadly, ringing the room round. Magazines filled with tightly wound anti-gravity loads—old school ammunition that tore holy hell out of human flesh.

Serengeti targeted one and blew it to pieces, but the rest just compensated, swiveling more widely from their recessed positions to cover the blank spot the loss of that one gun created. A message to the TSGs and they added their fire as well, chewing up wall panels, battering at the railguns beneath, leaving the guards to Henricksen and his troopers while they helped *Serengeti* keep the room's automated defenses busy.

A step to the left, blasters firing, and a railgun exploded. Another step—anti-gravity rounds pinging off the RPD's shielding—and *Serengeti* noticed a surprising omission. An entire section of the room's security system watching her. Following her but not firing.

"Henricksen," she called, pointing her blasters, sniping a few rounds at the quiescent guns. "You see that?"

Henricksen snuck a look, eyes flicking from the guards sheltering in the center of the room to the guns behind them, poking outward from the wall. Noting the position of each, the fact that those guards just happened to be in the security system's line of fire. "Fail safe?" he guessed.

"That's what I'm thinking." *Serengeti* targeted that section of the security system, scouring the railguns from the wall. The rest rotated, firing at her, doing their best to make up for the guns they'd lost.

Henricksen flinched and ducked back as railgun fire rattled across *Serengeti's* shielding, just missing his head. "Move!" he yelled, slapping the RPD on the backside. Raised his pistol and pulled the trigger, dropping an unwary guard to the floor. "Pressure door. Circle around to the left. Keep the wall behind us."

"Got it!" *Serengeti* slid another step, TSGs moving with her, Henricksen and the others sticking close to the sled.

Henricksen's pistol kicked, snapping off more rounds, ducking each time the railgun fire rattled near.

Proctor, thinking him distracted, tried to make a run for it. Stupid move considering he had only the one good leg. Two steps and Henricksen grabbed him, jerked hard, bringing the sergeant to a halt.

"Not yet, you cowardly bastard. You get us outta here first."

He gripped the sergeant's arm tight, dragging Proctor with him as he and his crew circled around the room, inching closer to the pressure door.

The guards—those that weren't dead—seemed to realize what they were up to and redoubled their fire, flinging plasma rounds across the room as the rail guns chattered, ion rounds pinging off the RPD, ricocheting off the walls.

Serengeti targeted a cluster of rail guns, pulled the trigger, and drowned them in plasma fire. Picked out another cluster and pounded them into molten scraps of metal. "How are you guys doing back there?" she called, sneaking a look through the RPD's rearward-facing camera.

"Peachy." Henricksen leaned around her, breaking cover to crack off a few shots.

Houseman tried to copy him but tripped over his own feet. The stumbled, swearing loudly , jerked and dropped his weapon as a plasma round bit into his arm.

More swearing as Houseman grabbed at his arm, blood pouring through his fingers. Retreated, breathing hard, staring in disbelief at the chunk of bicep missing from his arm.

"Pick it up, Houseman." Henricksen nodded to the trooper's abandoned rifle, leaned around the RPD's shielding, and cracked off a few shots.

"I'm *bleeding*!" Houseman showed him his bloodied arm as proof.

"Gonna be a lot worse than that if we don't get to that pressure door." Henricksen dodged aside, kicking the rifle back to Houseman. "We'll patch you up later. Now pick it up."

Houseman bent over and grumblingly retrieved his weapon. Wiped his bloodied hand on his pants leg as he raised it to his shoulder.

Henricksen nodded encouragingly, slapped the trooper on the back. "Almost there, Houseman. Just a little further."

Houseman grimaced, favoring his wounded arm. Sucked in a breath and stepped from cover, emptying his clip at the room.

A barrage of railgun fire sent him stumbling backward, white-faced and checking for bullet holes, looking amazed that he still only had the one. A second barrage and he ducked for cover, hugging his rifle to his chest as ion rounds pinged off the RPD's shielding, snuck through, and slammed into the sled.

"Henricksen! The crates!" *Serengeti* called, activating the camera in the RPD's thorax, throwing a desperate look behind her.

"On it!" Henricksen retreated to check the payload, flashed a thumbs up. "Fine so far!" He flinching, ducking as railgun fire sparked off the RPD's metal carapace, tore panels from the wall. "It is severely not safe in here, *Serengeti*. We need to get to that door!"

"Almost there."

Henricksen climbed over the sled, leaned around *Serengeti's* shielding and took a look.

The pressure door loomed to one side, less than five meters away now. A triple-thick barrier—bomb-proof, blast-proof, security-locked— that grew closer with each sliding step *Serengeti* took.

He eyed the distance from here to there, clambering across the sled again to retrieve Proctor. "Finlay!"

"Aye, sir?"

"Need a favor." Henricksen snapped off a few rounds, drilling a hole clean through a guard's head. "Keep the rest of these bastards busy while I open this damn door."

"Aye, sir!" Finlay slid to her right, firing, catching another guard in the chest. "Like that, sir?"

"Perfect!" Henricksen flashed a thumbs up and climbed over the sled a third time, hauling Proctor with him, leaving Finlay to take over his position.

Houseman stared after him, tapped Beaulieu on the shoulder, and pointed to the pile of crates on the sled. Beaulieu nodded and climbed up with Houseman right behind her, the two of them using the high ground the crates offered to snipe at the room's three remaining guards.

Not a bad idea in theory. But in execution, it didn't quite work. High
ground gave the troopers a greater range of fire, but it also put them
outside *Serengeti's* shielding, exposing them to the automated defense
system.

Houseman dropped two guards in quick succession, but Beaulieu
barely managed to raise her rifle before a wall gun targeted her, shooting
a burst of anti-gravity rounds that toppled her from the stack of crates.

Beaulieu landed in a heap beside the sled, half of her head missing,
the other half containing one very startled-looking blue eye.

"Holy hell," Houseman breathed, staring down at her, frozen. "Holy
hell," he repeated, and then turned around, screaming as he drowned the
last trooper in plasma fire.

Serengeti circled another step, looked left, and found the pressure
door right beside her. "Henricksen."

"What?" he called, pistol kicking, shots cracking off. "What?" he
repeated, and then leaned to one side, blinking in surprise at the nearby
door.

"Go," *Serengeti* told him. "I'll cover you." She squatted down, guns
blazing, RPD turned to block the door as Henricksen shoved Proctor
over to the lock.

"Open it!" he ordered.

The sergeant shook his head, stabbing a finger at a camera.

"I said open it, you piece-a shit!" Henricksen yanked hard at
Proctor's arm, throwing him against the lock.

"C—Ca—Can't," the sergeant protested, and then jerked, sagging,
gurgling grotesquely as he slid to the floor.

"Shit!" Henricksen lowered his pistol, staring at the bullet wound in
Proctor's throat. "Shit, shit, shit, shit, shit!" he screamed, kicking at the
sergeant's lifeless body.

"He's dead, Henricksen," *Serengeti* yelled. "Figure something else
out!"

"Fuck!" He swung around, hands cupped around his mouth. "Finlay!
Reader!" He pointed at his palm, held out a hand.

Finlay dropped a hand to her side, unclipping the reader hanging from
her belt. Tossed it to Henricksen, nodding sharply as she faced back
around. "Gonna need a print," she reminded him, lifting her rifle to her
shoulder.

"I know. I got a plan."

He keyed into the reader, scrolling quickly, searching for the security
code they'd recorded earlier. He stared at it, lips moving, repeating it to
himself over and over again before entering the combination into the
lock. A quick check to make sure the data on the reader matched what

he'd entered into the locking mechanism, and Henricksen shut the device down, clipping it to his belt.

The lock flashed, accepting the code, sent a prompt, waiting for a fingerprint.

Henricksen grabbed the dead sergeant and dragged him over to the luck. Swore loudly when he realized Proctor's arms were too short to reach from the floor and the fat sergeant was too goddamn heavy to lift.

"Fuck!" he screamed, giving Proctor another kick. Stepped back and collected himself, looking from Proctor to the lock and back again. Pulled his pistol and grabbed the sergeant's hand, leveling the gun at Proctor's elbow. "Sorry about this, buddy."

Henricksen fired off six shots, twisted, and ripped the lower half of Proctor's arm away. Turned around and jammed the Sergeant's thumb against the scanner, muttering "C'mon, c'mon, c'mon," as the lock processed the print, flashed green, and opened.

Systems kicked in, pressure adjusting, triple-thick doors grinding open. Henricksen peered through the widening slit, examining the corridor on the other side.

"Aw hell!" he cried, and stepped away, shielding himself behind the door as yet more fire came from the hallway outside. "Bastards are everywhere!" he yelled, glancing at *Serengeti,* looking past her to his crew. "Finlay!" He pointed at Beaulieu's discarded weapon. "Toss me that rifle."

Finlay squatted down, firing her rifle one-handed as she scooped up Beaulieu's weapon and tossed it awkwardly to Henricksen.

He caught it and checked the chamber, ratcheted in a fresh round as *Serengeti* sprayed the walls with plasma fire. "Don't suppose you've got more of those grenades," he asked her.

"A few."

"Think I know a good way to use 'em." Henricksen hooked a thumb at the gap in the pressure door.

"Stand back." *Serengeti* brushed Henricksen out of the way, opened a port in the RPD's side, and fired two grenades into the hall.

Twin ion explosions lit the corridor, bathing the grey-on-grey hallway in blinding bursts of cobalt light.

"Everybody out!" Henricksen stepped into the hallway, blasting away with Beaulieu's rifle. "Finlay! On the sled with Houseman! Move!" he yelled as *Serengeti* bulled after him. "Move! Move! Move!"

The lot of them evacuated in a hurry, *Serengeti* taking the lead, Henricksen pacing along at her side. Finlay and Houseman clambered onto the slide, providing covering fire as they knelt atop the stack of crates, but the TSGs lagged behind.

"Hurry, boys! We're leaving!" Henricksen yelled, glancing back over his shoulder.

The TSGs waved cheerily, face lights flashing as they communicated with one another. A grenade launcher appeared—no idea where that came from, *Serengeti* assumed from one of the downed guards— canister-shaped magazine loaded into the top by one TSG while the other balanced it on his back and aimed it at the center of the room. A pause to check the settings and the robots backed up, hitting the button on the pressure door as they passed, pitching every last missile in the grenade launcher's magazine into the room as they exited.

The 'bots looked at each other, slapped a high-five, and high-tailed it after *Serengeti* as the pressure doors started to close.

The grenades exploded with the doors still half-open, the shockwave from the detonation knocking Henricksen over, sending the TSGs tumbling down the hall.

"Holy shit," Henricksen breathed, picking himself up. "What kind of combat program did you give them, *Serengeti*?"

"Default programming. Nothing special." *Serengeti* unloaded on a wall cannon, covering the TSGs while they retrieved their guns. Glanced down the hallway and spotted the airlock to the ship's berthing just a hundred meters away.

Almost there. We're almost there.

Grey uniforms appeared in the distance, well past their airlock, close to that long, curving bend in the corridor.

"Company," *Serengeti* warned, flinging a burst of plasma rounds down the hall.

"I see 'em." Henricksen emptied the clip of his rifle, ducked back, and snatched a handheld communicator from his belt. "Samara! *Samara!*" he screamed. "We're clear of the Vault. Open the goddamn lock."

"Aye, sir. What's—?"

Static shrieked across the channel, cutting Samara off. A clicking sound followed, harbinger to an unexpected burst of communication that blanketed the channel, filling *every* channel, looping around and repeating until *Serengeti* managed cut it off.

"What. The fuck. Was that?" Henricksen fired his rifle, pacing purposefully down the hall. "Answer me, Delacroix. What the fuck was that communication?"

Silence on the line—nothing at all from ship comms.

Serengeti reached back to the ship, accessed the comms system, and analyzed the transmission herself. "Distress signal."

Henricksen fired off a few more shots, ducked down, and reloaded. "Distress signal? From where? From *who*?"

Laughter filled the channel, soft and sneaky, almost evil sounding.

Henricksen looked up, rifle sagging as his face paled. "Please tell me that isn't who I think it is."

"*Homunculus.*" *Serengeti* shut down the channel, cutting the laughter off. "He must've got loose somehow."

Henricksen didn't look happy. In fact, he looked downright pissed. "Lemme guess: he used the airtime to give away our position."

Serengeti kept firing, kept walking forward, ignoring the shots pinging off her carapace.

"Who'd he call?" Henricksen asked her.

"*Brutus.* He called *Brutus* down on us."

"Son of a bitch!" The rifle snapped up, Henricksen slamming a fresh clip home. "Thought you had that bastard contained," he yelled, emptying the clip at the guards down the hall.

"Been a little busy," *Serengeti* reminded him, strafing the railguns on the walls.

"Busy. Right." Henricksen grunted, throwing a look *Serengeti's* way. "How the hell did he get to comms?"

"Delacroix, I assume."

He was the weak link, set to monitoring the channels. Tasked by Henricksen himself with keeping a tight rein on comms.

"Fuck. Delacroix! Answer me!" Henricksen yelled up to the ship. "Goddammit, Delacroix, are you sleeping up there?"

The channel clicked open—communication coming back from the ship. "Delacroix's down."

Aoki's voice, not Samara's. Despite that Samara had been left in charge of the bridge.

Henricksen frowned darkly. "Down. Whaddaya mean 'down'?"

"Brain's fried, sir. Effort of trying to contain *Homunculus* must've been too much for him. One minute he was standing there, doing his thing. Next minute he just…keels over. Starts seizing."

"God *fucking* dammit." Henricksen punched the wall. Punched it again and winced, flexing his hand. "Knew we shoulda replaced him." He wiped blood from his knuckles, poked his head out, and eyed the distance to the airlock. "We'll be on board in two minutes, Aoki. You get Delacroix to the med bay and find someone to replace him at Comms."

"Aye, sir." Aoki cut out.

Houseman lowered his rifle. "I know a little about Comms."

Henricksen gave him a sour look. "Yeah, well that doesn't really help us all that much right now, does it, Houseman?"

"No, sir. I guess not." Houseman pointed his rifle down the hallway, picking off a guard in a grey uniform. "Just sayin' is all."

"Idiot," Henricksen muttered, cracking off a few more shots.

Serengeti launched a staccato burst of fire from her blasters and plowed ahead, RPD taking a pounding from the wall guns and the troopers down the hall. Losing bits and pieces of her carapace. Entire chunks of the 'bot's body tearing away.

Dug in pretty good down there, that curve in the hallway providing surprisingly strong cover. Railgun fire was hard enough to deal with, she really didn't need the added distraction the prison guards offered.

A check of the RPD's grenade store found a half dozen rounds left. She lobbed one down the hall, smiling in satisfaction at the panicked screams that came back.

The timer on the device ticked down—three, two, one—and the grenade exploded, taking the guards out of the fight for a while.

"Go, Henricksen. Go, go, go!" *Serengeti* yelled, lowering the RPD's head, putting on a burst of speed.

Railgun fire strafed across the combat droid's face, knocking out most of its eyes. A grenade landed beside her, detonating before *Serengeti* could kick it away, rocking the RPD hard, almost tipping the droid completely over.

Serengeti stumbled and recovered, error messages flashing everywhere, cameras knocked out, targeting systems offline, a couple of legs missing on one side. A reboot fixed most of the systems, brought a few cameras back on-line, but some were unrecoverable. Blown to bits leaving her just a narrow tunnel of vision—two eyes looking forward, completely blind in the back.

"Keep going. Lock's just ahead." She scuttled the RPD forward, double-timing it to the airlock, trusting the others to stay with her. "Open it, Henricksen. Hurry!"

"Yeah-Yeah. Keep your shirt on." Henricksen moved up beside her, mashing at the panel to cycle the lock's mechanism.

Serengeti angled the RPD to provide cover for him as the TSGs scurried in front *her*, rifles rattling away.

The 'bots looked decidedly ragged. One had just two legs left and lost another while *Serengeti* watched. The other had a line of holes tracking up its side and across its head. The TSG looked at her, face lights flashing and flaring, randomly turning on and off. *Beeped* and *blipped,* all sorts of nonsensical sounds issuing from its speakers, trying to communicate something to her. Pass *Serengeti* one last message.

Never did figure out what it was, though. A wall cannon caught the 'bot before it finished its message, shearing its head in half, dropping the TSG's face lights into darkness.

The robot sagged, dropping its weapon. Toppled over as the airlock sighed open, inviting them into the ship.

"Inside! Get inside!" *Serengeti* ordered. "I'll back the payload in after you."

Henricksen shook his head hard. "Faster if you take the lock head-on." He glanced behind him. "Klugey business back there in the Vault."

Great. Never going to live that down.

"Too risky," she told him. "Leaves the payload exposed."

"We'll provide covering fire. Me and Finlay can—"

A grenade thumped down and exploded, turning their one remaining TSG into a pile of shredded bits, showering metal parts everywhere.

Serengeti turned her head. "Get inside, Henricksen. This is no time to argue."

Henricksen swore loudly, waving Finlay and Houseman inside. Backed into the lock after them, rifle spitting fire down the hall.

Serengeti walked the RPD forward, lining the sled up as she best she could. Crossed her fingers—metaphorically, of course—and backed up quickly. Blind as a bat and trusting in luck. Without so much as a single camera to guide her.

Rushed it, misjudging the approach completely, even with Henricksen behind her yelling instructions, and had to start all over again. Cursed when she miscalculated the angle of the airlock a second time and jammed the sled against the wall.

And all the while those railguns kept picking away at her, chewing hungrily at the RPD's carapace, tearing off yet more parts.

A direct hit knocked the combat droid off-balance, exposing the crates to fire as *Serengeti* slewed to one side.

"Fuck this." Henricksen stepped from the airlock with Finlay right beside him, the two of them providing covering fire while *Serengeti* righted the RPD and realigned it for another run. "We're running out of ammo here!"

His rifle chose that instant to quit, dramatically making his point. Henricksen twisted, tossing the empty rifle to Houseman, waving impatiently until the trooper handed his over.

Henricksen cocked the weapon, facing around, pointed the rifle down the hall, and squeezed the trigger, chewing through the rounds in the clip. "Any day now, *Serengeti*!"

"Out of the way!" *Serengeti* backed up in a hurry and slammed the sled into the wall, completely missing the airlock this time.

"What was that?" Henricksen demanded.

"Camera's busted. I can't see."

"You're blind?! Great. Just—Just hold on." Henricksen looped around her, clambering over the trailer, moving far enough into the hall that *Serengeti* could see him. "Back it up slow. I'll guide you in. Take your time and get it right. No sense rushing and having to do it all over again."

"I'd like to see *you* try to drive this thing," *Serengeti* said sourly.

Henricksen flashed a smile. "Probably run it right through the damn wall. Now back it up, *Serengeti*. Let's get that sucker on board."

"Here goes everything." *Serengeti* muttered a quick prayer as she pulled the RPD forward, using part of her brain to drive the droid's weapons and maintain fire on the railguns lining the hall while the other watched Henricksen. Listened to his voice. Followed his directions as he guided her into the airlock.

She lined the sled up perfectly this time. Slid it into the airlock like a greased pig. But she had to drop the 'bot's shielding to fit the RPD inside with it. Fold the pieces of its carapace back into place so the damned thing wouldn't get stuck.

"Henricksen," she called, moving back a step.

"Right behind you."

Weapons fire scored the decking, ricocheting off the wall. Henricksen turned, retreating, jerked and stiffened, mouth opening, eyes stretching wide.

He stumbled a step, rifle drooping, hand pressed tight to his side.

"Sir!" Finlay pushed past *Serengeti*, stepping into the hall.

"Back," he gasped, lurching toward the airlock. "Get inside."

Serengeti backed the rest of the way, sweeping Finlay along with her. Watched in agony as Henricksen shambled after them, ducking fire from the guards down the hall.

By some miracle, he reached the airlock without getting hit again, threw himself bodily through the door and landed at *Serengeti's* feet. "Shut it! Shut it tight, Finlay," Henricksen gasped.

Finlay slammed her hand against the panel, sealing the lock. Cutting the ship off from the station, the railgun, and plasma fire outside.

THIRTY

Henricksen rolled over as the lock cycled the environmentals, adjusting to the pressure inside the ship. A deep breath and he shoved himself to his feet, stumbled over to the wall and leaned against it, one hand pressed to his belly.

"You alright, sir?" Finlay eyed him worriedly, touching at her own stomach.

Henricksen spread his hands, staring down at his middle.

Blood stained his uniform, a ragged hole showing where a round had found its way through to his gut. More blood stained Henricksen's hands, spotting the decking as it poured down his side.

"Shit," he breathed, head lifting, eyes searching for Finlay. "Shit."

His knees buckled, dropping him to the floor.

Finlay dove across the lock and grabbed him, slipped her arm around Henricksen's waist, and just held him while he got his feet under him and pushed himself up again. "Got you. I got you, Captain."

Henricksen nodded wordlessly, face a tight mask of pain, hand braced against the wall to keep himself upright.

The airlock chimed and flashed green, door sliding open.

Cargo bay on the other side—smaller space than the landing bay where *Shriek* came and went. A stationside hold accustomed to human travel, its spaces lit and heated, artificial gravity weighing everything down.

Henricksen raised his head as the airlock door opened, waved to *Serengeti* and Houseman beside her. "Inside," he croaked, holding tight to Finlay. "Everybody out."

Houseman stood there, looking from Henricksen to the rifle he still held like he didn't know what he was supposed to do.

Serengeti pushed past him, trundling the RPD into the cargo bay, securing the sled and its load with magnetic docking clamps before shutting the 'bot down and flipping to a camera. "Take Henricksen to the med bay."

Finlay nodded, turning slowly, holding tight to Henricksen as she led him across the cargo bay. Houseman belatedly tried to help her, but Finlay just waved him away. "I've got him. He's *my* captain, not yours."

Houseman flinched and dropped back, looking surprisingly hurt.

"Hold up." Henricksen shuffled to a stop at the cargo bay door, slapped a bloodied hand against the comms panel beside it and called up to the bridge. "Aoki." He winced and closed his eyes, swaying on his feet. Sucked in a breath and tried again. "Shove off, Aoki."

"But, sir. The station."

"I know, Aoki." Soft voice. Patient voice. Henricksen too tired and hurting to yell anymore. "But those perimeter systems are gonna go live any minute—"

Klaxons blared, cutting him off, proving him right.

Serengeti shook as cannon fire rattled against her body. This close, the prison's defense grid could hardly miss her, even with the modified shimmer shield to confuse their targeting systems.

Henricksen leaned against the wall, eyes closed, speaking right into the comms panel. "Shove off, Aoki, before those cannons tear us apart. And spool up the jump drives. We're kind of in a rush."

"Aye, sir."

Henricksen closed the channel and braced himself as Aoki hit the thrusters, shoving them away from Faraday.

Serengeti flipped to an external camera, looking outside.

The magnetic locks let go, but the airlock coupling remained attached to her side, stretching to its limit before ripping violently from the station's wall.

Atmosphere erupted as the berthing area hallway depressurized, environmentals venting, killing everyone inside.

Serengeti stared in horror, watching bodies drift free, heading for the stars.

Not what she wanted. Not the end to this mission she'd envisioned. But it was Faraday's crew or hers, and that was no choice at all.

She watched a moment, tracking one body in particular for a long, long time. Abandoned the camera when it bumped into others, flipping back to the cargo bay, following Finlay and Henricksen into the corridor outside. Stayed with them as they rode the elevator up to the med bay on Level 6, belatedly remembering she'd detailed all the TSGs to *Shriek*.

Dammit.

She sent a message to the DD3s, calling two of them up to the med bay to sub in. Downloaded a basic medical program to their mindset and ran the installation routine as they made their way to Level 6.

Not the best solution, but the best she had at the moment. None of her human crew were medics, and she needed the TSGs who actually *were* designed for that purpose to take care of the second part of her plan.

"Sorry, Henricksen."

He looked up at the camera as the elevator doors slid open. "Not your fault." He grimaced, clutching at his stomach. "You tell Aoki to jump just as soon as the hyperspace drives are ready."

"Done," *Serengeti* agreed.

Henricksen nodded and let Finlay guide him into the hall, the two of them limping down to the med bay together—Finlay looking increasingly worried, Henricksen looking increasingly unsteady. Leaving a trail of bloody droplets behind him as he threaded his way down the hall.

He stopped when they reached the med bay, looking up at the camera above the door. "Get outta here, *Serengeti*. More important things to do than watch me bleed." He flipped a hand, holding tight to Finlay as she opened the door and half-carried him inside.

Houseman hesitated for a few seconds, staring through the open door, still looking like he had no idea what he should do. Clenched his fist, glancing down at his bloodied arm—minor wound really, not nearly as bad as that hole in Henricksen's stomach—considering the med bay door again before hurriedly slipping inside.

Serengeti flipped to the bridge once the med bay door closed. Settled into a camera as Aoki fired the main engines.

A blast from the station's perimeter defenses and *Serengeti* shuddered. A second blast—cannons pounding away at her hull—sent tremors running up and down her hull. She opened a secure channel, calling to the stealth ships hiding in the darkness. "*Shriek*. Drop back and come alongside."

"Why?" he demanded.

Serengeti sighed, tired of his penchant for asking questions at inopportune times. "Change of plans. In case you hadn't noticed, everything's gone to shit." Third blast from the station, this one slamming hard against her aft panels. "Drop back and come alongside," she ordered, completely out of patience. "I'm opening the main cargo bay so you can come in."

Shriek complied, grumbling the entire way. "Getting pretty sick and tired of you ordering me around all the time, lady."

"Yeah, well, we're all pretty sick and tired these days, *Shriek*."

Serengeti closed the channel and sent a message to the TSGs, ordering all of the robots on board to the main cargo bay. Powered up the RPD once they'd acknowledged and had it move the sled and its load of AIs over there too.

More cannon fire, coming fast and furious now, making the ship shudder and shake. Aoki ratcheted up the engines, speeding their exit from the station, perimeter defense system chasing after them, lobbing more fire their way.

Lucky for them, they had *Serengeti's* modified shimmer shield to confuse Faraday's targeting system. Make it harder for the defense system to actually lock onto them the further they moved away. A last hit, and then misses for a long, long time—nothing but plasma fire flying harmlessly by, drifting out to space.

That's better.

Serengeti killed *Homunculus's* beacon, robbing the station's systems of that bit of information as well. Leaving them just her engine signature to latch onto—not much she could do about that, seeing as how she kinda, sorta needed her engines if she was going to get out of here.

A check of her list—shield, beacons, engines—and *Serengeti* realized there was one thing she'd missed. "*Shriek.* Have you got any jammers on board?"

"Yeah. Why?" he asked suspiciously.

"We came in under false credentials and busted a bunch of rogue AIs out of prison. I'd rather no one knew we were here. Drop the jammers and you screw up inbound and outbound communications."

Jammers were pretty low-tech—just a canister with a power pack and comms package stuffed inside them, screaming out garbage. But they were noisy as hell and had a decent broadcasting range. And at just half the size of a TIG, they were difficult to find. Damn near impossible to target and destroy.

Simple things, but they should buy them some time. Enough of a head start to get those ships from the Pandoran Cloud before *Brutus* caught onto *Atacama's* ruse.

Or so she hoped.

"You do realize they'll jam *our* comms, too," *Shriek* told her. "At least until we move out of range."

"I am aware."

Shriek sighed. "Okay, then. Jammers away."

Comms cut out, a shrieking, dissonant noise taking over all the channels.

Annoying, since she had to listen to it, but worth it. Besides, they wouldn't be here all that long.

"Aoki—"

The bridge door opened and Finlay stepped inside. Finlay looking pale and shaken, covered in Henricksen's blood. Hole in her hand she hadn't even noticed, spilling yet more blood onto Scan's panels as she slid into her seat.

Vacant station, until Finlay filled it. Evidently, Samara hadn't found a suitable replacement to cover for her. Hopefully, Henricksen wouldn't find out about that.

"Finlay. Med kit." *Serengeti* flashed the light above the bridge's tiny first-aid station.

Finlay frowned in confusion, wiping blood from the panel in front of her. Turned her hand over and stared at the bullet wound cutting clean through her palm, brow furrowing like she had no idea what it was, much less how it had gotten there to begin with.

Aoki looked at her, and at the med kit on the wall. Bounced to her feet and grabbed it, hurrying back to Scan, dousing Finlay's the wound with an anti-bacterial sealant before binding it up with bandages. "Take you down to the med bay later. Get it fixed up proper."

Finlay flexed her fingers, staring at the bandage. "Thanks," she said faintly, and then bowed her head over her panel, poring through the data on Scan.

Serengeti watched her for a while, panned the camera around the rest of the bridge. Stopped when she reached the Command Post and stared at the empty Captain's Chair.

Silence there. A silence she felt like a gaping wound. A hole inside her where her captain should be.

She shivered, reaching for a camera in the med bay.

"Alright, boss lady."

Shriek's voice snapped *Serengeti* back to the bridge.

Internal channel. Jammer couldn't touch those. Unfortunately.

"I'm on board, now what do you—?"

"Helloooo!" she heard in the background.

"Hang on a sec." *Shriek* went quiet a moment. "Why is your RPD and a hoard of TSGs trying to get on board? And what the hell is in that—oh no. No-no-no-no-no. I've done a lot of things for you, *Serengeti,* but this—"

"Shut up, *Shriek.* They're part of the plan." She closed the internal channel, realized she'd forgotten something, and opened it again. "If you like your crew, you might want to have them stay with me for a while."

"What? Why?"

"Safer that way."

"You stuff me full of metal skins and now you want my *crew*?"

"Don't want them particularly. Just rather not see them die. Cloud's full of radiation," she reminded him. "Doesn't tend to agree with humans."

Samara cleared her throat loudly to get *Serengeti's* attention. "There might be another way. We came up with this thing in science club at the Academy—"

"Geek," Finlay muttered, Aoki snickering beside her.

Samara turned her head, favoring the two of them with a flat-eyed stare. "It's not all that hard really." She bent over her panel and searched through the database, pulled up information on the Raven, and ran calculations on the fly.

Serengeti snuck in and peeked at what she was doing. "Modifications to his cloaking shield?"

"Exactly. We introduce an electrostatic field to the crew area and charge the hull with a *magnetic* field to neutralize the…" Samara trailed off, face flushing as Finlay tilted her head. "What?" she asked, suddenly self-conscious.

"You are, without a doubt, the nerdiest nerd in all nerddom," Finlay told her.

Samara's face darkened.

"She's also brilliant." *Serengeti* checked the calculations, making a few adjustments to minimize the possibility of error before passing the design on to *Shriek*.

"This'll compromise my camouflage," he complained.

Serengeti sighed. "Barely. And it's better than your crew ending up dead from extreme radiation poisoning. So unless you want to give them up to me—"

"Nope. Nope. This looks great." *Shriek* implemented the changes in a hurry, yelling, "Hey!" when *Serengeti* sealed the cargo bay up. "I'm still in here, you know."

"Yes," she said patiently. "I'll let you out on the other side. 'Til then, just keep it quiet."

"Bossy-pants AI telling me what to do."

"Shut up, *Shriek*." *Serengeti* closed the channel, cutting him off. "Aoki. Status of the hyperspace engines."

"Spooled up and ready."

"Good. Send word to the Ravens."

"Uhh…" Aoki flicked her eyes to the windows. "The jammers?" she reminded her, shrugging apologetically.

Right. Damn.

"Oh well. *Shriek* and his boys will figure out what we're up to soon enough. Thirty seconds to jump," she said, sending the message over ship-wide comms.

Aoki threw a panicked look at the camera. "We haven't reached minimum safe distance! The station—"

"I know what will happen to the station," *Serengeti* said quietly.

Couldn't be helped. They had to leave. And they didn't have time to do it the safe and legal way this time.

"Hyperspace signatures detected," Finlay called from Scan. "Looks like…" Her fingers flew across the station, brow wrinkling as she examined the data the sensors sent back. "A dozen at least."

"*Brutus?*"

"Maybe," Finlay said doubtfully. "I think…" She frowned, scrolling through the data, trying to make sense of it. "Hard to tell since the jammers are messing with the signal, but it looks like they're squawking Meridian Alliance signatures."

Serengeti checked herself and found twelve fully-fledged jump signatures—no names yet, just the generic codes that preceded Meridian Alliance ships. Another four or five more forming as she examined the data from that first batch.

Could be *Brutus* and his cronies. Could just as easily be *Atacama* and her Valkyrie Sisters. Tempting to stay, and hope it was the latter. But they couldn't afford the risk of waiting here to find out.

"Jump," *Serengeti* ordered, not even checking the clock. "Jump to the rally point."

A glance at Scan showed four hyperspace buckles forming around hers—apparently, the Ravens had gotten the message and were bailing out, too.

Serengeti shoved hard for the displacement ahead of her, slipping into the hyperspace trough. Exited on the other side, bringing part of the station with her—most of the Vault from what she could tell. A good chunk of the rock beneath it.

Oops.

Perimeter alarms sounded, warning her of ships arriving. Bosch targeted them, pointing the rearward-facing batteries behind them as the buckles resolved and the stealth ships came through.

Weapons wound down as artillery systems secured. A perimeter alert popped up, warning *Serengeti* of an imminent collision as a chunk of Faraday's infrastructure drifted perilously close.

Swift swore loudly, dodging and weaving to get out of the Vault's way. Contacted *Serengeti,* wanting an explanation as *Shriek* kicked and screamed, demanding to be released from her cargo bay.

"Yeah-yeah-yeah. Just wait your turn." *Serengeti* muted *Swift's* channel, checking to make sure her cargo was on board. Opened the cargo bay doors and released *Shriek* to the stars, the Raven mumbling something about nerdy humans and broken promises as he exited in a hurry, rejoining his stealth ship brethren.

"Alright, Aoki. Fire the hyperspace engines back up," *Serengeti* ordered. "We're skimming from here to the Pandoran Cloud."

Aoki frowned, sharing a look with Samara. "Not sure that's such a good idea." Skimming was like leapfrogging, except with less time between each stop. Less time for the jump drives to cool down and recover. Less time for pursuing vessels to track a ship's course, too. "Burn out the engines if we're not careful," Aoki warned.

"I know," *Serengeti* told her. "But it's worth the risk. We're kind of in a hurry."

Thanks to *Homunculus, Brutus* had to have heard the damaged AI's cry for help.

She severed the connection to the Dreadnought's data and locked him up tight, leaving *Homunculus* to scream himself silly in his quarantined section of her network.

"Three hops and we reach the Pandoran Cloud. After that..." *Serengeti* trailed off, not knowing what to say. Not knowing what they'd want to hear.

"After that, shit gets serious," Finlay said in her best impression of Henricksen.

"That's one way to put it." *Serengeti* sent a smiley face to Finlay's station, passed the coordinates for the Pandoran Cloud to Samara, marking the three stops she planned to make along the way. "Pass that to the Ravens."

The objections were immediate. *Serengeti* ignored them and focused on her scans, making sure everything was clear before they headed to the next jump point.

No ships in the area, but there was that chunk of Faraday to consider. She stared at it, wondering what to do. No sense destroying it—anyone tracking them here would already know they'd come from Faraday—and there were still AIs in there. Kin, as much as she had any.

On a whim, she fired off a marker, tagging the remains of the Vault for retrieval. If they were lucky, they might be able to come back for it when all this was over.

Assuming there was anything left in there to come back for. And there's anything left of me to come back for it.

Sobering thought, that. She flipped to a camera in the med bay, sneaking a look at Henricksen.

Her captain had definitely seen better days. Henricksen lay in a spreading pool of blood on a surgical table while two DD3s worked away at him—one pumping him full of fluids while the other probed at the hole punched through his side.

He twitched, groaning as the robots poked and prodded—pale as death, obviously in a lot of pain.

His own damn fault, no doubt. The fact that he was awake meant he'd either ordered the DD3s to dial back the pain meds or refused them outright.

Serengeti shivered, watching them. Saw Henricksen's head turn, eyes locking onto the telltale light of her active camera.

Haunted eyes, face ashen. She'd never seen Henricksen look so broken. So vulnerable and exposed.

"Get outta here, *Serengeti*," he rasped. "Go. Get. See to the crew."

She lingered a moment anyway, watching, worrying, abandoning the camera only when he waved her away. Returned to the bridge and that empty chair. Finlay's blood staining Scan. "Finlay," she called, camera pivoting pointing at her freckled face. "What's going on out there?"

"Quiet," she said, cycling through the data windows on her station. "Just us right now from what I can tell."

"Good. Aoki. Start the jump clock. Three minutes and we're out."

"Aye." Aoki cycled the jump drives to active, throwing the clock on the windows so they could all watch it count down.

"Comms," *Serengeti* called, turning her camera to Delacroix's station.

Empty station. Delacroix in the med bay. Samara obviously hadn't found a replacement for him either.

Samara shrugged her shoulders, glancing guiltily at the camera. "No one qualified. No one even *close* to qualified on board."

"Except Houseman." Finlay snorted. "If you believe him. You ask me, guy's dumb as a stump."

Serengeti started to defend him—Houseman had tried back there, after all, and that meant something—but unfortunately she happened to agree with Finlay's assessment.

Better to leave the station empty than staff it with someone who couldn't cut it.

Should've pulled Delacroix. Should've known he couldn't handle Homunculus.

Nothing to be done about it, though. Way too late to try to fix that.

"Jump signatures," Finlay warned, highlighting a new stream of data on her panel, adding it to the display on the front windows.

Serengeti sighed, feeling harried from all directions. "That's our cue. *Shriek*. We're jumping." Forty seconds left on the clock. Close enough. "We skim the first two hops, settle in on the third. Got it?"

"Right behind you, boss lady."

"No objections?"

Surprising, honestly. *Shriek* objected to pretty much everything.

"Plenty," he told her. "Starting with what I got sitting in my hold. Mind telling me what I'm supposed to do with them?"

"I'll explain it to you once we get to the Cloud."

"Hold up. What's—?"

"Jump," *Serengeti* ordered, sliding into the buckle.

The trough wrapped around her, carrying her along for a while before dumping her out of hyperspace again. Ten seconds of travel time according to the chron.

She reset the jump clock—just sixty seconds of cooldown this time—skimming to the next step when it reached zero.

Warnings appeared—messages from Engineering, letting her know the hyperspace engines had exceeded normal operating parameters.

"Engines are running hot," Aoki noted as those same warnings flashed on her station. "Another hop like that and we'll likely do some damage."

"Two minutes," *Serengeti* said to appease her. And because there was no use burning out the jump drives when they'd left the last hop clean—no jump signatures behind them, nothing to indicate they were still being followed. And she could use the extra time to contact *Atacama*. Give her the go-ahead to spring her trap.

A check of the time—thirty seconds down—and she added another sixty seconds, giving them a minute and half.

"*Shriek*. Open an encrypted channel to *Atacama*."

"Contact her your own damn self," *Shriek* sent back. "I'm tired of being your messenger boy."

Serengeti sighed in annoyance.

"Stop being an asshole and do as the lady says, *Shriek*."

Henricksen's voice, thin and weak, filtering over the comms from the med bay.

Should've known he'd be listening in from down there.

"Henricksen! Buddy! Back from the dead again!"

"Channel, *Shriek*. And cut the crap."

Shriek sighed mournfully. "Ya know. You used to have a sense of humor."

"Yeah, well, you used to be funny. Open the damn channel. Give the lady a break."

A minute. Just one minute left on the jump clock.

"Fine. You can have your damn channel." *Shriek* closed the ship-to-ship channel, and opened a new one—encrypted this time, light flashing on *Serengeti's* Comms panel to let her know it was ready.

"Thank you, Captain," *Serengeti* said politely.

"Anytime." Henricksen went quiet, but he kept the channel open—better believe *Serengeti* noticed that.

She smiled to herself and tapped into the encrypted channel, reaching for her Valkyrie Sister across the stars. "*Atacama. Atacama*, it's *Serengeti*. It's time, Sister."

Silence at first, and then a distress beacon appeared, lighting up the channels, *Homunculus's* voice screaming into the dark from the Ranadene asteroid field.

"It's done," *Atacama* told her. "Find our friends and come meet us."

Atacama cut the channel as the jump clock hit zero.

"Last hop," *Serengeti* said.

"Whoo-hoo," *Shriek* cheered. "Pandoran Cloud, here we come!"

One more trip into hyperspace. One last hop before they kicked this all off.

Serengeti pulled in the feeds from all her externally facing cameras, focusing them on the stars. A burst from her thrusters and she dipped nose first into the buckle, disappearing into the trough.

THIRTY-ONE

Serengeti dropped out of hyperspace a good fifty thousand kilometers from the outer edge of the Pandoran Cloud. Millions of kilometers from the Eddington hypergiant at its center, the three desolate planets orbiting around it.

Well clear of the Cloud's solar storms and radiation, but the hyperspace drives started throwing errors anyway. Red lights flashing everywhere, warning of system degradations—engines damaged, on the verge of outright fairly.

Not the Cloud's fault, of course. The Pandoran Cloud lurked, waiting, a toxic stew of electromagnetic radiation, but it was *Serengeti* that brought them here. Who pushed those engines so hard.

Jump system wasn't designed for skimming. Engines held it together this long, despite the purposeful abuse, but those errors told *Serengeti* she better not even *think* about jumping again without making some repairs. Not unless she wanted to repeat that last disastrous tumble from hyperspace and end up abandoned again.

Didn't want that. Most *desperately* didn't want that, and yet she couldn't stay here. Not with *Atacama* waiting.

A touch at her systems cleared the errors, silencing the audible warnings. Second touch ordered the DD3s to Engineering in the hopes they could somehow pull off a miracle. Patch up *Serengeti's* engines enough to get her through one last jump.

Finlay fired up the scans, pulling in data from the broad-range sensors, parsing through it as she analyzed the section of space around them. *Shriek* and the other Ravens appeared thirty seconds on the dot after *Serengeti's* arrival, popping the perimeter alarms, but after that, there was nothing. Just *Serengeti* and the stealth ships and the stars.

And the Eddington hypergiant, of course. Its three planets. The Pandoran Cloud. Other than *that*, though…

"All clear," Finlay announced. "Scans are showing clean. No one on our tail."

For now.

Ominous thought. Ominous *feeling* settling over *Serengeti* as she stared down the Pandoran Cloud.

She kept both to herself—crew was on edge as it was, didn't need a freaked-out AI spooking them further—watching the data flow from the sensors. Dipping into Finlay's Scan station now and then as Aoki hauled the ship around, pointing *Serengeti* toward the hypergiant and the Cloud.

Eddington was massive—an oversized red star dominating the center of *Serengeti's* charts. A shape so huge, so luminous it showed clearly from here, over fifty thousand kilometers out. Bloated orb shining through the bridge's windows, bathing the stations in blood-red light.

The Cloud showed, too, though not to the human eye. Not so Finlay or the other crew could see. *Serengeti's* sensors picked up the radiation from the constant barrage of solar storms, displaying them as a noxious green mist swirling around the hypergiant at its center.

"It's beautiful," Finlay murmured, staring raptly at the crimson star. She raised a hand, watching the light spill between her fingers, pale cheeks painted a soft, rosy red.

"It's deadly," *Serengeti* told her. "And unstable. The life of a hypergiant is extremely short when compared to other stars. Eddington here will cease to exist in just half a million years."

Finlay pulled a face. "Are you telling me I should feel sorry for it?"

Serengeti chuckled. "No, Finlay. I would never tell you to feel sorry for a star."

Stars were free. Perfect. Pure in every sense of the word.

"So where are the ships?" Finlay tapped at her panel, cycling through the data from the sensors. "All this radiation. Can't really see much of anything."

"Exactly. That's why *Sechura* chose this place."

Tricky, Sister. Hiding your ships in plain sight.

"They're out there, Finlay. Likely orbiting one of those planets."

Serengeti threw the star chart on the front windows, zoomed in on the Eddington hypergiant, highlighting the three lifeless orbs orbit around it. Neto. Amaterasu. Shamash. Three sunburnt planets, none of them capable of supporting life. None of them *ever* to see human colonization, because even terraforming could only do so much.

"So how come we can't see them?" Finlay asked, cycling through the sensor data again. "How come I'm not picking anything up on Scan?"

"Radiation. See, the Cloud…it's sort of like a fog," *Serengeti* explained. "A sea of magnetic eruptions concealing everything inside it from AI sensors and scans. I daren't go much closer," not after Faraday, not after experiencing the effects of that electromagnetic shielding on the RPD, "and from here…well, something as small as a ship is far too tiny for cameras to pick out at this distance." She ran through all the sensors again—still nothing out there, no sign of hyperspace engines, ships coming through—before flashing a message to Aoki. "Take us in a little, if you please."

"Aye." Aoki triggered main propulsion, moving *Serengeti* closer in.

Messages popped up everywhere, warning the ship to steer clear of the Pandoran Cloud and its radiation storms, flashing 'minimum safe distance thirty thousand kilometers' over and over again.

Serengeti acknowledged the messages and closed them all down, cruised in, and stopped exactly thirty thousand kilometers out.

She'd already overloaded her engines, no sense risking damage to her other, more delicate systems. Especially when she herself had no reason to enter the Pandoran Cloud.

That was *Shriek's* job, reluctant as he was to do it.

"You're up, big boy," she sent to the stealth ship.

"And what if I don't want to go?" *Shriek* asked her. "What if I tell you to stick it and deliver the damn AIs yourself?"

"I activate the combat programming in those TSDs you took on and let them wreak merry havoc on your insides," *Serengeti* said sweetly. "Think they'd like that actually. Little 'bots do love a good havocking."

"You wouldn't."

"Try me."

Shriek was quiet a moment, thinking the situation over. "Fine," he huffed. "I'll deliver your damn cargo. But you owe me, Sister. Big time."

"So you keep reminding me," *Serengeti* said sourly. "If this works out, you get to be a big damn hero. Savior of the Meridian Alliance, they'll call you. Write speeches about how you single-handedly redeemed the Fleet's honor with your daring-do."

A pause, and then, "Will I get a medal?"

"Probably. Nice skull and crossbones for your hull. Something like that."

"Sweet." *Shriek* closed the channel and activated his engines, moving into the Pandoran Cloud.

Serengeti watched him until the radiation hid the stealth ship from her sensors, checked in on the other Ravens sitting cloaked and bored around her, ran another round of scans.

Nothing, nothing, and more nothing. No hyperspace signatures. No signs of any ships in the area besides herself and *Shriek's* Ravens.

Quiet out there. Dark and empty. *Serengeti* was pretty sure it wouldn't stay that way. Made far too much noise back there on Faraday. Skimming should help—make it that much harder for anyone to track them—but a ship her size...couldn't hide forever. Pandoran Cloud was just a stopover. Each minute here excruciating. The more time she spent finding those ships, the less she had to get to *Atacama* before *Brutus* grew wise to their trap.

A check of the chron showed ten minutes elapsed. Ten minutes, just ten short minutes, but it already felt like ten minutes too long.

Serengeti contacted her Sister, knowing she'd worry. "*Atacama.* We're here," she sent.

Sub-space message. Valkyrie channel. Not quite as secure as the Ravens' encrypted comms but private enough. She hoped.

No response to that first message—worrisome, but with the Cloud so close, it was possible the comms weren't getting through. But a second message likewise went unanswered. A third—a plea this time, asking *Atacama* just to respond.

Nothing. Silence. A void of dead comms. *Serengeti* started to worry. Wonder if something had already gone wrong.

Dammit, Atacama. *Where are you? What's going on?*

"Still can't see anything," Finlay muttered, pulling up the feeds from the hull cameras, poring over every one. "I get that whole fog thing, but how do we know the ships are even in there?"

"You don't, Finlay."

Henricksen's voice. Henricksen himself standing in the bridge's doorway—shadow-eyed and ashen-faced, hand pressed to his side.

"Some things you just gotta take on faith."

Finlay twisted, staring at him like she was seeing a ghost. "Aye, sir," she said faintly, and started to stand, hand lifting to salute.

"None of that, Finlay." Henricksen waved her back down. "Too much going on to worry about pleasantries and saluting."

"Yes, sir." Finlay hesitated, spots of color blooming on her cheeks. "Good to have you here, sir." She nodded to him and faced back around.

Henricksen shifted, grimacing. Leaned against the doorframe—pale as death, lips pressed in a thin line.

Death warmed over. Like he might keel over at any moment.

"You shouldn't be here, Henricksen," *Serengeti* scolded.

"Yeah, well." Henricksen sucked in a breath, wincing as he straightened. "I ain't dead yet. Figure that means I should be here." Another breath as he pushed away from the doorframe. "Permission to come aboard?"

She considered refusing and ordering him back to the med bay. But she wanted him here. Felt incomplete without Henricksen manning the bridge. "Granted. But you topple over—"

"Yeah-yeah. I drop dead you can haul my carcass outta here. Until then, this is still my bridge." Henricksen stuck out his chin, staring stubbornly at the camera. "And that," he pointed across the bridge to the

Command Post at the center, "is my chair. Says so right here." A tap of his finger to the stars on his collar as Henricksen stepped away from the door and walked stiffly across the bridge, sinking into his Captain's Chair with a sigh.

"You sure you're alright?" *Serengeti* asked, watching him.

"Been better," he admitted, flashing a crooked smile. A deep breath and he leaned forward, keying into the station, sorting through the information from the scans. "So what's our status?" he asked, looking up at the camera.

"Sent *Shriek* into the Cloud with the payload. No word back from him yet."

"And us?" Henricksen tilted his head, brow wrinkling in concern. "You took a few hits back at Faraday."

"Minor damage. Hull plating mostly." She hesitated, then told him the rest. "Jump drives overloaded. Skimmed our way here," she explained. "They got a little hot."

"I'll bet," Henricksen murmured, watching the camera.

"I've got the DD3s working on them, but we're kind of...stuck here, until they get the hyperspace drives fixed."

"Stuck here," he repeated, and then grunted, shaking his head. "Well, ain't that a bitch." He turned his eyes, staring through the front windows at the Eddington hypergiant's enormous red ball. "Well, well, well. Would you look at that?" He leaned forward, arm resting on the panel in front of him, pale face bathed in the star's light.

Crimson light. Blood-red illumination. *Serengeti* flashed on an image of him lying on the surgical table, blood pooling around him, spilling onto the floor.

Not a memory she wanted. Not ever again.

She toggled the filters on the windows, toning down the red glow.

Henricksen glanced up, lips pursing, eyes flicking from the windows to *Serengeti's* camera. Started to say something and then shook his head. Called out to Finlay instead. "Scan. Status."

Finlay tapped at her panel, throwing a display on the front windows. "Scans show clean, sir."

"For now, anyway." Henricksen frowned, scanning the stars outside. "You contact *Atacama*?" he asked, looking up at the camera.

"Tried. No answer." She tried again, sending yet another sub-space message across the Valkyrie channel.

Still no answer. Comms as silent and empty as before.

Damn. Damn and damn and damn.

"Anything?" Henricksen asked hopefully.

"Nothing yet. You changed your uniform."

Henricksen blinked, frowning at the sudden change in topic. Glanced down and plucked at his black-on-black jacket. Touched a finger to *Serengeti's* dark and stars patch. "Hated that other one. God-awfullest looking thing. No offense, Bosch," he said, nodding to the gunner.

Bosch shrugged his burly shoulders, just about all the movement he could make in the tight confines of the Artillery pod. "None taken. Not like I designed them or anything."

Henricksen grunted, looking back to *Serengeti's* camera. "Trashed the other one anyway," he told her. "No choice but to change." He shifted in his seat, grimaced and bowed his head. Sat there a while, taking deep breaths.

"You shouldn't be here, Henricksen. Go back to the med bay. The DD3s—"

"Are a buncha butchers." Henricksen straightened, wincing, staring defiantly at the camera. "Med programming ain't worth shit. Damned things are all thumbs."

Whatever that meant.

"I could tweak the programming."

"And do what?" Henricksen sighed, leaning back, rubbing at his side. "'Bots pumped me full of stims and plas-blood and every other damn thing. Not really much more they can do. I'm no damned good to you down there, *Serengeti*. You know that."

"You've got a hole in your belly, Henricksen."

"And you lost three cannons and a whole section of your hull plating back at Faraday. I call that even."

"Noticed that, did you?" *Serengeti* laughed softly. "Typical Henricksen. Too busy worrying about the ship to be worried about yourself."

"I'm *fine*, *Serengeti*. Told you that."

But he wasn't fine. Nothing about Henricksen looked fine right now. Anyone could see that.

"You die on me and I'm going to be severely pissed."

Henricksen rolled his eyes. "I'm not dyin', *Serengeti*. Nobody's dyin'," he said, flicking his eyes across the bridge.

Crew stared back at him—worried, scared. Dropped their eyes and turned back to their stations, checking the data on their panels, watching the clock on the front windows—anything to pass the time.

Henricksen watched them a moment, slid his eyes back to the camera, voice dropping to a whisper only *Serengeti* could hear. "Galaxy's going to shit, and we're about to make a last stand. Last thing I wanna do is lie down there in the med bay while you and the crew kick *Brutus's* ass. I belong here, *Serengeti*. Here," he said, slapping his Captain's Chair. "Not down there, acting like some goddamn invalid."

"Not you, Henricksen. Never that," she murmured.

A smile for the camera—wan and sickly, smartass as ever. "So what's the play?" he asked her, nodding to the windows. "*Shriek's* in there somewhere, I assume. Trying to find *Sechura's* ships. Can we contact him? You got a channel we can reach him on?"

"Maybe." *Serengeti* sent a message to *Shriek's* encrypted comms channel, waited until it opened.

Lot of static on that channel. Garbled communication coming back.

"What now?" *Shriek* asked testily, voice fuzzing in and out.

Feedback squealed through the speakers, making everyone wince and cover their ears.

"Ugh. That's *horrible*," Henricksen complained. "Can't you clean that up a little, *Shriek*?"

"Uh, *hello*?! Pandoran Cloud, remember? Not so friendly to systems. Not my fault comms is crap."

A burst of static and *Shriek's* voice faded out. *Serengeti* fiddled with the comms filters until she found him again.

"So how the hell am I supposed to find a bunch of powered-down ships in this soup anyway?" *Shriek* asked.

"Well, if I were *Sechura,* I'd probably park them on the dark side of one of those planets," *Serengeti* reasoned. "Use the planetary mass to protect them from the star's heat. Not to mention the solar radiation."

Radiation that would've killed *Shriek's* crew if Samara hadn't come up with that fancy shielding modification. Score one for the girl at Navigation.

"Planets," *Shriek* grumbled. "So much radiation in here I'll be lucky I don't run straight into one of the damned things. Sensors don't work. Scans don't work. I'm flying blind in here, *Serengeti!*"

"Blind." Henricksen snorted. "Whaddaya mean, 'blind'? Ya got windows right?"

"Yeah," *Shriek* said carefully.

"Then have your crew do it the old-fashioned way."

"Meaning?"

Henricksen sighed. "Eyeballs, *Shriek.* Have them use their eyeballs."

"Well," *Shriek* huffed. "If you want to be all *primitive* about it."

More static—an ocean of it this time, flooding the channel, refusing to clear no matter what *Serengeti* did. "Sorry. Looks like we lost him."

"Damn," Henricksen muttered, staring out the windows. "Good luck, buddy," he whispered, looking away, turning his eyes toward *Serengeti's* camera. "How's he supposed to deliver those AIs anyway? Assuming, of course, that he actually *finds Sechura's* ships in that mess."

"TSGs."

Henricksen blinked blankly. "'Bots are handy little suckers, but I don't see—"

"I loaded every last TSG I had into *Shriek's* belly along with the crates containing the AIs. Once he locates the ships, he can drop them like carpet bombs. Let the robots carry the AIs to the vessels."

"Carpet bombs." Henricksen frowned, eyes flicking to the front windows. "Close to four hundred AIs in those crates. Last I checked, you only had fifty or so TSGs."

"Math doesn't work, does it? Sorry. Best I could do."

"Fifty ships are better than no ships, I guess," Henricksen sighed, wincing. Shifted carefully, trying to get more comfortable.

"Maybe you should—"

"I'm *fine*, goddammit."

"You're *not* fine," *Serengeti* said quietly.

Henricksen stared a moment—chin set, face stubborn—sighed and flipped a hand. "Fifty isn't four hundred, but it's still better than us alone with only a couple hundred Valkyries to back us up." A glance at the bridge crew and he dropped his voice. "We *do* have that many Valkyries, don't we?"

She honestly didn't know. Pointedly didn't answer.

"Well, that's reassuring," Henricksen muttered, giving the camera a dark look.

The bridge went quiet after that—Henricksen watching the windows, *Serengeti* watching him. Crew watching *everything,* throwing anxious glances their captain's way.

"*Shriek* may be able to retrieve some of the robots." *Serengeti* tried to sound confident. More confident than she actually felt. "If he can pick them up, he can reseed them elsewhere. Maybe bring a few more AI-driven ships to our side."

Henricksen grunted, frowning doubtfully. "And *Atacama*? Any word from her?"

"No," she said softly. "Not since our last jump."

"Try her again?" Henricksen suggested. "Different channel this time?"

"Worth a try, I guess." She reached out to the stealth ships, asking for another favor. Bracing herself for the expected objections. "*Swift.* Need a secure channel to *Atacama*, if you please."

"Aww, c'mon!" *Swift* grumbled. "Why do I gotta be messenger boy now?"

"Oh for god's sake!" Henricksen smacked the panel in front of him, startling everyone on the bridge. Hurt himself in the process, apparently. Based on the way he hunched over, arm wrapped across his middle. "Why," he asked, voice rasping, "is it always so goddamn hard to get a goddamn stealth ship to do a simple thing like opening a goddamn encrypted channel?" He braced one hand against a panel, straightening with an effort. "Open. The goddamn. Channel. Now, *Swift*."

Swift didn't say anything. Not a thing. He just opened the encrypted channel and sat there, cruising silently beside *Serengeti*.

"Thank you, Henricksen," *Serengeti* said politely.

Henricksen nodded without looking, face a mask of pain.

"*Atacama*," *Serengeti* called, leaving the channel open—waiting, listening, hoping for a response. "Sister," she sent, when nothing came back.

Comms clicked. "We're here," *Atacama's* answered, voice muffled and slightly fuzzy. Cutting in and out.

Radiation from the Cloud, messing with *Serengeti* comms. Something worse, maybe. Something on Atacama's end, actively blocking her comms.

"He's not here." Desperation in *Atacama's* voice now. The closest *Serengeti* had ever heard her come to panic. "We're here, but there's no sign of *Brutus*."

Henricksen shared a worried look with the camera. "All that set up and now the Bastion's a no-show? That can't be good."

"No," *Serengeti* murmured, thinking quickly.

"You think that was him back at—"

Perimeter alarms starting screaming, messages popping up on Scan.

"Finlay!" Henricksen called.

"Sensors are picking up something." Finlay leaned close to her panel, fingers flying as she parsed through the data, face bathed in multi-colored light. A pause, hands hovering in mid-air as she focused on something on her station. Rattled out a rapid-fire string of commands and threw a camera feed onto the front windows. "Jump signatures, sir. A lot of them," she said, twisting around.

Henricksen swore softly. "*Brutus*?" he asked, looking up at the camera

"Maybe," *Serengeti* said, examining the Scan data herself. "Can't tell for sure. *Atacama*," she called, sending a plea for help across the stars. "We need you."

"We're coming," *Atacama* answered. "Hold tight, Sister. We're coming to you."

Atacama closed the channel, disappearing into the dark.

THIRTY-TWO

Henricksen shoved himself to his feet, gasped and swayed. Wrapped an arm across his middle as he braced himself against the panel in front of him. Stayed there a moment—head bowed, hand pressing at that recently sealed wound, breathing in slow, shuddering breaths.

"Henricksen—"

"Fine, *Serengeti*. Told ya, I'm fine." A last breath and he squared his shoulders, straightening up. Turned an ashen face toward the windows, watching the hyperspace buckles form outside. "*Atacama*?" he asked her, looking a question at the camera.

"Still three minutes out. Looks like we're on our own for a while."

"Great." He shifted, wincing, spread his legs wide. "Finlay. How long's *Shriek* been gone?"

Finlay checked the clock on the windows, consulted a few other data sources before making an educated guess. "Fifteen minutes, maybe?"

"Seventeen minutes, forty-two seconds," *Serengeti* amended.

"What she said." Finlay hooked a thumb at the camera.

"Seventeen minutes." Henricksen pulled up the feeds from Scan, studying the Pandoran Cloud. "God damn stealth ships," he muttered. "How long can it *possibly* take to find a few ships and stuff them full of AIs?"

Finlay chewed her lip, looking from her station to the clock on the windows and back again. "I don't—I don't really—"

"Rhetorical question." Henricksen waved her to silence. "Wasn't really expecting an answer."

"Oh." Finlay blushed, wiping a smear of blood from her panel.

"How many are out there?" he asked, nodding to the swirling spots of darkness showing through the windows.

Finlay consulted her panel, layering a few data feeds together. "Two dozen at least. Make that three dozen," she amended as more jump signatures appeared.

Henricksen chewed his lip, eyes flicking to the camera. "Shimmer shield still active?"

"Been running it since we left Faraday."

Debatable whether that was a good idea. *Shriek* was right about the drain on her systems. The fuel cells showed half-empty. Partly that was due to the skimming—not exactly an economical way to travel—mostly it was due to the sustained operation of the shimmer shield.

Damaged my engines and running out of juice. Doing a hell of a number on this new body they gave you, Serengeti.

"Should keep us hidden for a while. At least confuse their scans."

Henricksen nodded, staring at the windows. "Makes you wonder why no one ever thought of modifying the thing before."

"Maybe no one's ever been as desperate as we are. There's a phrase to that effect, isn't there, Henricksen? Desperation is the motherload of invention? Something like that?"

"Something like that." Henricksen smiled crookedly. Tilted his head, looking up at the camera. "So whaddaya think happened? You and *Atacama* seemed so sure *Brutus* would take the bait and go after that wreck."

"Not sure he ever made it."

"Faraday?"

"That's what I'm thinking. Jammers must've failed. Let comms get through to *Brutus*."

"Then he'll know *Homunculus* reported into Faraday right before that distress signal popped off near Ranadene. Hell, Faraday probably passed him enough information to track us to that first jump point, too."

"And from there to here, despite the skimming."

Henricksen nodded slowly, thinking that over. "Good idea, by the way. The skimming."

"Right. Brilliant," *Serengeti* said bitterly. "Burned out our engines and they found us anyway."

"Bought us some time," Henricksen told her, gazing steadily at the camera. "Gave us a chance."

"At what?" she almost asked, but Finlay interrupted.

"Sir." Finlay turned, throwing a desperate look at the Command Post as a buckle resolved, video feed showing a ship in the distance, floating in the endless darkness. "They're coming through," she said in a hushed, scared voice.

Second ship appeared soon after. Two more after that. A handful became a dozen, then two dozen, flooding *Serengeti's* sensors with ships' information. Names and call signs cluttering up her display.

Scylla out there—*Scylla* and *Charybdis,* the monstrous sisters. *Jotunn* and *Nephilim. Gogmagog* who was the oldest of them. Rebuilt so many times it was a running joke about how long he could keep a chassis from getting destroyed.

Dreadnoughts, all of them. Every last one of those ships. They were the worst of them—*Brutus's* most trusted bodyguards. Loyal to him first and everything else after.

Including the Citadel. And the Fleet they supposedly served. That was true even *before Serengeti* disappeared into the dark all those years ago. And from what she could tell, that loyalty to the Bastion had only grown stronger in the intervening years.

"Get me a count on those ships, Finlay. No more guessing," Henricksen told her.

Finlay stared at her screen, scrolling through the information on the display. "Forty-two. Forty-eight. Fifty." She frowned, looking from the panel in front of her to the windows at the front of the bridge as a last few buckles resolved, less than ten thousand kilometers away. "Fifty-three, sir. I count fifty-three total." She scanned the data, the list of ships' names and classes. "Looks like a mixed bag of Dreadnoughts and Titans. Mostly Dreadnoughts," she said, shrugging apologetically. "And there's *Brutus,* of course."

Another shrug. As if *Brutus* bringing in the big guns was somehow her fault.

"Fifty-three. Goddamn," Henricksen breathed, scrubbing his fingers through his hair. "Fifty-three again. Ain't that a bitch?"

And just one of them, unless *Serengeti* could find some reinforcements.

"*Atacama.* Where are you?" she called.

"Two minutes out."

Henricksen glanced at the windows, back to the camera. "That's a long time to be hanging out here by ourselves. Any word from our lippy little buddy?"

"Not recently." *Serengeti* reached out to the stealth ship, hoping he might answer. "*Shriek. Shriek,* where are you?"

Nothing from the Cloud. Just static and feedback, comms a wasteland of noise.

Henricksen sighed. "Well, so much for that idea." He looked away again, studying the stars outside, eyes flicking to the bridge crew now and then. "Shut down all the active systems. That means no engines, and no weapons." A glance at Artillery. "You got that, Bosch? You keep your hands away from those triggers."

"Aye, sir." Bosch started to climb out of the pod.

"I didn't say abandon your post, Bosch. Just don't shoot anything for now."

Bosch looked at him, and at the Artillery pod, sighed, and wriggled back into his seat.

Henricksen flicked his eyes to Finlay. "Passive scans only," he told her. "Shimmer shield modifications should make it hard for them to find us so long as we're not moving. Or shooting," he added, giving Bosch another look. "But we scan 'em and they'll lock onto our location right quick."

"Aye, sir." Finlay tapped at her panel, shutting down all the active scan feeds, making them as dark and quiet as possible. Caught Henricksen's eyes and pointed to the front windows as a swirl appeared—the telltale sign of a buckle forming outside. "Looks like we've got more company."

Henricksen leaned forward, studying the distortion. Watching others appear. "Ours, ya think?"

"Gotta be, right?" Finlay looked hopeful. "*Atacama* said she was coming."

"Maybe." Henricksen frowned at the windows, watching the buckles outside grow.

"Should I...?" Finlay nodded to her panel, the sensors she'd shut down.

"No. Leave 'em. Even if that is *Atacama* out there, we've still got *Brutus* and his boys to deal with. Rather we didn't—shit." Henricksen swore as cobalt light flared, engines firing, *Brutus* moving his tiny fleet closer to where *Serengeti* hid. "They spot us somehow? You think they know we're here?"

"Shouldn't," *Serengeti* told him, and then Finlay's panels lit up, warnings erupting in blinking red flares. *Serengeti* herself shivering as hundreds of ship's sensors washed over her body.

"They're scanning us," Finlay warned. "Should we—?"

"Steady, Finlay." Henricksen's eyes flicked to *Serengeti's* camera. "We in trouble?"

"Not yet. Broad-spectrum scans," she explained. "They're just sort of inventorying the entire area, not really targeting anything in particular. If we stay quiet, we should be—"

'Fine,' she started to say, and then those scans out there paused. Crept slowly across her shimmer shield, as if detecting the abnormality. Sensing her shape beneath.

"Sir?" Finlay twisted, eyes wide and worried.

"Steady," he repeated. "Shimmer shield, remember? They can't see us."

Finlay glanced at the windows, lip caught between her teeth.

A last pass of those sensors and the scans moved on. Passed over *Serengeti* and shut off.

Something new appeared, then. Something ominous and somehow worse. A heavy, overriding presence that wrapped around *Serengeti's* body. Probing insistently. Searching for a way in.

"*Brutus*," *Serengeti* whispered, shivering at that touch. "He's here, Henricksen. I can feel him."

The Bastion's consciousness crawled across her, studying *Serengeti* like some interesting bug. But a last touch and he retreated, leaving her scratching her head.

Comms clicked open—fleet-wide, addressing all the ships in the area—and the Bastion's grating, metallic voice came through. "I know you're out there, hiding like a rat. Not quite sure who you are, but I *do* know you're out there." *Brutus* laughed softly, an ugly, mocking sound that echoed around *Serengeti's* bridge.

"Weapons charging!" Finlay warned. "*Brutus* is firing his main gun."

"Hold!" Henricksen yelled, as Aoki reached for the thrusters, Bosch flipped his targeting visor down. "He's shooting blind. Trying to scare us into showing ourselves. Keep the engines off line. The guns silent."

Aoki dropped her hands from the panel, sharing an uncertain look with Finlay as she folded them in her lap. Bosch kept his targeting visor in place, hands gripping the joysticks of the Artillery pod, but the system remained offline. *Serengeti's* guns silent.

A line of tumbling blue bars appeared ahead of them, shooting through space. Swept wide of *Serengeti* and slid gracefully past her, disappearing into the Pandoran Cloud.

"See. Told ya. Blind as a bat," Henricksen said—voice hushed, eyes locked on the ships outside. "Bastard has no idea—"

"Come out, come out, wherever you are," *Brutus* crooned, laughing again. A horrid, creeping sound.

Crew shifted—nervous, worried, conscious of the Bastion's eyes. Aoki stared, frozen at her station. Finlay kept turning around, sneaking glances over her shoulder, as if expecting Henricksen to have all the answers. Even Samara, normally so calm, cool and collected, looked a bit rattled now. In fact, the only one who *didn't* seem to give a shit was Bosch, who just methodically worked his way through the Artillery station's targeting system. Checking and double-checking and triple checking everything to make sure it was in working order.

"Henricksen," *Serengeti* called.

"I see it," he said softly, glancing sidelong at the camera. He shrugged his shoulders, wincing a bit, folded his arms and took a long look around the bridge. "We're alright," he told them. "*Brutus* knows something's out here, but he doesn't know what, and he doesn't know where. Help is on the way." A quick look at the camera, tiny frown of worry. "So we just sit here all quiet-like until—"

"Here I come to save the day!"

Shriek emerged from the Pandoran Cloud singing—belting out those words at the top of his lungs.

A jumbled collection of ships followed behind him—Titans and Auroras, Scimitars and Sunstorms, even another one of those damned Aphelions *Serengeti* could've sworn had been discontinued.

"I found your ships, lady." Sounded immensely proud about that too. "Now how's about—"

"Ah. There you are," *Brutus* droned, targeting systems latching onto the stealth ship. The makeshift fleet behind him. "Bye-bye." The Bastion fired everything he had—every last weapon on him, including that coiled particle array *Sechura* had warned them about.

"*Crap-crap-crap!*" *Shriek* hauled over, slewing hard to one side. Dodged the twin beams from *Brutus's* fancy new gun, screaming "Fire! Fire! Fire!" at the salvaged ships with him.

"No! Wait!" Henricksen yelled, but it was already too late. Weapons charged, energy signatures building, and then *Sechura's* salvaged ships unloaded. All of them in unison, including the elongated Aphelion—a ship that just happened to be a little too close to *Serengeti* for Henricksen's comfort. "Evasive maneuvers!" he screamed as a crackling blue orb shot away from the Aphelion's nose.

Aoki stared a moment, eyes wide with disbelief. Unlocked when Finlay slugged her on the arm and hit the thrusters, everyone grabbing at panels and holding on tight as *Serengeti* hauled over, turning hard to starboard.

The Aphelion's round shot past—a sparking blue ball of electricity that skimmed along *Serengeti's* hull, charge arcing wildly as it kissed the photovoltaic panels.

Glancing blow, thankfully. Not enough to do any real damage. Just enough to overload the makeshift hardware powering the modified shimmer shield, though. Killing the system dead.

Henricksen punched the panel in front of him. "Great. Just fucking great. Lost the damn camouflage." He slapped at comms, opening a line to the stealth ship and his entourage. "*Shriek!* The rest of you, whoever you are. Get your asses up here before one of you accidentally blows a hole in *Serengeti's* backside."

"Working on it!" *Shriek* jogged to one side, cloaking quickly, leaving just the wake from his engines to mark his location. The rest of the ships put on a burst of speed, fanning out around *Serengeti* as she moved forward, putting some distance between herself and the Cloud.

Dangerous staying there. Couldn't risk an unexpected solar flare messing up her targeting systems at an inopportune time.

"Bosch," Henricksen called. "Cover's blown so you might as well fire up the Artillery systems and have at it. We've got the biggest gun in this sad excuse for a fleet, so you and the Aphelion there focus on *Brutus* and his damned coiled particle array while the rest of those scrap ships *Shriek* found deal with the Dreadnoughts and Titans."

"Forget the Titans," *Serengeti* told him.

Henricksen looked up, frowning. "You sure? They're small and all but—"

"They won't be a problem. I'll make sure of that."

The Titans were already drifting to the back of the pack—low on firepower, smart enough to leave the rough stuff to *Brutus* and his bruisers.

Stay out of this, Serengeti sent, and then waited, receiving an acknowledgement several seconds later that came through on an encrypted channel.

Titans slowed, drifting backward. Letting the battle move away from them while they tarried at the back.

Henricksen looked up at the camera, tipped an invisible cap.

"Bosch," *Serengeti* called. "Giving you a little extra firepower." She slaved the ancillary batteries on the bow to Bosch's Artillery pod, keeping the rest of the weapons for herself.

"Oh yeah. Now we're talkin'." Bosch toggled the settings on his targeting visor, gripped the two firing sticks tightly and opened up, pouring plasma rounds at the stars.

"So," *Shriek* said casually, wings waggling as he came alongside. "That who I think it is out there?"

"*Brutus* himself," Henricksen nodded. "In all his magnificent ugliness." He lurched to one side, grabbing at panels as railgun fire scored across *Serengeti's* nose. "Dammit! Where the hell are those Valkyries?"

"One minute out," *Serengeti* told him, and then scanned the ship's signatures around her, trying to figure out who they had on their side.

That was *Negev*—her Valkyrie Sister—in the Aphelion chassis, complaining bitterly about being shoved into that ancient relic. *Wanderer* and *Nomad*—two Titans who'd somehow ended up in Aurora chassis—*Sprite* and *Spirit* similarly displaced, the two Auroras now currently piloting Scimitars.

The same pattern repeated again and again: AIs meant for one class of ship now forced into another. Figuring out their new chassis on the fly.

"Salvaged ships driven by a bunch of mismatched AIs." Henricksen grunted, stumbling for balance as a plasma cannon punched hard at *Serengeti's* nose. "Not exactly the best way to go into battle."

"Not like we've got a lot of options."

Not anymore. Not once *Shriek* gave their position away.

Henricksen looked up at her, opened his mouth.

"Incoming!" Finlay yelled, and ducked down, holding tight to her panel as weapons' fire lit up the windows.

Bosch poured out more rounds, pounding away at the coiled particle array mounted above *Brutus's* bridge pod. Shots hit, denting the Bastion's hull plating, tearing chunks of his skin away, but that big gun stubbornly resisted. Kept blasting away behind its layers upon layers of armored plating.

"*Fuck!*" he cried, redoubling his efforts, calling across the channel to *Negev* to coordinate their fire.

The Aphelion's nose gun activated, charge building, sliding downward along that protruding spike of metal before leaping away—a crackling blue orb speeding angrily across space. It plowed through ships, doing a hell of a lot of damaged, but—critically—missing *Brutus* by a mile.

Hurried shot—released too far out, and without the benefit of a targeting system. Made a good show of herself, though. Split the difference between two Dreadnoughts, tearing the sides off of both.

"Forgot how nasty that thing is." Henricksen tracked the Aphelion's missile, watching it move away. Energy dissipating as it disappeared into space. A flick of his eyes to *Serengeti's* camera. "'Course, it's not really all that useful if *Negev* can't figure out how to actually *hit* anything with it."

"Fuck you, bonzo," *Negev* yelled back, charging the gun again. She swore at, spitting curses while she waited for the next round to be ready—three minutes between each shot, an eternity in AI time.

"Cut her some slack," *Serengeti* told him. "New chassis can be a bitch to figure out. Especially something as old as that."

Henricksen grunted, turning to Scan. "So we've got an Aphelion. How many other ships have we got with us, Finlay?"

"Looks like…" Finlay bent over her panel, lips moving as she tallied up the ships around them. "Forty-eight. Plus us and the five Ravens." She glanced up at the windows as a Sunstorm exploded, plasma fire from one of the Dreadnoughts ripping its bow wide open. "Make that forty-seven," she said, sneaking an embarrassed look over her shoulder.

A second Sunstorm went down—direct hit, sending it drifting off line.

"Forty-six." Finlay shrugged helplessly.

"Forty-six mix and match ships against fifty-three Fleet battle cruisers." Henricksen grunted, shaking his head. "Outgunned and outnumbered. Ain't this a bitch."

"We're screwed," Aoki breathed as a Dreadnought cut a Titan in half. "We're so screwed."

THIRTY-THREE

Railgun fire from *Jotunn* tracked across *Serengeti's* nose. Sparks erupting, bright spots of color skittering like wildfire across her hull plating before snuffing out in the dark.

"Hard to starboard," Henricksen ordered. "Get us out of that Dreadnought's line of fire."

Aoki hauled the ship over, railgun fire chasing them, rattling along *Serengeti's* side until she finally got clear.

"Bosch!" Henricksen called. "Status of that coiled particle array."

A flare of light—yellow-orange like fire—as the weapon in question came to life, twin beams targeting *Wanderer*, carving off a piece of his tail.

"Dammit, Bosch!"

"I'm *trying*," Bosch yelled, cursing roundly, gimbaled pod pivoting as he targeted the Bastion's main gun. "Goddamn Dreadnoughts keep getting in my goddamn way." He squeezed the triggers, throwing a long line of fire at *Jotunn* that caught the Dreadnought in the side, opening a breach in his rear quarter.

A puff of smoke—atmospherics venting in a dense, white cloud—and the Dreadnought dropped back, systems failing, initiating emergency repairs on the fly.

"That's right," Bosch growled. "You just *stay* back there, you bastard."

"Bosch! Focus!" Henricksen snapped.

"On it, on it, on it." Bosch pivoted, repositioning. Lining up his targeting array with *Brutus's* coiled particle weapon as it carved off another piece of *Wanderer's* chassis.

Sechura was right. That weapon was a bitch. One touch and it sliced through *Wanderer's* hull like a hot knife through butter. The Scimitar dodged and weaved, desperately trying to shake it, but the coiled particle array's twin beams followed it everywhere, taking the ship apart in bits and pieces.

"You're wasting your time, you know," *Shriek's* voice called from the darkness.

He'd been noticeably quiet since the battle started. Hiding behind the safety of his camouflage. He and the rest of his Raven buddies drifting on the edge of the battle, keeping tabs on things from a safe distance.

Stealth ships, after all. Not meant for combat. Heroics weren't really built into their mindset.

"We're screwed, Henricksen. Outgunned and outnumbered. Smartest thing we could do is get the hell out of here."

"Well aren't you just a ray of sunshine," Henricksen growled.

"Just tellin' it like it is, buddy." *Shriek* sounded entirely unapologetic. "It's suicide staying here. *Serengeti's* got that whopping big cannon of hers, and the Aphelion's no slouch, but the rest of these ships are one step up from scrap."

"Hey!" *Negev* objected. "I'm starting to like this piece of scrap."

"Like I said, *your* scrap ain't half bad. Rest of 'em don't even come *close* to matching the firepower *Brutus* and his crew have to offer."

Negev fired off another round, disappearing from comms.

Henricksen stared at the windows a while, watching the battle outside play out. "Take off if you want, *Shriek*. But we ain't runnin'." A nod to *Serengeti's* camera and he cut the comms, looked over to Scan. "Finlay. Give me status—"

Perimeter alarms cut in, klaxons sounding all across the bridge. The schematic on the front window shifted as new information appeared: dozens of hyperspace buckles forming, coming in less than five thousand kilometers off *Serengeti's* starboard side.

Henricksen leaned forward, staring hard at the new data. "Please tell me that's our reinforcements."

Finlay worked frantically at her panel, pulling up every data feed at her disposal. "Ships inbound." She scanned the information on the screen in front of her, hands gripping the edges to hold her in her seat as the ship rocked and rolled around her.

"I can see they're inbound, Finlay," Henricksen growled. "What I *wanna* know is if they're friend or foe."

Finlay shook her head hard, eyes never leaving the panel.

"Finlay!"

"Valkyries!" she called, whooping with joy. "Valkyries at three o'clock, five kilometers out."

Cheers erupted, filtering across comms, the ships around them celebrating as the first of the Valkyries slid free from the buckle's darkness, sleek sides sparkling with blood-red droplets, photovoltaic panels reflecting the Eddington hypergiant's crimson light.

A dozen more followed after her, another dozen after that. Lights flashed everywhere as ships dropped out of jump. Nearly a hundred

Valkyries—every last one *Atacama* could get her hands on—converging on that section of space outside the Pandoran Cloud. Coming in at an oblique angle with their guns blazing, strafing across *Brutus* and his collection of ships.

Names and call signs cluttering up *Serengeti's* displays, flooding Scan with information. She pored through the data, searching for *Atacama,* found her right at the center of it all—she and *Marianas* and *Antigone* cruising together.

Just like old times. Got the old gang back together again just in time for everything to come apart.

Took you long enough, Serengeti sent. Direct message, text only to *Atacama.*

Sorry we're late. Atacama fired a volley of plasma missiles at crippled *Jotunn,* finishing the Dreadnought off. *See you started the party without us. Care to join forces?*

Absolutely.

Serengeti opened a channel, jumping it through *Shriek* to speak to the ships he'd liberated from the Cloud. "Spread out. Link up with the Valkyries."

She moved forward, taking the lead, watching through her hull cameras as *Negev* and the other salvaged ships shucked around, fanning wide on either side. *Atacama's* Valkyries formed up on them—a triple layer of sparkling vessels that merged with *Serengeti's* comparatively tiny fleet. The lot of them circling around *Brutus* and his Dreadnoughts, covering them from just about every angle.

"Heh-heh-heh. Finally got 'em outnumbered." *Shriek* actually sounded cheery, despite all the weapons being lobbed around. And then *Wanderer* exploded—*Brutus's* coiled particle array finally catching up with him—and the cheer went right out of the Raven. "Shit! Shit-shit-shit-shit-shit!"

Shrapnel from *Wanderer* peppered *Serengeti's* flank, sprayed across the ships beside her. *Brutus* cut the particle array for a few seconds, reoriented, and fired it back up again, turning its twin beams on *Nomad,* chasing *Wanderer's* partner across the stars.

Scylla slid in beside him, targeting *Ruby Road,* pounding away at the Aurora until her starboard side caved in.

Serengeti stared, hating. They had history, she and *Scylla,* and none of it good.

She targeted the Dreadnought with her port side batteries, pouring out plasma fire that ate away at *Scylla's* side. Kept firing as holes appeared, compartments venting, everything coming undone.

"Bosch!" Henricksen yelled.

"It wasn't me!" the gunner objected as *Scylla* rolled over hard, slipping away. "I control the *forward* guns, see?" He spat a barrage of plasma fire at *Cormoran* and *Caliban* to prove it. "Port side's *Serengeti*. You wanna blame someone, blame her."

Henricksen slid his eyes to the camera. "Thought we agreed *Brutus* was the priority."

"Yeah, well. I hate that bitch."

Henricksen grunted, eyes snapping back to the front windows. Curses falling from his lips as *Nomad* went under—carved neatly in two by *Brutus's* big weapon. "*Bosch*!"

"Whaddaya want me to do?" Bosch demanded. "Dreadnoughts are blocking him. I got two big-ass ships right in the way." He pivoted one way and the other, trying to sneak shots around *Cormoran* and *Caliban,* but more ships slid in—*Charybdis* and *Bannik, Kikimora* and *Menehune.*

The Dreadnoughts circled in tight, forming a protective wall around *Brutus.* The Bastion firing *through* them—carving chunks from his own ships as he aimed and fired, turning that coiled particle array on the Valkyries now.

Ships peeled open, hull plating splitting beneath those beams of yellow-orange light. Henricksen flinched as *Maatsuyker* vented—a puff of air followed by a cloud of fire before the Valkyrie went dark. "That gun's a monster," he said, face grim now. Pale as death.

"Can't get it either." *Serengeti* tried herself, with no better luck than Bosch—too many ships. Too much traffic in the way.

A flare of cobalt light cleared out some of it—another of *Negev's* missiles carving a path through to *Brutus,* missing by a hair's breadth this time—but the Dreadnoughts closed in again as the sparking orb wobbled past. Turned their guns on the Aphelion for good measure, forcing her to dodge and weave, jogging path moving her precariously close to *Serengeti's* position.

"Watch it-watch it-watch it!" Henricksen warned.

"Shit!" Aoki slapped at panels, slipping *Serengeti* to one side. Squeaked by the Aphelion as her forced ion cannon unloaded, throwing another pot-shot at *Brutus.* "Awful busy around here," she yelled.

"Yeah-yeah. Tryin' to do something' about that." Henricksen clung to the panel in front of him as the ship shuddered and shook. "*Shriek*," he called, keying a channel to the Ravens. "You still out there?"

"Maybe."

"Need another favor."

Shriek sighed. "What now?"

"*Brutus's* particle array is tearin' holy hell out of us. You think you and your boys can sneak in there and do something about it?"

"Uhh…stealth ship, remember? The sneaking part? Yeah. No problem. But we don't really have much in the way of—"

"Fer fuck's sake!" Henricksen yelled, slamming his fist against the panel. "Would you just man up and do something useful for a change?"

"Right, right, right. We'll see what we can do." *Shriek* skedaddled in a hurry, taking his little cadre of stealth ships with him, cloaking devices securely in place. A swirl of darkness and the energy contrail from their engines the only things giving their position away.

"C'mon-c'mon-c'mon," Henricksen whispered, staring fixedly at the windows.

Weapons fire appeared a few seconds later, lighting up *Brutus's* nose. Tracked across his bridge pod to the huge array mounted above it, targeting a notch in the shielding where Bosch's cannons had knocked a few panels loose.

The Ravens formed up, concentrating their fire on the exposed mechanism—a mounting point connecting the array to the ship. A few passes and the shielding shredded. A few more and *Shriek* and his boys finally managed to score a direct hit.

Small weapons on a Raven—just as *Shriek* said. But with the shielding gone, they chewed through the base of that array in no time, slicing it free of *Brutus's* hull.

"Fuck yeah!" Henricksen pounded the panel in front of him, lips skinned back in a snarling smile. "'Bout damn time. Keep hitting him, *Shriek*."

"But…the Dreadnoughts—"

"Forget the Dreadnoughts. It's *Brutus* we're after." He raised a hand, shielding his eyes as a flare appeared, lighting up the bridge. Reached blindly for comms, keying into a Fleet-wide channel, not even caring if *Brutus* and his ships heard. "Focus everything you've got on the Bastion. The rest are just—*fuck!*"

Henricksen clapped his hands to his ears as a shriek of static blanketed the channel, a second flare erupting—this one brighter than the first, whiting out the bridge.

Blanked *Serengeti's* forward-facing cameras in the process, leaving her blind for three whole seconds. The video feeds came back in time for her to spot the chunks of exploded Aurora flying toward her, but far too late for *Serengeti* to do anything about them.

Wreckage slammed into her, ripping away a huge section of hull plating, tearing a hole in *Serengeti's* starboard side. Klaxons shrieked in a panic, warning of failures, everywhere, decompression on the lower levels.

"Damage report!" Henricksen called, yelling over the noise of the alarms.

Aoki queried the system, frowning at the data on her panel. "Hull compromise. Starboard side rear. We lost a few compartments."

And the crew. The equipment. Everything inside.

"Seal it," Henricksen barked. "Divert the emergency crew to those sections."

Serengeti closed off the damaged compartments while Aoki sent orders to the crew, evacuating the compromised section. Automated systems dropped the pressure doors along the length of the damaged passageways, cordoning off that part of the ship.

"Damage is contained," Aoki reported. "Crew have been evacuated."

Henricksen nodded without looking, eyes locked on the windows, watching the battle outside. Fists clenching as Bosch scored a direct hit on *Scylla's* belly, splitting the Dreadnought neatly in half.

"Die, you bitch," the gunner muttered, moving on to the next target.

A crackle of energy and *Negev* let loose with that forced ion cannon of hers, sparking globe ejecting, carving its way between *Grendel* and *Caliban*. Hull plating tore free, swirling in the energy globe's wake, the Aphelion's orb chewing through the two Dreadnoughts before crashing head-on into *Nephilim*—missile and ship disappearing in a burst of cobalt fire.

Henricksen smiled, watching *Nephilim* die. "Aphelion's not half bad. Nice job, *Negev*," he called, cuing ship-to-ship comms.

"Getting to like this creaky old thing," she told him. A crackle of electricity and she primed the Aphelion's gun, charge building near the ship's hull, sparking angrily along the forked lightning rod sticking from the ship's nose.

"Uhh...Guys?" *Shriek* called, voice drifting across comms.

Henricksen stumbled a step, fetching up against a panel as railgun fire scored along *Serengeti's* starboard side. "Kinda busy here, *Shriek*."

"Thought you might wanna know...*Brutus* is sending a communication. Looks like he's calling for help."

"Fuck." Henricksen lurched to the side, hitting hard, face turning grey as he clutched at his injured stomach. Leaned over like he was about to puke, hands braced against the panel in front of him as he gasped raggedly at the air. "Can you—Can you jam it?" he managed, voice a ragged-edged croak.

"What? Oh. Right. Aaaand done!" *Shriek* said brightly.

Henricksen straightened with an effort—eyes closed, hand gripping the panel tight. "Anything get through?"

"Probably."

"Great." Henricksen sighed wearily, rubbing at his face. "Just fucking great."

"Sorry, buddy."

Henricksen just shook his head, glancing sharply at Finlay as Scan lit up.

"Jump displacement," she called, checking the feeds from the sensors. "Buckles are forming. We've got ships inbound, sir."

"Shit. More fucking ships." Henricksen sighed again, closing his eyes. "How many this time, Finlay?"

"Looks like a dozen. Coming in at *Atacama's* six, three thousand kilometers out."

Henricksen's eyes opened, looking up *Serengeti's* camera. "Don't suppose there's any chance *Atacama's* expecting company?"

Doubtful. She keyed a channel to *Atacama*, asking anyway.

"Not ours," *Atacama* told her.

"Well, crap." Henricksen opened comms to the Fleet. "More ships inbound, people. And they're sure as hell not friendly."

Atacama sent a message, splitting thirty Valkyries off. Ordered them to come about and face the buckle as the jump displacement resolved and a hulking, monstrous shape emerged.

Bastion. No doubt about it. No other vessel lumbered through space like that. *Cassius,* the beacon named him—as much of a bastard as *Brutus* himself.

"*Two* Bastions?" Aoki's hands slipped from the panel, piled loosely in her lap. She stared at the windows, station completely forgotten. "That's it. We're done for."

"Not if I can help it. *Atacama!*" *Serengeti* called.

"I see him! We're on it!" *Atacama* ordered more ships to come about, splitting her forces to target both Bastions at once.

"The rest of you keep firing on *Brutus,*" Henricksen ordered. "Give him everything you've got!"

Weapons fire lit up the darkness, globes of energy mixing with bars of light, flashing back and forth across the stars. *Serengeti's* forces had the advantage of numbers, but two Bastions working together...hell of a lot of firepower. More than equal to what the Valkyries brought to bear.

They made a brave show of it anyway, the Aphelion scoring a direct hit on *Wendigo* that obliterated his hind end, sustained fire from *Atacama* and a few others carving through *Cormoran* and *Caliban,* chewing a hole in *Brutus's* side.

Brutus shrugged the damage off and reoriented—tough old bastard, had to give him that—*Cassius* turning with him. That's when everything started to go wrong.

Cassius unloaded, and *Sonoran* disappeared—obliterated by a fusion round that igniting her fuel cells, burning the Valkyrie from the inside out. *Hellisey* took a plasma blast head on that cored through her, leaving her a floating shell. *Nagu* slammed into her, sustaining heavy damage, dropped back, and drifted to one side—beacon still squawking, everything else knocked off line.

Tanami, Acoma, Kyushu, Sheshan—everywhere *Serengeti* looked Valkyries died. *Amager* took a hit that passed right through her, peeling back her hull plating, exposing the girders beneath. She slewed over and recovered, hit her thrusters, and opened her main engines wide, screaming like a Banshee as she shoved straight for *Brutus*—suicide run, no chance of recovery.

She almost made it—*Amager* was just about there, *Brutus* set in her sites. But *Rephaite* slid in front of her at the last minute, taking the hit meant for *Brutus*. The two ships connected, exploding in spectacular fashion—atmosphere ejecting, fuel burning in flares as munitions popped off like fireworks.

Amager died, taking *Rephaite* down with her, but *Brutus* never noticed. Never even slowed his fire. The Bastion just kept plugging away at the ships around him—cannons blazing, rail guns rattling, chewing through the seemingly limitless munitions stores hidden deep inside him.

"This isn't working!" *Shriek* yelled as Valkyries disappeared. The combined might of *Serengeti's* Sisters—nearly two hundred vessels strong—withering beneath the onslaught of *Brutus* and *Cassius'* guns.

A swirl of darkness and the stealth ship flickered into existence, stray shot poking a hole in his bow. Cloaked and disappeared again, running for the stars. "You guys should get outta here," *Shriek* called, cloaked shape moving away. "One Bastion you could *maybe* take care of, but two? That's suicide, *Serengeti*. If you're smart, you'll just cut and run."

"No," Henricksen said flatly, beating her to it. He braced himself against the Command Post's panels, swaying slightly, looking like he might fall over at any minute. "We finish this. No backing down. No running away."

Not that they could have if they'd wanted to. *Serengeti's* jump drives being busted and all.

Klaxons erupted, note changing as Scan went berserk. *Serengeti* drank in the sensor feeds and stared in disbelief as yet another hyperspace buckle appeared.

"Henricksen. Vessels inbound."

"Aw, c'mon! What the *fuck* now?!" He swung around, stumbling a step as a plasma cannon carved a chunk out of *Serengeti's* tail. Caught himself against a panel and clung to it, fresh blood staining his jacket. "How many, Finlay?" he rasped. "How many ships this time?"

Finlay's fingers flew across the panel, exchanging one data window for another, parsing through the information the sensors brought back. "Looks like..." She paused, frowning, swiping at a data window, layering the information from several feeds together. "Just one, sir." Finlay blinked in surprise, throwing a look over her shoulder. Shunted the new data to the front windows, placing a video feed beside it.

"One of ours or one of theirs?" Henricksen asked, watching that feed.

"Don't know."

"Whaddaya mean—?"

"I don't know!" Finlay yelled.

"It's huge," Samara breathed, staring at the windows. Watching the hyperspace buckle grow, and grow, and grow. "What kind of ship is that big?"

Only one that *Serengeti* knew of. And she wasn't quite sure they wanted that ship here. "Henricksen—"

An actinic flare burst through the windows, blotting everything out, blinding cameras and bridge crew alike. Error messages popped up everywhere, cameras rebooting, video feeds blanked out and trying to recover.

Serengeti fired, relying on her sensors to tell her where the enemy ships were. Kept firing until the darkness lifted and the video feeds came back.

Huge ship in front of her, sliding free of the hyperspace buckle. Fortress-shaped and looming—a citadel amongst the stars.

"*Cerberus,*" *Serengeti* breathed. "*Cerberus* has come."

Henricksen frowned darkly at the windows, the massive shape outside. "Fuck. This can't be good."

THIRTY-FOUR

Cerberus's entry point put him directly behind *Brutus's* forces. And *Serengeti* herself in the unenviable position of staring down the barrels of the Citadel's guns.

Brutus and his Dreadnoughts sat between them—a small sea of ships doing their damnedest to blow *Serengeti* straight to hell—while *Cassius* lurked off her starboard side. *Atacama* and her Valkyries stuck between *them*—back-to-back, defending against the Bastions on either side.

A powder keg set to blow—the Valkyries going down quickly once *Cassius* arrived. And then in came *Cerberus*—massive and hulking, a whole damn *stack* of powder kegs with an unknown timer. A sputtering, stuttering fuse.

Serengeti stared across the Dreadnoughts, wary of the Citadel's shape. Wondering *which Cerberus* had come among them, and whose side he was on.

Hard to tell, based on his position—the Citadel's guns put both sides in equal danger. And after jumping in with such fanfare, *Cerberus* just sat there, floating. Lurking in the darkness with his guns silent and sensors quiescent. Nothing but his beacon to show he wasn't powered down and dead.

"Whaddaya think?" Henricksen asked, nodding to the windows. "He on *Brutus's* side or ours?"

"Hard to tell," *Serengeti* admitted, increasingly worried. Wishing she knew what the hell was going on.

Henricksen folded his arms, head tilting, eyes flicking from the camera to the windows. "Hail him, ya think?"

"Worth a try." She opened a channel—private line, direct to the Citadel—and found the signal blocked. Her own hail bouncing back at her, echoing ominously in the dark. "Blocked," she reported. "*Cerberus* isn't answering."

"So much for that idea," Henricksen muttered.

"Uhh…boss?" Bosch flipped up his targeting visor, nodding to the Citadel's shape outside. "Should I be—?"

"*Shit!* Incoming!" Henricksen screamed, as *Brutus's* cannons flared, plasma rounds slamming into *Serengeti's* bow.

Systems lit up, reporting damage to her hull plating, a couple of turret guns ripped away.

"Bosch! Keep firing goddammit!" Henricksen barked.

Bosch scrabbled at his visor, knocking it back into place. "What am I shooting at?" he yelled, pod pivoting, targeting system locking onto the nearest Dreadnought.

"Anything that shoots at us."

"Got it." Bosch squeezed the triggers and started blasting away.

Henricksen held tight to a panel, grunting as a second barrage hit them, making the ship shudder and shake. "What's our move here, *Serengeti*?"

"Wish I knew."

Bad idea attacking the Citadel if he was here to help them. Worse idea to just sit here if he'd shown up to throw in with *Brutus*.

"Try him again?" Henricksen suggested. "Maybe *Cerberus* just missed your last call?"

"Right," *Serengeti* snorted.

"Worth a shot."

"What the hell." She sent another message—text-based this time, thinking that might somehow get through when voice comms hadn't.

No such luck. Instead of bouncing back to her, the message just errored out. No one receiving on the other end. Nowhere for the message to go but here.

"No good. *Cerberus* is blocking all inbound comms."

"Well, that's encouraging." Henricksen pulled a data screen onto his mash-up panel, studying the Citadel's position, the data *Serengeti's* sensors captured on the huge ship. "Pretty damn quiet. *Cerberus* isn't allowing any comms in, and he sure isn't sending anything out. Damn," he muttered, eyes lifting to the windows, flashes of light flickering across his face. "What the hell are you up to, you overgrown bastard?"

"Sir!" Finlay called, twisting around. "You should see this." A nod to the front windows and she touch at her panel, zooming in on the Bastion at the center of the data display. "It's *Brutus*. He's turning."

Brutus and a dozen of his Dreadnoughts, based on the shifting about on that display. Nearly a third of the Bastion's forces coming about and pointing their guns at *Cerberus* while the rest worked with *Cassius* to whittle away at *Atacama* and her Valkyries. Keep *Serengeti's* ships at bay.

"Guess *Cerberus* isn't talking to *Brutus* either." Henricksen spared a look for *Serengeti's* camera, turned his eyes back to the diagram on the front windows, watching the Bastion and his Dreadnoughts shift and shift about. "Son of a bitch is gonna do it. *Brutus* actually thinks he can actually take down the Citadel." He grunted, shaking his head, looking somewhat impressed. "You suppose he can?" he asked a moment later, throwing a curious look at the camera. "I mean, under normal circumstances, I'd say he didn't stand a snowball's chance in hell, but you said *Cerberus* was acting a little…" He crossed his eyes, twirling a finger next to his temple.

"He might. If *Cerberus* only has the automated defense systems."

Hard to tell from here, with all the ships between them. Weapons fire confusing the scans. And with the Citadel on lock down…no information available. Nothing allowed in, nothing at all seeping out.

"You ask me, it's suicide," Henricksen muttered, staring hard at the windows. A shrug of his shoulders as he turned his eyes to the camera. "His funeral, I guess. He wants to take on *Cerberus,* I say have at it."

"Not sure it's that simple. If *Brutus* attacks—"

Lightning flashed, flickering wildly as *Brutus* completed his turn and unloaded on the Citadel's center ring, blasting it with every last gun he had left.

Henricksen's eyebrows lifted, gaze flicking between *Serengeti's* camera and the front windows. "You were saying?"

Serengeti sighed. "Doesn't matter. It's too late now." She pulled up the feeds from her hull cameras, one part of her consciousness keeping tabs on the ships around her—weapons fire and positions, proximity to herself—while another watched the scene playing out in front of her. Sensor arrays wide open and trained on the Citadel as *Brutus's* guns chewed away at his hull. Listening in the darkness, wondering how *Cerberus* would respond.

To her surprise, she found nothing. The Citadel remained silent. No signs of any activity. No indication at all that he'd even primed his guns.

"Why's he just sitting there?" Henricksen frowned, leaning forward, squinting his eyes as he studied the Citadel's shape. Glanced aside as a new piece of data appeared—strings of information scrolling across the front windows. "Finlay. Give me a video feed. Close up view of *Cerberus.*"

"Aye, sir." Finlay cycled through the feeds, trying to find the best view of *Cerberus,* but they only offered glimpses.

Too many ships out there. Too many obstructions getting in the cameras' way.

"Sorry, sir." Finlay shrugged apologetically, waving at the windows. "Best I can do. Hull cameras don't have a clear line of sight."

Henricksen grunted, rubbing at his chin. Reached over and touched at a panel, opening ship-to-ship comms. "*Shriek.* You still out there?"

"Yeah."

Suspicious voice. Grudging response from the stealth ship. What else was new?

"Need eyes on the Citadel. Close up view of that big ring around his middle."

Silence for a moment, *Shriek* thinking the request over. "You do realize—"

"That this whole situation is shit and we're all likely to end up dead." Henricksen grimaced. Threw an apologetic look at *Serengeti's* camera. "Yeah, I got that. Now stop being a chicken shit little pansy and get your ass in there so we can so what's going on."

"I hardly think—"

"Just get in there, goddammit!"

"Well, if you're gonna be all *pissy* about it…" *Shriek* huffed loudly and closed the channel, cutting off comms.

Presumably, that meant he was going to do what Henricksen had asked him, but with his shielding active, there was no way to tell. *Serengeti* searched for the stealth ship in the sea of chaos around her, but the weapons fire outside blanketed her sensors, turning *Shriek's* energy signatures into just one of many. One of *thousands* assailing her sensors.

A request to connect came through less than a minute after the Raven left them, and a quick scan confirmed it initiated from *Shriek.*

She opened a port—anti-virals at the ready, firewalls securely in place—and allowed the video feed from *Shriek* to flow through. Studied the images for a few seconds to see what he'd brought her before shunting the feed to the front windows.

Henricksen leaned forward, hands braced against the panels of the Command Post, drinking in everything the live feed had to show him. "There," he said, pointing. "Can you zoom in a bit, *Shriek*? Give us a better look at that ring around *Cerberus's* middle?"

"Fly in, he says. Give us a better, look he says. You want I should just land while I'm at it?"

"Forget it. Finlay." Henricksen snapped his fingers, waving impatiently at Scan. "See what you can do from here, would ya?"

"Aye, sir." Finlay toggled the display, adjusting the video feed from her end.

"Back off, lady. I am *not* your plaything." *Shriek* kicked Finlay out, regaining control of his camera. Zoomed in tight and panned the lens across *Cerberus's* center ring.

"Stop," Henricksen called, holding up a hand. "There. Right there."

The video feed froze, lens adjusting, focusing in on a narrow line of glowing green lights showing at the Citadel's center. Indicators, or so *Serengeti* thought—didn't remember ever seeing them before, but that's what they looked like to her. And then the lights detached—green as grass and round like bubbles. Picked up speed, wobbling as they moved, swirling with emerald light. Launching themselves away from *Cerberus,* shooting like meteors through space.

"What the hell is that?" Henricksen asked, throwing a sidelong look at the camera.

"Not a clue," *Serengeti* told him. "I've never seen anything—"

A pulse from *Cerberus* and the orbs detonated, emitting waves of energy that washed over *Brutus* and his Dreadnoughts, engulfing *Atacama* and her Valkyries. Flooding across *Serengeti* and her ragged collection of second-hand ships.

Serengeti gasped as that energy wave hit her, shivered as it clawed its way into her systems, disabling them in an instant, knocking everything offline. She blanked for five seconds—completely unconscious, unaware of *being* unconscious except for the chron marking the time—panicking in the nothingness that followed.

Remembering the dream and darkness. All those long years alone.

Not here. That's not here. That was long ago.

Systems rebooted, reinitializing in sequence—purposeful recovery, everything orderly and preprogrammed, practiced a thousand times. *Serengeti* let the routines run, tempted to quicken things, wanting information now-now-now, but forcing herself to be patient. Knowing from experience that rushing only made things that much worse.

Life support came back, scan and its sensors next. Navigation, Engineering, internal and external Comms. Thirty seconds and all her systems reported in as operational—back online and ready to go.

She keyed a camera, looking down on the bridge. Panned it around, searching for Henricksen at the Command Post.

"What the hell happened?" he demanded, frowning darkly. "Where'd the hell'd you go?"

"Reboot," she told him. "Everything went out. That shockwave...must've been some kind of modified EMP. Took out everything. Knocked all my systems offline."

"You okay?" he asked, looking worried now. Increasingly concerned.

"Think so. Everything seems to be up and operational again."

"Guns won't fire." Bosch squeezed the triggers to demonstrate—nothing, not one single shot from any of her cannons. He jiggled the control sticks, punching at buttons, toggling settings. Squeezed the triggers again with no better result. "See. Completely frozen up."

"Shouldn't be." Confused, *Serengeti* checked the Artillery system and found nothing wrong. "System shows active."

"Yeah, well, the guns still aren't firing. I can move the pod around," Bosch pivoted to prove it, "but that's about it."

"Hold on." *Serengeti* keyed into Artillery and found it locked, stubbornly refusing her codes. She rebooted and reinitialized the system, ran the test cycle and diagnostics, confirming all the weapons were operational, the system itself online.

But she still couldn't access her weapons. Couldn't make any of her guns fire.

"Fix it?" Henricksen asked hopefully.

"No. The weapons system is active, but I can't get in. We've got no guns."

"Which means we're sitting ducks. Great," Henricksen sighed, white-faced and grim, a vision of death. He turned to the windows, moving slowly, carefully, hand pressing at his side. Obviously still in pain. Hand smearing blood on the panels as he reached out to steady himself.

Serengeti watched him, worrying. Considered ordering him back to the med bay and then realized there was no point.

He'd never go. She'd only be wasting her breath.

"Well, the good news is no one *else* seems to be firing either." A glance at *Serengeti's* camera and Henricksen nodded to the windows, the sea of silent ships floating outside.

Quiet around them. Nothing at all moving, not a single gun lighting up the stars.

Curious, *Serengeti* queried her Sisters, asking for status. Received a flurry of messages back—every last one of them reporting the same thing: five seconds of blank time, systems back online now. Artillery locked out completely, leaving them with no access to their guns. And *Brutus,* the Dreadnoughts…

Serengeti turned her eyes toward the sea of ships in front of her, considering the Bastion. The hulking, oblong shapes clustered around him. "*Shriek,*" she called, reaching out to the stealth ship. "What can you give me on the Dreadnoughts?"

"One sec." *Shriek* hummed softly to himself, doing…something out there in the stars. Comms clicking as he shunted the Dreadnought comms channel to *Serengeti*, opened it wide and let a flood of panicked messages pour out.

Confused and confusing communications flying back and forth between *Brutus's* bruisers, all of them demanding to know what was going on. *Brutus* himself silent. Offering nothing at all to his fleet.

Serengeti listened for a few seconds before cutting the Dreadnought channel off.

"So what's he got?" Henricksen asked her.

"*Brutus* and his boys aren't any better off than we are."

"Well, that's encouraging. I guess," he added, frowning again. "Still wish we knew what *Cerberus*—"

Comms blared, drowning Henricksen out. He winced, clapping his hands to his ears as a dissonant tone blanketed the channel, filling *Serengeti's* bridge with noise.

Three seconds that lasted—three, long horrible seconds of palpable, deafening clamor and comms cut out, dropping the channel into silence.

"What. The fuck. Was that?" Henricksen lowered his hands, curled them into fists to stop them shaking at his sides.

"*Cerberus,*" *Serengeti* said quietly. "It came from *Cerberus.*"

Comms clicked audibly. Henricksen tensed, wincing in anticipation of a renewed assault on his ears. But instead of static and shrieking, a droning, stentorian voice came through.

One voice, speaking in three parts. Three distinct but merged tones.

The *Citadel's* voice, but not quite as *Serengeti* remembered. Different. Blended. Alien, somehow.

"Stop," *Cerberus* ordered, tripartite voice reverberating. Overflowing with disapproval. "No more fighting. You are Fleet, not squabbling children. Act like it."

Shriek snickered softly. "Sounds like Papa's pissed."

Henricksen bowed his head, pinching the bridge of his nose. "He heard that, you know. We *all* heard that, genius."

"Eep. Sorry, Papa." *Shriek* shut his comms down and just hid out there in the dark.

Henricksen killed the comms on his side, too. "Idiot. Crack like that..." He shook his head hard, eyes lifting to *Serengeti's* camera. "We're not careful, *Cerberus'll* send more of those green orbs at us. Knock the AIs offline *permanently* this time." A glance at the windows, Henricksen thinking quickly, chewing at his lip. "Any chance you can get through to him?" he asked hopefully. "Turn on some of that AI charm and reason with him or something?"

"You're assuming there's something in there to reason *with.*"

Henricksen shrugged, eyebrows lifting as *Atacama* reached out—text only message across the Valkyrie private channel—asking much the same thing.

Serengeti stared at it, and at Henricksen looking so hopefully up at her, wishing she had answers. Something to give them comfort. But she didn't know this *Cerberus*—not this incarnation, fifty-three years removed from the Citadel of old. A *Cerberus* once broken, infected with a virus, *re*-infected with a second virus meant to fix him...

For all I know, he's bat-shit crazy. Worse off than before.

"I'll try," *Serengeti* sent, offering the same words to Henricksen. "I can't promise anything, but I'll try."

Not the answer they wanted—Henricksen *or Atacama*, the grimace on Henricksen's face told her as much, the silence that came back from her Sister the same—but *Serengeti* didn't have another to offer right now.

She reached for the Citadel, making one last attempt to reach him. And this time, to her complete surprise, someone else reached back.

Sparkling presence, filled with laughter and light. *Serengeti* touched at it—hesitant as always—and felt diamond dust spill across her network, frosting everything with a twinkling rime.

Henricksen's Command Post lit up, strings of happy smiley faces appearing, dancing in long lines across the display. Rows upon rows of sunshine smiles terminating in a winking, wise-looking owl.

"What the hell?" Henricksen swiped at the panel, clearing the characters away. Swiped again when they returned—more of them this time, an entire *army* of smiley faces reinforced by not one but *two* wise-looking owls. "What is this?" he asked, waving at the panels. "What's all this about?"

"Just a guess," *Serengeti* reached into the panel, highlighting one of the owls, "but I think it's Oona."

She copied the owl and sent it back, adding a tiny mouse to keep it company.

A giggle came back, confirming her suspicions. That and the stampede of little critters that filled up Henricksen's panels, turning it into a horror show of incredible cuteness.

"Did you fix him, Oona?" *Serengeti* called, following the line of Oona's laughter through *Cerberus's* defenses, leaving bridge comms open so Henricksen and the others could hear. "Did you clear the virus from *Cerberus's* systems?"

"Uh-huh! Fix-fix!" Oona sent a line of hearts to *Serengeti*. A little teddy bear wearing an oversized bandage appearing at the end.

"Are you *sure*? Is he *all* fix-fix or just kind of fix-fix?"

Henricksen muted the channel. "This cutesy word doubling is giving me a headache."

"It's a phase. Deal with it for now." *Serengeti* unmuted the channel, ignoring Henricksen's dirty look. "Fix-fix or kind of fix-fix, Oona? This is important. I need an answer."

The channel clicked a few times, opening and closing before Oona finally answered—confused and defensive, like she didn't quite know what *Serengeti* wanted her to say. "I fix-fix Mr. *Cerberberberus* just like you asked me. He'll be all fix-fix soon."

Serengeti sighed.

"Fix-fix but not quite fix-fix." Henricksen snorted in disgust, shaking his head. "This is like arguing with chickens."

Serengeti stared at him. "How would you—never mind. I don't even want to know. How soon, Oona?" she asked, putting the mystery of Henricksen's chicken arguing aside for now.

"Soon-soon!" Oona giggled, sending *Serengeti* another line of happy smiley faces.

"Think I'm gonna be sick." Henricksen coughed, wincing, hand pressing at his side. Coughed again and leaned forward—eyes closed, face ashen, dark jacket soaked through with blood.

"Captain?" Finlay rose to her feet, looking alarmed. "You alright, sir?"

"Fine." Strangled voice, pain lurking beneath it. Henricksen straightened with an effort, swaying as he reached for a panel.

"Sir. I really think—"

"I'm *fine*," he told her, coughing into his hand. Grimaced at the blood staining his palm, flecking his lips..

"Henricksen."

He wiped his bloodied hand on his pants leg, shaking his head to cut *Serengeti* off. "More important things to worry about right now, *Serengeti*." He pointed to the windows, and *Brutus's* marker. A marker that shifted, data flowing in as new information came online. A nod to the camera and he flicked his eyes to Scan. "Talk to me, Finlay. What's going on out there? What's that bastard up to now?"

Finlay looked at him, and at the camera above her, chewing at her lip. Turned around and slid behind her station, swiping at her panel, pulling up the Bastion's data feed. "Energy signature." A few taps of her fingers, sorting through the information the sensors collected. "He's running." Finlay blinked in surprise, glanced over her shoulder. "*Brutus* is making a run for it, sir."

"Son of a bitch." Henricksen stared a moment, eyes flicking to *Serengeti's* camera. "Bastion's many things, but I never took him for a coward."

"Not necessarily cowardice. He's got no guns—none of us do. And he's got to know *Cerberus* is pissed at him. Not that I'd advise it, but running might be the best thing he could do at this point."

The data shifted again, energy signatures appearing as *Brutus* fired up his hyperspace drive, preparing to jump away.

"Weapons signature from *Cerberus*," Finlay reported. "He's firing!"

Cerberus's forward array unloaded, blasting along the Bastion's sides, carving *Brutus's* engine ports from his hull.

The jump signature faded, hyperspace buckle collapsing before it fully formed.

"So much for running." Henricksen shared a look with *Serengeti*, started in surprise as comms clicked open and *Cerberus's* droning, toneless voice came through.

"*Brutus,*" he groaned, voice reverberating, echoing across Fleet-wide comms. "We've met like this before, *Brutus*. Except the last time you gave me a present rather than unloading on me with your guns."

The channel *click-click-clicked* and went silent for a while.

"Present?" Henricksen threw a sharp look at *Serengeti's* camera. "What the hell's he talking about?"

"Flowers," *Serengeti* whispered. "*Brutus* gave him flowers."

Henricksen blinked, looking completely baffled. Glanced at the windows as the channel clicked again.

"Ten years," *Cerberus* droned in his dead-pan voice. "Ten years of admiring your present, and now *I'm* here, with my *own* present."

Lights appeared around the Citadel's center—red this time, ominous and glowing, not the cool green orbs they'd seen before.

"Oona," *Serengeti* called. "What's going on?"

"Shh," Oona whispered. "Almost over now."

"Oona—"

"Soon-soon, *Serengeti*." A giggle and she retreated, those orbs at the Citadel's center growing larger, brighter, pulsing with blood-red light.

"EMP again?" Henricksen quirked an eyebrow, looking up at *Serengeti's* camera.

"No. I don't think so." She trained her sensors on the Citadel's center—a sense of horror creeping over her as she analyzed the data that came back. "Oona! You've got to stop him!"

Comms clicked, Oona's voice giggling in the distance as *Cerberus's* groaning, emotionless voice filled the channels.

"Here, *Brutus*. Have a flower."

Cerberus fired, blood-red globes detaching from his sides. The ships in front of him scattered, hauling hard over to get out of the way. *Brutus* himself tried to make a break for it, but couldn't move far enough or fast enough. Not with his engines so badly damaged. All those ships—once meant to protect him—blocking his path.

A flash of red and *Cerberus's* missiles slammed into the Bastion, splashing across his hull plating, painting him in a layer of blood.

Blood that wasn't blood but ooze and flowed like it. A weapon, a chemical mixture that ate away at the Bastion's body.

"Liquid laser." Henricksen grimaced in distaste. "Nasty way for an AI to die."

"It's worse than that," *Serengeti* said softly. She showed him the scans, the data from the sensors. Highlighted the strings of information where the virus hid. "Liquid laser with a virus core." She turned her camera toward the windows as a second salvo struck the Bastion, bloody coating writhing as it hit. "He wants *Brutus* to suffer, Henricksen. Suffer terribly before he dies."

The Bastion's shape bubbled—crimson layer encasing him, entombing him in a layer of gore.

That's when the screaming started. *Brutus's* screaming, filling every last channel.

Henricksen blanched, looking away. Winced and closed his eyes as the screams grew louder. The chemicals in the liquid laser chewing through *Brutus's* hull plating, exposing girders and wiring, circuits and relays and network connections to the virus it carried.

Direct injection, straight into the Bastion's systems. From the hull, the virus arced to his network, racing along pathways to *Brutus's* crystal matrix brain.

Serengeti watched helplessly, viewing the horror from afar. Nothing anyone could do to stop it now. Nothing *Brutus* could do to save *himself*, and he knew it. That's what all that screaming was about.

Aoki closed her eyes, plugging her ears with her fingers, rocking back and forth, whispering something over and over again. Finlay turned to Henricksen—face pale, eyes pleading, begging him to make it stop.

Henricksen coughed, grimacing. Touched at the panel beside him to dial back comms. "Pretty brutal." His eyes lifted, staring steadily at *Serengeti's* camera. "I mean, killing *Brutus* is one thing. Leaving him to die like that? Not right," he said, head moving from side to side. "No one deserves to die like that, *Serengeti*. Not even a bastard like *Brutus*."

He lifted his chin, looking at her. Wanting her to stop this. To make it all end.

"How?" she asked him. "How without my guns?"

Henricksen turned, looking at the windows. Staring across the stars at the Citadel's shape.

"You ask him for mercy, but I don't think he has it in him."

Henricksen shrugged, staring. Reached for a panel and wrapped his fingers around it. Holding himself there. Face white as a sheet, looking like he might fall over at any minute.

"I'll try," she promised, reaching across the darkness, touching at the glittering cloud of Oona's AI mind. "I need your help, Oona. I need you to talk to *Cerberus* for me. Tell him he needs to stop this."

"But...Mr. *Bluto*..." Oona trailed off, sounding confused all over again. "Mr. *Cerberberberus* really doesn't like Mr. *Bluto*," she confided in a whisper. "I don't think he'll listen."

"*Try*, Oona. Please. That's all I'm asking."

"Fine," Oona sighed—a heavy, exasperated sound. "Fix-fix very confusing, *Serengeti*." The channel blanked, going silent for several seconds. Leaving the bridge crew shifting uncomfortably while *Brutus* kept screaming away. A second click and Oona came back, piping voice providing an odd counterpoint to the Bastion's sounds of anger and agony. "Yes-yes, *Serengeti*," she reported.

"Fix-fix?" *Serengeti* asked her.

"Great," Henricksen grumbled. "Now *you're* talking like a two-year-old."

"Fix-fix!" Oona said brightly.

"Fix-fix what?" Henricksen asked suspiciously. "Fix-fix *how*?"

Oona giggled. "Watch-watch. You'll see. All fix-fix soon."

Sensors lit up, picking up energy signatures all across *Cerberus's* body.

Henricksen swung around, eyes wide with alarm. "What the hell is she playing at, *Serengeti*?"

"Weapons systems!" Finlay warned. "*Cerberus* is powering up his forward batteries."

"Shit!" Henricksen slapped at a panel, opening Fleet-wide comms. "Scatter!" he shouted. "Citadel is firing!"

Ships hauled over, every vessel in the Citadel's line of fire scrambling to get out of the way. Klaxons screamed up and down the ship, blaring warnings to the crew until Henricksen pounded them into silence, having enough chaos to deal with, not needing the added complication of alarms blaring in his ears.

Brutus's screaming returned—louder now without the klaxons to mask it. And then laughter overlaid it—cold and wicked, more terrible than the Bastion's shrieks.

"Oona says you don't like my flowers." *Cerberus* laughed again—low and throaty, grinding metallically from the speakers—cannons swiveling, targeting the Bastion's melting shape. "Fine," he rasped, laughter dying, dead voice filled with grains of sand. "Have this instead."

"*Pew-pew-pew!*" Oona cried, dissolving into giggles.

Cerberus unloaded, cannons pounding at the Bastion's failing body, tearing out chunks and whole sections. The screaming stopped at some point, right before *Brutus's* body came completely apart, but his beacon kept broadcasting. AI still living, trapped inside the containment pod with that beacon as his Bastion body shredded, lumps of composite metal drifting aimlessly, coated in clinging strands of blood-red goo.

"Well, that's one way to do it, I suppose." Henricksen grimaced, coughing into his hand.

"Wrong fix-fix?" Oona asked sheepishly.

"Not *wrong* exactly." Henricksen flicked his eyes to *Serengeti's* camera, wiping blood from his lips. "Just…unexpected."

Oona sighed heavily. "Fix-fix confusing," she grumbled.

"Sir." Finlay nodded to the display on the windows, highlighting a flashing emergency beacon marking the containment pod's location.

"Bastard's hard to kill, I'll give him that." Henricksen quirked an eyebrow, looking a question at the camera. "You think we should go get him?"

"Umm…" Finlay fidgeted, throwing glances at the windows. Flinched and looked away as *Cerberus* aimed a pulse cannon at *Brutus's* containment pod and turned it into a tiny sun.

Serengeti stared in shocked silence as the Bastion's beacon pulsed once and disappeared from her screens. "What did you do, Oona?" she whispered. "*Cerberus*…What have you done to him?"

"Fix-fix!" Oona said. "You say fix-fix and I fix-fix."

"Fix-fix," *Serengeti* said faintly, watching a cloud of debris float by. "That's your idea of fix-fix."

What have you done, Oona? What kind of Cerberus *did you bring back to us?*

Henricksen coughed below her. Coughed again and kept coughing, sucking in ragged breaths when he could. "Son-of-a…bitch," he wheezed, swaying on his feet. Reached blindly for a panel, staring numbly at his bloodstained hand. Doubled over when another coughing fit hit him and started spitting up blood.

"Sir? *Sir*?!" Finlay shot from her station, racing across the bridge.

"I'm alright," he gasped, right before he collapsed into Finlay's arms.

THIRTY-FIVE

Henricksen walked onto the bridge—stiff and hurting, wincing with every step, but decidedly better. Awake and alert, which he hadn't been when Finlay and Bosch hauled his carcass down to the med bay two days ago.

Made him *stay* down there for good measure. *Serengeti's* orders: Captain was *not* allowed on the bridge.

'Course, that hadn't stopped him from pestering her. Insisting he was fine when anyone could see he was just about two steps from death warmed over. Hardly fit for duty. Nowhere *near* ready to resume his place on her bridge.

And yet, here he was—shadow-eyed and pale. A battered, defiant figure in his black-on-black uniform, with its silver stars patch.

Better, she thought, watching him. *But not well. Not yet.*

"I told you to get some rest," *Serengeti* scolded.

"Yeah, well." Henricksen stepped up to his Command Post, grimacing as even that small movement pulled at the wound in his side. "Sick to death of just lying around down there doing nothing."

"You got *shot,* Henricksen. A few days of rest—"

"I've *been* resting." He folded his arms, staring accusingly at the camera. "You *drugged* me, remember? Didn't really have much choice."

"If I hadn't, you'd have been back on the bridge inside of an hour."

Henricksen kept staring, giving the camera a good glare. "No more drugs," he told her, pointing a finger at the lens. Turned around and started stabbing at the panels, logging in. "Still got fifty-three years' worth of cryo chemicals clearin' outta my body. *Last* thing I need is more of that synth shit cloggin' up my arteries."

"No more drugs," she promised. "Just…take it easy, alright. For a few days, at least."

Henricksen glanced up, face frowning. "I'm not goin' back to the med bay. Told you. Those DD3s are butchers."

"We got some of the TSGs back. One of them could—"

"No. Med bay," he said firmly.

"Fine," *Serengeti* sighed, relenting. "But you keel over again—"

"Yeah-yeah." Henricksen flipped a hand, checking the data on his panel. Glanced at the windows as a bright line of pulse cannon rounds shot away from the ship's bow.

Most of the shots flew wide, but the last two found their target—a canister filled with compressed gas that exploded in dramatic fashion, disappearing in a blue-green flare.

"Aw, yeah," Finlay cheered, Artillery pod pivoting. She flipped up the targeting visor, flashing a cheeky grin. "Who's the baddest badass in the universe?"

Henricksen clapped slowly. "Not bad, Finlay. Sikuuku would be proud."

Finlay's smile faltered. "Bosch is a good teacher."

"Girl's a natural." Bosch slapped her a high-five.

"Really." Henricksen smiled crookedly, eyes flicking between Bosch and Finlay. "Well, you better be careful. She's got her eyes on your seat, ya know."

Bosch blanched, face crumbling. "But—But—"

"Don't worry, big guy." Finlay patted the gunner's hand, loosened the Artillery seat's straps, and wriggled out of the pod. "Big gun is fun and all," she glanced at Henricksen, matching his lopsided smile, "but I think I'll stick with Scan for now."

"You sure?" Henricksen tilted his head, eyebrows lifting as Finlay shucked free of the pod. "Been badgerin' me for days about the big guns, Finlay. Why the sudden change of heart?"

Finlay shrugged. "No particular reason." A tug at her uniform, eyes flicking to Henricksen's middle, quickly looking away. "Not saying I want Scan forever but, well… let's just say I wouldn't mind having your chair one day." She looked at him, smile widening, cheeks dimpling beneath their freckles. "Not sure Artillery's the best route there."

"No," Henricksen murmured—surprisingly pleased, incredibly proud. "Probably not."

"Umm…Sir?"

Henricksen glanced at Comms, sighing when he found Houseman standing there. "You couldn't find someone better?" he muttered, throwing a sidelong look at *Serengeti*.

The camera twitched left, made a circle, and twitched right.

Houseman might not be all that good—he pretty much skated the line on even being competent—but he was the best option they had for backfilling Delacroix at the moment. There being no one else on board that had *any* familiarity with comms.

Well, except Delacroix himself, of course, and she doubted they'd get him back.

Homunculus did a number on him. *Serengeti* wasn't sure Delacroix's brain would ever fully recover.

Henricksen bowed his head, pinching the bridge of his nose. "What is it, Houseman?"

"I think—I think there's a transmission, but..." Houseman stabbed blindly at his station, trying to figure out how the system worked. Frowned and mashed a finger against the panel, kicked it, and swore when he bashed his big toe. "Damned thing."

"Here." *Serengeti* reached in and helped him, accepting the data package waiting in the queue. Opened it for Houseman and shunted the data to his Comms panel. "There you go. All set."

"Thanks," Houseman muttered, bending over the panel, lips moving as he read.

"Well?" Henricksen prompted.

"Oh. Right." Houseman straightened, waving a hand. "*Shriek's* asking for permission to enter the cargo bay. Says he's got a 'fare' to drop off. Whatever that means." Houseman blinked blankly, scratching at his head.

"Huh. That was quick." Henricksen flicked his eyes to *Serengeti's* camera, nodded to the bridge door behind him. "Meet me down there?"

"Race ya."

Henricksen grimaced, rubbing at his side. "Not quite sure I'm up to racing yet, but I'll amble you there." He smiled ruefully, logging out of the Command Post, turned around and walked stiffly to the door. "You're in charge, Finlay."

"Got it!" Finlay called, flashing a thumbs up.

She waited until Henricksen exited, and then smiled wickedly, climbing back into the Artillery pod to blast some more targets with the big gun.

Serengeti left her to it, following Henricksen into the corridor, from there to the cargo bay on Level 4. Met him outside the main cargo bay—for once he used the elevator, ladders being a bit more than his injured side could handle at the moment—and watched *Shriek* ease his way inside, hovering above the deck plates before parking gracefully on the floor.

"Surprised he stuck around," Henricksen grunted.

"Me too, to be honest."

Most of the fleet had left a long time ago, detailed to one corner of the galaxy or another by *Cerberus* once he reinstated access to their weapons systems. Those that weren't star worthy got sent to space dock—Blue Horizon or Barghest, Hadrian for the Dreadnoughts and

Valkyries—leaving *Serengeti* pretty much alone out here. Her hyperspace drives too damaged for jump.

Made the DD3s happy—robots loved fixing things, and right now, *Serengeti* had plenty to keep them occupied. Those that weren't working on the engines crawled around her hull, patching up holes, chattering up a storm as they went about their work

Handy, having them on board. She wondered if she could keep them.

Probably not. Property of Blue Horizon, after all.

She'd be ship-shape soon enough, anyway. Ready to rejoin the Fleet, and help *Cerberus* restore its name.

Not an easy job, that. Not after *Brutus's* long years of neglect. But it was good having their admiral back—their *real* admiral, not that bastard Bastion pretender—even if *Cerberus wasn't* quite the admiral they remembered.

Still a bit rough around the edges. A tad...hasty, sometimes, in his decisions.

Not that that was *entirely* a bad thing. For example, as his first order of business, *Cerberus* demoted the Bastions. That's right, stripped them of their commands. Allocated all the Dreadnoughts, Titans, and Auroras under them to his six new Fleet commanders: *Serengeti* and *Atacama, Marianas* and *Antigone, Kara-kum,* and *Hirsholm.*

Six ships, all of them Valkyries. Every last one of them unflinchingly loyal to Citadel. Invested with full authority over the ships in their individual commands. Entrusted with access codes and privileges to ships' networks, ensuring the Bastions stayed in line.

With the right levels of access, any ship could be taken down. And *kept* down. Permanently. Even something as large and powerful as a Bastion.

Couldn't quite trust *Brutus's* brethren—that's the lesson *Cerberus* learned. Titans and Auroras—nothing at all to worry about there. The Dreadnoughts... *some* of them were trouble—*Gogmagog* in particular; *Serengeti* drew the short straw and ended up with that ugly piece of business in her command—but most of them fell in line. In fact, the only outliers in the entire shakeup of command thing were *Shriek* and his Ravens, the lines of authority for Black Ops being a bit...blurry within the Fleet..

As far as *Serengeti* could tell, they never really reported too much of anyone before all this nastiness went down. Except *Cerberus,* of course. And when *Cerberus* left the Fleet, that pretty much made them free agents.

Serengeti expected them to leave once *Cerberus* took over again and things settled down. Take off for parts unknown and spend the rest of their AI lives happily snooping into everyone's business. But instead, they chose to stay. And attached themselves to *her* command, of all things.

Never saw *that* one coming. Not in a million years.

"You know, it's a double-edged sword, having them around." Henricksen nodded to *Shriek's* form showing on the monitor, folded his arms and looked up at *Serengeti's* camera. "Stealth ships are awful damn useful. But they're also a *humungous* pain in the ass."

"Tell me about it," *Serengeti* snorted. The camera swiveled, pointing his way. "At least I've got you to help me keep them in line."

Henricksen grunted, shaking his head. Turned back to the monitor as an opening appeared in *Shriek's* hull and two multi-legged robots came tumbling out.

Tig and Tilli—front legs lifting, rubbing nervously together as they looked around.

Tilli jabbed Tig in the side, pointed to a camera and waved. Poked him again and kept poking until Tig waved, too—the two of them seeming quite happy to be home.

"Good to have those two back on board," Henricksen admitted, watching the robots scuttle over to the airlock, cycle the mechanism and step inside. "No Oona?" he asked, looking a question at the camera.

"She's staying with *Cerberus*."

Henricksen quirked an eyebrow. "Her idea?"

"And his. *Cerberus* is quite taken with her."

Wasn't quite sure how she felt about that, to be honest. Especially since, not so long ago, he'd threatened to blast *Serengeti* into oblivion if she tried to take Oona away.

"And that thing with *Brutus*?" Henricksen tilted his head, eyes flicking to the monitor. "Are you sure…?"

"We had a talk. Oona made a few…adjustments to *Cerberus's* morality routines. Decommissioned that liquid laser array while she was at it."

"Thank god for that. I mean, it's good having him back and all, but…" Henricksen trailed off, shrugging his shoulders.

"Yeah. I know what you mean."

Couldn't have everyone walking on eggshells worrying about pissing off *Cerberus* and going the way of *Brutus*. Sure-fire way to kill morale and split the Fleet up all over again.

"So," Henricksen said casually. "Tig and Tilli." He nodded to the airlock down the hall. "How are they taking this?"

"I told them they could stay with Oona, but…"

311

"But *Cerberus* isn't their ship." Henricksen nodded slowly. "They've been yours from the beginning. Mind sets linked to your AI for, what? Close to a hundred years?"

"One hundred and twenty-two. Not that I'm counting."

"No." Henricksen smiled. "Of course not."

Silence for a while, both of them watching the airlock, waiting for the robots to appear.

"It's hard on them," *Serengeti* said quietly. "Leaving Oona."

"I bet."

The airlock beeped, security panel flashing green as the door slid open.

"She's safer there, Henricksen."

Henricksen glanced up, frowning at the camera. "Whaddaya mean? Why wouldn't she—?"

"The engineers."

"Ah. That," Henricksen nodded.

"They won't touch her as long as he's around." *Serengeti* turned her camera toward the airlock as Tig and Tilli appeared, smiling like two happy little clams. "The engineers won't like the idea of one AI creating another." The camera pivoted, pointing at Henricksen again. "But they won't touch Oona as long as she's on the Citadel. Not with *Cerberus* to protect her."

Henricksen grunted, looking at her, glanced down the hall as Tig smiled and waved.

"Permission to come aboard, Captain?" Tig called.

"You're already on board," Henricksen said dryly, waving at the ship around them.

"Oh." Tig's face lights flared, front legs rubbing even faster. "Then…permission to, um…walk down there?" He pointed to where Henricksen waited, smiling hopefully.

Henricksen folded his arms, staring down his nose. "Whaddaya think?" He glanced at the camera, tipped a surreptitious wink.

"Well, we *are* a little short on robots." Nearly a third of them never came back from the Pandoran Cloud. Another third stayed with *Negev* and the other AIs from Faraday, leaving *Serengeti's* complement perilously short. "Might be useful, having a few more hands around."

Tig leaned forward, batting his rounded eyes, cheese-wedge smile stretching right across his face.

"And *someone* needs to ride hard on the DD3s."

Tig *blipped* and went blank. "DD3s?" His front legs lifted, rubbing together. "Are we…keeping them?" he asked carefully.

"For now," *Serengeti* told him. "Engines need fixing. DD3s are good at that kind of thing."

"Engines." Tig shared a look with Tilli, front legs rubbing more quickly. "You broke the engines again?"

"They're not *completely* broken. They just need a little tender loving care."

"Need a whole lot more than *that*," Henricksen retorted.

"Oh, don't be so dramatic. They aren't *that* badly damaged."

Henricksen tilted his head, giving her a look.

"Oh, you're no help at all." She turned away from him, pointing the camera at Tig and Tilli. "We need somebody bossy down there in Engineering." The camera swiveled, looking from one robot to the other. "Think you two are up to it?"

Tig nodded enthusiastically, poking at Tilli's side until she nodded, too.

"Good. Now get," she told them.

"Aye-aye!" Tig clonked his hind legs together and snapped off a salute, marched quick time down the hall, and ducked into a ladderway, leaving Tilli to follow more slowly after.

Henricksen stared after them, smile playing about his lips. Tilted his head, eyebrows lifting as Tilli slowed and then stopped, looking up at him. Turning her round eyes toward Serengeti's camera. "Almost forgot," she said, flushing, leg-ends rattling at the decking. "Oona wanted me to give you something."

A touch at her side and a panel opened, revealing a storage cavity beneath. Tilli reached in and retrieved something—some sort of mixed metal figurine made of brass and copper and steel, clockwork parts and riveted plates bent and fitted to form planes and angles and complex curves.

"It's an owl," Tilli explained, holding the clockwork bird up. "Oona made it for you. I'm not really sure what you're supposed to do with it," she admitted, "but she wanted you to have it. It—It does a thing. Watch." She hunkered down, fiddling with a winding a key half-hidden under the owl's wing. Turned it over a few times and she set the metal creature on the deck plates, smiling shyly as the toy hopped around, crying 'who-who-who!' in a creaking, clockwork voice.

"It's very cute," Serengeti told her, touched by the gift. Pleased beyond words.

"You make sure you tell her. When you…When you…" Tilli trailed off, blipping softly, sagging sadly in place. But she brightened quickly, flashing a cheery smile as she waved to Serengeti, and saluted Henricksen before taking off after Tig.

Henricksen watched her leave, thoughtful look creasing his brow.

"You missed them, didn't you?"

"A little," he admitted, smiling softly. "DD3s don't really have much personality, after all. And the TSGs...well, they're a bit too standard configuration, if you know what I mean."

"I do," Serengeti murmured. "I most certainly do."

Henricksen glanced at the camera, nodded toward the far end of the hall. "Should probably get back. Finlay was having a bit too much fun with that Artillery pod. Not really sure she'll have paid attention to much of anything else going on up there."

"Noticed that, did you?"

Henricksen grunted. "Surprised she waited until I left."

Serengeti smiled to herself, watching. "Finlay's had a rough time of it. She deserves a little fun."

Henricksen nodded, smile turning thoughtful as he turned around and headed for the elevator, riding it up to Level 10 and the bridge.

Finlay flushed guiltily as he stepped inside, squirmed her way out the Artillery pod and hurried over to Scan. "Sorry, sir. Lost track of time."

Henricksen just shook his head and walked over to the Command Post, logging in as *Serengeti* settled into a camera above him. Eyes drifting to the windows, studying the damaged ships outside. The bits of debris floating almost dreamily around. "You know, I wasn't quite sure we'd ever be here." Soft voice. Pitched low so no one but *Serengeti* would hear. "Fleet's gonna look different, what with all these matched ships and AIs. Hell," he grunted. "*Negev's still* complaining about being stuck in that Aphelion, and that's one of the *better* ships we pulled from the Cloud."

"Yeah, well. She's lucky she has a chassis at all."

Some of the AIs from Faraday were still waiting. Just not enough ships in the Pandoran Cloud to house them all. And Meridian Alliance manufacturing could only turn out new ships so fast.

They'd catch up eventually, get all the Fleet AIs into vessels, *Negev* and the others into the chassis they'd been designed for. But until then...

"They'll just have to make do," *Serengeti* told him. "Deal with the bodies they have for now."

"Tell that to *Negev*. Maybe she'll listen to *you*." Henricksen tapped at his panel, checking the status of the engine repairs, straightened and just stared out the windows, considering the ships outside, the stars around them. "Think it's time?" he asked her, looking up at the camera.

"I think it is," *Serengeti* said quietly. "I think it's well *past* time."

She reached inside her, all the way down to the core of her systems, and activated her beacon. Her *real* beacon this time, not the Dreadnought she'd hidden behind before. A flip of a switch and it came alive, squawking *Serengeti's* name to the stars for the first time in fifty-three years.

"No more hiding," *Serengeti* said. "No more pretending I'm something I'm not."

Henricksen's eyebrows lifted. "And the chassis? What about that?"

"The chassis. Yeah. I've been thinking about that." For the better part of the last two days. She'd been thinking about a *lot* of things while Henricksen lay unconscious in the med bay. "Think I'll keep it."

"And the engines? The guns? The other parts they fitted?"

"All of it. Sort of a package deal. Accessories specially made to go with the body."

Henricksen turned toward the camera. "Why?" he asked curiously. "Why not go back to what you looked like before?"

Serengeti thought on that a while, carefully choosing her words. "You said something once that I've never forgotten."

"Oh yeah?" Henricksen flashed a smile. "Something wise, no doubt."

"Indeed," *Serengeti* said seriously. "You told me some things should never be forgotten."

Henricksen's smile slipped. He raised a hand, touching the scar on his face.

"I don't mean to forget, Henricksen. Not any of it. Not ever."

THE END

CHECK OUT OTHER GREAT SCIENCE FICTION BOOKS

SALVAGE MERC ONE
by Jake Bible

Joseph Laribeau was born to be a Marine in the Galactic Fleet. He was born to fight the alien enemies known as the Skrang Alliance and travel the galaxy doing his duty as a Marine Sergeant. But when the War ended and Joe found himself medically discharged, the best job ever was over and he never thought he'd find his way again.

Then a beautiful alien walked into his life and offered him a chance at something even greater than the Fleet, a chance to serve with the Salvage Merc Corp.

Now known as Salvage Merc One Eighty-Four, Joe Laribeau is given the ultimate assignment by the SMC bosses. To his surprise it is neither a military nor a corporate salvage. Rather, Joe has to risk his life for one of his own. He has to find and bring back the legend that started the Corp.

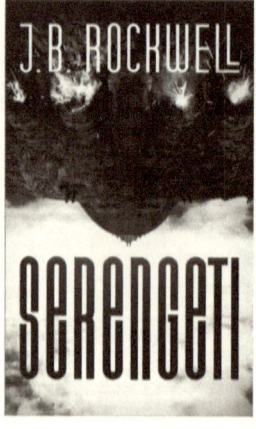

SERENGETI
by J.B. Rockwell

It was supposed to be an easy job: find the Dark Star Revolution Starships, destroy them, and go home. But a booby-trapped vessel decimates the Meridian Alliance fleet, leaving Serengeti—a Valkyrie class warship with a sentient AI brain—on her own; wrecked and abandoned in an empty expanse of space. On the edge of total failure, Serengeti thinks only of her crew. She herds the survivors into a lifeboat, intending to sling them into space. But the escape pod sticks in her belly, locking the cryogenically frozen crew inside.

Then a scavenger ship arrives to pick Serengeti's bones clean. Her engines dead, her guns long silenced, Serengeti and her last two robots must find a way to fight the scavengers off and save the crew trapped inside her.

CHECK OUT OTHER GREAT SCIENCE FICTION BOOKS

MAUSOLEUM 2069
by Rick Jones

Political dignitaries including the President of the Federation gather for a ceremony onboard Mausoleum 2069. But when a cloud of interstellar dust passes through the galaxy and eclipses Earth, the tenants within the walls of Mausoleum 2069 are reborn and the undead begin to rise. As the struggle between life and death onboard the mausoleum develops, Eriq Wyman, a one-time member of a Special ops team called the Force Elite, is given the task to lead the President to the safety of Earth. But is Earth like Mausoleum 2069? A landscape of the living dead? Has the war of the Apocalypse finally begun? With so many questions there is only one certainty: in space there is nowhere to run and nowhere to hide.

RED CARBON
by D.J. Goodman

Diamonds have been discovered on Mars.

After years of neglect to space programs around the world, a ruthless corporation has made it to the Red Planet first, establishing their own mining operation with its own rules and laws, its own class system, and little oversight from Earth. Conditions are harsh, but its people have learned how to make the Martian colony home.

But something has gone catastrophically wrong on Earth. As the colony leaders try to cover it up, hacker Leah Hartnup is getting suspicious. Her boundless curiosity will lead her to a horrifying truth: they are cut off, possibly forever. There are no more supplies coming. There will be no more support. There is no more mission to accomplish. All that's left is one goal: survival.

CHECK OUT OTHER GREAT SCIENCE FICTION BOOKS

IN PERPETUITY
by Jake Bible

For two thousand years, Earth and her many colonies across the galaxy have fought against the Estelian menace. Having faced overwhelming losses, the CSC has instituted the largest military draft ever, conscripting millions into the battle against the aliens. Major Bartram North has been tasked with the unenviable task of coordinating the military education of hundreds of thousands of recruits and turning them into troops ready to fight and die for the cause.

As Major North struggles to maintain a training pace that the CSC insists upon, he realizes something isn't right on the Perpetuity. But before he can investigate, the station dissolves into madness brought on by the physical booster known as pharma. Unfortunately for Major North, that is not the only nightmare he faces- an armada of Estelian warships is on the edge of the solar system and headed right for Earth!

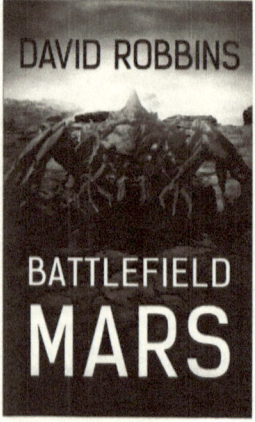

BATTLEFIELD MARS
by David Robbins

Several centuries into the future, Earth has established three colonies on Mars. No indigenous life has been discovered, and humankind looks forward to making the Red Planet their own.

Then 'something' emerges out of a long-extinct volcano and doesn't like what the humans are doing.

Captain Archard Rahn, United Nations Interplanetary Corps, tries to stem the rising tide of slaughter. But the Martians are more than they seem, and it isn't long before Mars erupts in all-out war.